Buttermilk Book Publishing

Myrtle Beach, South Carolina

This book is a work of fiction, craziness from the author's
wild imagination. While some locations and venues
might exist, the characters and plot are purely fabricated.

Typecast in Times New Roman

ISBN 978-1-7331576-9-8

Acknowledgement

A special thanks to Judy Cannon who took time out of her busy life to proofread this book, even though it was not her genre for reading material. My dear friend is penning her first book after losing the love of her life a few short years ago, Sammy Cannon. Cuz as I called him, my brother, a man I loved like no other man ever in my life. Her book will be one of coping with that loss, a book that might help others while documenting her journey for family and friends. It will be my honor to publish hers when completed.

Foreword

Last Stand on the Grand Strand crosses boundaries with two other T. Allen Winn fictional series. Characters from the Detective Trudy Wagner series interact with new characters of this book. There are also ties and references to the Foot series, the Bigfoot trilogy. While the plot is a standalone story, readers familiar with the other two series might get a kick out of the crossovers entangled in this new adventure.

Last Stand on

the Grand Strand

"Whoever fights monsters should see to it that
in the process he does not become a monster.
And if you gaze long enough into an abyss,
the abyss will gaze back into you."
— Friedrich Nietzsche

"What would an ocean be without a monster
lurking in the dark? It would be like sleep without dreams."
— Werner Herzog

Prologue

The closest house was at least a quarter mile north of where the three young surfers enjoyed the seclusion. While the three to four feet waves offered no great challenges, beggars could not be choosey along this stretch of Grand Strand beach. The pack made up of Cody, Tanner and Newt, sixteen-year-old best buds, were content riding the bumps, pumped just to be on the ocean. Tanner had just pulled off a duck dive as he approached the other two straddling their boards.

"These are lame bumps today," commented Newt.

"It's tough to do much carving, for sure," added Tanner.

"Where's your dream waves," asked Newt, paddling up beside the pack.

Tanner bobbed his head up and down. "Got to be the Trestles in Orange County, California. Supposed to have easy paddle-outs and high-quality breakers."

"No man. Numero uno is the Pipeline in Oahu. Threading the needle, how cool would that be. Hell, just bobbing the perfect crest would be awesome." Cody gave the hang ten sign.

"I would do the box," said Newt. "It has late takeoffs and right-hand barrels."

"Yeah, right, sharky place to surf, dude," scoffed Tanner.

"I would. Sure, it's sharky as hell but it would be worth it. Anywhere in Australia is going to have those great whites. Double daring makes it cool. Same goes for the Supertubes of Jeffrey's Bay in South Africa. Surfing Magazine said that's where the best right-handed rides in the world are."

With that, Newt broke off and caught one but misjudged his dismount, hamming his left wrist against the sandy bottom. He held his left arm trying to shake off the stinging pain. One thing for sure, he wasn't going to let on to the others. He bellied down on the board and paddled back out. Once there, he flipped over on his back and decided to take a break, sponge in some rays. He rode the bumps, facing towards the ocean while Cody and Tanner searched for the next dune, wishing they actually existed along the Atlantic Grand Strand.

"Look," called out Tanner, pointing to an enormous swell, "Got to be a rogue."

The ocean piled up, a small concentrated mountain forming and heading directly toward them. Newt, 15 yards away was still lying flat. The splashing water to the side of his ears had obstructed him from hearing Cody and Tanner's excitement. They had already turned, belly down, paddling towards shore, timing to catch the once in a lifetime big one, clearly now stacking upwards of 15 feet. It was upon them quicker than they had anticipated. Tanner managed to make it just ahead of the potential crest, while Cody was still paddling like hell.

White water broke like no other they had ever experienced. A gaping hole opened in the wave; a dark cavity lined with rows of gigantic razor-sharp teeth. Cody, surfboard, and all was sucked into the hole in the wave, swirling as if caught in a giant flushing toilet. Tanner was up, balancing on his board, but something wasn't the norm. He glanced over his shoulder to see why. Caught off guard by something entirely un-wave like, he fell off his board just as his board disappeared inside the nightmare. Still attached at the ankle he was towed along for the ride. A Tsunami crashed on shore washing away their street clothes and cooler resting on the beach, any signs of them ever being there.

Newt, now aware of the pattern change in the water, up righted himself, straddled the board, and then paddled to face the shore. A huge bump was now moving ocean bound. He had never witnessed a wave this large, one moving away from the shore. It was maybe 20 yards wide and heading in his direction. Screams made him shift his stare. Thrashing about just behind the crest of the wave was Tanner being dragged helplessly behind it? Newt was spellbound. It was unclear what he should do about the approaching bass-ackward's wave and his friend in distress. The wave crashed inward, and Newt watched helplessly, too late to react.

Seconds later the Atlantic Ocean was as if nothing had ever happened. The pack, boards, and all, were gone. Three young surfers with aspirations of hanging the perfect ten would never be found. Only their beat-up Ford parked on an old beach access dirt road would mark the last place they had visited. A search would turn up nothing, surf boards reduced to tiny pieces that would wash ashore eventually but would never be recognized for what they once were.

1

The Atlantic Ocean off the South Carolina coast is a mega for fishing and shrimping. Nothing beats the Grand Strand for fun in the sun, toes in the sand and sea, a tourist destination for many. An honest living can be made by those harvesting catches from the ocean. Nothing can be more challenging than those shrimping on the trawlers off the coast. Captain Joe and his mate Ken prepare for a new day of just such a life.

"A wonderful day for shrimpin, mate," announced Captain Joe, slapping his first mate and best friend Ken on the back.

"Not until after I've at least had my third cup of java," responded Ken, lids heavy and eyes still crusty from his early wake up call.

"Tough to beat a morning like this anywhere; thank God I live in the Palmetto State. Georgetown is first class in my book, even with that stinking pulpwood mill," boasted Captain Joe. "Ken, just take a gander at that sunrise over the marsh there. You can't improve on perfection."

"Reminds me. I need to get my sunglasses out of the truck," muttered Ken.

"Hop to it, son. We will be shoving off in ten minutes. Round up that sorry excuse for a shrimper, young Vic. I saw him puking up last night's menu in the john. I have warned him about tanking it on during the work week. I know he's your nephew, but he won't be worth a crap today to us, belly all churning like that."

"I'll have another talk with him," mumbled Ken. "And it won't hurt my feelings if you cut him loose. He's my sister's boy and a real pain in the butt, but I don't owe him or her nothing. I'm not his dang keeper, that's for sure."

"We'll see how he does today but if he doesn't pull his weight, he can puke his guts out on somebody else's watch and that's just a fact."

"Fair enough, I'm getting tired of doing the job of two."

Captain Joe Wilson watched his long-time friend Ken Simpson make his way across the dock to retrieve his glasses and that sorry nephew. He and Ken had been friends for over 25 years and had been shrimping together for nearly two thirds of that friendship. He would have never thought Ken would make it as a shrimper, being so overweight and a chain smoker, but no denying it, he could hold his own amongst the best of them. To Joe, he had always reminded him of that character on the sitcom Cheers, Norm. The exception, he wasn't a boozer and didn't bar hop, unlike that sorry nephew of his.

Captain Joe, the opposite end of the spectrum from Ken, was lean, sun baked, a hardened sailor at the young age of 53. He didn't smoke and would only partake of his one glass of Apricot Brandy before retiring each night. He claimed it helped him welcome sleep and stifle that awful ringing in his ears, tinnitus brought on by years of loud music and deer hunting. His jet black hair only recently showed signs of white speckles along the sides of his temples. Standing at only five ten and 175 pounds, he came across as much larger. With bulging muscles and baby face features he caught the eyes of the female population when he was in port. Captain Joe was not a womanizer though and didn't take advantage of his gift. His heart belonged to the sea. Only occasionally did he crave female companionship and he never ever entered a serious relationship.

He certainly hoped today would be a better day. The small fleet of seven shrimp boats calling Georgetown their port had not done too well in the past couple of weeks. Captain Dick had commented that the ocean seemed spooked to him. He didn't elaborate and Joe didn't ask him to. Another shrimp boat captain, Sullivan, had one of his nets snatched free from his boat just yesterday. He still couldn't lay claim to the critter that had wreaked havoc. He said he had never had it happen before and hoped it didn't happen again, couldn't afford it. Times were hard for everyone.

Many of the charters had been struggling too. It just didn't make any sense that the fish were so tough to locate. It made even less sense that the charters and shrimpers would be experiencing the same woes. Talk concurred, it could not be weather related because conditions had been perfect. No one could ever remember it being this bad but for the last few weeks it had been just plain terrible. If things did not change soon, they would all be hurting. Captain Joe looked out over Winyah Bay. The water was almost flat. Very few white caps chopped the surface.

He eyed Captain Dave waddling in his direction, cigar protruding from the corner of his mouth, his white crew neck t-shirt already stained from the morning's preparation and perspiration. A long white bushy beard and barrel-chested physic had earned him the nickname of Saltwater Santa. Captain Joe could read the frown lines on Captain Dave's forehead even from the 30 feet that still separated them. Captain Dave, the chronic complainer, always painted a picture of gloom and doom every time shrimping went south on them. Joe expected such rhetoric this morning.

"How's my favorite Salty Santa doing this glorious morning?"

"How can you be in such a cheerful mood, you old piece of cut bait? We are losing our butts and we are all going under if things don't flip."

"We've seen worse. We even survived Hugo, so I expect we'll come out of this slow spell just fine."

"Hugo slammed us pretty damned good, wiped out everything down in McClellanville but I don't reckon we can blame our misfortune on the likes of Hugo this time," said Captain Dave.

Young Vic had finally arrived and overheard the conversation. "What's a Hugo? Isn't that a car?"

"You have your head up your ass or something, boy?" asked Captain Dave. "You've never heard of Hugo?"

Captain Joe chimed in. "Hurricane Hugo, Vic; September 1989, it slammed the coast as a Cat 4. It might near ruined the shrimpin' business. Hugo wiped out all the boats in McClellanville and sent

14

people scurrying for their lives from a twenty-foot-high storm surge."

"That was a couple of years before I was born so how am I supposed to know anything about a Hurricane Hugo?"

"I tried to get your mom to pinch your head off then, but she never listens."

"Funny, Uncle Ken!"

"Nasty storm it was. People high tailed it inland and Hugo followed them," added Captain Dave. "It blew out windows all the way up in Charlotte. The governor back then said enough trees were felled to build a house for every family in West Virginia. There was so much timber available in the marketplace; it caused the pulpwood industry to suffer."

"All up and down the coast it was a wreck. Houses were wiped off the face of the earth in Surfside and Garden City where the storm surge worked its evil destruction," stated Captain Joe.

Vic seemed worried and asked, "We don't have a hurricane out there now, do we?"

"Nope, weather is pretty much clear from here to the coast of Africa right now," confirmed Captain Joe.

"We did have that near miss a few weeks back, but it stayed well off the coast. It was a monster Category 5 but didn't make landfall and turned back out to sea," said Captain David. "I forget the name of that one."

"Not important in my book if it don't make landfall," said Captain Joe. "Just maybe it churned everything up and that's why we're down on our luck."

Vic, standing there shirtless and in cut off jeans, pretended to be captivated by the stories of the two old timers, but he could care less. He figured it was in his best interest to pretend like he did though. Sucking up was never a bad thing to exercise. Vic, a master in the art of sucking up, had met his ultimate challenge in this bunch of ocean slugs. They weren't so easily taken in by his attempted cons.

Captain Joe asked, "Reckon you done purged your system now?"

"I think it was just something I ate last night," replied Vic.

Captain Joe eyed him suspiciously. The scrawny little chap probably didn't weigh 140 soaking wet. Badly in need of a haircut, his golden locks reached his shoulders but while on the boat, Joe insisted he wore it in a ponytail. It wouldn't do for him to entangle it in a net and have his butt jerked overboard. At 18, he still wasn't able to muster up any facial hair. Joe doubted if he had any hair on his ass either. The boy was way too soft for this line of work. It was probably going to be his very last trip unless he really stepped up to the plate and showed some gumption. He didn't expect any miracles.

Now sporting his dark *Blues Brothers* sunglasses, Ken returned with news to share with them. "Did you guys hear about Marvin Brown?"

Everyone shrugged.

"Coast Guard went out looking for him just before dark last night. He sent out a distress signal, but the message was garbled and short before everything went dead. He had four guys from New Jersey on board," recapped Ken.

Captain David asked, "Did they find them?"

"Not yet," answered Ken. "They haven't found hide or hair of them or the Serendipity. Heard they were supposed to continue searching this morning. They said he was about 11 miles out when he radioed the mayday. Clear weather and calm seas."

16

"I like old Marvin," added Captain Joe. "Always a straight shooter. He has been chartering longer than most of us have been shrimpin. It must have been something really bad for him to yell for help."

"Screaming is dead on the money from what they've been telling," clarified Ken. "Rumor has it they heard all sorts of yelling in the background when he radioed his SOS."

"Could have been something like a fire," said Captain Joe. "You don't want to think fire when you're on a boat 11 miles out."

"Rogue wave maybe," said Captain Dave. "It seems we hear more about them lately."

"Well, one thing for sure, we're not going to solve it here and I hear shrimp screaming my name, so how about we shove off," winked Captain Joe.

"Race you," smiled Captain Dave with not so much as an ounce of pep in his step, ambling back towards his vessel.

Vic grabbed his stomach and then clung to a moor as he heaved ho into the water, vomiting up mostly clear liquid, just a hair away from the dry heaves. He wiped his mouth with his t-shirt he had wrapped around his waist and then turned to face the inevitable music.

"Hold some of that chumming until we get to our spot," smirked Captain Joe.

Ken shaking his head, said, "When are you going to learn your lesson, Vic? Hope it was worth it."

"Seemed like it last night, but not so sure right now," gagged Vic, turning to face the water again.

"You know you've just about screwed up this gig and I promised your mama to help you get settled," Ken lectured him.

"You did what you had to do," smarted off Vic, insinuating that Ken had no balls when facing up to his sister. "And I live my life the way I want to."

"Some life, puking your guts out half the dang morning and looking like a dead man stumbling."

Vic started to mount a come back but gag reflexes held him firmly in their grip. He just shrugged and continued his attempted vomiting to no avail. He felt as if the inside of his stomach would spew from his mouth next. He had nothing else to offer the gods of the sea. Captain Joe boarded his vessel, Shrimp Cocktail, and fired up the engines. Ken prepared them for casting off while his nephew clung to the side.

An hour and half later they had reached their destination. Soon, one bag like trawling net with its two boards connected to the mouth of the net had splashed the water. The Shrimp Cocktail was equipped with duel nets but today they would only be using one. Ken monitored the angle of the boards controlled by the chain bridles to regulate the spread of the net's mouth. Ensuring the trawl remained on the bottom was crucial. The trawl bridles kept the towlines in check. Weights ensured the net remained on the ocean floor while floats attached to the top of the net regulated the buoyancy to tickle the shrimp from ocean bottom. Vic should have been helping Ken but had camped out in the head instead. That most likely sealed his doom. A pink slip was in his future.

A typical drag of about two hours would transpire before they would haul in the net with the power winch. The net would be hoisted along side then onto the shrimp boat's deck where the crew would empty, sort, and store their bounty in the hold. Ken sure hoped Vic was over his puking by then because he needed his help to complete that portion of the task. He sensed this would most likely be Vic's last trip too.

Captain Joe in the wheelhouse operated the steering and the throttle to maintain the fifty-foot vessels' position and keep the otter trawl in check. The powerful diesel engine purred with perfection. Joe had sunk his life savings into her and while not yet completely paid for and almost five years old, he treasured her and kept her in immaculate shape. The remaining six ships in the shrimp fleet couldn't hold a candle to her. Sadly, Joe was almost two payments behind and that would only worsen if they came up empty on this trip.

He could see Captain Dave almost a half mile north, both nets in the water. Hindsight, Joe thought, he should have probably dipped both of his but with Vic next to worthless, he didn't want to burden Ken with the extra net. He had to stand at the controls and could be of little assistance. Joe had already decided he would give Vic his walking papers after they docked, today's performance sealing that for sure. He just hoped he could find a warm body to take his place. It wasn't easy to find anyone willing to take on such a tough and thankless job.

Watching the Holy Grail, captained by Dave, it suddenly struck him as odd that he didn't see any birds flocking around the boat. Gulls should be swarming it as they do all shrimp boats, but he saw none. He was beginning to believe they might just be hexed out here, but the birds dipped and circled his own vessel relentlessly. He could see activity on board the Holy Grail. They were hauling in the nets. He glanced back at his own, figuring to give them about another 30 minutes before they'd do the same. Vic was back on the deck but even from his view in the wheelhouse, the boy still looked pale and puny. Joe certainly didn't feel sorry for him. He was reaping what he had sowed. The absence of birds continued to haunt his thoughts. Something just wasn't natural about that picture. He contemplated radioing Salty Santa to see what was up but decided best not to interrupt him. Dave was very superstitious and didn't take kindly to radio talk while in the middle of a trawl. He decided he would ask him about it after they docked tonight.

It caught him completely off guard. He wasn't quite registering what he was witnessing at first. The Holy Grail began moving strangely seaward. Even from this distance he could tell the nets were the culprits, pulled tight and turning the vessel. Before his very eyes, the Holy Grail completed a one eighty turn. He now faced wheelhouse to wheelhouse with Captain Dave. He could no longer see the rear of the Holy Grail but could still barely make out Dave moving about in the wheelhouse.

Without any warning the bow launched almost vertically into the air. He could see two thirds of the hull's underbelly. It remained in that position what seemed to be forever. Probably no more than ten seconds passed before it came crashing back into the water, spraying enormous rooster tails. He could no longer see Captain Dave. Possibly he had fallen or had shimmied down to the deck to assist his crew. He reached for the radio microphone and this time hailed the Holy Grail, once, twice, and then a third time. No one responded.

He reached in the overhead compartment and retrieved his binoculars. Affirmative, Captain Dave was not in the wheelhouse unless he was sprawled unconscious or injured on the wheelhouse floor. He tried again to hail the missing captain, but the radio remained silent. He couldn't rush to the rescue because his net was still submerged. He signaled to Ken that they would be hauling in the net. Confused, Ken looked at his watch and suspected something was up, because it was still too early yet for them to hoist up the net. Captain Joe confirmed his orders, haul it in. Ken complied and barked instructions to Vic.

Time crawled like a sea slug. To make matters worse, shrimp were few and far between in the net. The Shrimp Cocktail appropriately lived up to its name because that's about how many shrimps they had snagged. He scoped out the Holy Grail again, but he still saw no movement on board. It bobbed like a cork in the water now drifting toward the shoreline. Joe sat their helplessly unable to speed up the process of hauling in his own net.

Better than an hour had expired by the time he pulled up along side the Holy Grail. He still saw no one on board. He directed Ken to take control of the wheelhouse while he and Vic launched the skiff and pulled along side her. Clambering on board, Joe called out to Captain Dave and his crew, but all remained silent. A quick search confirmed the Holy Grail was unmanned. Joe radioed the Coast Guard from the Holy Grail, and while he waited for their arrival, he conducted an inspection of the vessel. What he found defied his imagination. Both nets were empty and shredded to pieces. The boat offered up no signs of the occupants' where-abouts. Fact, this was not the Bermuda Triangle, so how had they just disappeared?

Captain Joe heard a loud splash and returned aft where he had last seen Vic. The boy was gone. He called out. No answer. He radioed over to Ken, but Ken had not seen what had happened either. He didn't know why he said it, but he did. "Ken, secure the door in the wheelhouse and stay put until the Coast Guard arrive." He did the same on board the Holy Grail. They were both still there when the cutter arrived, alive and well.

2

Chad and Liz Reynolds arrive in Myrtle Beach where they will be joining family for a well-deserved vacation along the scenic Grand Strand. Nothing could be finer than to be in Carolina, as the catchy tune goes.

"Come on Chad, at least act like you're having a good time. My folks did invite us here so please try to make the best of it for the next two weeks. For me, pretty please," said Liz Reynolds.

"Heaven on earth, fun in the sun, Myrtle Beach waves, the Grand Strand exploding with scantily clad little nymphs frolicking in the sand, who could wish for anything more?" replied Chad.

"You forgot *nothing could be finer than to be in Carolina in the morning*," sang Liz.

"What are you now, an American Idol wantabe? You're just a little too pitchy I'm afraid."

"And who are you all of a sudden, Simon fricken Cowel?"

"How close are we?"

"I think just a couple of more blocks. Relax, the place does come with an ocean, so you should be thankful," smiled Liz. "But, no serious work, you promised!"

"Sand in my sandals, I got it."

"Sorry your mom couldn't join us this year," said Liz.

"She called from the west coast and him-hawed around, so I know she's up to something. You know Mattie Reynolds, the lone wolf Sasquatch hunter. She's probably out there in the great northern woods stalking her legendary prey, trying to prove Bigfoot actually exists. What a crock. What pisses me off even more, it's so ridiculous how she tries to keep her passion hush, hush like I don't know what's she's up to," blasted Chad. "I wouldn't think any less of her if she confessed. I mean, people chase UFO's and the Loch Ness Monster, why not a missing link?"

"Be nice. She is your mother after all."

"I read that journal of Matt McGregor's, the one written by our renowned ancestor documenting his adventures in the 1800 wilderness. She doesn't know I did. It was sort of spooky, cowboys and Indians and the Bigfoot twist. It would make a great movie I suppose. Guess those folks back then had wild imaginations too. I'm sorry. It just frustrates me that she never had any intention of sharing it with me like she's ashamed or something."

"She probably has her reasons."

"Yeah, she didn't want me to think Looney Tune cells run in our gene pool. I get it. She still refuses to talk about that time when she was lost and almost got whacked by the eruption of Mount Saint Helens. Something bad happened to her then but she absolutely will not talk to me about it. Dad never would either, even when I asked him about it; rest his soul. Whatever happened, it dramatically changed both of their lives. You'd think she'd be buzzing to tell those stories to her children and grandchildren."

"You're an only child and unless you've been keeping secrets from me, we don't have any children."

"Not yet," he replied.

"Does that mean you're ready?" She inquired, excited about the possibility.

"Don't start on me, how about it?"

"I know, first comes the astounded career. You should have been my father's son."

"We'll have kids, I promise, but not now."

"Guess I'll have to settle for the uninhibited, wild and raunchy, sweaty marathons," she said, reaching over to remind him.

"Unless you want to cause me to wreck the car, you'll refrain from doing that."

"You used to be so good at multitasking behind the wheel."

"I used to be a horny adolescent and took every opportunity to score."

"So, you're no longer that young and virile young man."

"I'm just no longer an adolescent. If we had more than two blocks, I would prove it to you."

"Two blocks are more than enough time"

"Hold on Liz, you're going to cause me to miss my turn!"

"Then drive around the block," she responded.

One spin around the block had done it. Chad now pulled into the parking garage craving a cigar.

"Look, there are my folks," she pointed to them unloading the Black Escalade.

Professor Chad Reynolds, influenced by the gene pool from both parents, had obtained degrees in marine biology, physical oceanography, and marine chemistry. An accomplished California surfer, Chad had followed his dream, the ocean. He had grown up living and breathing what the sea had to offer. It just seemed fitting that he'd build his career around what he loved the most. That's the only reason he didn't kick and scream about coming to the Grand Strand of South Carolina on the two-week family vacation. Besides, it was only a hop, skip and a jump from the Keys where they had called home for the past two years.

He and Liz had met in college and had bonded immediately. She had a degree in chemistry and directly after graduation had landed a job in the pharmaceutical industry. She started out in the developmental side of the business but quickly found her niche in testing and marketing. Her constant traveling had tested the strength of their marriage, not that either contemplated being unfaithful. It just created a void that required kick starting their relationship after long intervals apart. They had learned to make a dating game out of it and embraced the technique of role play and acting out fantasies to spice things up. So far, this method worked wonderfully.

Liz's father, Frederic J. Bornfreund, both an archaeologist and paleontologist, after years of teaching and gaining his tenure, had accumulated his vast wealth as the famous author of over 20 books and as a lecturer. He frequently pulled in six figures for a single appearance. Chad worshipped his father-in-law He strived to follow his example and was presently penning his first book. Unfortunately, he didn't share the creative juices for theological research and the intensity or time required to study the mysteries of the sea and science behind it. Instead, his was a novel, pure fiction and more entertaining he hoped, dreaming of a best seller. So far, he had only outlined a potential plot but then again, he had a lifetime to complete his masterpiece.

Teal, Liz's mother was the real treasure. She had no formal education and had never worked outside the home. With the assistance of nannies, Teal had raised Liz and her sister Corinne and brother Robert. They say you should always meet the mother of the woman you plan to marry to determine how she will age. Well Chad always said if Liz turned out half the woman as Teal, he would be a lucky man. She was drop dead gorgeous. There was nothing fake or fabricated. Teal was a red headed, full figured vixen of precise proportions. Frederic was indeed fortunate.

Corinne Bornfreund, the youngest of the three siblings, never married and was a wild child still, even at age twenty-four. Many families have their closet secrets. Corinne took that status to new levels with her antics. Supposedly she would be bringing a friend with her. She had a history of going through guys like a bag of potato chips and couldn't settle for having just one. It was no surprise that her family didn't know who she had invited. One thing for sure, with Corinne in the mix, unpredictability was guaranteed. She thoroughly enjoyed pushing Frederic J. Bornfreund's buttons, oil, and water from start to finish.

Robert, his wife Cody and their two kids Abilene and Corey would be rounding out the merry band for two weeks of forced family fun. Chad didn't particularly care for Robert. He was too snobbish, but Cody was about as down to earth as they get, a Blue Ridge Mountains girl from Maggie Valley, North Carolina. She was the former Miss Chattahoochee. Robert too often treated her like a mountain hick though and that disturbed Chad. He had been tempted many times to kick Robert's butt but out of respect for Liz had let things slide, so far. He felt sorry for Cody and never understood why she stuck it out with him. She wasn't a material girl, so the money had no hold on her. Chad figured she lived and died by her principles and didn't believe in divorce, especially with the two children to think about. He admired her for that.

"Elizabeth, Chadwick, I'm so glad to see you two have arrived safely. You must come over and assist Teal and I with carrying up the luggage and provisions," shouted out Frederic, giving no consideration to the fact that Chad and Liz had their own vehicle to unload.

Teal on the other hand rushed over and gave both big hugs, whispering, "Don't bother, we can manage. You take care of your things first then freshen up, so we can visit for awhile. I'll have the Margaritas iced and waiting."

"Mother, it's only eleven o'clock," said Liz pointing to her watch.

"We're on vacation dear. Let a woman indulge if she wishes to," smiled Teal.

"Make mine on the Rocks, Teal," added Chad.

Liz asked, "Are Bobby and Cody here yet?"

26

"Plane delays. They'll be joining us tonight hopefully."

"Why didn't they just drive? It would have been less than eight hours, much shorter than our drive up here," said Liz.

"Bobby had frequent flyer miles he wanted to use, and you know how that boy loves first class."

"First class, that's big brother all the way."

"Please, don't start dear. We're here for a non confrontational family gathering."

"Just rehearsing Mother Dearest, you know how he is, and the games will start once he arrives."

"Please try to be civil to your brother, for me, just for two weeks."

"I'll do my best, but it takes two and he doesn't play well with others, especially me, and you know how he rubs Chad the wrong way."

"Chad doesn't lash out at Bobby like you, dear."

"I wish you and father would settle on a name for big brother. You always call him Bobby, but father must call him Robert. I have a few choice names but will refrain from using them unless he pushes it."

"Your father and I see him differently, that's all. He'll always be my little Bobby and Frederic…"

"Forget it mother, I don't really need to hear this again. You just make little Bobby behave and I'll follow suit, I promise, but the gloves are off if he starts pulling his crap."

"Fair enough dear. We're going to have a wonderful time."

"Welcome to Fantasy Land," whispered Liz, "It'll be more like dysfunctional hell."

3

Chad, like every man, had been lured to the bedside remote control and while unpacking had flipped on the television to one of the local stations. He had stuffed most everything in drawers or the closet and now stood on the balcony staring out at the ocean and beach ten stories below. He was only half heartedly paying attention to the breaking news flash. It only drew his attention when he heard the Coast Guard mentioned. He stepped back inside to catch what the reporter was saying.

"We're live at the Georgetown marina where they've just towed in the shrimp boat. We're purposely blocking out the name of the vessel and are not disclosing the names of the missing until their immediate family have been notified. The mystery surrounds what happened to the crew and one of the rescuers under sunny skies and calm seas less than a mile offshore. Another shrimp vessel captain witnessed the mishap, but authorities are not releasing any details. The search continues for the missing men. Sadly, they have already switched this from a rescue to a recovery mission. This follows on the heels of another maritime tragedy, the Serendipity operated by Captain Marvin Brown. Captain Brown and four men charting his boat disappeared several miles off the coast. The captain did issue a distress call. Again, the weather didn't appear to be a factor. The Coast Guard is still investigating the disappearance of those on the Serendipity but hope of finding survivors has expired. We understand that some debris has been located but we have no further details. This is Shannon Brinkley reporting live for Channel 15 News."

Liz walked into the bedroom and stood there, arms crossed and patting her foot. Chad, mesmerized by the report had not noticed her standing there.

"Off limits remember," she spoke up. "No television in the bedroom, we agreed."

"I didn't place the TV here. And our agreement was no television at bedtime."

"Bedtime could be anytime, so let me have that remote," she said, holding out the palm of her hand.

Chad clicked it off and handed her the remote like a good boy. "Couldn't help it, they've had a couple of bad boating accidents over in the next county the last few days. The Coast Guard is puzzled, haven't found any of the missing."

"I'm sorry for the families but there's nothing we can do about it."

"But a charter boat and the people on board just vanished, and then today, all the people on a shrimp boat have gone missing too and the boat is intact. That's just too weird, don't you agree?"

"Look, we're here to have fun with the family and not solve the mysteries of the sea, Chad. Let the authorities take care of the problem. Just because it has to do with the ocean, it doesn't mean you have to be involved."

"Family fun. I want to hear you repeat that out loud and often when your brother and sister arrive."

"I'd finish what I started if Mother Dearest wasn't already expecting us to join them for cocktails," she said, pulling up her shirt and flashing him.

"Tempting fate with that little maneuver aren't you," said Chad, closing the distance between them and pulling her into his arms.

"Just a tease to keep you primed," she said.

"You'll get yours soon enough," replied Chad, pulling her close.

"Promises, promises, bad naughty professor" she said, breaking free and leading him back to the den.

"Your sister called," said Teal. "She just exited off 95 and should be here within the hour."

"If she doesn't become too distracted between there and here," finished Liz. "She still has to pass those outlet stores and you know how she loves to shop."

"We all have our vices, dear," responded Teal, always the peace maker.

"Tell me, Chadwick, just what has the professor and acclaimed oceanographer been up too? Are you still penning that great American novel of yours?"

"When time allows," answered Chad, wishing he would not call him Chadwick. "The Navy presently has me contracted studying the decline in the natural reefs around the keys. We are losing them at an alarming rate. As humans we focus more on our fun and leisure and don't give it much thought to how we're impacting the marine life. I'm not too proud of my surfer past and how I had little regard for nature and how adversely I impacted it."

"But you have reformed my son. Sowing our oats is a rite of passage. We are all guilty of it I'm afraid. I could share with your stories of my adolescence that would make you question my integrity, but we learn from our ill-fated mistakes and move on. The world hopefully appreciates the final product once we have."

"How's the lecturing circuit, sir?"

"Always in demand. I have the luxury of choosing my poison. I opt to travel less and stay in the lower 48 when possible. I deploy the pain and anguish inflicted from airplane travel these days."

"Unlike your infamous son," chimed in Liz.

"Youth has no limitations my dear, but he will one day see it my way, I assure you. How's the pharmaceutical world my dear, Elizabeth, still boring as usual?"

"I don't recall every saying it was boring, father."

"One man's perception," replied Frederic. "You should have remained in research, not a peddler of the goods, my dear."

"I'm a wonderful snake oil peddler. My clients cry uncle whenever they see me coming."

"I'm sure you are excellent at what you do, Liz," assured Teal, not catching the sarcasm being traded between the two.
Changing the subject, Chad asked Frederic, "I don't suppose you happened to catch the local news did you sir? A charter boat has been lost at sea just off the coast and thus far they have not located the ship or any of the crew."

"I'm not one for watching television, my boy. Is it really so uncommon for ships to fall prey to oceanic disasters?"

"Not so uncommon, but just today another ship, a shrimp vessel lost its entire crew," continued Chad, "But the shrimp boat appears to be fine. This time they apparently have a witness to the mishap."

"Chadwick, very interesting events but why do these have you so captivated?"

"I'm not sure. I suppose two accidents so close together costing the lives of nine or ten individuals seems a bit odd, don't you think?"

"Are you drawing the conclusion that the two are somehow related?"

"No. I have no such evidence. I don't have any evidence at all come to think of it. I just overheard a two-minute news segment and it just caught my interest. You know me sir, if it's on the ocean, it automatically lures me into the situation. Force of habit."

"I'm sure the local authorities will solve the mystery without our intervention or interference," stated an unconcerned Frederic.

"Their poor families must be devastated," added Teal.

"I'm sure they are mother," agreed Liz.

Frederic changed the subject. "Are you up for a little fishing tomorrow? After all, this is supposed to be a time of recreation and relaxation. I suggest when Robert arrives, we charter a boat and commence enjoying the Atlantic Ocean."

"You need not twist my arm, sir."

"You promised, no oceanic exploration."

"Elizabeth, this will be pure male bonding at its best, fellowship among comrades," clarified Frederic.

"Boy's day away from the women folk you mean," replied Liz.

"Exactly," smiled Frederic, "And you, your sister, your mother, and the amazing Cody can benefit from our absence and complete the female ritual equivalent."

"Corinne and Cody under the same roof, I feel so cursed."

"You boys have your fun out on the great blue yonder," said Teal. "We girls will do just fine without you."

"Wild blue yonder refers to the sky, Teal," Frederic corrected her.

"I see no reason why it can't apply to the ocean too. Blue is blue."

"Have it your way my lovely. Chad, would you be so kind as to call and arrange a charter for in the morning?

"Shouldn't we wait and see if Bobby wants to do this too?"

"Robert will be keen on the idea, I assure you. We'll invite Corrine's friend along with us to make the perfect foursome."

"Four it is then," said Chad. "Let me get busy and see what I can do."

Reaching for his wallet, Frederic retrieved a credit card. "Here Chadwick, use my card."

"I wouldn't think of it, sir. You have already provided the accommodations. The fishing trip is my treat."

"As you wish Chadwick," stated Frederic, replacing his card in his wallet.

"Please try not to throw my brother overboard," whispered Liz to Chad.

"You sure know how to spoil a man's chumming," whispered Chad back.

"He's a pain but he is still my flesh and blood."

"I draw the line at baiting his hook."

"What are you two whispering about over there?"

"It's a surprise, mother," answered Liz.

"Marvelous, you know how I love surprises, but your father despises them, so plan accordingly."

Liz just rolled her eyes and grabbed Chad by the arm and pulled him toward the balcony, but not before she refreshed their Margaritas. Looking down at the beach Liz suggested that they change into their bathing suits and take a walk. Chad agreed. It sounded like a wonderful idea, cherishing any opportunity to be near the water. Minutes later they returned dressed for the beach, having fought back the desire to make love while in the confines of their boudoir, figuring best not to push their luck right now. As a gesture, Liz even invited her parents to join them, selfishly glad when they declined, saying they would wait for Corinne and her latest boy friend to arrive. The descent to ground level seemed to take forever with the elevator stopping on almost every floor, accumulating an assortment of people along the way. Finally, they reached their destination. Liz spotted Corrine at the check-in counter decked in a custom fit blouse, shorts, sandals, and hat with matching sunglasses.

"See you made it sis. Nice outfit."

"Lizzie, Lizzie, my dear sister and Chad, aren't you both just looking quite touristy," replied Corrine, eyeing them head to toe. "Has everyone arrived?"

"Everyone is here except for Bobby and Cory and their rug rats," said Liz.

"Yeah, mother told me they were flying in."

"Did you end up coming alone?"

"Oh no, Alex is in the restroom, should be back any second."

"So where did you meet this Alex?"

"We met during New Years in Aruba. I think I'm in love."

"Again," commented Liz, rolling her eyes.

"I mean it this time," bragged Corrine. "Alex has taken me where no other has ever taken me before."

"Spare us all the graphic details, sis."

"Speak for your self," spoke up Chad, receiving a complimentary elbow to his ribs.

"There's Alex now," said Corrine, smiling and waving like a little college co-ed.

"Where, I don't see him?"

Liz and Chad searched the crowd for Alex but did not manage to pick him out of the assortment of guys meandering in the lobby. "Where?"

"Here," said Corrine. "Alex, I would like you to meet my sister Liz and her husband Chad."

"Could have picked you both out in a crowd; Corrine described you perfectly, plus I must confess, I have seen photographs."

Alex was not what they had expected. She was quite beautiful, tall, and lanky, very black, and possessed a distinctive, British sounding accent.

"Father is going to crap a brick," blurted Liz.

Corrine frowned, "Why, because she's black?"

Alex smiled, "Certainly, he has nothing against Britts, does he?"

"You're a woman," exclaimed Liz. "This is going to be worth the price of admission. Corrine, you've outdone yourself this time"

"I apologize, Alex. My sister can be so crude."

"I certainly hope this will not inconvenience anyone," spoke up Alex. "I warned Corrine that she should have confirmed this with her family first."

"Nonsense. Corrine always brings someone with her on these annual family outings. You need not worry about an invitation. Any friend of my sister is a friend of mine. A matter of a fact, we will help you with your luggage," said Liz, then whispering to Chad, "I wouldn't miss this for the world."

Chad eyed her. She was gorgeous to say the least; possibly the prettiest black woman he had ever seen. She could have just leapt from the pages of Sport's Illustrated, swimsuit edition quality. Close, he discovered on the ride up in the elevator. Alex confessed that she had appeared in Playboy, Miss August 2008. He thought she looked vaguely familiar. This vacation was looking up.

"Tell you what, if you ladies can handle the luggage, I think I'll head on to the beach. I need a little fresh air. Liz, I'll walk south toward that pier if you decide to join me later."

"We can manage. Have a nice walk and I'll see you when you get back," said Liz, then she turned with her back to the others and whispered to Chad, "Sorry, I just can't pass this one up. It's going to be so good. Father is going to flip out."

"Knock yourself out," whispered Chad, choosing not to be a participant in this little three ring circus. He respected Professor Bornfreund too much and didn't want to be party to or witness the ordeal anticipated by Liz. Besides, it was a gorgeous day and a shame to waste an opportunity to stroll down the beach and take in the sights, sounds, and smells of the Atlantic Ocean. He had brought his surfboard but didn't really see any waves right now that beckoned him to take the plunge. Maybe later if he was lucky. Chad paused after passing through the pool gate and onto the beach. He had removed his sandals and placed them beside the entryway shower. He wiggled in toes in the fluffy sand. It was hot but not unbearable yet. Come summer you would have to quicken your pace until reaching the more packed version of the beach sand. This was his domain, sea salt running though his veins.

Scanning north then south, the beaches didn't appear to be too crowded yet, but it was just the first week of May. Tourist season was not in full throttle yet on the Carolina Grand Strand. This suited him just fine. It was a pleasant break from the Florida Keys where there never seemed to be a lull time for tourist. As planned, Chad headed south toward the pier, an estimated mile and half away. He opted to walk in the shallows, the tiny waves breaking over his ankles. Gulls squealed their high pitch squawks darting along the beach ahead of him and then taking flight to land just behind him. Tiny spindly legged Sand Pipers played dodge ball with the incoming waves, moving to the rhythm of the tide. A line of Pelicans flew in formation about 50 yards beyond the breaking surf, riding the winds like motor-less gliders.

In either direction Chad saw boats hauling large parachutes behind them. The canopy style chutes were used in the parasailing attraction. Some distance away from shore Chad could make out at least two people per parasail, their feet dangling below their harnessed carriage. He had often seen those in the Keys with up to three people suspended. He had tried it once but didn't receive the rush he had expected. Chad did not like the aspect of not being in control of the parachute. He liked even less the toying of the boat's commander slowing down until your feet dipped into the water and then speeding back up to launch you upward. Chad had recently witnessed news footage where the cable had broken, sending the people floating freestyle to a not so pleasant landing. One such incident had resulted in death as the occupants crashed inland onto the balcony of a hotel. Lawsuits were pending of course, but the industry itself still thrived.

Even though the peak tourist season still lay ahead, the ocean attractions lured their marks whenever they could. A wave runner tugged a Banana Boat as four people clung onto it for their dear lives, whooping and hollering to express their glee. A splattering of kayakers and a wave runners speckled the horizon. A group of four Sea-doos, PWC, Personal Watercrafts of choice, launched airborne over the waves, the drivers weaving and rooster tailing their way through what the ocean had to offer them.

Chad refocused. All the activity wasn't reserved for the ocean. An array of bathing attire was sported by the hodgepodge of sun seekers. Some were most revealing and quite sensual while others revealed entirely too much, bellies hanging over their waste bands and unflattering bulges protruding from precarious regions. No matter what shape or size the sun worshippers were in search of the perfect tan, many settling for that painful burn instead. Noticeably, it was still too early in the season for most of the beach's hard bodies. The older and middle-aged crowd dominated the sandy turf. Just the same, Chad took in what nature had to offer, the good, the bad, or the ugly.

He, himself, was no hard body but at least he had no flab overhanging his belt line. His muscles were fairly toned from surfing, swimming, and skin diving. He was not a fitness freak but kept in shape. He did sport a dark tanned body with no signs of tan lines, compliments of his and Liz's private pool offering them the freedom to sunbath in the buff. Chad kept his brownish hair cropped short. His boyish almost whiskerless face made him look 10 years younger than his 40 years on this earth. Not a big guy at five feet, ten and 165 pounds. He was two inches shorter than Liz who stood at an even six feet. They were a perfect fit. Their bodies seemed to conform to one another in every possible way.

Four approaching girls, each clad in colorful bikinis, caught Chad's eye; not because he had lustful thoughts, but because their attention was focused on four guys walking just ahead of him and in their direction. The girls giggled and whispered, maintained off and on eye contact with the boys. Chad couldn't see the reaction of the four boys but suspected it to be similar. After the four met and passed, Chad smiled at the comical sight of the four boys turning to catch butt shots of the girls, remembering how he had walked in those shoes in his youth. Seconds later, as if having a sixth sense, the girls peeked back at the boys who had turned and were now not looking at them. The eight would most likely remain strangers. Such was the life. The boys then broke away running down the beach toward a crowd congregated about 100 yards further down the beach. From his vantage point, Chad could not make out what commotion had the people so preoccupied. He quickened his pace as more onlookers arrived. He could now make out something in the surf; no, more than one something in the surf. He sure hoped it wasn't any of those missing fishermen.

Through breaks in the crowds he could make out five, possibly six figures in the shallows. His heart skipped a beat, thinking his worse nightmares may be about to be confirmed. A lone black man was attempting to wave the crowd back, but few if any paid attention to his pleas. Chad took a deep breath and politely elbowed his way through the wall of people. He counted seven in the surf and exhaled, relieved that none of them were human. Bottle nose dolphins had beached themselves, small waves lapping against their motionless bodies. At first observation he assumed the mammals were dead but as he drew closer, he saw the blow holes opening and closing.

The black man announced his authority, proclaiming to be a detective of Horry County. The crowd reacted reluctantly to his request to stand back. Chad noted that the dolphins appeared to range in length from around six to twelve feet. He stepped in to assist the detective.

"Folks, I'm Chad Reynolds, a marine biologist. Please do as the detective has instructed and give these creatures a little room. There is no need to traumatize them further."

"I'm Detective Sylvester Stone. I welcome your assistance in this matter, Mister Reynolds."

Chad attempted to lighten the mood, "What crime did they commit to bring you to the scene, detective?"

Falling in line Detective Stone said, "Nude sunbathing. We do have laws against that here in Garden City." The crowd irrupted in laughs and snickers.

Taking a more serious tone Chad asked, "Does anyone know how long they have been beached?"

"I saw them come scooting on shore from my balcony about ten minutes ago," said an elderly woman in an oversized straw hat and a wild colored flowery sun dress. "I teach dance and I must say their arrival almost looked choreographed."

A young boy asked, "What kind of fish are they?"

"They're not fish. They're mammals. Atlantic Bottlenose Dolphins to be exact," answered Chad.

"They look like fish," repeated the young lad.

"If you don't mind, I'd like to examine them for any signs of injury or possible sickness," said Chad.

"Please, by all means," answered Detective Stone. "Let me know if I can help."

After about ten minutes moving from one to the other Chad announced. "Odd, I found no signs of injury on any of them. They appear extremely healthy, alert and well fed."

"Why do you think they beach themselves?"

"Now that's an excellent question, detective. Often one or more is stricken and intentionally beach themselves and because of stressful clicking, others sometime follow suit."

"But you said you didn't think any of them are sick," stated Detective Stone.

"And I stick by that statement. We are going to need a few volunteers from our onlookers to see if we can assist our friends in getting to deeper water. These larger ones probably weigh over 800 pounds and the smaller ones around two hundred. This won't be a walk in the park, so let's tackle the two larger females first. Once we get them back in the surf, hopefully the others will be easier and more willing to venture into deeper water."

Chad, the detective, and four young men along with an energetic middle age lady wrestled with the first twelve-footer. They moved it back and forth until finally wiggling it into deeper water. Once the waves were breaking over its back, they maneuvered it so that its nose pointed toward the open ocean. Oddly, even when the water covered half of the dolphin's dorsal fin, it refused to swim. The volunteers under Chad's guidance walked the dolphin out to waste deep water and pushed it forward. It disappeared under the breaking waves and the crowd cheered triumphantly.

"Okay, one down and six to go," announced Chad, wadding back to the other large female.

Just as he reached her, people in the crowd began yelling and pointing. Chad turned to see the twelve-footer launching its body airborne to again anchor itself in the shallow water. Chad rubbed the back of his neck, distraught by the disturbing behavior. Ten minutes later they had successfully forced it back into the ocean and had managed to steer the second one into the surf. A scream from the shore alerted Chad that both had again beached themselves. Over the span of the next hour they returned each of the dolphins to the ocean only to have them beach themselves again. The crowd of rescuers had become too exhausted by their efforts to continue trying.

Chad realized their attempts were in vain. Convinced they were not sick, he derived that something had the dolphins spooked and fearful of returning to open ocean. Clueless, he could not picture a predator that could instill such fear in the much faster prey. Sharks, even a great white, was not a real threat to them. No orca swam in these waters, so what out there had driven them aground and to a sure death rather than face what lurked in the deeper waters? He had no answer.

He flopped down in the water next to the largest one and tried to splash water onto its skin. He asked others to do the same. The detective informed him that he had contacted the local aquarium. A team was on the way with the equipment to rescue and relocate the dolphins to a holding tank at the aquarium until they could diagnose their problem. Chad hoped they would arrive soon. They had already lost two young females to exposure or possibly shock. Chad watched helplessly as they lost a younger male and one of the larger females, leaving only three dolphins clinging to life. He saw a series of vehicles enter beach access. One sported a crane type sling lift, the other an open water tank. The Calvary had arrived but most likely too late to save the weakened three survivors.

"You got to be kidding me," whispered Chad at first sight of the rescuers.

"Chadwick Reynolds," shouted the man approaching him.

"Roth Niederwerter," responded Chad, stunned to see Roth here on the South Carolina coast.

4

Only the large female that Chad had coddled vigorously had survived long enough to be loaded into the rescue pod as Roth had dubbed his aquarium tank on wheels. His staff now transported it back to the local aquarium where Roth was the curator and a partner with 52% controlling interest. Roth hung around to talk old times with Chad. There wasn't much to talk about though. The two had been bitter rivals in college and in their early careers in the private sector. They had both courted the same young lady in college, but she had entered the military after they graduated leaving them both high and dry to pursue her dream job in the Navy. Chad had met Liz by then.

"Sorry you didn't have more experience in rescue of marine mammals," stated Roth Niederwerter, taking the first jab.

"Experience had nothing to do with it, Roth. These creatures were totally stressed and freaked out about something in these waters. They thwarted all attempts to assist them back to deeper water."

"Probably infested with an invasive parasite," rebutted Roth.

"I don't believe so. I assume you will conduct a complete autopsy on them. I believe you will find them to be extremely healthy. I found no signs of disease or parasites in any of them."

"Dead in my book doesn't equate healthy. Not to fret, my expert team and I will diagnose their problem, I assure you. We should learn much from the survivor if she does indeed make it."

"I'm sure your Cracker Jack team won't allow the creature to die, especially after I nursed her and kept her alive until you arrived."

"One out of seven, not good odds for a seasoned marine biologist, especially if they were all as healthy as you claim," snipped Roth.

"These dolphins were stressed about something. They do not appear to be diseased."

"And what pray tale could have threatened their existence and forced them to face death here instead? Sorry, I am not buying your theory. I know these waters. They have no natural predator."

"That I can't answer," said Chad. "Your territory, I'm sure you will find the answers, Roth."

"You never were that good at solving the large problems were you, Chadwick?"

"At least I didn't cheat to get where I am, Roth."

"What are you implying, Chadwick?"

"Not implying anything. I deal in fact, not assumption."

"Mister Always Color Between the Lines, you're pathetic."

"At least I sleep well at night. How about you?"

"Like a brick," said Roth. "I'll let you know what we find. Are you in town for awhile?"

"For the next couple of weeks, I'm here with Liz's family."

"Ah, I forgot, your father-in-law is the renowned Professor Frederic J. Bornfreund, how convenient for your career? You have learned how to play the game, haven't you? Too bad it took you so long."

Chad ignored that comment. He didn't feel like wagering a verbal debate with his long-time nemesis. He never enjoyed it back then and surely would find no pleasure in doing now. He figured he would just allow Roth to purge it from his system and be done with it.

"Sorry to learn that your father passed a few years back. And how is that mother of yours? Is she still chasing; now what was it, I forget, werewolves or vampires or was it little green men in flying saucers?"

Chad balled his fist, tempted to bash that smile off Roth's face but instead he flexed and opened his hand. He absolutely refused to allow him to push his buttons and completely control the situation. "Mother is doing wonderfully. Thanks for asking. Normally she would have been here with us, but her research does keep her busy. She still lectures and teaches part time."

"Hope she didn't get beamed up to the mother ship," chuckled Roth.

"Oh, she doesn't do that anymore," mocked Chad. "Not since she designed her own craft. She's quite the pilot I must say. She's even thinking about commercializing flights. You know the public is just giddy, anticipating the opportunity for space travel."

Roth ignored the sarcasm. "How many of you are here for our wonderful bike rallies?"

Roth's bike week references meant nothing to Chad. He replied, "Frederic and Teal Bornfreund, Liz's brother and his wife, their two children, her sister and a friend, Liz and me. That would make ten of us if you can still do math."

"Excellent," he said, reaching inside his windbreaker pocket. "Here you go, complementary tickets for admission to the aquarium for one and all. I can guarantee that you and your family will thoroughly enjoy the visit. Here is my card. Call me when you plan to attend, and I will arrange the VIP tour and cater dinner. I so look forward to conversing with Professor Bornfreund and meeting the siblings of Elizabeth. Again, sorry for the loss of your father, my condolences go out to you and your mother. It saddens me that she could not be here for your family festivities. I would have enjoyed her tall tales of mythical creatures and folklore."

"I'll be sure to tell her of our meeting. Thank you for the tickets. I'm sure the children will enjoy looking at your fish once they tire of the ocean and the beach."

"Come by, I'll give you the exclusive private tour and you can check on the progress of your sole surviving dolphin," said Roth, hopping into his Land Rover.

"You're a better man than me, Mister Reynolds," stated Detective Stone. "I would have decked Roth Niederwerter ten minutes ago. I'm off duty, so who would care?"

"Detective Stone, so you know Roth."

"The entire Grand Strand knows that arrogant a-hole. Please, drop the formalities. My friends call me Sly."

"I'm Chad and I share your sentiment."

"Sounds like you were old college buddies or something."

"Or something," replied Chad.

"I take it you don't much care for our aquarium curator either."

"It shows," smiled Chad.

"Just a tad."

An eruption of rumbling thunder abruptly filled the airwaves. Chad frowned and finally asked "What the heck was that?"

Sly smiled. "Welcome to bike week."

"Bike week?"

"Actually, two of them, back to back. You and your family picked the two weeks that we have the spring motorcycle rallies here at the beach."

"Is that what Roth was referring to?"

"Exactly, and that's why I'm taking a few days off right now because come this weekend and for the next two weeks, every cop

45

on the force will be stretched to the limit. We will have nearly half million bikers in town for both events."

"Both events?"

"We have the Harley Rally coming up this weekend and then the Atlantic Beach Bike Fest the following week."

"Why two, can't they be combined?"

"If you're here both weeks you'll notice the difference," smiled Sly. "The Harleys are what you've been hearing. Next, the rice cutters arrive whining their way through our streets. I'm black so I can say this. The youngsters during what the locals have dubbed Black Bike Week are much more disrespectful to the community and introduce somewhat of a thug element. The city council has been lobbying for years to boot out the bikers because the locals say they wreak too much havoc."

"Do they?"

"This is a tourist town and they pump a lot of money into the community, so why shun them I say? Who's next, the golfers, and spring break crowds, then the Canadians and northerners, where do you draw the line? I think the locals despise the black bikers the most, but they can't get rid of one rally without getting rid of the other. The NAACP would be on them like a bunch of banshees if they tried to shut down the Atlantic Beach Fest and not the Harley one. The Harley bikers are the older, white crowd, and while we have our issues with them too, they're not as bad as my black brothers."

"I'm shocked they even still call it the National Association for the Advancement of Colored People. To me that sounds so racist."

"It's sort of funny. Atlantic Beach residents try to hold on to that poor black people persona refusing to allow developers to really make something out of the community. Atlantic Beach was the black man's beach and they want to forever remind everyone of that fact. You know, it's one of those see how you treated our

46

people little grudges, I think. They need to let go of that idiotic concept and join the rest of society. It can be a darn circus at town meetings. It's so embarrassing to be a black man and see them behaving as they do."

"If you feel so strongly, have you considered running for some office there?"

"I'm no damn fool. You definitely can't fight that city hall. Enough of the history lesson, I need to let you go back to trying to have an enjoyable vacation and me back to my day off."

"Thank you, detective. This has been a most enlightening experience."

"I believe in keeping it real. I'm not into my people verses your people and do you know how your people treated my people back on the southern plantations. None of us lived that life back then, time to let it go. I don't personally know any slave owners or slaves. This is an equal opportunity country if you're willing to set your goals, get off your butt and work for it. That's how my parents raised me."

"You had very wise parents."

"Nice to have met you Chad Reynolds and I hope you solve the beached dolphin mystery."

"Pleasure has been mine Detective Sly Stone. I'm on vacation. It's not my problem to solve."

"Here's my card if you ever need my assistance."

"Thanks. I hope I never do," smiled Chad, as he watched Sly turn and jog down the beach.

He gazed at the six carcasses as were plenty of onlookers. These poor creatures were terrified of something in that water; he was convinced of it. The rumble of heavy equipment alerted him that Roth had summoned help to remove the dead dolphins. The

47

aquarium's logo was plastered on the sides of the crane and truck. Chad decided to cut his walk short and headed back toward the hotel, but not before he scanned the ocean for any signs of an intruder. He saw nothing out of place and shrugged. He was on vacation and it wasn't his problem.

5

Captain Joe sat on his boat, still troubled by what he had witnessed. The Coast Guard was not completely buying his depiction. Four men were missing, and the shrimp net had been shredded. What more proof did they need he wondered. Something horrific had happened to old Salty Santa and the rest, but he had no idea what. He had not seen whatever had attacked the Holy Grail. No denying it though, something had indeed attacked it. One does not see the underbelly of a shrimp boat on a calm day at sea if something extraordinary is not influencing the buoyancy.

Young Vic was a worthless turd, just fact, but he had not deserved the fate he had received. Joe had ordered the young man to accompany him to the Holy Grail. That made him responsible for his disappearance, even though his Uncle Ken did not blame him. Divers had not found a trace of the missing men. People just don't vanish in plain sight and in broad daylight in calm seas without even finding any shred of clothing or something. Even sharks could not have completely consumed all the evidence that quickly. And no shark could have tipped that shrimp boat up on end like he had witnessed. This was not a cinema production of *Jaws*. There was no monstrous shark large enough to take out a trawler.

Captain Joe was back to square one. He had no answers; not even a wild guess as to what had happened. Neither Ken nor young Vic had seen what he had seen. And if Vic had, he was gone now. Whatever had gotten Captain Dave and his two men had most certainly taken Vic, probably while he was hanging over the side of the Holy Grail puking out his guts. Both Vic and Ken had been too busy with the Shrimp Cocktail's net to have seen what he had witnessed from the wheelhouse. Poor Dave had not even had a chance to make a distress call. It had happened too quickly. What could do that, and the captain not have time to react? Sea monsters did not exist. Something sinister did though, but what.

Now down to a one-man crew, Ken, he couldn't resume shrimping and that posed a new dilemma. And with what had happened aboard the Holy Grail, there weren't exactly a slew of volunteers scrambling to take Vic's spot and venture onto the open sea. Ken had told him he would ask around. At least he wasn't bailing on him. With his nephew now missing and a funeral pending whether they found his body or not, his ability to do any shrimping had been compromised in the near future. Joe poured a second glass of Apricot Brandy, sipping on his nighttime brew much earlier than he had ever done before. Strangely enough he felt none of the soothing affects. A long night awaited him once it did arrive. A longer day had already haunted him. What had attacked the Holy Grail and what would prevent it from attacking again? This dogged him relentlessly. Questions deserved answers. He had none.

Captain Joe had weathered hurricanes and rode out thirty-forty-foot swells. He had even overpowered an attacking nine-foot hammerhead while snorkeling in the Bahamas, escaping with not so much as a scratch. He once had to abandon ship, not his own, due to a destructive out of control fire. He had floated for four days clinging to a boat paddle until finally been rescued by a passing charter boat. That same charter boat had been skippered by Captain Marvin Brown, now among the missing. Captain Joe had never feared the sea, not until now. Chills raced up his spine as he recapped what he had witnessed with the Holy Grail. Evil lurked in these waters. Of that he was certain. What was he going to do about it? That was the six-million-dollar question.

6

The young runaway sat in the sand of the secluded stretch of beach, soaking in the rays. She loved listening to the crashing waves. They didn't have an ocean in central Ohio where she had escaped the living hell of an abusive stepfather and half brother. Her mother had never defended her against the onslaught of the males in the family. She had remained in denial. After her mother had died it had only gotten worse. What they had taken from her fifteen-year-old body for free she now parlayed for drugs, food, and pocket money. Her body was her lifeline. At least now she chose when to offer it and received pay for the swap. It had funded her trip from Ohio to the Carolina beaches. She now reaped one of life's little pleasures, Methamphetamines, her escape from the only world she had known.

She had made her camp 100 yards south of the State Park. By doing so she avoided park authority, didn't have to pay the park fee for camping, and still made use of the public facilities. Plus, she could forage for food among the countless campsites. When the campers slept, she took what she wanted. She had mastered her technique and had never gotten caught. She had even managed to turn a trick or two from the more adventurous vacationing campers, dirty old men mostly, with the cash to pay. This had turned out to be a very profitable gig having prompted her to remain in the same spot for almost a week now, longer than she had resided anywhere since leaving Ohio. It was her version of paradise, the best she would ever have given her circumstances.

The Meth helped sooth the cramps brought on by her menstrual cycle. The first signs of her period had been welcomed by joyful tears. She possessed no birth control and always encouraged her tricks to use a condom. If they didn't have one, which was often for some of her teenage clients, she gave in to their desires. Rolling the dice had thus far paid off. She often wondered if all that abuse inflicted by her stepfather and half brother had somehow damaged her inside to prevent a pregnancy. If so, that was the only good thing that had come out of it. She didn't need a child and couldn't afford an abortion. But some facilities offered free abortions if the time ever came. She hoped it never did though. She did not want to take a life even though she couldn't provide a home for a child.

51

She chose to live an anonymous life and carried no identification. She always used a different alias when she arrived at a new location. Currently she went by the name of Dakota Williams. She liked the name Dakota. It sounded so in control, so independent, like a woman who knew who she was, fearless and not one to be crossed. Men liked that name too. It beckoned them to her web. Dakota, they wanted Dakota, had fantasies of Dakota. Dakota would fulfill those wild fantasies while taking everything they had. Come to Dakota and let her quench your thirst. She would remain Dakota Williams until she decided to leave. She currently had no such intentions. She liked living here.

Right now, she needed to wash off the stench and nastiness of the blood flowing from her. She currently had no feminine hygiene products and really had no desire to waste her hard-earned money on such luxuries. Taking a dip in the ocean now and then would take care of it. She would avoid offering herself to any prospects in the meantime. There were other ways to satisfy her customers. The money was good either way. Before advancing onto the beach she scanned the northern direction toward the park front. She was in luck. She only saw three or four people, all in beach loungers and none facing in her direction. With bike week approaching, most of the usual tourist crowd had gotten the heck out of Dodge. The next couple of weeks should be quite profitable for her with the bikers coming to town. They would enjoy their time with Dakota Williams. She could possibly hitch a ride with one of them. The destination wasn't important providing it wasn't central Ohio.

Dakota tiptoed into the water, still a little too chilly for her liking. She turned her back to the breaking waves and eased backwards. The first waves tickled her ankles. Ten yards further out, the waves crashes on the back of her knees. She shivered but continued to back her way to at least waste deep. There she could dip down, remove her panties, clean herself and them. She had done it a thousand times effortlessly. In warmer weather, she would wait until dark and skinny dip while washing her things. Too bad it wasn't warmer and dark now.

Finally, she reached the level she desired but this posed new challenges. Every other wave crashed hard against her backside. She managed to retain her balance and remove her cloths from the waste down. The cool rushing water did feel good. She glanced every so often up the beach, but no one appeared to have seen her. She dipped her head under quickly, submerging her entire body underneath the cold salty ocean. Now shivers overcame her, the ocean breezes chilling her to the bone. Next challenge, with the ebbing tide and heavy wet clothes, she had to manage to replace the removed garments.

Her back still facing the open ocean, she felt the rush of what she assumed to be an exceptionally large wave crashing toward her. She leaned backwards against the flow, legs spread, clutching her garments, and bracing for the impact. The young runaway currently named Dakota Williams was no more; plucked from her bathing spot in one clean swoop. At the tender age of fifteen she would join the countless number of runaways never to be seen again. Even worse, the authorities would never know to include her among their mounting missing. The encampment of the nameless homeless person would draw little interest if ever discovered. At least she had died with clean underwear, even though they were in her hands and not on her bottom.

7

Chadwick Reynolds returned to the hotel disturbed by what he had witnessed on the beach. He was still convinced that the dolphins had been trying to escape when they beached themselves, but escape from what? Riding the elevator to the 10th floor he struggled with if he should share this information with Liz. He knew she would challenge him getting involved while on vacation. But how would he explain the encounter with Roth and the tickets if he didn't confess the entire story? Liz had only briefly met Roth in college and only then after Chad and Roth had parted ways after their intense courtships to win the hand of Vanessa Daetwyler. Vanessa had indeed left both high and dry to join the Navy before completing her last couple of years of college. She had written both men a brief Dear John letter providing no valid explanation for severing the ties with either of them. Chad had considered himself the front runner and was heartbroken by her swift exit. Roth had blamed Chad for screwing things up and causing her to run.

Chad certainly would never have met and married Liz if Vanessa had remained in the picture. He thought he had found his soul mate, even with all the interference from Roth. He had always believed that Roth had been pursuing her just to prove to him that he was the better man. Chad never believed for a second that she could ever have been interested in Roth. Then again, Roth had produced those photos of him and her to prove he had indeed bedded her. From the angle of the camera, Vanessa obviously had not known Roth had photographed their liaison. He never told Vanessa what Roth had done and that he had seen the evidence. Crushed, he had stepped back to catch his breath and that's when Roth had moved in and taken charge just as he had intended.

Roth could be so ruthless. He had planned and calculated this little maneuver and had banked on Chad reacting just as he had done. Once Roth had gotten his foot in the door, he had rooted Chad out and somehow convinced her that Chad was not good for her. He didn't know what Vanessa had been told but for a while she kept her distance from him. Still reeling from those explicit photos Chad had allowed Roth to win her hand. Only when it was too late had he tried to regain what he has lost. Vanessa apparently confused, had decided it was best for her to leave. Roth's plan backfired and they both were taken out of the running.

He and Roth had competed on everything; academics, sports, you name it, and they had battled tooth and claw for the win or recognition. Chad constantly kicked himself in the ass for allowing Roth to manipulate him like a puppet. As if possessed by a demon he had to one up and out-do everything Roth attempted. The loss of Vanessa just made Chad's urge to defeat Ross devour him like a cancer. Their rivalry became intense, often malicious and over the edge, both pushing the envelope to take it to new limits. And now, here there were again.

Chad intended to take the high road and not allow Roth to do what Roth did best and push him to do something he would surely regret. They were no longer stupid immature kids and there was no Vanessa up for grabs. Roth had nothing in his arsenal that he could use to get under his skin. He could thwart off the dolphin digs. After all, in two weeks he would be back in the Keys and Roth would be a distant memory. The best way to defeat Roth was be cordial and polite, maintain a poker face, and ignore any challenges. Chad decided to take that strategy, but could he pull it off? It had never worked in the past. The elevator door opened and there stood Alexis Clarke in a shear beach robe and an extremely tiny hot pink bikini. Chad had flashes of her Playboy spread. Time seemed to freeze. She spoke and snapped him out of it.

"I'm not sure you want to go in there right now," she said in her British accent.

"Didn't go well, huh?"

"Still going on, that's why I decided to give them room to air it out," she smiled. "I now see where Corrine gets her tenacity."

"Corrine is a piece of work indeed," admitted Chad, still holding the elevator door open. "Mind if I ride back down with you? I don't think I care to witness this either."

"You're a very wise man, Chad," she said, caressing his chin between her fingertips, sending a series of electrified chills throughout his body

Chad twitched nervously on the return ride back down, reacting too much like a high school kid in awe of being in the presence of a Playboy pinup. He tried his best to control his wondering eyes, but the eyes were winning the contest. Alex had noticed, smiling her approval, a gorgeous full lipped, picture perfect smile. Her jet-black complexion enhanced the experience.

"So, Chad, Corrine tells me you're some sort of scientist," she said, breaking the silence.

"Marine biologist actually."

"So, you swim with the fishes," she replied, trying to sound like Marlon Brando in the Godfather.

Chad chuckled. "Sharks can be found everywhere."

The elevator door opened on the 4th floor and a mother and three badly sunburned children entered carrying an assortment of bags, towels, and toys worthy of a pack mule. Mommy gave Alex the look up and down, expressing her distaste or possibly envy for the chocolate goddess. While she was no living doll in her one-piece bathing suit, the woman still held her own having had what Chad assumed to be three children. The kids maybe ranging from two to five years old were remarkably well behaved. Chad knew Liz wanted kids, so he always observed children behavioral habits preparing for the day when they would have their own. Finally, they arrived at the ground floor. He allowed mommy and the children to exit first before cordially motioning to Alex, her turn.

"Care to walk on the beach?"

Thinking about his last journey he almost declined, but instead suggested that they walk up the beach and away from the dolphin clean-up. She removed her robe and sandals, leaving them on a pool chaise lounger. Chad felt sweat breaking out on his forehead, still having imagines of her in Playboy. Like Chad, she headed directly to the ocean to wet her feet in the ebbing tide.

"Tell me Alex, how did you and Corrine meet?"

"We met at one of those all inclusive adult themed resorts in Jamaica," she replied, kicking up water with her long slender toes.

"Interesting," said Chad. "Never been to one. What do you do at an adult all inclusive?"

"It's not what you might be thinking," she winked. "It isn't an orgy fest or anything like that, but nudity is permitted. They have regular swimming areas and swimming pools where clothes are optional. No children are permitted at the resort."

"Which one did you choose?"

"It may surprise you but I'm really shy when it comes to total exposure. I do go topless to avoid tan lines but prefer to keep my buns private. Yes, I do have tan lines. Corrine, now she's quite the exhibitionist, you know?"

"Actually, I haven't seen that side of her; no pun intended."

"Too bad, you would definitely enjoy every inch of her exquisite body. But, then again, she is your sister-in-law, isn't she? I shouldn't be referring her to you in that manner. Please excuse my rudeness."

"That's okay. Liz has shared a few Corrine stories with me. It's no mystery that Corrine is a wild child."

"That girl takes it to a whole new level," smiled Alex, obviously wanting to share the intimate details with Chad. "She embraced the full nudity option."

Chad again surprised himself with his next question. "Have you always been into women?"

"Never. Corrine is my first and only experience. I could never imagine being with another woman. I have never been attracted to women at all until Corrine came into my life. She made the first move and swept me literally off my feet. I think I'm in love."

Chad hated to spoil the moment for her and burst her bubble, but he had firsthand witnessed Corrine go through lovers like pairs of shoes. Granted, this was the first female he had ever seen her with but with Corrine why should this be any different than any of her other brief affairs? He certainly hoped his sister-in-law did not end up breaking Alex's heart, because he did like her and not just because she had been in Playboy.

Déjà vu, Chad saw a large crowd accumulated 50 yards up the beach. He almost suggested to Alex that they should head back, but curiosity always nails the cat. As they approached, he caught whiff of the stench as did Alex now holding her nose and almost gagging. From less than 15 yards away Chad could now see it was not dolphins this time. These beach strolls were becoming way too adventurous for a vacationer.

Chad told Alex, "You should probably stay here why I go and take a look." She nodded, totally okay with not getting any closer.

Chad wasn't as prepared as he thought he was for what was beached this time. The bile rose without warning and he leaned over, grabbed his knees, and began vomiting. He wasn't the only one. Many of the onlookers had already done the same. Between heaves he caught quick looks of the lower torso of a person. The real shocker, the body had been severed almost cleanly at the belt line. What remained was an intact pair of faded jeans, white socks, and brown loafers with slivers of flesh above the waste washing in the surf, an eerie sight to say the least.

Some one patted him on the back and asked, "Are you okay, Chad?" Still unable to straighten up he managed a quick look and saw Detective Sly Stone standing beside him. "So much for taking a couple of days off," he added.

Chad managed to cough out, "What a vacation…"

8

By the time Alex and Chad had returned to the condo the fireworks from Corrine and Frederic had subsided. Neither were present in any of the condo common areas. Chad spotted Liz and Teal sitting on the balcony. Alex opted to retire to her assigned bedroom. Chad reluctantly joined his wife and mother-in-law on the balcony.

As if acting all was well, Liz asked Chad, "What's going on up the beach?"

"A body or what's left of it has washed on shore. Authorities have it blocked off now and are investigating."

"Did someone drown? I heard them warning of riptides this morning on one of the local television stations."

"Possibly, Teal" lied Chad, not believing for a minute what he had seen resulted from a drowning but figuring he would save them from the gore.

"You didn't get involved, did you?"

"No Liz. Not unless you call puking on the sand being proactive. Alex was shaken by the incident too."

"You were walking on the beach with Alex," exclaimed Liz

"Not to worry, she only has eyes for Corrine," blurted out Chad before thinking.

"Oh my," commented Teal, fanning her face with her hand.

"This will really thrill father," snickered Liz.

"I don't think we should share this little tidbit with your father, Liz. He's not in the best of moods."

"Alex is really a nice person."

"And you formed your opinion solely on your brief walk on the beach," questioned Liz.

"Between puking, must I remind you."

"Did you know she has posed nude in Playboy?"

"Heavens no, Teal. She doesn't seem like the type to do something like that," Chad said, acting surprised.

Liz gave him the look only women possess, "Not the type Chad, are you blind?"

"Just kidding. I still have that issue actually."

"Maybe she can autograph it for you," spouted Liz

"Only if Corrine brings her to visit us in the Keys," said Chad, egging it on. "I didn't bring it with me."

"I better go check on your father."

As Teal exited, Corrine appeared from the bedroom. "Was that the boss or what, the old man is so pissed at me. Don't you just love it."

"I can't believe you get your rocks off of making him angry," said Liz.

"You wouldn't," replied Corrine, rolling her eyes. "You're his favorite after Bobby that is."

"Where's Alex?" Chad quickly regretted the inquiry.

"Why are you so concerned about Alex?" Liz was in no mood to have conversations about the ex-Playmate.

"Yeah," added Corrine, elbowing Chad in the side. "She's really hot, isn't she?"

"She just saw a dead body washed up on the beach is the only reason I asked," clarified Chad.

"Right," snapped Liz.

"The body, yeah, she told me you guys saw that. She's fine, just showering. What happened to the stiff?"

"I don't know. Detective Stone is investigating."

"Detective Stone," questioned Liz. "I thought you said you hadn't gotten involved?"

"Oh, I met him when we were trying to save the dolphins," blurted out Chad.

"I thought that was save the whales," said Corrine.

"Sorry, I forgot to mention that a group of dolphins beached themselves earlier. We managed to save one of them."

Liz was now furious. And said, "You've had a mighty busy day on the beach, haven't you?"

"But I have these free passes for everyone to visit the aquarium. The kids should love it," said Chad, digging his hole deeper.

"Did the nice detective give them to you?"

"Got them from Roth Niederwerter," said Chad.

"Not 'The' Roth Niederwerter from college," stated Liz.

"One and the same. He is curator and part owner of the aquarium here in town. He transported the surviving dolphin to the aquarium and said he would give us the VIP treatment when we visited."

Ignoring the part about the dolphins, Corrine asked, "Who is this Roth guy?"

"A real smock according to Chad," answered Liz. "He and Chad couldn't get along at all in college. They always tried to one up one another."

"Who ended up winning that one?"

"Depends on who you ask," said Chad.

"No more walking on the beach without me," proclaimed Liz.

"You opted out of this one if I remember correctly."

"Admit it sis, you wanted to see the old man blow his top too, didn't you?"

"I wanted to see him kick your butt, Corrine."

"Didn't happen, did it? The old man isn't quite so intimating anymore, is he? I think I can take him every time now."

Liz crossed her arms and then commented, "So, you brought her here just to get under his skin?"

Corrine smiled, "And it worked perfectly, didn't it?"

"You're just using Alex to get at your father then," stated a perturbed Chad.

"Oh, I'm using her all right and loving every minute," nudged Corrine. "I bet you like what you see too, don't you brother-in-law. She is every young man's fantasy, a Playboy centerfold. I for one can strike that fantasy off my list."

Corrine had pissed Chad off. He could see where this was now headed. Poor Alex was going to have her heart broken at the expense of his revengeful and spiteful sister-in-law. He would just have to do something about that. Teal returned from their bedroom without Frederic.

"Is he still stewing?"

"No Corrine. He's reading and prefers not to be disturbed. He will be joining us for dinner when Bobby and Cody arrive," answered Teal sheepishly.

"He's still pissed. I knew it," smiled Corrine.

"Why do you insist on treating your father in this manner?"

"It's just a game we play, mother, and I'm winning."

"For now," said Liz, leaning against the rail, "I wouldn't count on that lasting though. He doesn't like to lose, and he won't go down without a fight."

"Bring it on, this girl is ready," boasted Corrine, holding both fist in front and striking a boxer's pose.

"Have you forgotten about Alex," Chad reminded her.

"Apparently you haven't," snapped Liz.

"I just think it's unfair the way you're using her just to spite your father."

Teal eyed Corrine, "Is that true?"

"Chad just wants her too. He'll say anything to win her hand, isn't that right, Chad?"

"You're one insane piece of work," scoffed Chad, trying to avoid eye contact with Liz. "You must be adopted or something?"

Teal's face reddened. Adoption was not far off the mark. Only she knew that deep dark secret or so she thought. Skeletons in any closet tend to escape sooner or later.

Alex stood in the balcony doorway. Her expression indicated she had not overheard any of the conversation relevant to her. "When do we eat dinner? I'm famished."

Alex in a bra-less ruby red mid drift and khaki high cut shorts struck quite the pose and indeed was every man's fantasy, thought Chad. It saddened him to know how Corrine was using her and how she had confessed her love for Corrine to him. That put him in a very awkward position. It was a no brainer, however, as he had no intentions of siding with his evil sister-in-law. He wasn't ready to break that news to Alex quite yet and spoil her vacation. This was going to be an eventful family vacation for all the wrong reasons.

"Bobby and Cody and the kids should be arriving at Myrtle Beach National within the hour," confirmed Teal. "We have dinner reservations at eight. Alex, there are plenty of snacks in the kitchen. Please make yourself at home and nibble on something until we dine."

"I have something you can nibble on," whispered Corrine, loudly enough for only Chad to overhear.

He shrugged. "I think I'll go shower."

"You might want to go with him sis," announced Corrine.

"Bite me," snapped Liz.

"Girls," broke in Teal.

This vacation had gone to hell in a hand basket in record time, thought Chad. That's why he despised these forced family fun events. Two weeks would not end soon enough.

9

Roth's team had settled in the surviving dolphin in a holding tank at the aquarium and had begun examining it. Roth planned to bait Chad with the creature. He knew he had him where he wanted him. He asked one of his associates about the dolphin's condition.

"The dolphin is fine best I can tell," said Russell.

"Did you do the test I requested?"

"Look at him Roth. This is a healthy dolphin. He almost appears relieved to be here."

"Russell, just complete the damn lab work like I asked. Don't, and I repeat, don't ever question my authority again or you'll find your ass on the street. Do I make myself clear?"

"Perfectly, I'll complete the test but I'm telling you…"

Roth interrupted, "Russell, you're fired. Get the hell out of here now."

"But…"

"Now," demanded Roth.

After Russell exited, Roth eyed the remaining employees and said, "I will not tolerate insubordination by anyone, understood? Tyson, complete the lab work on our dolphin and have the report on my desk in the morning."

"Will do sir," replied Tyson.

"Colby, how were the crowds today?"

"I'm not sure we had enough to rank them as a crowd. The approach of bike week is already taking its toll on normal tourism and school still is not out. Both are impacting the numbers."

"What are we going to do about it, Paige?" Roth turned to his PR person demanding answers and results.

"Offer a biker special," she responded to the laughter of the others.

"Biker special," repeated Roth.

"Yes sir, a two for; the old buy one get one free if you ride here on a Harley or any motorcycle," stated Paige.

"You do know I hate freebies and discount prices. This aquarium is world class. We should not resort to such extremities. Those peasants should be begging for the privilege to visit."

"The next few weeks are always our toughest I'm afraid."

"We could dress Paige in a bikini and advertise a bike wash," snickered Kevin.

Roth's look at Kevin required no comment. "Paige, I pay you to be creative and innovative. A six-year-old could have suggested buy one, get one free. On my desk in the morning, I expect a solution that doesn't bury us deeper."

"Yes sir, miracles will be on your desk by morning." Paige despised him and hated this pathetic job. Of course, no one liked him or working for him, but the pay caused them to look past it.

"Sir, I heard on the scanner that a body had washed up on the beach north of where the dolphins had beached," said Beth.

"Another wayward dolphin," stated Roth.

"No sir, human and I called my cousin at the morgue. He said the person had been severed at the mid section. He added he had never seen anything like it before on this coast."

"Boating accident," inquired Roth.

"He seemed to think it might have been a shark, a huge shark."

"Interesting, possibly we have a Great White in these waters. There are no adult ones in captivity. Now that would be the perfect draw."

"Sir, no one has ever captured a mature Great White for an aquarium and even the younger ones have a zero survival rate in captivity," mentioned Colby.

"We're not just any aquarium, now are we? Besides, we only need to keep it alive for a couple of weeks until after these horrid bike weeks have expired. Paige, why didn't you think of this?"

"We've got to capture it first," said Tyson.

"Paige, work up a campaign and offer a reward for the capture of a live mature Great White that is suspected to be off our coast. Play up the man killer angle."

"But we have no evidence to support that theory," stated Paige.

"You have my say. You don't require evidence."

"Shouldn't we run this by the local authorities first?"

"Call the mayor and inform her, but don't try my patience sweetheart; I'm not in the mood."

"What if she denies the request?"

"Better still, it's easier to ask for forgiveness than permission. We'll secure our investment first."

"What if there's no shark," added Kevin

"Then I'll fire you next," replied Roth.

"But I couldn't possibly have any impact on finding a shark, why would you fire me?"

"Because I can," smiled Roth. "Now where's my wife?"

"She's pulling duty this afternoon meeting and greeting. They were shorthanded, and she volunteered," answered Paige.

"Milk that for some free publicity," ordered Roth.

"I had a photographer accompany her, sir. I anticipated a photo opt. Channel 13 will be doing a news segment at eleven tonight."

"And why not at six o'clock? There are more viewers at six. Call them and arrange the earlier time."

"I'll try but…"

"Do it Paige and obtain a recording for my library."

"Yes sir."

Roth Niederwerter, born into life with the proverbial silver spoon, had never wanted for anything, except power. Hungry as they came, no one or no obstacle stood in his way; at least not for long. The aquarium, a mere steppingstone, had no sentimental value. It simply served as smoke and mirrors, concealing his real agenda. Roth had not divulged his intent. He trusted no one, not even his wife. Since his competitive college days with Chad he had become much more ruthless and extremely dangerous. He won at all cost now and used whatever means available to ensure his success. In the rare occasion that he did not win, the winner paid a horrific cost for obstructing his agenda. Eventually he reconciled the loss one way or the other. Winners never win unless the winner was Roth.

Roth was well spoken, handsome, possessed an athletic physique at 6'2" and 178 pounds. He had wavy blonde hair and intriguing dark blue eyes. He oozed charisma. This he used quite effectively to snare his prey. Once you had stumbled into his web and eventually discovered the true darker sinister side it was typically too late. The spider showed no mercy and systematically relinquished you of your life force. As any insect in the web, once sucked dry of your life-giving juices, you were cast aside if you were lucky.

The discovery of Chad Reynolds arrival had revitalized Roth. He relished the thought of doing battle again with his old rival. Who was he kidding he thought? There would be no battle, no war waged; only the slaughter of the lamb and with it would come closure to an open festering chapter. Yes indeed, he had surprises in store for Chad Reynolds and the first one just strolled in the door. He could hardly contain his joy anticipating the reaction on Chad's face when he dropped the first bomb. He hoped Chad brought his in-laws for the VIP treatment. His loved ones witnessing his reaction would be equivalent to Ross achieving a category five orgasm. He became giddy at the thought.

10

Bobby, Cody, and the kids had arrived 40 minutes ago. After allowing ample time for them to refresh from their flight, they would load up in two vehicles and head to the Gulf Stream Restaurant. It was Frederic's favorite local spot. It was nestled between the ocean and the marsh. As goes tradition, the men would ride in one vehicle and the women and children in the second. The arrival of Alexa Clarke had shuffled the deck but not the order. The four men would ride in the lead car. A stickler for protocol, only the men were allowed in Frederic's ride for such outings. The remaining seven, five women and the two children would cram inside the second one. Luckily, Bobby's rental had a third seat. Cody opted for Corrine to do the driving. The four-mile drive would be inconvenient but not unbearable. Frederic, other than a cordial nod, had completely ignored Alex. He had not spoken to Corrine either, but she intended to shake things up once they arrived at the Gulf Stream.

"Chad, how do you and my little sister like living in the Keys? It sort of removes you from the mainstream of life, doesn't it? Have you achieved beach bum status yet?"

Chad sighed, thinking here we go, right out of the chute, a double dose; first Roth, now Bobby. This was turning out to be the vacation from hell and he was just on day one. "I'm just a Hemmingway at heart. Life there suits me perfectly."

"Liz is allergic to cats, so I hope you don't go totally Hemmingway," Bobby chuckled.

Frederic asked, "Did you reserve our charter for in the morning?"

"Sorry sir, none are available until day after tomorrow," answered Chad, dreading to break the news.

"Damnations! I had my heart set on fishing tomorrow."

"Suits me just fine, I can sleep in," said Bobby.

"Did you try Little River, my boy?"

"Little River and Murrells Inlet, nothing, all booked; suppose we could fish from the pier."

Frederic turned up his nose. "Disgusting! I deplore competing elbow to elbow with all those grimy tourists and gawkers. I'd rather be stranded on that poor deplorable highway, death trap 501, than participate in such a despicable act with the bottom feeders of life." The old man was quite opinionated and thought of himself as the ruling crust of humanity. Chad tried as best he could to overlook it but at times it could be most difficult to swallow.

"Another reason I fly here," added Bobby.

He was his father's son indeed, thought Chad.

Frederic wasn't happy and asked, "How will we fill our agenda for tomorrow?"

Reluctantly Chad blurted, "I do have free passes for the entire family at the new aquarium. I understand that it's state of the art."

"An aquarium, I haven't visited an aquarium in ages," said Frederic.
"I've been promised VIP treatment and a free catered lunch," added Chad, trying to reconcile this disappointment.

"VIP, less interaction with the tourist, that sounds like a marvelous idea, Chadwick. Let's do plan it."

"Hope we're not doing this early," sighed Bobby.

"Robert, do you intend to sleep your life away?"

"Only two weeks worth," replied Bobby, leering over at Chad. "Way to go Hemmingway."

Compromising, not for Bobby, but for the kids, Chad had phoned and made an afternoon appointment to visit the aquarium tomorrow. Chad dreaded seeing his nemesis again but tried to put aside his differences for the family outing. The kids should be excited and hopefully it would be a distraction from the constant bickering between Frederic and Corrine. For now, the Gulf Stream would be a welcome change to the confines of beach condo life.

"We're here," Chad gladly announced, locating an open spot to park.

Corrine followed suit but had a more difficult time finding a parking place. Eventually a van with New Jersey plates backed out, offering a spot almost directly in front of the steps. With Alex's arm looped through her own, she intentionally strolled pass her father and even gave Alex a little peck on the cheek for good measure. Without even looking over her shoulder she could feel the anger surging from her father like a flash fire. She cherished that moment and prepared for her next move.

The young lady seated them outside at Frederic's preferred table, a huge round one offering an ideal atmosphere for conversation and excellent views of the ocean and marsh. Corrine made sure she commandeered the two seats to her father's left, seating Alex between her and her father. His face reddened but he said nothing derogatory. Corrine assumed her mother had persuaded him to at least try to act civil, but she doubted it would last, especially with the current seating arrangement. She didn't have long to wait.

"Chad has most graciously scheduled a trip for us to the local aquarium tomorrow. He assures me we will receive VIP treatment and a catered meal. Everyone mustn't feel obligated to go," said Frederic, making eye contact with Corrine. "Dear, please feel free to enjoy the beach tomorrow if you'd prefer."

"Alex simply loves aquatic life, don't you sweetie," said Corrine, placing her hand on top of Alex's hand.

Alex smiled but said nothing, refusing to take part in this tryst between Corrine and her father. Frederic frowned and continued to avoid any contact, both visually and verbally with Alex. For all practical purposes she did not exist as far as he was concerned. This angered Corrine, so she stepped up her game.

"I must say you've outdone yourself this year, father. The bedroom is simply gorgeous, and the view is breathtaking. Alex and I cannot wait to tryout that huge spa tub. I sure hope we don't disturb anyone."

Teal spoke up instead in response to the provocative raunchy talk. "Corrine, we have little ones present, so please refrain from your graphics."

"Sorry mother. I'm so taken by Alex; I sometimes forget everyone doesn't share my sentiment." She glanced over at her father, but he never looked her way or acknowledged the comment. He proved a tough egg to crack tonight.

"Excuse me, I must visit the facilities," pardoned Chad, pretending he had the urge to go. All this combativeness had begun to stifle him. He decided to get a breath of fresh air on the opposite side of the second story deck where no one could see him. A gentleman standing a few feet away raged at his cell phone too loudly for Chad to ignore.

"Can you believe it, Frankie? The worthless piece of whale crap fired me. His way or the highway and I had worked for the inconsiderate bastard for what, almost seven years. I just voiced my opinion about the condition of that stupid beached dolphin, and he axes me without hesitation or remorse. Just watch me. I'll show the mighty Roth Niederwerter that he can't mess with Russell Craig." Russell paused, receiving an earful from Frankie which he took with a grain of salt.

"He's planning to pay big bucks for the capture of that large great white," continued Russell. "Oh, you haven't heard. Maybe it hasn't made the news yet? A gigantic shark supposedly bit a person slap dab in half and the mighty Roth wants to catch it and display it at the aquarium. He thinks it will boost revenue. Can you imagine the expression on his face when I catch it and collect the money? Yeah sure, if you help, I will cut you in. Meet me at the Marina in Murrells Inlet at five in the morning."

Chad waited until Russell had ended the call before speaking. "Sorry, I didn't mean to eavesdrop, but I couldn't help overhearing your conversation. You say a shark bit that man in half?"

"What do you know about it? I guess you're going after the bounty too."

"No, I'm not interested in any reward for a shark, but I was there. I saw the body on the beach or what was left of it. And you say it has been confirmed that a great white did that?"

"That's what they're saying," replied Russell.

"If that's the case, trust me, you don't want to tangle with that fish. It has to be of record proportions to have made the bite I saw."

"Even better, Roth would probably pay double for a trophy like that."

"I hate to be the barer of bad news but there aren't any charters available anywhere along the coast until Wednesday."

"I don't need a charter. A friend of mine works for this guy that owns and operates his own boat. He just told me the other night that times are tough right now and that this boat captain had mentioned trying to find other means to make ends meet. I bet he would jump all over a charter offer."

"Be careful out there. I wish you the best of luck."

"Keep this under raps, buddy, if you don't mind. I need to get the jump on the competition before it hits the public airwaves."

"Mums the word. I'm just here on vacation."

Retuning to the table, tension still prevailed between Frederic and Corrine. Chad had to hand it to poor Alex, a mere pawn in the chess game, she appeared to be maintaining her composure. Chad thought, she's a better woman than I am a man. He decided to kick

74

up a little dust and hopefully deflect some of the attention away from her.

"I just met a gentleman on the deck who tells me that they believe a great white is responsible for the death of that person that washed up on the beach earlier."

"Carcharodon carcharias, in these waters, I hardly think so," stated Frederic.

"That was my thought exactly. While the species can be found almost anywhere, they're not typically known to patrol these waters. A pair had been spotted off Charleston a few years back, but they posed no threat to the general population. They were studied for about a week by local marine biologist until they moved on. I'm sure others probably migrate well off the coast as well."

"The Cooper River in Charleston is probably best known as the home of their ancestor, Megalodon," stated Frederic. "In the early seventies it was a treasure trove for Magalodon teeth. Individuals were so hungry for these prizes, harvesting the teeth became commercialized. At the peak, tractor trailer loads of teeth were being hauled from the river."

"Amazing," commented Alex, "Why were so many teeth discovered in one area?"

"Spawning grounds and at one time that portion of the coast was submerged," replied Fredric. "I dived there a couple of times in my youth and never left empty handed. The pride of my collection exceeds five inches."

Alex asked, "Just how large were these fish?"

"Most agree a mature female could have easily exceeded 40 or 50 feet in length. Some experts believe they could have reached lengths twice that. My studies have pointed towards 100 feet not being out of the question. One thing for sure, life on the ocean would be much different if they still ruled the seas."

"A hundred-foot fish sounds astounding," said Alex.

"Blah, blah, blah father, boring! I've heard this story too many times," said Corrine, mocking a yawn.

"I think it is simply fascinating Professor Bornfreund," smiled Alex.

"From what I read, those waters were pretty treacherous with poor visibility," stated Chad.

"I assure you Chadwick, those waters certainly didn't compare to the crystal-clear waters you are accustomed to in the Keys. I must add, the currents were indeed unpredictable. At 20 to 30 feet deep the murkiness consumes you. Even with a powerful underwater lamp it is difficult to see beyond four or five feet. Best strategy is to find a way to anchor in one spot and just dig through the bottom mud until you find a triangular shape. Teeth were not difficult to locate if you were up for the challenge. I'm almost tempted to travel down there and give you boys a treat."

"And girls' chimed in Alex. "I haven't been diving for years. I thoroughly enjoy the rush."

Frederic nodded his approval. That steamed Corrine. This was not going as she had envisioned.

"No one is going diving in those waters," spoke up Teal. "Not with a man-eating shark lurking in the ocean. Besides, we planned our vacation here, not Charleston."

"But Teal, we're talking less than a two-hour drive," said Frederic. "And, might I add, dear. The Megalodon have been long extinct."

"Dead or alive doesn't matter, and it may as well be an airplane flight away, no one is going to Charleston and that's it!"

"Fine, I concede, my dear. We'll do the aquarium instead and Alexis, you are cordially invited to join us if you like," said Frederic.

Corrine was not liking this, realizing that her father was taking a shine to Alex now.

"How big do you think this shark is," asked Cody in her mountain girl twang.

"To have severed that torso so cleanly I suspect it would have easily exceeded 20 feet. I'm still not convinced a great white is the culprit," spoke up Chad.

Cody squinted and then asked, "You don't think one of those Meg things did it do you? A hundred-footer is a mighty big shark."

"As I stated, they've been extinct for millions of years, my dear" stated Frederic.

Alex asked, "Other that one of these great whites, what in the ocean can chomp a person in half like that? We saw what was left of that person that washed up on the beach."

"No idea without examining the remains," said Chad.

"You're on vacation Chad," spoke up Liz. "You promised to remove the nutty professor marine biologist hat for the next two weeks, remember?"

"I have no intentions of getting involved I assure you. I'm simply curious, that's all."

"I don't recall ever hearing of a great white being in captivity;" stated Bobby. "Isn't all this Mutual of Omaha Wild Kingdom stuff a load of crap?"

"Well you're half right;" said Chad thinking half wit, "In 1984 the Monterey Bay Aquarium did showcase a great white during their grand opening. Unfortunately, the creature died ten days later. So much for their star attraction."

"No one has been successful then," inquired Alex.

"The California coast, infamous for their great whites, has several attempts in the history books. I believe around 2003 researchers managed to capture a young female and contained her in a net pen for almost a week before releasing her. They were not able to get the female to feed and feared for her health and released her. A couple of years later a young female was caught and kept alive in a massive aquarium at the Outer Bay Exhibit for six and half months before they released her. There were several others over the next few years, but none remained in captivity for exceptionally long. The most famous, dubbed Sandy, a seven-foot nine female had been housed at the Steinhart Aquarium in San Fran. She had to be released for refusing to eat and constantly slamming into the walls."

"Sounds to me these creatures are not destined for containment," commented Alex.

"Yes, I believe something in their genes program them for life in the open sea. The apex predator will not be confined to the likes of an aquarium," replied Chad.

"Roth Niederwerter is making a tragic mistake placing a bounty on the head of Carcharodon carcharias," stated Frederic. "I deplore such behavior."

"If indeed we have Carcharodon carcharias in these waters," stated a skeptical Chad, "And by the way, excuse my French but, Roth is a pompous arrogant self-serving a-hole."

"Sounds as if you don't like this gentleman," stated Alex.

"Gentleman, not hardly; dislike is not a strong enough term."

Liz spoke up, "Either way, Chad, father, it is none of your business, correct?"

"Correct," Teal answered for both. "This is a family vacation. It is not going to be the great fish hunt."

The waitress arrived with their order. Fortunately, no one had requested shark off the menu. Chad watched as she served the table while thinking he had an uneasy feeling about this, recalling the fear displayed by the dolphins. I'm on vacation and should leave matters to those that are not on vacation, he reminded himself. Fair argument, but he was struggling to remain on the sidelines.

11

Nothing could be finer than to be in Carolina in the morning. The tune rang loud and clear through Chad's head, sitting on the balcony at dawn, sipping his first cup of coffee. A spectacular sunrise greeted him exploding over the ocean like a firestorm. A few early morning walkers and joggers scurried like ants on the beach ten stories below. At least he saw no crowds massing and huddling around some tragedy as had been the theme yesterday, however, the day was still early.

Images of the Griswold's do the aquarium crept into his head. The dysfunctional Bornfreund clan could give the fictitious family of National Lampoon a run for their money. At least it appeared that Alex and Frederic had buried the hatchet and to the dismay of Corrine, not in each other's back. Chad still regretted the fact that Corrine was still using Alex. He should tell Alex and expose Corrine. Thus far he had a cowardly streak running up the center of his back. He tried to convince himself that it really wasn't any of his business. A shrill sound to his right diverted his attention. A soaring osprey passed just one story below, less than ten feet from the balcony, a large fish clutched in its talons. He smiled thinking how interesting to marvel the bird in flight from his view from above.

Hearing a scream below shocked him back to reality. A boy held a fully clothed girl in his arms in knee deep water pretending to toss her into the crashing waves. The young man laughed loudly satisfied that his bluffs were affective. Further down the beach, he saw a pickup truck loaded with umbrellas and beach chairs. Two diligent individuals worked vigorously to dig holes for planting the umbrellas and placed two chairs at each configuration before moving to the next. A lady walking three small dogs passed them. One dog hiked its leg on the truck's tire apparently marking its territory.

A trio of small speeding boats headed northward about a quarter mile offshore, each containing two people. All three were the same color and configuration. Chad surmised they had some sort of commercial value. They were too small for parasailing, but he wasn't sure of their intent. Moving quickly, leaping the waves, they were soon a distant memory. Chad had not expected so much activity this early in the morning. The patrons of the condo remained quiet. After all, they were on vacation and sensed no urgency to rise. Chad managed on less than six hours of sleep each night and just couldn't fathom why anyone would want to sleep their life away. He was about to step back inside for his second cup of java when something odd caught his eye directly below.

Half dozen large shadows streaked effortlessly just beyond the breaking waves. Only dolphins typically traveled that close to shore, but the shadowy blobs did not appear conducive with those of dolphins. These were too large even for mature dolphins. Schools of fish broke the surface just ahead apparently fleeing from the pursuing oceanic predators. Chad watched as the group of shadows broke off reminding him of a pack on the hunt. He guessed that whatever skimmed below the surface to be in the range of 14 to 16 feet. In a matter of ten seconds or so the shadows disappeared. He scanned the surrounding area but never saw anything break the surface like dolphins do. Could the phantoms have been responsible for the beached dolphins he wondered? They certainly appeared fast enough to have intimidated them. Drawing blanks, he had no logical explanation for what he had just witnessed. He had estimated again that the originators of the shadows had indeed easily reached 16 feet in length but from ten stories up and with the defection underneath the surface he couldn't bank on the accuracy of his estimates. Shrugging, he opted for another cup of coffee to clear the morning cobwebs. Alex stood in the kitchen by the coffee maker pouring a cup. Wearing dingy white socks and an oversized tee shirt, no make-up and bad hair, she looked nothing like a Playboy centerfold. Turning she saw Chad entering the balcony doorway and she held up her coffee mug in a mock toast. She could have passed as the poster child for housewives international.

"Pour you another cup," she offered, still holding the pot.

"That would be wonderful. You missed a beautiful sunrise."

"Been there, done that," she answered, "Seen one...you've seen them all."

Accompanying Chad back to the balcony Alex collapsed onto a chaise lounger. "Are we the only ones up?"

"Appears so. Are you normally an early riser?"

"Never, but my little Corrine was snoring like a bear in the middle of hibernation. I love her but that gal sure sleeps noisily. I don't have the heart to tell her. She can be quite sensitive. She wears her emotions on her sleeves."

"Not Corrine! You must be having a positive influence on her."

Alex shrugged and then asked, "When do we visit this aquarium?"

"Noon. That will allow ample time to get the troops up and moving."

"What do you really think happened to that person that washed up on shore yesterday?"

"I don't know. I didn't really examine the body closely. I was too busy puking. What I could tell, it had been severed in half cleanly. It certainly had not been gnawed in half."

"A shark did that, just chomped a person in two pieces with a single bite."

"Only two creatures could have come close to making that bite, a shark or an orca. It had to be a monster of either to have done that. I have never heard of Orcas being in these waters and probably only a tiger shark or great white could have pulled it off cleanly. I think something is spooking these waters. Adult dolphins don't beach themselves for the hell of it. I'm convinced none of them were sick."

"Have you ever done any diving here?"

"No, it's my first time on the Grand Strand. What about you?"

"All of my diving has been in the Bahamas on spring breaks and holidays, and once during a Playboy shoot in Hawaii."

"Tell me. How did you enjoy your reign as a centerfold?"

"Paid the bills," she smiled. "Everyone thinks we're sexually obsessed just because we pose nude. If I had blonde hair, I would have been a ditzy blonde-haired black Britt with sex maniac tendencies for those fantasy seekers out there."

Chad chuckled visualizing the image.

"What," she asked. "You can't picture me as a blonde?"

"I'm sure it would have brought you an occult following. Tell me though, how long have you been away from the homeland?"

"Why do you ask?"

"Your accent isn't heavy."

"Very perceptive," she nodded. "I've spent most of the last ten years in the states becoming Americanized I suppose. I did a little modeling before the Playboy offer. I do love this country of yours and hope to be a citizen one day."

The condo entrance door opened and in walked Frederic carrying two grocery bags. After setting them on the counter he approached Chad and Alex on the balcony. "Well, finally someone is stirring. I have purchased ingredients for preparing omelets for one and all. I must admit. I'm a bit of a closet chef and omelets are my specialty."

"I didn't realize you were up, sir."

"My dear boy, I'm always up by four. I find such solitude at that hour. This may sound silly of an old man, but I feel as if I'm the sole survivor at that time between mere hours before dawn. I do my best contemplating and reflecting while the world sleeps. And besides, one can find the most unique characters roaming the aisle ways of Wal-Mart if you dare venture out. I have studied human behavioral habits during this time. I've been tempted to document my findings in a publishing."

Alex smiled. "I must agree with you professor, the gifted ones do indeed prowl those all night shopping venues. I have had many a chuckle and strange encounter doing exactly the same."

"Marvelous my dear, we must share stories sometime."

"I would much enjoy that."

She had the old man eating out of the palm of her hand all right thought Chad. He had been a much easier nut to crack than he had anticipated. Corrine's plan had blown up in her face. It couldn't have happened to a more deserving person as his sinister sister-in-law.

"Let's make some noise and wake the dead," grinned Frederic. "The vacationers have slept long enough, don't you agree? It's time for a pot and pan drum roll. Let's bring the kitchen alive."

Teal stood in the doorway yawning, arms crossed, barefooted and wearing Betty Boop lounging pants and a matching tee-shirt. She said, "Let's roust them. I know how you live for these moments, Freddy."

Chad had to stifle a laugh and sarcastic comment when Teal addressed Frederic as Freddy. It didn't deter Alex. "Let's do it Freddy," she giggled

Frederic shot her a false glare and said "Let's, shall we."

By ten everyone had been fed a hearty specialty omelet breakfast and were now dressed and assembled as requested by Frederic in the den. Frederic compulsively controlled the activities, embracing his role as the alpha male. "Chadwick has made arrangements for us to tour the aquarium at 12:30. Our itinerary will include a late lunch, compliments of our host Mister Roth Niederwerter, curator and owner of the aquarium. He is a former colleague of Chadwick.

84

Dare I remind you that we will conduct ourselves in a most cordial and professional manner and pay homage to our most gracious host." Frederic eyed Robert and Cody then the kids to ensure they understood. For good measure he shot Corrine a warning glare.

Corrine responded to the comment. "What do you think we're going to do father, skinny dip in the fish tanks and go sushi on the unsuspecting captured creatures?"

"I expect you to behave yourself, Corrine."

"Such expectations must not go unrewarded, "replied Corrine in her best rebellious attitude.

"Do something with your daughter," insisted Frederic of Teal.

My daughter thought Teal, but she said nothing.

"Let's get this touristy crap over with," spoke up Bobby, "Then we can relax around the pool."

"Please don't feel obligated to participate in this family gathering, Robert," snapped Frederic.

"And be banished from the land," replied Bobby.

"Ease up brother dearest," said Liz, "The kids will love this. For once do something for them and not yourself."

Cody almost put her two cents in, but she thought better of it. Bobby didn't take too kindly for her taking anyone's side but his. He absolutely would not allow her to get away with belittling him in public, not without consequences. She had faced too many consequences in their life together; more so than anyone would ever know. Bobby, a master of concealing the abuse could be quite malicious if crossed. Thankfully, he had never shown any aggression towards the children; not that she had ever seen, but she on the other hand had survived her fair share. Bobby made sure that no signs of his uglier side were ever visible. He strategically concealed evidence of his physical abuse. No one saw the bruises except for Cody in the isolation of her bathroom while standing in front of the mirror. She went to great pains to ensure she never wore the type of clothing that would advertise she was the spouse of a wife beater.

12

Prompt and on schedule, the traveling caravan pulled into the parking lot at ten minutes after twelve. The ride to the aquarium had been alive with the thunder of rumbling motorcycles. Thousands upon thousands had begun arriving for the Harley Davidson rally. Clad in leather and club logos, riders of all shapes and sizes, genders, and races, speckled the highways giving way to a hint of what lay ahead. The patrons of the two vehicles had taken in the spectacle as free entertainment. Cody frequently warned the children not to look when scantly clad women were encountered riding on the back of the hogs.

Chad presented the free passes at the aquarium entrance prompting a phone call from the ticket collector. Within minutes Roth appeared all smiles and oozing charm. Chad saw through the ruse. Roth announced that he would personally conduct the guided tour of his pride and joy. Chad would have preferred roaming freely, but he wasn't willing to challenge Roth in front of family. Before the tour commenced, he did pose one question for Roth, "How's the Dolphin doing?"

"Sadly, it did not survive the trip here. Your coddling only prolonged the inevitable. As I predicted, it and all the dolphins were infested with parasites."

"You've completed an autopsy of all the dolphins this quickly," questioned Chad.

"I have an exceptionally large and competent staff. They completed the task with great expediency."

Chad wasn't buying it, but he didn't push the issue. "Could I see the bodies?"

"Sorry, we've disposed of them already. There really was no need to keep them once we identified the root cause of their demise. Their carcasses posed health and environmental risks."

Too damn quickly thought Chad but again he held his tongue. "I understand that you're offering an award for an alleged great white in these waters."

"News does spread rapidly here, doesn't it? Don't you think it would be simply monumental if we displayed a gigantic man eater at this facility?"

"Are you positive that a great white is responsible for the human remains that washed ashore?"

"My sources confided in me that the coroner has all but confirmed it."

"Did you examine the body?"

"I have not been consulted, but I assure we have an extremely competent coroner. Shark bites are not that difficult to identify."

"You're absolutely correct, but I don't think your typical coroner has the experience for identifying the species of shark, do you?"

Roth obviously becoming quite frustrated at Chad's drilling quickly changed the subject. "Speaking of sharks, the kiddies and adults alike will surely enjoy our exhibit, Dangerous Reef. You will experience being under water enclosed within our acrylic tunnels underneath two million gallons of water. Our state of the arts moving 340-foot long glide path will wind you through our tunnels where you will be part of the sea. We have an impressive array of large sharks; Sand, Tiger, Sandbar, and Nurse Shark to mention a few. The Sand Sharks can reach lengths of 13 feet. You will come face to face with these wondrous creatures not to mention many other species of fish such as giant stingrays, great green sea turtles, a not so often seen saw fish, and assortment of tarpon, grunts, and snappers."

"Sounds quite impressive Mister Niederwerter," stated Frederic.

"Call me Roth, please, but that is just the tip of the iceberg. There are thousands of marine lives in our facility. To make sure they receive the best quality of life in their new home, our completely computer-controlled system filters more water in a day than the city of Myrtle Beach. My staff tests millions of gallons of water that is continuously circulated to simulate life in the aquatic world. I assure you; they are treated to a better quality of life than they would ever be exposed to in the real sea. No pollution or deadly toxics. I am sorry for my embarrassing display of exuberance. As you can tell, I am proud of my accomplishment."

"And so, you should be," added Frederic.

Chad felt like puking. "Can we get started?"

"Certainly, please follow me."

"Roth is a weasel," whispered Corrine to Alex, "And an arrogant pompous ass." Alex nodded and tried to remain focused on the tour. "He and Chad hate one another's guts. This should be fun seeing them go at it."

Just over an hour later they arrived at a lunch spread fit for a king and his court. Roth announced that after lunch his guests could feel free to roam throughout the aquarium at their leisure. He thanked them for coming and then he pulled Chad off to the side. "Chadwick old comrade, did you enjoy the digs?"

"Very impressive," Chad managed to choke out, but truthfully it was. "But you can't be serious about capturing a great white."

"Not me. I am merely offering monetary reward to anyone who can deliver a live adult specimen. I have no intentions of utilizing my resources chasing this creature. You must admit, it is a great gimmick for publicity."

"You do realize you could be contributing to a very volatile situation. Amateurs have no business shark hunting."

"You are absolutely right. I do not expect anyone inexperienced in landing a live shark of any significant size. I hope to draw in more than just amateurs."

"I guess you expect a Sam Quint to show up like in that movie Jaws. News flash. Roth, Robert Shaw is dead, and it was only a movie."

"So skeptical," scoffed Roth, "Why don't you take your clan out and give it a try. Capturing a record-breaking fish might pluck you from your pathetic life of obscurity."

"I thoroughly enjoy my pathetic life of obscurity. Thank you very much."
"You could even work for me, Chadwick. I assure you it would bump your status in the scientific community being associated with me and my endeavors."

"I can tarnish my reputation without your help," professed Chad.

"Ouch, now that left a deep gash. I had hoped we were over our immature attacks on one another. I suppose you harbor ill feelings against me for being so successful. I cannot help it. I've always been destined for great things."

"Again, thank you for the hospitality but I think I'll round my family up before you decide to put them in one of your exhibits."

"Chadwick, please don't punish your family because of how you feel toward me. Did you not see the sparkle in your niece and nephew's eyes? It was quite priceless to touch young minds."

"Young impressionable minds I'm afraid and it is an uncle's job to protect them from such corruptive influences. Please excuse me."

"Jealously is not becoming on you, old friend."

"Trust me Roth, there's not a jealous bone in my body; only one of complete empathy. You must live a lonely life and I've never been or ever will be your friend."

"On the contrary," he smiled, nodding toward the opposite side of the room. "Not lonely at all."

Chad could not believe his eyes. There stood Vanessa Daetwyler, his college crush, looking more radiant than he remembered. He soaked her in as she waved and approached them. He felt flushed and nervous anticipating her arrival to where he stood on trembling legs.

"Chad Reynolds, Roth told me you were here. I so looked forward to seeing you again," she spoke in a simply sensual voice.

"Vanessa Daetwyler," choked out Chad.

"Niederwerter," she said, holding up her ring finger sporting a gargantuan diamond. "Vanessa Niederwerter. Roth and I wed last spring. Can you imagine that?"

"Sorry, I failed to tell you that Vanessa and I were married. Well I intentionally did not disclose it to you. I decided seeing the look of surprise on your face when you saw her would be too priceless to pass up."

Chad stifled his tongue. "Married to Roth, who would have ever figured."

"I certainly would have to agree with you on that," admitted Vanessa, "The two of us finding one another after all these years was certainly a surprise to me as was learning you were already married."

"How did you know I was married?"

"Roth told me, silly. We had just stumbled upon one another out in San Diego last year where I was stationed. During supper he informed me that you were blissfully married. I'm certainly happy for you."

Her eyes told a different story. Chad could see sparks in those baby blues. He felt it and he knew so did she. Roth had parlayed him being married into courting Vanessa, convincing her to settle for the runner up. It crushed him to know that she was now with Roth.

91

Suddenly he realized; that was Roth's intent all along. The bastard wanted to rub his nose in it. Final victory and the ultimate prize belonged to him.

"You mentioned stationed. Are you still in the Navy?"

"Retired as of three months ago. Life as a Navy Seal is not as it was when I first achieved the status. The work had changed and so had that role. Roth convinced me to opt out, so I did."

"Is your wife here?"

Chad nodded and pointed to the group standing at the far end of the room. "Stunning," commented Vanessa, "She's quite beautiful. I had never taken you for one interested in an African-American."

Flattered Chad blurted out, "No that's Alex, my sister-in-law's girlfriend. Liz is standing to the far left, next to her father."

"Oh, quite charming as well," said Vanessa. "She looks to be the homebody type. Do you have children?"

"No children, and actually Liz is in the pharmaceutical field."

"Oh, does she work in a local CVS?"

"Marketing and Developing for a rather large firm," explained Chad, "She does travel quite a bit I'm afraid."

"And that must lend to a lonely existence for you."

"I'm sure Chadwick stays busy diving for sunken treasure off the Keys," chimed in Roth.

"We make it work."

"I see," she answered, her tone indicating she really wasn't interested in the arrangement. "Roth tells me you are in town for a couple of weeks vacationing."

Chad nodded. "Well deserved R&R with the family."

"Maybe we can meet the two of you for dinner one night while you're here."

"Lot of family stuff going on, not sure it will be possible," Chad replied as his cell phone rang. "Excuse me while I take this," he said Chad, walking away. "Yes, this is Chad Reynolds. Well hello Sly. Sure, that shouldn't be a problem providing we keep it just between you and me. I have promised the family I would enjoy this vacation if it killed me. Give me about an hour. Yeah, that's fine. Pick me up in front of the hotel. Don't mention it."

Chad retuned to the presence of the happy couple. "Business always has a way of reaching us now days with all this modern technology. Again, thank you for your hospitality and maybe you can drop by our hotel if you have an opportunity. Here's my card with my cell phone number.

"Let's do plan to go over, Roth, so we may spend time with Chad's wife and family," said Vanessa.

"Certainly, my dear, they are quite an interesting assortment of individuals I assure you," said Roth.

13

Upon returning to the condo, most went their separate ways. Cody took the children down to the pool. Teal did the grandmotherly thing and joined her. Liz, Corrine, and Alex opted for the beach. Frederic insisted that Bobby and Chad accompany him to Dick's Sporting Goods to purchase appropriate fishing gear for the charter they had secured. Chad tried unsuccessfully to convince his father-in-law that the charter boat would furnish what they needed. Giving up, he told them to have at it, but he passed on the venture. Instead he descended to the ground floor and waited out front for Detective Sly Stone. He arrived as promised.

"Thank you, Chad for agreeing to conduct the examination."

"Have you had any luck identifying your John Doe? I'm sure it must be difficult with his upper torso missing; no opportunity to search fingerprints or dental records."

"On the contrary, we had no problem identifying the corpse. His wallet was still tucked inside the back pocket of his jeans. His name is Salvatore Provenzano, a caporegime, for one of the notorious Jersey crime families."

"A what?"

"A caporegime, sort of the next in command reporting to the sotto capo, underboss who reports directly to the head honcho, crime boss leader," explained Sly. "Typically, there are several of the caporegimes each commanding ten or more foot soldiers. Provenzano was one mean sonofabitch. This ties him to a missing charter boat. His cousin, a brother and an associate along with the captain disappeared several days ago just before that shrimp boat incident."

"Are you thinking that charter incident was no accident; possibly a hit or something?"

"Very good deduction, junior detective, that's exactly what the sheriff thinks, but your examination should help shed light on our theory."

"How so?"

"Well if you don't think the cadaver's condition is a result of a fish attack then we may be on to something. I mean, look what we have here; four crime figures gone just like that or at least until Provenzano washed up on shore. It was almost the perfect crime."

"What does the coroner think?"

"Inconclusive, or so goes his story."

"Roth Niederwerter seems to think a great white shark is the culprit."

"That's why I asked you to assist rather than him. He is trying to utilize this tragedy for his own gains. I'm not so sure he doesn't have the coroner in his back pocket."

"You've seen the body. What do you think?"

"Never seen anything like it," replied Sly, rubbing his chin. "I suppose the missing top torso could be contusive with attempting to hide the identity, but someone had to go to great lengths to perpetrate it. What really puzzles me is the mayday recording."

"Why so?"

"The captain radioed for help not saying why. In the background you could hear all these blood curdling screams. These guys are real bad asses. They would not have been screaming like that, not even if the ship was taking or water or was on fire or had some how capsized. Whatever caused that charter to go down, terrified the crap out of these men who never fear anything. What out there could do that?"

"Same thing that could severe a man in half I suppose. Guess we'll have an idea after I examine Mister Provenzano or what's left of him."

"We'll be at the morgue in five."

Fifteen minutes later, Sly, Coroner Al Roberts, and Chad Reynolds viewed the remains of one, Salvatore Provenzano, minus his jeans now. Chad took in a deep breath as he stepped forward for a closer look. Silently but methodically he examined the alleged bite and took measurements. He jotted down notes then wiped sweat from his brow. Sly and Al handed him equipment as he asked for it. After 45 minutes he sighed and proclaimed, "It wasn't a shark."

"Yes," said an exuberant Detective Sylvester Stone. "I knew it!"

"Don't get too carried away. No known species of shark did this nor did any known mammal."

"Are you saying it was staged by some mechanical device or a very sharp instrument?"

"I don't believe that is what Mister Reynolds is indicating at all," added Al Roberts.

"If it wasn't a fish or animal then what did it?"

"I honestly can't say, but I can confirm this is indeed a bite from one hell of a biter, not mechanical or staged."

"Is there some new species out there that we are not aware of it?"

"I don't really know what I'm saying, Mt. Roberts. This baffles me. I have to say it's inconclusive, but definitely not a shark bite."

"This isn't what I had hoped for, Chad. My superiors are not going to be very happy and worse still; the Jersey clan is going to demand answers once we make the phone call. It will most certainly hit the fan. They'll be out for revenge."

"Good, then maybe they can tell us what did it," Chad smiled.

Once the cat was out of the bag that this wasn't a great white attack, Roth's publicity stunt would blow up in his face. He relished being the one to debunk the alleged allocations and bring Roth down a notch or two, game on. As for the mob, they would have to draw their own conclusions.

14

Roth Niederwerter stared into the huge glass viewing window of the containment tank. The dolphin suspended effortlessly stared back at him. He tapped lightly on the glass and the dolphin reacted, touched the glass with its sleek nose. The rogue shark had apparently forced the dolphins to beach themselves he surmised. It must be one hell of a monster specimen to have impacted them in such a manner. Dolphins can out swim and out maneuver sharks. Why had this one terrified them so, he wondered. He smiled. It had brought him great pleasure to have informed Chadwick Reynolds that this dolphin, his dolphin had died. It had brought him even greater pleasure to have shown him he had claimed the trophy, Vanessa Daetwyler.

Energized, Roth intended on making Chadwick's two weeks on the Grand Strand a living hell. He had forgotten just how much he despised Chadwick until he had laid eyes on him at the beach. Their rivalry in college had started off friendly enough but by the end, it had evolved into anything but friendly. He now had an opportunity to tidy up unfinished business, long overdue. Next on Roth's agenda, discredit Chadwick in the eyes of the entire Bornfreund clan. His dear wife, Vanessa, would be instrumental in Chad's final destruction. People were just tools, pawns to be used and abused by the anointed one. He was the self-appointed king and the others would do his bidding. His pawns really had no choice; at least not one of their liking.

He saw her approaching by her reflection in the containment tank window. She was quite breath taking but she had been so easy to manipulate. Bombarding her with his natural charm then crushing her by announcing Chadwick's marital status had wooed her into his awaiting web. While the prize had been worth the winning, the conquest behind him now, only a flicker of flame remained for him for her. Roth required life challenges and she no longer posed one. Prenuptials, man's best friend, would be exercised when necessary.

Vanessa wrapped her arms around Roth's waste and kissed him on the nap of the neck unaware that her advances no longer aroused her husband. "It was nice to see Chad again, wasn't it?"

"Indeed, it was."

"You two were so extremely competitive in college. I sure hope those days are behind you; both of you."

"What is there to compete for now? We have gone our separate ways and no longer share the same goals."

"Good, you two did take it too seriously. Let's do plan a night that we can go out; just the four of us, if they can pry themselves away from family."

"As you wish. I think dear Chadwick is still quite taken by you. He resembled a little lovesick puppy."

"Come now, I'm sure you're reading too much into his reaction. After all, we have not seen one another since college."

"You two never really had closure due to the circumstances."

"Please, let's not go there, Roth. Decisions were made and we have no choice but to live with the consequences."

"Do you have any regrets?"

"Please, let's not do this. I beg you."

"If you hadn't become pregnant with my child," Roth reminded her.

"It happened. We took care of it and we moved on with our lives."

"And look at us now; we've come full circle. This time you're with me instead of Chadwick."

"I am a firm believer in destiny. Everything happens for a reason."

"And now, is the destiny that the three of us find ourselves intertwined again?"

Vanessa didn't answer. She feared destiny more than ever right now. Chad showing up spelled trouble for her and she knew it. She sensed Roth knew it too. Did Chad feel the same way? Roth said he had seen it in Chad's eyes. She thought she had too. After leaving Roth to his work, she strolled through the aquarium fumbling with Chad's business card. He had said to contact him via his cell. She shoved the card back into her pocket and sighed.

15

Sly drove Chad back to the condo. He remained quiet on the return ride, still floored by the sight of Vanessa, and devastated by the fact she was now married to Roth. Further complicating matters, the identity of the mystery creature lurking the waters of the Grand Strand; just what could it possibly be? Sly had provided him with a copy of the autopsy report, complete with vivid images of the mobster cadaver. He wondered what could have taken a charter boat down along with its five screaming occupants.

"We're here…Chad…uh…we've arrived…this is your hotel…right?"

"Excuse me," asked Chad, snapping out of his death spiral.

"We're back at your hotel. I hope I haven't screwed things up by getting you involved?"

"No, that's not a problem. I'm just as intrigued as you by the events surrounding that boat's disappearance and discovering just exactly what did attack the men on board."

"Unbelievable, just what could have taken down a charter boat with a seasoned captain at the helm and it being loaded with fearless wise guys?"

"If I come up with any theories, I'll give you a call, Sly."

"Please exercise discretion before sharing those photos and file with anyone. This is an ongoing police investigation and it's likely to heat up once the wrong people are informed. We have identified the body and still can't determine the precise cause of death. Those mobsters are going to be demanding answers and I'm not sure they are going to buy what we currently have to offer them."

"Will do and please keep me posted if you have any new clues as to the cause."

"You can count on it. Now go enjoy your vacation."

Chad nodded, thinking how in the hell would he do that now. "You really should put out a statement debunking the great white theory before this reward thing gets out of hand."

"First thing on my agenda; can't you just imagine the reaction from your friend, Roth Niederwerter?"

"He's not a friend, but yes I can, and it is well deserved."

"Totally. Now go spend some time with your family."

Before going upstairs Chad walked out to the pool area located beachside. He gazed out over the ocean searching for answers but came up with none. A boat towing two people suspended from a parasail headed southward. The boat occasionally stalled causing the two riders to come close to dipping their toes in the water before lifting them again. A lone kayaker in a bright red kayak paddled no more than 100 yards offshore. A cluster of colorful sailboats dotted the horizon north of his location. A group of boys body-surfed in the breakers and a Seadoo waited patiently while a swimmer swam out to join the operator. A second swimmer swam toward shore. Gulls called out soaring above the scene. All appeared so peaceful and tranquil. Chad wished he could shake the feeling; one of pending doom.

"Chadwick, my boy, I see you have returned. Robert and I have purchased what we require for tomorrow's fishing excursion. I am quite happy we secured a boat."

Chad shifted the autopsy folder to his left side, concealing it from Frederic. "Wonderful, so you, Bobby and I should be up before daybreak then."

"And Alexis," added Frederic. "She's such a wonderful lassie."

"And Corrine?" asked Chad

"Not hardly, my boy, she has decided to remain behind. She's not the adventurous type."

Much more adventurous than you could ever imagine thought Chad, but glad she had declined. "Have you seen Liz?"

"She, Teal and Cody have taken the children to that horrendous tourist trap theme park. I just don't understand what motivates them to do such things."

"Your grandchildren," pointed out Chad.

"Yes, the little munchkins do have their way."

"Indeed, they do," replied Chad.

"Robert has concocted this crazy scheme that we could possibly land a great white and collect the bounty," stated Frederic.

"There is no great white," blurted out Chad.

"Of course, there isn't. I informed Robert but he is in denial. Besides, he certainly is not qualified to attempt capturing one alive. What convinced you, my boy?"

Chad reluctantly handed over the folder. "It's the autopsy report of the man they found yesterday. That's where I've been. I examined the body and it wasn't a shark bite. I'm unsure what did that to the deceased, but I am sure that some sort of creature snapped him in two," stated Chad, pointing to the photographs.

"Interesting, so what of nature's wonders do you suspect?"

"That's just it. I don't have a clue or even a logical guess. And those are confidential, sir. The death is still under investigation by the authorities."

"How did you acquire your copy?"

"Detective Stone asked me to assist if I could. He gave it to me."

"Oceanographer turned sleuth," smiled Frederic.

"I suppose, but we must keep this between ourselves," warned Chad, already feeling guilty he had broken his promise to Sly.

"Certainly, my boy, confidentiality must be of the utmost importance during any crime scene investigation, however, might I suggest we utilize all resources available for identifying the perpetrator of this horrific attack? I have a couple of colleagues that could possibly assist us. Of course, we would not divulge to them the location and specifics of the case."

Chad took a deep breath. Ensuring confidentiality was snow balling out of control. "I'm not so sure about getting others involved."

"Allow me to send copies of the photos. We can edit out much of the specifics on the report and just include those pertaining to size and measurements of the bite."

"Okay, I suppose that would work."

"Wonderful. I believe the hotel has everything we require for scanning and e-mailing."

"Then let's do it before the ladies return."

The two young women squealed with delight each time their toes dipped into the ocean. The parasail boat pilot reacted to their screams and sped up lifting them upward and then slowed, causing them to drift downwards toward another wet rendezvous. This time their screams reached new levels. They began scrambling and jerking on the framework of the parasail, jeopardizing keeping it airborne.

Art tapped the boat pilot, Jesse on the shoulder, motioning that something was happening. Even from his present distance Art could see the reddish discoloration on one of the lady's feet. He tried to wave them off, prevent them from squirming so much. They were on the brink of causing a crash. Their boss would have both his and Jesse's ass if they damaged the parasail apparatus. Jesse gave him the signal to reel them in. The gals were not helping with all their tugging and scrambling about the parasail frame. Jesse pulled off several saves by speeding up and preventing them from spiraling into the ocean. What seemed like an eternity but had been seven minutes, they had the two safely back on board? That's when Art noticed the severity of the injury on the larger of the two girl's right foot. All but one of her toes was missing and the stub of her foot was a stringy mass of shredded flesh. The other girl while hysterical appeared physically in tack.

Art quickly wrapped up her foot to stop the bleeding. Jesse radioed ahead requesting medical assistance. He motioned for Art. "Did you see anything?"

"Nothing. Do you think it was a shark?"

"Probably, wrong place at the wrong time."

"They were kicking up water pretty good."

"Barry can't blame us for this," spoke up Art.

"You want to bet on that? If business suffers, we're toast."

"Anything like this ever happened before?" This was Art's first season working at the beach.

"Not on my watch and I have been doing this for almost six years. Stick with them and make sure she doesn't go into shock."

"How do I prevent her from going into shock?"

"You can't, but don't let her go to sleep. Just keep her talking and awake, Art."

"What can we talk about?"

"Just talk about anything, the weather, the beach, who the hell cares."

"Okay," answered Art, turning, and asking the two ladies, "What do you think of the weather we are having?"

16

With an early morning wake up call looming for the four fishermen, they opted to cater in instead of venturing out for dinner. Dough Boys had just delivered their assortment of pizzas. No one had objected. They had put in a full day. Poor Cody and the kids had fried in the sun and each sported a glow in the dark painfully looking red sunburn. Liz and Teal showed no signs of the sun's affects, both having already obtained deep dark tans prior to their arrival. The only ones not joining them were Corrine and Alex. They had opted to visit one of the local hangouts to toss back a few and indulge in a little dancing.

Liz and Chad decided to have their pizza out on the balcony. A combination of the setting sun and shadowed side of the building had provided a cool breeze. Liz had become chilled and slipped on lounging pants. "Tell me about this Vanessa," encouraged Liz. "She attended college with you and Roth, but I don't seem to remember her or you ever talking about her."

"She was before us. I met her in college as well. She ended up leaving college."

"Dropped out?"

"Guess you could say that. She joined the Navy."

"Bad grades?"

"Not that I know of, she just had this hankering to be a Navy Seal."

"Navy Seal, that's pretty tough, isn't it?"

"That's what I hear. She is retired from the service now. She gave it up and married Roth."

"I can tell by your tone that you don't seem too pleased with her decision."

"What, to retire from the Navy."

"No, her marrying your nemesis, Roth."

"She deserves better."

"Like whom…you?"

"Why would you say something like that?"

"I saw how you looked at one another. You had a thing for her, didn't you? You still do, don't you?"

"How ridiculous! I was just shocked to see her after all these years and to find out she was married to Roth. It just caught me off guard. That's all."

"Did you love her?"

"What's all this really about, Liz?"

"Answer me. Did you love her?"

"I don't know…first time away from home. College, lot of crap going on…Roth to boot…"

"You did, didn't you? Do you still love her?"

"Cut me a break, Liz. We're supposed to be on vacation."

"And you never felt the need to tell me about her."

"What does it really matter? I married you." Oh, he knew that had been a stupid thing to say the minute it left his lips.

"So, you settled for me when you couldn't have her. Is that it? I was your rebound. Now here she is, and you are stumbling all over your tongue. Are you thinking of a little stroll down memory lane?"

"I'm thinking of no such thing, Liz. You are making a mountain out of a mole hill! We are married. They're married." He had done it again.

"I didn't detect a happily married in that statement."

"You're picking apart my words. That's not a fair thing to do."

"What's not fair is you concealing this relationship from me all these years. You lead me to think I was the only one, the love of your life, your soul mate."

"Damn it, Liz. You act as if you caught me in bed with her. She's just a part of my pass. Why dig it or her up?"

"Because she obviously impacts our future, doesn't she? You know it. I know it and I damn well believe she knows it too." Liz flung her slice of pizza over the balcony rail and stormed back inside. It landed in the pool with a large slap just inches away from a ten-year-old boy swimming with goggles. He looked up as if thinking God had rewarded him. He picked off and ate the pepperoni then floated the crust toward the steps where he appropriately sunk it with a barrage of squirts from his water gun.

"What's eating Elizabeth?"

Chad turned to see Teal standing in the doorway. He just shrugged.

"It's that young lady at the aquarium, isn't it? Sorry, I saw how you two looked at one another. She's an old flame, isn't she?"

Chad just sighed.

"Best keep it that way is my only advice," said Teal with a warming smile. "Can I bring you another slice of pizza?"

"A shot of Scotch would be better."

"I'll make it a double. Give her time to brood then she will be okay. Just make sure you keep it in your britches where that old girl friend of yours is concerned," winked Teal.

Chad thought, Lord, if I ever do consider doing another family vacation, please give me a swift kick in my butt. He shook his head and whispered, "I thought vacations were supposed to relieve stress?"

Bobby came out and flopped down beside him; just what he needed to top off his day. "Appears you pissed off my dear sister. Nice going. What did you do?"

"That's between me and your sister."

"Trouble in paradise, what a shame that is…"

"Between me and Liz," repeated Chad.

"All the women in this family are fruit cakes," commented Bobby.

"If so, what does that make us?"

"Don't know but it's for damn sure we're lower on the food chain than fruit cakes for marrying them."

"Hear you're gunning for a great white tomorrow," said Chad, changing the subject.

"I figure I have just as good a chance as anybody."

"Have you run this idea by the charter boat captain?"

"Not yet, but I'll pass him a few green spots and he'll go along with whatever I want to do."

"Have you ever seen a great white or any shark up close?"

"Seen them on National Geographic and in the aquarium today," boasted Bobby. "On the National Geographic episode this diver just stuck his hand outside the cage and grabbed it by the snout. He stopped the shark dead in its tracks."

"Picture this, a shark two and half times longer than you are tall and exceeding 2000 pounds. How do you propose hauling that in with a charter boat?"

"I don't know. We'll figure it out once we hook it."

"Where are you getting this we crap?"

"Well you and the old man will be there too."

"You're a piece of work. I'm going for a walk."

"Damn sure you're not going to your bedroom right now," chuckled Bobby.

"And I wouldn't bet the bank on landing Jaws if I were you." Chad was tempted to tell him there was no shark.

17

"I can't believe you're actually going to hunt for that shark," mumbled Ken. "This is a shrimp boat, not a big game vessel."

"Look, we're hurting right now, so why not give it a shot, at least for a couple of days until we round up a new mate," replied Captain Joe.

"Chumming, it doesn't get any nastier," complained Ken, elbow deep in fish heads and guts.

"Nastier and smellier the better," stated Captain Joe.

"Then I must have primo stuff in this bucket. I can't believe you're going to risk destroying one of the nets to snag one."

"We're not going to try to catch it in the net. We will hook it then we'll use the net to contain it and haul it back to the dock. Remember the reward is for a live shark not a dead one."

"What about Salty Santa and that nephew of mine; you think the monster shark got them?"

"That crap only happens in the movies," replied Captain Joe, thinking back on how he had seen that shrimp boat tip up exposing its under belly.

"I'm taking my 30-06 Remington just in case."

"You know I don't allow firearms on my vessel."

"It goes or I stay. That's the deal. Bend the rule, Joe. We're not trawling for shrimp right now."

"All right, but we keep it in the wheelhouse and you best not use it on our shark," conceded Captain Joe.

"I won't unless it tries to take us down."

"And only if I give you permission to shoot."

"My mama always professed it easier to ask for forgiveness than permission."

"I'm not your mama, so don't even think of pulling that bull crap with me."

"My mama is prettier anyway."

"Make way," Captain Joe shouted the command. "Nighttime is supposed to be the best time for shark hunting."

"Aye, aye Captain."

"Once we're off, you can return to your favorite job, Mister Chum Master."

"I need a third mate to boss around."

"Let's just go catch us a shark and collect that bounty."

"And try not to end up like that guy that got chomped in half from Captain Marvin's boat. You think that the shark sunk his charter?"

"Possible I suppose if it is as big as they say. It might have damaged his boat and sunk it. Don't worry, this vessel isn't likely to be taken down by any shark. They don't grow sharks that big."

"Tell that to Salty Santa."

"The Serendipity is still afloat," Captain Joe reminded him.

"Like I said, tell that to old Salty wherever the hell he is."

Captain Joe would never admit it to Ken or anyone else but for the first time, going out to sea just didn't feel right. His normal invigoration had left him high and dry. The darkness suffocated him. His breathing was labored, and his heart pounded in his chest, neither brought on by the normal excitement of returning to the open water. He could smell fear oozing from his pores. The stench was sickening and degrading. He thought about taking a shot of Brandy but quickly discounted it. Tonight, he must remain clear headed for what might be waiting for them out there. Even the slightest edge might be a life saver. "God help us if this goes bad," he whispered.

18

The radio woke him to the tune of Bad Moon Rising. Chad sat straight up in bed listening to the lyrics being belted out by John Fogerty and CCR, a 1969 classic. He reached over and shut off the radio glaring 5 AM, the digital display illuminating the darkness. Liz laid with her back to him almost hanging off the edge of the opposite side of the king size bed. She had gone to bed still pissed at him. An unwritten law, never go to bed mad at one another, but they had. He fumbled in the darkness for his clothes and then headed to the bathroom opting to skip shaving and jumped directly in the shower instead.

Adjusting the shower head to massage mode he stood with his back to the stinging beads recounting the events that had landed him in the doghouse. Hopefully, time away from Liz today would help mend the fence. If not, he would have to come up with a plan B. Not helping his cause, flashes of Vanessa disrupted his logical thought process. Worse still, he had become aroused by his stroll down memory lane. He heard the toilet flush signaling Liz was now in the bathroom. Funny thing about an erection, you can't just command it to go away. He could see her shadowy figure through the opaque shower stall washing her hands. He prayed she did not open the door. She didn't.

She returned to the bedroom without as much as a good morning or have a nice day. Prayers had been answered. As he passed back through the bedroom, he could see she had pulled the covers over the top of her head. Again, this suited Chad just fine. He did not relish a confrontation before heading out. She didn't stir. Second prayer answered. He was on a roll. He found Frederic sitting at the kitchen bar sipping on a cup of coffee and reading the morning paper. His attire looked as if he had stepped from the cover of GQ.

"Your man Roth should be quite angry when he reads the headlines this morning," stated Frederic in his matter of a fact tone. "The authorities have discounted the rumors that your cadaver had been attacked by a shark. Reports are inconclusive as to the cause of death. The authorities did confirm the person as being one of those missing from a charter boat."

"I would love to be a fly on that wall when he finds out," said Chad, pouring a cup of coffee. "Is Bobby up?"

"Better be," replied Frederic. "He knows I'm a stickler for punctuality. Alexis is on the balcony taking in the sunrise. Teal prepared us a lunch before retiring last night. How's my number one daughter this morning?"

Chad took the low road and replied, "Still sleeping."

The bedroom door creaked open and out stumbled a half-awake Robert Bornfreund, rubbing his eyes and clothes looking like he had slept in them. Like brother like sister, without as much as a good morning, he made a bee line to the coffee pot just as Alex stepped in from the balcony.

"Good morning gents. I do believe we have a simply fabulous day for fishing," she announced. "Does anyone care to wager on who lands the largest catch?"

Frederic chuckled, "You continue to amaze me, my dear."

"I am quite the amazing type," she confessed "Any takers?"

"Fifty bucks say I clean your clock," spoke up Bobby.

"One hundred for largest, another hundred for quantity," barked Alex.

"My boy you may have met your match," laughed Frederic.

Red faced and not to be made a fool of, Bobby countered with. "Two fifty, both categories."

"Wow, you American chaps can be quite cocky, can't you? If this is going to be a *who has the largest cock* contest, then let's do make the wager worthy of such arrogance. Five hundred for each says mine is larger than yours."

The look on Bobby's face indicated he was in over his head, but he couldn't back down now. "You're on bitch."

"Robert, I'll not condone such language directed toward our guest," stated Frederic. "You owe Alexis an apology."

"Thank you very much sir but none is required. We'll know by the end of the day who really has the largest set."

"So much for fellowship on the seas," said Chad.

"I think we should be on our way," added Frederic. "This is getting too much out of hand."

There were no further confrontations during the short drive to Murrells Inlet. Frederic had insisted separating the two, Bobby in the front seat and Alexis in the back with him. Within 30 minutes of arrival they had cast off. Tommy's Gal was captained by Tommy O'Hara, a red haired and red bearded wiry little guy, no taller than five foot five. He probably weighed in wet at no more than 140 pounds. Chad guessed him to be in his fifties but with the constant influence of the salt water and coastal sunshine, his leathery weathered skin could be that of a younger man.

"You men could not have picked a better day for an adventure on the high seas," barked Tommy in a mocking pirate dialect. "Calm seas and temperatures in the eighties await us. My mate, Carlos will tend to your needs." Carlos, even shorter than the captain, nodded and smiled then said something in broken Hispanic English.

"We'll be at our first honey hole in less than two hours. Please relax and enjoy the ride and the scenery. For those adventurous, we have ice cold beer and an assortment of adult beverages on board. Carlos is also your bartender. Gratuities are most welcome and appreciated."

The two-hour ride to the first fishing spot had been uneventful as had the fishing once they had dropped their lines. Alex had managed to catch three small sea bass and one puffer fish totaling less than seven pounds. All were tossed back. Fredric and Chad had landed one sea bass apiece but weren't in on the wager. Bobby had come up empty handed. Captain Tommy announced for everyone to pull in their lines, they would be moving to a new spot.

The morning sun reflecting off the ocean had begun to bake the fishermen foursome. Alex, now sporting a skimpy bikini top and skintight shorts, seemed unaffected by the heat. She had sprawled out on the bow soaking it in. Chad, accustomed to the ocean hardly broke a sweat. Frederic while not fairing as well as them, shading his head with a wide brim straw hat, still looked in much better shape than his son. Bobby. Sweat was pouting off him like a running faucet. He had swigged down his third beer further contributing to his dehydration death spiral.

Chad joined Captain Tommy in the wheelhouse and struck up a strategically planned conversation with the old salty dog. "Captain, what's your spin on what happened to that missing charter?"

"The ocean, she poses many challenges and far more mysteries. It is a tragic thing what happened to a good man, Captain Marvin Brown. He will be missed by his fellow mates."

"It sounds to me like you are skirting my question."

"Are you asking if I believe in sea monsters, lad?"

"Do you have a reason to believe in mythical creatures? I was just wondering what you thought really happened. And what about those people who vanished from that shrimp boat?"

"My you are the curious one. Do you represent one of those tabloid papers?"

"I'm on vacation. I am just concerned about the sudden disappearances, but if you must know, I am an oceanographer and scientist."

"Ah, a studier of the sea," he smiled. "And do you believe in mythical creatures, lad?"

"I believe in only what the data supports. The ocean is a vast unexplored world and I suppose there are many things yet to be discovered given the time."

"Stranger things I have not seen in my fifty-some odd years of sailing," replied Captain Tommy.

"Fifty years, just how old are you?"

"Sixty-eight come October and I have had salt in my veins since a wee teenager. My father and grandfather and his father before him made an honest living from the sea."

"And you say you have seen things, just what sort of things?"

"Sea serpents…no…but even I must admit the ocean here has undergone a transformation. The once reliable honey holes have suddenly gone dry, now yielding hardly a minnow. Something else is definitely fishing these waters."

"Like what?"

"That I can't say but my gut tells me it is something different, something we have not laid eyes on and it has an insatiable appetite."

"Do you think it's linked to those missing people?"

"If it has gained an appreciation for human flesh then I fear we are in a world of trouble," he winked.

"Have you seen any strange new creatures, Captain?"

"Me, no. I have witnessed no sea monsters. To answer your earlier question though, I do not believe the recent events are random. I think they are connected. Those captains were seasoned veterans and chance mishaps do not happen to souls such as them. Yes, a ship can sink, and yes it can go down with no survivors, but Captain Marvin had the time to send a mayday. He should have had time to ensure his paying customers reached the safety of a life raft or as a bare minimum had life jackets. No wreckage, nothing was found; at least not yet."

"Haven't you heard? Remains of one of his paying customers washed up on shore."

"I did not. No one else was found?"

Chad shook his head no. "I saw the body. Local law asked for me to examine it. It was severed at the waist, the bottom half completely in tack."

"Shark ten," added Captain Tommy.

"No shark; I could not identify the bite marks, but the bite was clean."

"You are the expert and could not ascertain the identity of the guilty one?"

"I could not, and I can't get it out of my mind. I've probably said too much. It is still under investigation."

Captain Tommy crossed himself with the sign of the cross. "Mother of God, what has the sea unleashed on us?"

Chad shrugged. "Do you think it is safe for us to be out here?"

"I did until now," answered Captain Tommy with a glimmer of uncertainty in his eyes.

"Still no guesses," asked Chad of the old man.

"Like you, lad, I deal in fact not fairy tale. It does concern me that we could be facing something man has never seen before."

"Sea monster," asked Chad.

"Unless you have a better name for it. We will make one more stop then I suggest we head back in. I'll reimburse you half fare for half day of fishing."

"Like hell you will," spoke up Bobby, standing behind them. "I have a bet to win. You committed to a day of fishing, old man."

"Don't disrespect or anger this old man, lad. You may find your ass tossed overboard," warned Captain Tommy.

"You can't talk to me like that," growled Bobby. "I'm a paying customer."

"I am captain of this ship. I can and just did. Aboard this vessel I make the calls as I see fit."

"Robert," stepped in Frederic. "Mind your manners."

"Me, this old coot wants to head back in," fumed Bobby.

"He knows best," spoke up Chad.

"I concur," added Frederic.

"And me makes three," yelled Alex, joining in on the conversation.

"You would," remarked Bobby.

"If it makes you feel better, we'll cancel our wager," said Alex.

"Like hell we will. He said we had one more stop."

"Suit yourself. I have no problem relieving you of your money."

"Captain, take us to that last spot," demanded Bobby.

"Feisty little she devil, isn't she?" commented Captain Tommy

"Yes I am," answered Alex. "The loser's going to pay the price for calling me out."

"I can't wait to make you eat those words," mouthed Bobby.

19

Rhonda Pinkerton and her students, all 31 of them, disembarked from the ferry that had scuttled them out to Bull Island. Her fifth-grade classes always looked forward to the annual outing. Bull Island, a 64,000-acre Class I Wilderness located northeast of Charleston and just a 30-minute ferry ride off the coast, stretched over 7 ½ miles. It offered the perfect forum for introducing her students to nature's wonders. A cloudless sunny spring day made the perfect setting for their trek.

The Cape Romain National Wildlife Refuge established in 1932 offered an array of wildlife viewing. Rhonda always prepared her class before arriving. She had told them they were apt to see an abundance of wild birds, including bald eagles and their nests. She told them to be on the watch for wood stork, osprey and peregrine falcon, the glossy ibis, and least tern to mention a few. The island was home to alligators and even a red wolf population that resulted from a recovery assistance program for the species. Loggerhead turtles nested on the island boasting on average, 1000 nests per year, second only to Florida. Typically, the ferry ride was accompanied by playful dolphins but for one of Rhonda's few trips to the island she had seen none. Her students were disappointed after Rhonda had all but promised them they would see the mammals. The ferry boat captain admitted dolphins had been scarce lately.

"Okay kids, listen up," called out Rhonda. "No one wanders off alone. I have assigned groups of four, me rounding out the last group. Each group has a list of items and animals. Identify and check off as many as you can. You will be graded on the experience. Photographs of each creature and various shells are provided in your handouts."

Kyle asked, "What if we run into a wolf?"

"Consider that a bonus point because of all my visits here the best we've ever done is finding their scat."

Rachel turned up her nose, "Scat?"

"Wolf crap," whispered Wanda.

"Collect the scat in your Ziploc and that too will earn you bonus points. Might I remind you to not disturb any nesting grounds, especially those of the loggerhead turtle. Do feel free to collect items like sand dollars, conchs, cockle shells, or any other shells you feel like bringing back for a souvenir, providing it is not alive."

Bart spoke up, "What if we get lost?"

"You're on an island, Bart. I think becoming lost is not a major concern. Stick to the marked trails. There are 16 miles of clearly marked trails inland and each of you has a map, a compass, and a watch. Use your compass like I have taught you. We meet back here no later than 3 PM for lunch. The ferry leaves at 4:30. Please do take time to visit Bone Yard Beach."

Frankie raise his hand, "Is that some sort of elephant graveyard thing?"

"No stupid, didn't you read your brochure," said Doris. "The Bone Yard is where all the trees have washed up on what they call a Barrier Island. The sun has bleached them white to look like bones."

"Very well said, Doris" commended Rhonda. "You have done your homework."

"Suck up," whispered Frankie.

"Jealous," answered Doris.

"Okay, everyone please make sure you have your sunscreen, a couple of bottles of water, insect spray, and snacks in your back packs. Please use the facilities before you go because there are no other bathrooms out there."

"Who needs one," laughed Mike, holding his finger like a penis.

"Girls do," snapped Doris.

Rhonda just smiled. "Okay, divide and conquer, and have fun out there, but remember, you are in nature's home. Please treat it with the utmost respect."

Most of the kids visited the facilities first but within ten minutes the beach was a virtual ghost town. Luck of the draw had saddled Doris with Frankie, Claude, and Kendra. Doris, an intellectual and straight A student had little tolerance for shenanigans and stupidity. Petit as they come, sporting large black rim glasses and a ponytail, she made no fashion statement in her baggy kakis and oversized long sleeve t-shirt. Confident, she asserted herself and took the lead.

Claude certainly did not mind. He was a runt for a fifth grader, 20 pounds lighter than most of his male peers. Possessing a chalky white complexion and enough red freckles to make him look like he had the measles, he had layered on the sunscreen. His red hair was spiked but still served to make him look geekier. Frankie was the athlete of the group, destined to be a jock as he matured. Wavy black hair and solidly built, large for his size, he never hit the books and barely got by with C's and D's.

Kendra, a product of a mixed marriage, her father extremely black and her mother white, had produced a lovely daughter of almost olive complexion. She wore her hair shoulder length and had been blessed with the body of an eighteen-year-old. Like Doris, she was a straight A student but chose to be a follower, not a leader.

"Let's go to Bone Yard Beach first," said Frankie.

"According to the map it's on the opposite side of the island. We may as well follow this path and explore the interior on the way," stated Doris, pointing to the map.

"Come on Claude, let's go that way," said Frankie, preferring not to take his marching orders from Doris.

"Mrs. Pinkerton said we were supposed to stick together," answered Claude.

Franky boasted, "She's not here, now is she?"

"Come on Frankie. Don't mess this up for all of us," begged Kendra.

"What is this, three against one?"

"Democracy rules," smiled Doris, standing defiant with her arms folded.

"Fine, let's go. Maybe we'll spot some red wolves," said an angry Frankie.

"I hope we don't see any alligators," whined Claude. "I don't like alligators. They look like mean dinosaurs, like a T-Rex."

"T-Rex, you're crazy, they don't look anything like a T-Rex," scoffed Frankie.

"We'll stay away from any inland water and swampy areas," spoke up Doris. "That's where alligators live."

Kenda asked, "How will we see the waterfowl if we avoid the wetlands?"

"I'm with Doris, no swamp, no alligators," said Claude. "I don't like alligators."

"Whatever," said Kendra, rolling her eyes and tossing back her head to flip her hair.

Finally, everyone fell in line and followed Doris. The first thing they crossed off their list was a bald eagle perched high on a branch overlooking a second eagle roosting in a massive nest. Kendra pointed to a circling osprey, check mark as well.

"Hey guys, look over here," leaned down Frankie. "I think I found wolf crap."

"Scat, it's called scat," Doris corrected him. "Nope that's not wolf scat. It looks like maybe a raccoon or something."

"I didn't hear anyone mention raccoons," said Claude.

"Well it doesn't look like this picture of red wolf scat," pointed Doris.

"Maybe its alligator crap," stated a concerned Claude

Frankie just rolled his eyes.

"Let's bag it and take it back. Maybe Mrs. Pinkerton can identify it for us. Here, scoop it up and put it in the Ziploc," ordered Doris.

"You scoop it up," said Frankie. "I'm not picking up that for anybody."

Doris using rubber gloves from her backpack did and placed it in her backpack. She shrugged her shoulders and said, "Nothing to it and it could be bonus points."

"Who cares," snipped Frankie, "Let's head to the Bone Yard."

"We'll get there soon enough," said Kendra.

"We'll get there soon enough," repeated Frankie, mocking her tone

"Frankie, bite me," snapped Kendra.

"Come on team, let's not bicker," spoke up Doris.

"Doris Pinkerton, teacher clone, she speaks," laughed Frankie.

"Look," interrupted Claude, pointing toward the edge of the marsh, "It's a red wolf!"

"I'll be," exclaimed Frankie.

"It's a wolf cub," stated Kendra.

"Look, two of them," whispered Doris.

"Over there," yelled Claude.

"The mother," said Doris. "And she doesn't look very happy."

"Let's go," whined Claude.

"I think you're right,' said Kendra, "But mark it on our list, three of them."

"You heard Mrs. Pinkerton. No one has ever seen one before," said Doris. "We'll be famous."

"Whoop-Dee-Do," said Frankie. "Can I have your autograph?"

"Let's go," snapped Doris.

Forty minutes later they emerged on the beach but saw no bleached wood. "Where's this so-called Bone Yard?" Frankie was addressing this to their fearless leader, Doris.

"Well, I followed the map," she defended herself.

"I knew it. We're lost," whined Claude.

"We're not lost," chimed in Kendra. "The island is supposed to be too tiny for us to be lost."

"We're just on the wrong beach," said Doris. "Let's follow the shoreline in that direction."

Less than a hundred yards down the beach they discovered strange marks in the sand. "What made these?" Claude thought they looked like tire tracks.

Doris smiled, "A logger head turtle."

"It sure looks big for a turtle," said Claude.

"I think they get pretty big," said Kendra. "Let's follow them."

"Okay but remember if we find a nest, we can't disturb it," Doris the mother hen reminded them.
Moving inland about 30 yards they indeed discovered a large mound. Markings indicated it had been recently covered. The mother had returned to sea to allow nature to take its course.

"A nest all right," stated Doris.

Claude kept his distance but asked, "How do we know it's not an alligator nest?"

"Alligators are fresh water. The mother returned to the ocean so it can't be an alligator," explained Doris.

"Let's dig it up," said Frankie, poking at it with a stick of driftwood.

"Leave it alone, Frankie," warned Kendra. "You'll get us all in trouble."

"I'm just messing with y'all," laughed Frankie. "Mark it off your list and let's hunt for the Bone Yard."

"Done," said Kendra,

They had walked for a couple of minutes when Frankie announced he had to pee. "We're not near the bathroom," stated Doris.

"Don't need one," smiled Frankie.

"You better not do that here in front of us," warned Doris.

"Let him," giggled Kendra.

"Go ahead. I'll go over there in the bushes and then I'll catch up with you," said Frankie, running over the dune and out of sight.

"Hope he doesn't cross paths with an alligator or a wolf," sighed Claude.

Frankie quickly backtracked to the nest. He un-shouldered his backpack, knelt, and began cupping hands full of sand, excavating the site. Soon he hit paydirt and found the first cluster of eggs. He retrieved one. It was huge; about the size of what he had remembered seeing pictures of an ostrich egg. He shook it then slammed it onto the ground. It didn't break. He figured the soft sand had cushioned it.

He heard a weird shriek from somewhere behind and it sounded awfully close. He looked at the breaking waves and thought he saw something. Whatever he had glimpsed had not looked like a turtle and sure hadn't sounded like a turtle. He didn't think turtles were supposed to make sounds. Maybe this was a gator nest.

He decided best not to stick around because he remembered seeing on one of those nature shows that gators protected their nest. He hurried to join the others but decided not to mention what he had heard or seen. No good would come of him admitting returning to the nest. He still heard that strange cry in his mind and flashes of something weird in the breakers. He soon forgot about it after they finally located Bone Yard Beach. Three other groups were already there. Soon they all headed back to the rendezvous point where they would picnic and wait for the ferry.

20

Tommy's Girl lolled about on the ocean as Captain Tommy positioned it over another of his supposedly honey holes. This spot had yielded the best catches in the past and his fish finder indicated that more of the same should be expected for his patrons today. He could detect thick masses of fish directly below the vessel.

"All right, last chance for you to claim your prize," announced Captain Tommy. "Snap on the squid and lower your hooks for the hungry mouths waiting below."

"Are you ready to have your buns spanked?" Alex eyed Bobby when she said it.

"That sounds like something your kind would be into," spouted Bobby.

"Robert, I've warned you about such talk," asserted Frederic.

"Don't disobey daddy, Bobby boy," whispered Chad. "He may turn you over his knee too."

Bobby leered at Chad and lowered his line, wads of squid dangling from both hooks. Alex had already beaten him to the punch and had been rewarded with her first strike. She began reeling hers in to his dismay. Her smile cut through him like a butter knife as she hauled in two large black sea bass. Both were keepers.

"Go deep my boy," said the captain, "It appears we have some large grouper just to our port side."

Alex asked, "Whose side are you on there captain?"

"My policy is not to become involved and just guarantee satisfaction, bounty of fish for everyone. You may wish to go deeper too."

Frederic managed to land a striper while Chad towed in a medium size trigger fish. Over the next 45 minutes everyone hauled in their fair share of fish; grouper, bluefish, drum, one small lemon shark, and plenty of sea bass. Captain Tommy sized up the fish determining the keepers and ensured that he weighed Bobby and Alex's before tossing them back. Just as quickly as it had started, the fishing ceased.

Chad asked the captain, "Have we moved off our spot?"

Captain Tommy shook his head, his face expressed confusion. "They're gone. I have never seen anything like it. There's not even a blip on the screen right now."

"Can't you relocate them?"

"That's what I've been trying to do but they're no longer here. Fish do not behave in this matter...unless..."

"Unless a natural predator has moved into the area," finished Chad.

"And I picked up no activity on the finder," added the captain. "Some species might become spooked but not every fish is fair game for just any predator. I see no fish at any depth right now."

Chad scanned the open waters for any sign to point out the identity of the intruder or intruders but spotted nothing peculiar breaking the surface. He agreed with the captain. This was not a normal event and very strange behavior for marine life.

Frederic joined in, "What seems to be amidst?'

"We don't know, sir," replied Chad. "The fish detector detects no fish. They have simply vanished from the screen and the area apparently."

"Maybe we've just caught all of them," commented Bobby, gloating over his catch.

"No, there was an abundance of fish here just a few minutes ago and now there isn't. Something has definitely spooked them."

"Then where did they go?"

"Don't know, my dear. They're just gone. You may as well haul in your lines."

Captain Tommy stepped on deck to assist with securing the gear as his customers reeled in their lines. Frederic's reel whizzed in the opposite direction. Something had snatched his bait. The lever on his reel spun out of control and he had difficultly stopping it. Chad leaned over and assisted him. Whatever had taken the bait had to be huge because the gigantic rod succumbed to the assault, the tip touching the ocean surface as Frederic labored to gain control.

Chad yelled to the captain, "Check the finder and see what we have here."

Captain Tommy rushed into the wheelhouse. "Out of range, nothing on the finder," he yelled back.

"Keep an eye on it as we reel it in," shouted Chad, "Maybe we have our culprit."

"Nothing in view yet," yelled the captain.

"It's a fighter whatever it is," reported Chad, still assisting his father-in-law.

"Glad you're not in on our little wager," commented Alex.

Two, three, five minutes passed and the fish on the other end gave little leeway. Chad asked again, "Anything yet?"

"Not in range. Wait, something, there is something…"

"Can you make out the size?"

The line went slack.

"It is swimming directly underneath us," shouted the captain.

"And the line is not coming with it," reported Chad. "Can you identify it yet?"

Captain Tommy stared at the object dumbfounded and said nothing.

"What do you see, captain?"

"I don't know," mumbled Captain Tommy.

Now it was Bobby that asked, "What's that supposed to mean?"

"It means what I just said. I don't know what it is but it's better than twice the size of Tommy's Girl," reported Captain Tommy in a trembling voice, "And it's directly below us and surfacing fast. God help us. Brace yourselves!"

21

On board the Holy Grail, Captain Joe ranted loudly at his first mate Ken. "I told you not to shoot, you damned fool!"

"You told me not to shoot the shark. It wasn't a shark that we hooked,' screamed Ken.

"Why didn't you wait for me? We could have hauled it in and secured it with the net."

"Trust me captain, you didn't want that thing in your net."

"Just what the heck did you shoot, Ken?"

"Too dark. I have no idea."

"Did you hit it?"

"Three times at least and then it broke loose," shouted Ken, still reeling from the encounter.

"What did it look like?"

"Like a damn sea monster," shouted Ken.

"A what," yelled Captain Joe

"You heard me. It looked like the Lock Ness Monster or something."

"Have you been in my Brandy?"

"No, but I could use it now," he said, trying to calm his voice. "You didn't see it."

"How the hell was I supposed to see something from here? Why didn't you yell for help?"

"It happened too fast. I didn't believe my eyes. Even worse, I think I saw more than one."

"What's that supposed to mean?"

"Another one swam up beside the first one, like maybe it was trying to help it get free."

"Did it?"

"Did it what?"

"Did it help set the first one free?"

"Maybe. I suppose it could have severed the line or something. Did you see anything on your screen?"

"I was watching you, not the dang screen," yelled Captain Joe, "I don't see anything on the screen right now. Whatever you think you saw is long gone and with it, our chance at fame and fortune."

"Sorry but I've never seen anything like that before. Those things must have been 15 or maybe 20 feet long from best I could tell."

"And you're sure it wasn't a shark."

"Since when do sharks have necks? Since when does anything that big have a neck?"

"Did it have a head to go along with the neck?'

"Couldn't see it real good because I was too taken by its girth but what I did see reminded me of a bird's head."

"You're so full of crap, mate!"

"I'm just telling you what I saw. You can believe it or not. When have I ever lied to you Joe?" Ken rarely ever addressed him as Joe so that alone convinced him that he believed what he thought he had seen.

"Let's pack it in," advised Captain Joe. "It has been a long night."

"Do you think what I saw could have attacked those other vessels?"

"What do you think, mate? You saw it. I didn't."

"What I saw could not have sunk the Serendipity, not even a pack of them could have brought her down. I didn't witness what you did with the Holy Grail but these things, whatever the hell they were, couldn't have done what you said you saw to her, unless..."

"Unless what..." asked Captain Joe.

"Unless those were just babies," finished Ken.

"What would make you say something like that?"

"Like you have said. Something attacked the Holy Grail and snatched everyone on board and most likely took my nephew after the two of you boarded her. The Serendipity disappeared under strange consequences and that poor man was found bitten in half from what we have heard. What I saw couldn't have done any of those things."

"Which means there is something out here bigger and more dangerous," stated Captain Joe.

"Let's get to shore; the sooner, the better as far as I'm concerned."

"Make way," replied Captain Joe.

The return trip offered Captain Joe an opportunity to think and ponder the events. He came up with way too may questions and very few answers. Furthermore, the ride to shore seemed endless. He caught himself scanning the horizon and looking over his shoulder. He wasn't sure what he expected to see; what he hoped not to see. Making his way back down the coast toward Georgetown, the going had been slowed by an electrical malfunction. It had turned out to have been nothing serious. It had only delayed them for less than an hour to track it down and to patch a wire short. Still, sitting helplessly in the open water had been unnerving for both.

Just past noon he received a startling radio call from Tommy's Girl. She was taking on water and required assistance. Captain Joe made brief contact with Captain Tommy, plotting the location before the radio went deathly silent. Tommy had just been able to tell him that they had been struck by something. He thought how odd he hadn't said they had struck something. No, he reported having been struck. Captain Joe headed in their direction and hailed the Coast Guard. The Coast Guard confirmed they had heard the mayday too. They were assisting in the rescue of a downed beach banner plane near Cherry Grove and requested for the Shrimp Cocktail to commence with the rescue, saying that they were the closest vessel to the scene.

Within just over an hour, The Shrimp Cocktail approached Tommy Girl's last reported location. Captain Joe saw no such vessel on the horizon. He plucked his binoculars from the compartment and began scanning the horizon. After several passes he located the dingy of passengers and steered in its direction. As he got closer, he counted five stranded soles on board. He recognized one, the captain.

22

The aquarium wasn't the happiest place to be right now.

"You're not going to like hearing this, sir," warned Paige.

"No games please, just spit it out dear," snapped an impatient Roth.

"After investing in the advertising to promote the reward for capture of the alleged great white, it appears there is no such creature stalking our shores."

"You have my full attention. Where did you hear this preposterous news?"

"Channel 4 stated that the coroner reported the autopsy inconclusive, but for the record stated that the person did not die of bites from any known shark. We have invested in a lost cause, sir, newspapers, television, and flyers, all for nothing."

"And what could the coroner possibly know about shark attacks?"

"The report said a consultant had confirmed the coroner's suspicions. The death had not resulted from a shark attack."

"Consultant! If the coroner required a second opinion, why did he not contact me?"

"I don't know sir. The report did not divulge the name of the consultant but…."

"But what…get on with it, girl."

"Our inside sources said it was Professor Chad Reynolds, an oceanographer."

"The bastard, this was intentional to make me look bad, I'm sure of it."

"So, what do we do about the reward?"

"We can't withdraw it now or we'd appear even more foolish. The reward stands. Maybe we will luck out and some poor fool will stumble onto a great white or possibly a large Tiger, and if no one does we still win by not having to cough it up. Tell the person who had a reliable snitch at the coroner's office he is fired. Escort him to the door and tell him if I ever hear that he has promoted me or this aquarium negatively there will be hell to pay."

"Yes sir, anything else?"

"Contact Chadwick Reynolds and arrange plans for dinner, he and his wife, Vanessa and I. Plus get your hands on a copy of that coroner's report, pronto."

"Any plans for the dolphin in the holding tank, sir?"

"Oh yes. I have plans but nothing that you should worry yourself with right now, dear. And Paige, come back here when you've finished. I require a bit of stress relief."

The things I do to hold onto this job thought Paige, so disgusting. Oh well, the pay is good, and I do have those videos if I ever need them, she smiled, but only as a last resort.

Roth still fuming thumped his fingers loudly on his computer keyboard. He absolutely would not allow Chadwick Reynolds to one up him. The task at hand, how to humiliate him? Simple, Vanessa would do it for him. He would simply prod her along. What Chadwick needed, maybe deserved, was a journey down memory lane. A knock on the door disrupted his scheming.

"Come in," he commanded, and Colby entered carrying a piece of paper

"I thought you might be interested in this," stated Colby, handing Roth the printout.

"What the hell is going on here," expressed Roth, reading the report out loud. "Coast Guard is responding to another ship in

140

distress. A second charter, Tommy's Girl, was taking on water when it called in the mayday. It reported it had been struck by something. A shrimp boat, the Shrimp Cocktail, is the closest to the vicinity and is responding and has located survivors."

"That's three incidences in less than a week," stated Colby. "The first two resulted in the disappearance of all passengers and one boat, the Serendipity."

"What makes you think this one is connected with the other two?"

"I didn't say they were, but don't you think this is just a little too strange in such a short span of time? Charters don't just go under for no reason and what happened to those three on the Holy Grail, vanished without a sign. And that report says something struck Tommy's Girl. What collides with a charter boat in open water and causes it to take on water?"

"Maybe they're being abducted by little green men," smirked Roth. "And must I remind you, half of a person did wash up on shore, so the aliens only needed the upper torso for their experimentation."

"Maybe I'm just reading too much into it," replied Colby.

"Or maybe the monster white shark has returned. Send Paige back in here. I may have a way to milk this to our advantage."

23

All safely on board The Shrimp Cocktail, Captain Tommy discussed what had happened with Captain Joe in the wheelhouse out of ears shout of the others. He even poured the two of them a shot of Apricot Brandy. "Tell me Tom, what happened?"

"As God is my witness, I'm not really sure, Joe."

"Strange, Tommy, you said on the radio that something had struck your vessel. Did you lock horns with a whale or a submarine or something?"

"Or something," replied Tommy, tossing back the Brandy. "She's gone. My life, Tommy's Girl is on the bottom. What the hell am I supposed to do now?"

"Count your lucky stars you're not down there with her and don't give me that bull crap about you should have gone down with your ship."

"Don't get me wrong, Joe, I am thankful to be here and no, I would not have foolishly gone down with her while my passengers sailed away in that dingy, too theatrical for my taste. Pour me another please."

"So, exactly what happened?"

"Fish were begging to get in the boat. My passengers were pulling them up left and right then suddenly the fish were gone. They vanished. The screen went blank. I've never seen anything like it I tell you, Joe."

"I guess we can rule out that a school of fish sunk you," smiled Joe.

"One of my passengers hooked something and they commenced to battling it. Whatever it was, it had no intention of being reeled in. It was over about as quickly as it started and whatever the hell it was swam right underneath Tommy's Girl. It filled the screen on my fish finder I am here to tell you. And it commenced to surfacing straight for her under belly. It slammed us and the shutter took our feet right out from under us. She started taking on water, belly split wide open. I barely got the call off before she went down."

"Did you see what *done* it to you?"

"I feared whatever it was would take out the dingy next and readied for it, but it never came. Joe, nothing surfaced. I never saw the slightest ripple. Whatever took my Tommy's Girl just swam back into the deep. Maybe it thought she was a rival or something and took out the competition."

"And you say it was how big?"

"Like I said, it filled the view of the finder's screen, so my best guess is it had to be 50, maybe 60 feet in length and I'm not sure of its girth."

"Then it had to be a whale. Sperm whales are not uncommon in these waters. Younger ones get beached from time to time."

"Whales don't normally attack without provocation."

"Well maybe you were fishing its territory, or it was protecting its young."

"Wasn't no whale that *done* this. It never surfaced the whole time we floated around out there, and a whale would have had to come up for air."

"Maybe the head butt inured it and it died."

"Sorry Joe, I'm not buying that whopper, and neither are you."

"Ken thinks we have the Loch Ness Monster out here," chuckled Joe. "We snagged something just before dawn."

"What were you doing out here shrimping in the dark?"

"Nets were dry. We were chumming for that great white shark."

"What did you catch?"

"I didn't see it, but Ken said it looked like a sea serpent, long neck and all. Whatever it was, Ken said it was not big enough to sink a boat. He thinks he saw more than one of them."

"What happened to it?"

"Broke the line. Ken plugged it two or three times with his rifle, but it got away."

"There are some mighty queer things going on out here, Joe."

"You don't have to tell me," agreed Joe, as he recapped what he had seen happen to the Holy Grail.

"What are your passengers saying?"

"That one over yonder is a fish expert," said Tommy. "He saw that body of the man that got cut in half from the Serendipity and said what *done* it was no shark."

"What does he think did it?"

"He doesn't know."

"What about the other three, what did they see?"

"The old man is some sort of famous dinosaur bone digger. He's the father-in-law to the ocean guy and that one over there is his piece of crap worthless son. I'm not sure about the good-looking darkie but she doesn't like the son. They had some sort of bet on who would catch the most fish. She's a tough one I'm here to tell you."

"So, none of them saw anything."

"They felt whatever slammed us from below and that's about it."

"Who won the fishing contest?"

"Neither one seemed too concerned about it now. I'm calling it a tie," he laughed.

"Yonder comes the Coast Guard, a day late and dollar short, I would say," said Joe. "How much are you going to tell them?"

"The truth I suspect. Something sunk us and I have no idea what. Maybe they can send divers down to check out Tommy's Girl. She might have more to say about what really happened than me."

Chad poked his head in and asked if he could join them. Joe motioned him to enter." Do either of you have any idea what may have sunk us?"

"You're the fish expert, from what Tommy has been telling me. What do you think happened?"

"My gut reaction, a sperm whale but we never saw it blow afterwards. Now I know they can stay down for a long time, but a whale never surfaced the entire time we drifted in the skiff. I'll have to rule out anything in the whale species."

"What does that leave," asked Joe, "A damn kraken?"

Chad smiled. "If it was a kraken then one of us must have really pissed off the gods."

"No more guesses," inquired Joe.

"Not off the top of my head. What about you two, you must have a guess?"

"I thought whale like you but ruled it out just like you said. Now a shark has been known to attack a boat from time to time, but I don't know of one that could have sunk us in one single blow."

"Okay, so we've ruled out whales and sharks, what's next?"

Chad tossed out another, "Any subs running exercises off the coast?".

"If there are, it must be a secret," said Joe. "And they need to learn how to steer them u-boats better because they've done run into three ships already, The Serendipity, The Holy Grail, and now Tommy's Girl."

"Once the Coast Guard is done with us, we're heading in," stated Captain Joe. "You're welcome to ride along."

"No offense but if the Coast Guard will take us back, I think we'll ride with them," answered Chad.

"You afraid what's out here has a taste for shrimp," said Joe.

"No, slow moving wood," replied Chad.

Joe laughed. "I guess I can't hold that one against you."

"Thanks for rescuing us, Captain Joe," said Chad.

"Likewise," chimed in Frederic.

Alex gave Ken and Captain Joe a big hug then turned to Captain Tommy and did the same. "We will forever be in you chaps' debt."

After the four of them departed from The Shrimp Cocktail, Joe turned to Tommy and said, "We need an extra hand, Tom. I know it's not much and I'm not trying to insult a fellow captain."

"Thanks Joe. I might just take you up on that. A man has got to eat. Something tells me the insurance company is not going to be too quick to settle until they can determine what sunk Tommy's Girl. I'm mighty curious too."

"You're more than welcome then to join us until you get things worked out or you tire of shrimping," said Joe, patting Tommy on the back.

Ken decided to stay away from the railing just in case. He had no intention of being the next victim of the sea monster or whatever the hell lurked the waters of the Grand Strand. He reloaded his rifle and took up watch on the bow. The ride back to Georgetown proved to be uneventful, thanks to the prayers of the entire shrimp boat crew.

24

Russell Morgan, disgruntled by his abrupt firing, had decided to proceed with his revenge on his former employer, Ross Niederwerter. Originally, he had entertained the idea of capturing the great white and collecting the reward but that would only put more money in Niederwerter's pocket. That's the last thing he wanted to do. He palmed the duplicate keys and eyed the bar-coded badge on the table. Gaining access to the aquarium would be a piece of cake. He first required a diversion, a distraction to throw old Ross off balance. Having worked with Ross for almost six years, he knew what pushed his hot button. The egotistical maniac thrived on being in the limelight and deployed negative publicity. Russell smiled, already envisioning several fronts of attack. He motioned for the waitress to bring him another draft then changed his mind. "Bring me a pitcher, honey." She obliged.

The biker walked in the bar, clad in a dingy white tee shirt, leather vest, and leather chaps. He sported a bushy reddish gray streaked beard, its length reaching his breastbone. Hair from the back of his baseball cap reached about the same length down his back but was neatly braided. Of average height but possessing a barrel chest and gut overhanging his waste band, he looked angry, a disturbing scowl on his face. Without hesitation the biker walked directly over to Russell's table. He grabbed the pitcher like a beer mug and turned it up as Russell did nothing but quietly watch. Beer drool ran through his beard and dripped down his shirt and onto the table. He slammed the drained pitcher down on the table and growled, "Taste like horse piss to me, best you order us up something better than that."

"Lost my job; that's the best I can do," spoke up Russell, the biker still standing over him, appearing none too impressed by his response.

He leaned over and placed both hands on the table tilting it toward him. "Then horse piss it is. Order us another one and tell me what's on your mind, Bro."

"Thanks for meeting me here, Luther," smiled Russell, standing to shake his old buddy's hand.

"Luther is fine here, but anywhere else I'm Copper Head and don't forget it."

"You still think you have those biker pals of yours fooled?"

"Damn straight and I parlay that into plenty of snatch and drugs," he grinned.

"Road whores and Viagra maybe," countered Russell.

"Hey man, you can't get it in if you can't get it up," he laughed. "So, what's so damned important that you interrupted my beauty sleep?"

"You better sleep more then, it's not working."

"Don't make me kick your ass just to uphold my reputation."

"And if I kick yours then your reputation is history," chuckled Russell.

"Okay, enough of this crap, why did you get canned, little brother? I thought you had it made at that fish tank."

"I crossed the line and bucked Ross and that's something you just don't do, so he fired my ass."

"Just like that," said Luther.

"Just like that, and he's not going to get away with it, big bother."

"That bastard is too snotty for my taste anyway. He always treats everyone like shit. You're better off, trust me."

"You're probably right but I loved that job."

"What do we plan to do about it? That's why I'm here, right?"

"That's why you're here, Copper Head," grinned Russell. "My brother is no dumb ass."

"But mine is still a smart ass. Order another pitcher and let's get down to business. That fish tank dude can't screw over one of the Morgan boys and get away with it not without hell to pay."

25

"I am so thankful that all of you are okay," said Teal hugging her husband.

Frederic was not one for open displays of affection, but he did not pull away this time

"We're no worse for wear, my dear" stated Frederic "I found the experience quite exhilarating given the circumstances."

"You would," snipped Bobby. "We could have all drowned out there or worse, we could have been attacked by whatever godforsaken creature sunk that charter boat." Cody clung to him like the caring wife while assuring the children that their father was fine.

"I'm so sorry," begged Liz for Chad's mercy. "Proof why people should never go their separate ways while still angered. One never knows if it might be the last time you see one another."

"We're fine, Liz. Captain Tommy loaded us safely in the skiff before the boat ever went under," said Chad kissing Liz on the cheek

Corrine, exploiting the situation as usual, kissed Alex square on the lips. She watched her father from the corner of her eye the entire time, hoping to see him appalled. Frederic never flinched and said, "She acted like a true champion out there, Corrine. You should be proud of her."

Corrine pulled away, stunned by his reaction. "I would expect nothing less of my lovely."

Liz interrupted, "What actually happened?"

"We were struck by something from the ocean's depths," answered her father, "But sadly we haven't identified our assailant."

"Yeah, Mister Oceanographer doesn't have a clue what tried to have us for lunch," smarted off Bobby.

"What could it have been, Chad?"

"Liz, Bobby is correct for once. I don't have a culprit to hang my hat on at the present."

"And it's the second charter sunk in less than a week," added Bobby. "We're lucky we didn't end up like that last one."

"Our captain viewed it on his sonar as it surfaced underneath our vessel. He could not identify the image. He said it filled the sonar's view screen and estimated it to be colossus in size," explained Frederic.

"Well, we surely know a minnow didn't sink us, Father," wise cracked Bobby.

"Robert, please refrain from those embarrassing outbursts of sarcasm. You should instead be thanking the Almighty above that you are here to tell the tale."

"Father, I didn't want to go fishing in the first place."

"And bet my Alex kicked your butt, didn't she?

"Under the circumstances, we called it a tie," spoke up Alex.

"You called it a tie," added Bobby.

"Actually, the captain called it a tie," clarified Chad.

"Whatever," shrugged Bobby.

"And I bet you're glad of it, aren't you? It would have killed you to have had to fork over that cash to Alex."

"I can't believe the two of you would quibble over a silly bet when you're lucky to have your brother here," said Teal, directing her outrage at Bobby and Corrine.

Corrine rolled her eyes. "You heard Father and Chad. They were never in any real danger, Mother."

"We were in the middle of the damn ocean and our boat sunk, Corrine. Just how dangerous do you want it to be?"

"Come on, Bobby, you look fine unless you need a change of underwear," egged Corrine.

"I think we all require a change of underwear after that episode," chuckled Alex.

Chad tiring of this, "Frederic, could I have a word with you?"

"Sure, my boy, what's on your mind?" They walked out onto the balcony.

"What do you really think attacked our boat?"

"I have been giving that considerable thought, Chadwick."

"And…"

"I'm no detective but I fancy my ability to reasonably deduct and derive given enough information to reach a plausible explanation. Let's review the evidence we have before us, my boy."

Chad nodded.

"Let's begin with recent events. There have been at least three boating incidences in the past few days. The extraordinary circumstances surrounding the disappearance of that first charter and its crew of five and that one gentleman severed in half. We have an alleged attack on a shrimp boat. Everyone on board vanished. Of course, we have our experience and regardless to the stupidity displayed by my son, we are indeed lucky to be here. And then there is your dolphin beaching compounded by the comments that the fishing patterns have dramatically been impacted."

"You're thinking they're all tied together some way."

"Possibly, the pieces do fit, would you not agree."

"Yes. I have been thinking the same thing. Let's dissect these incidences. The first thing that jumps out at me is the fact that these incidents are so widespread and not centralized. I have a difficult time assigning a single root cause."

"Chadwick, you're a scientist, an oceanographer, and you're approaching this with known facts, territorial boundaries of species you are familiar with. That my boy would be precisely the proper means for deduction, but what if we are experiencing the emergence of a new species?"

"Like what?"

"Ah, we must give that more thought."

"I do deal in fact; actual data and we don't have much of that right now."

"Don't deceive yourself my boy. Fact, we have something capable of destroying and sinking thirty-foot vessels and wreaking havoc on a fifty-foot trawler. Our dear Captain Tommy witnessed this creature on his sonar. He estimated it to exceed 50 feet and an impressive girth. Our creature has extremely aggressive tendencies which rule out whales, don't you concur?"

"Yes. I agree. Whales are only aggressive if you disrupt their breeding or possibly impede on a cow and her calve. These waters are neither breeding grounds nor known to harbor large pods of whale. I don't think we're dealing with a Moby Dick here."

Frederic chuckled. "And I'm certainly not the revengeful Captain Ahab type."

"Pondering the various species, we have the blue whale, adult male reaching lengths of over 100 feet. A finback can exceed 80 feet. More matching our fifty-footer would be a right whale, the humpback, a sperm, or a gray and none of these are typically that dangerous unless disturbed. Even with that, you might receive a bump or a tail slap. Furthermore, whales must surface for air. No whale sunk our boat. Nothing ever surfaced."

"Exactly," agreed Frederic. "And you have discounted the possibly of a rogue Orca."

"Well, an Orca could fit the build as far as temperament. They can measure up to 32 feet. No Orca reaches 50 feet. Orcas don't attack thirty-foot vessels, much less shrimp trawlers. And let's not forget, the victim from the Serendipity was not bitten in half by an Orca."

"Can we absolutely rule out shark?"

"Bite marks did not match any known shark species."

"Could we have an unknown species of shark?"

"Are you thinking megalodon?'

"Megalodon is not an unknown species; however, any bite marks from our extinct fish would match those of present-day sharks. You have already discounted that possibility by ruling out shark attack."

"Then we're back to square one," sighed Chad, "Unless…"

"Unless a new species has emerged from the ocean's depths," finished Frederic.

"Exactly. Something that can frighten dolphins into beaching themselves. Roth lied to me. Those dolphins were not infested with parasites and he damn well knew it."

"What did he have to gain by falsifying the results?"

"His way of ensuring I wasn't right," fumed Chad.

"Does this Niederwerter fellow dislike you that badly?"

"College rivalry and yes. I am his Moby Dick. I'm embarrassed to admit that the sentiment is mutual."

"That saddens me. He certainly has the resources to assist us in exploring the possibilities. One would think that a man of his stature would leap at the opportunity to discover a new life form in the sea."

"I'm sure he would, sir, however, he would not share that credit with either of us. We could never turn our backs on him."

"How does it go? Keep your friends close and your enemies even closer or some rhetoric such as that."

"So, you're asking me to ask him to help us?"

"I ascertain that this is most difficult for you to consider, isn't it son?"

"With all due respect, sir, please do not judge me on this alone. I have my reasons for hesitating."

"We each have our demons, son. I do not hold this against you, but if you could somehow look beyond yours for the greater cause…"

"I can only promise you that I will think about it, sir."

"Fair enough, in the meantime, I'll make a phone call to my associates and how do I phrase it; ah yes, I will light a fire under their posteriors to expedite their examination of your autopsy report. I must confess. I do not normally enjoy these family vacations, but I am invigorated by our most intriguing mystery."

"I confess too, sir. Forced Family Fun is not my bag either. Two weeks of this is ten days too much for me; no offense."

"None taken my boy. I'd rather be digging up T-Rex bones in 120-degree temperatures than doing what is morally required of me to muddle through this."

Chad laughed and offered Frederic his hand. "Thank you for your candidness, sir. Now let's see if we can discover the identity of our new species before another boat becomes victimized."

"An excellent idea, Chadwick, and we should probably exercise confidentiality or face the wrath of those who otherwise still believe forced family fun is beneficial to all."

"Amen to that," said Chad.

"We should probably research other events that might be associated with our creature."

"Or creatures," stated Chad. "I'm not so sure we're dealing with just one."

"Geographically speaking you could be right in your assumption. Why should we conclude that if a new species has surfaced that it would be a lone survivor?"

"And where have they been hiding and why have they just materialized? Why along the Carolina coastline?"

"We are here for a reason my boy, divine intervention."

"We should research any recent natural phenomena such as quakes, changes in weather patterns, ecological impacts, water temperature shifts in the gulf stream, something that would explain their arrival."

"A thought," added Frederic, "The ocean once harbored some of the most vicious creatures, worthy of plucking a mature T-Rex from its shores. What if one of these species still existed in the unexplored fathoms of the sea and has now invaded our world for the very first time. It could be a formidable foe to mankind."

"Captain Tommy mentioned sea monsters," recanted Chad. "I sure hope we're not talking Jurassic Park here and some corporation is cloning dinosaurs."

Frederic smiled. "You give science too much credit my boy. Only Michael Crichton and Stephen Spielberg could accomplish this feat."

"And make millions while pulling it off," chuckled Chad.

"Chadwick, we should probably go back inside if we intend to masquerade this forced family fun charade."

"FFF, here we come."

26

Vanessa Daetwyler Niederwerter sat in her office drinking her second cup of morning coffee. She held her cell phone in one hand and Chad's business card in the other. Her pounding heart and labored breathing deafened her senses as she contemplated phoning him. Seeing him had rekindled a long-extinguished fire. She had thought she had seen it in his eyes too; however, circumstances were different now. Both were married. Did this equate to both being happily married? She knew her answer but not his. A rap on her door disrupted her thoughts. Paige stepped in and informed her she might want to switch on the television to channel four. Paige offered no explanation, but Vanessa acted to her request. A reporter was conducting an interview.

The young blonde newswoman asked the gentleman, "And you have no idea what struck your boat causing it to sink?"

"No missy. We didn't see anything, nor did we have any warning," answered Captain Tommy.

"You must be devastated at your loss," she continued.

"I'll know just how devastated when I hear from my insurance company. I just lost by livelihood and my only means of income but hey. I'm alive, so no need to complain too much I suppose. And so are all my passengers. I'm thankful we didn't meet the same fate as Captain Marvin Brown and the Serendipity."

"The captain is referring to those who charted his boat, archeologist Frederic Bornfreund, his son, Robert and son-in-law oceanographer Chadwick Reynolds, and a family acquaintance, ex-playboy centerfold, Alexis Clarke. Are you suggesting that your incident and that of the Serendipity are related, captain?"

"We both sunk didn't we and in open water, that's all I'm saying. I don't know what caused the Serendipity to go down and we might never know. God bless Captain Marvin's soul."

"As I understand it, you were rescued by Captain Joe Wilson of the shrimp trawler, Shrimp Cocktail. This was the same vessel that witnessed another strange phenomenon, the attack on the Holy Grail and the odd disappearance of its crew."

"Captain Joe did indeed come to our rescue. As for all that other stuff, you best ask him."

"We solicited the preliminary report from your incident, and it states that you observed something rather large beneath your boat just before it was struck. Is that correct?"

"You said you had a copy of the report, didn't you?"

Trying to remain composed she asked, "Do you know what this object might have been?

"You mean you didn't see that in your report."

She smiled as she read his quote, 'I'm not Jonah and that weren't no whale,' it states you as saying."

"There you have it," he replied with a wink.

"So, you confirm that your boat was attacked by a sea creature of some sort."

"Are you one of them ventriloquist or something, honey? I don't recall saying nothing of the sort."

"Then what caused your vessel to sink, captain?"

"Guess my insurance company will let us know once they finish their investigation, now won't they."

"To coin the captain, there you have it. Just what is attacking the boats along the Grand Strand remains a mystery. We will update as this story unravels. This is Raven Mallow, Channel 4 News, reporting live from Georgetown Marina. We now return you to Days of Our Lives, in progress."

"Oh my," exclaimed Vanessa.

"Yeah," replied Paige. "Hopefully, this will help ease the blow a little. We were getting slammed by the media for our great white promotion, especially after the coroner said the dead guy was not the result of a shark attack. Hope your hubby cuts me some slack now that we do definitely have something out there chomping on boats."

"They could have all been killed."

"Glad Mister Reynolds made it. Roth wants me to schedule dinner for the Reynolds duo and you," stated Paige, unaffected by Vanessa's comments.

"Have you talked to him?"

"Next on my agenda," replied Paige.

"Where is Roth?"

"In a meeting over at the Barefoot Landing Resort. He can't be disturbed right now. I hope he is near a television. He has this thing for that Reynolds guy."

Vanessa almost blurted out that she did too. 'Why don't I call him?"

"I said he can't be disturbed," repeated Paige.

"No silly. I mean call Chad. I'll arrange the dinner plans."

"By all means…please be my guess," answered Paige, winking, and smiling.

"What was that supposed to mean?"

"Girl's intuition," she responded. Paige then turned and exited the office.

Vanessa took a deep breath then keyed in the number on her cell. She felt as nervous as a little high school girl waiting for Chad to answer. Instead she got his voice mail. "Chad, I just heard. I'm so glad you weren't hurt in that incident. Please call me when you get this message. My number is 843-349-6829."

Chad had received another anonymous phone call. The messenger in a disguised voice said, "The dolphin is alive and in the containment tank at the aquarium. Roth lied."

27

Morning took on a new meaning for Chad after yesterday's ordeal. From the balcony, alone with his thoughts, he peered out over the beach and ocean inhaling the salty air. Cody, Teal, Liz, and the kids had gone down to the pool. Neither Corrine nor Alex had emerged from their bedroom. Frederic had departed to meet with a former colleague to further explore what lies beneath. He wasn't sure where Bobby had gone and didn't really care. He was sipping a Bloody Mary, something he rarely ever did before noon. After all, he was on vacation and could indulge if he wished. Liz had insisted that he enjoy his vacation.

Ant like creatures scurried about on the sand ten floors below. A group of young mean and women tossed bean bags at a wooden target attempting to land their bags in the open cavity. Corn hole seemed to be the latest craze. Further up the beach several seniors played botchy ball. Obesity ran wild. Even from this height he could see their overhanging bellies. A clanging sound in the other direction alerted him to a horseshoe match. Scantly clad girls squealed at every toss. Young and old played volleyball further down the beach. Two kids tossing Frisbee in the surf almost collided with a boy body surfing. The ocean shallows were peppered with people, young and old, every shape and size. A young girl hocked her goods pushing a shaved ice cart. She had very few takers but appeared undaunted, probably just happy to be on the beach. Tranquility prevailed. The sea shimmered under the blue cloudless sky as a couple of gents cast their fishing lines into the incoming tide. Chad activated his cell phone having switched it off before going to bed last night. He had three new messages. He entered his code to retrieve them.

First Message left at 8:22 AM: "Chad, I just heard. I'm so glad you weren't hurt in the incident. Please call me when you get this message. My number is 843-349-6829."

He recognized Vanessa's voice. It sent chills down his spine, nice chills.

Second Message left at 9:13 AM: "The dolphin is alive and in the containment tank at the aquarium. Roth lied."

"I knew it." He did not recognize the caller or the number on the display. "Roth lied."

Third Message left at 9:20: "Captain Tommy just checking in on you gents to make sure you're okay. You can reach me at my work number. I'm going to hook up with the Shrimp Cocktail. Joe Wilson has offered me a gig until I get back on my feet and find out the fate of my boat. Something tells me this thing isn't over yet by a long shot either. There's something awfully bad in that ocean and it's got one ferocious appetite for sea captains. I should have my ass kicked for just thinking about going back out there. I don't know any other way though. Hope to hear from you."

Yep thought Chad, there is something out there with one hell of an appetite and it doesn't fear humans. And he too believed it was far from over. First task. Identify the perpetrators then formulate a plan to contain and possibly study them. Destroying whatever it might be did not enter his thoughts. Any new species deserved a fair shake. It was his job to ensure they got one. He may even find it necessary to file a request to place whatever it might be on the endangered species list. Chad figured surely there couldn't be many of these creatures or they would have been discovered before now. And why now had they chosen to emerge? He almost sounded like his mom, forever hunting for evidence that Bigfoot existed. Mattie Reynolds was a skeptic searching for truth.

The one scary aspect, with their arrival, they had brought death and destruction if indeed they had been responsible for the three boating incidences. This would pose a difficult picture for him to paint to protect them if they continued to wreak havoc and mayhem on humanity. And if this was the work of one new rogue species, how could he possibly allow it to be destroyed? He was getting ahead of himself. First, identify it, and then worry about the rest.

Chad again thought about his mother, Mattie and how she would simply relish being in his situation. She had for most of her adult life searched for an elusive creature, for any evidence that a new species existed. Here he stood with no aspirations of following in her footsteps, faced with the opportunity of a lifetime. He contemplated calling her but remembered she was off on another excursion, probably following a Sasquatch lead. He didn't like her going off on her own but knew better than to butt heads with a hard head. He instead stared at the recent call list of the received numbers on his phone's display screen deciding who to call first. He toggled to the unknown caller's number and pressed the call button. After a seventh ring he halted the call, figuring it must have been initiated from a pay phone since no answering service picked up. The snitch wanted to remain anonymous. Best guess, he worked for Roth.

Next, he returned the call to Vanessa. She picked up on the second ring. "Sorry, I just heard your message. I had switched off my phone last night and had just switched it back on. To what do I owe the honor?"

"Are you okay?"

"Not bad for a survivor of a sunken ship I suppose."

"Do you know what attacked you?"

"It wasn't Roth's great white shark if that's what you're asking."

"Roth doesn't even know I'm calling you. He'd be furious at me if he knew."

"We never were too good at sharing you."

"It was good to see you. I've thought about you a lot over the years."

"I can tell. Is that why you married that asshole? He reminds you of me?"

"That was a crappy thing to say even for you."

"Sorry, you didn't exactly leave the best taste in my mouth, exiting so abruptly and leaving me the Dear John letter."

"Things were complicated. I had no choice."

"We always have choices, Vanessa. Why did you wait so long to marry Roth if he was the chosen one?"

"He wasn't my first choice," she blurted out.

"And I was? You certainly had a way of pleading that case, didn't you? Just up and left, no real explanations. That really hurt."

"I had no intentions of hurting you, Chad. I loved you."

"Past tense?"

"Like I said, things were complicated."

"Why did you call, Vanessa?"

"Can you meet me so I can explain?"

"I'm listening, explain. It beats reading it in a letter."

"No, can we meet, now?"

"What's the point? You're a happily married woman and I'm a happily married man."

"Please," she begged.

"Look, I don't know what good could come out of us meeting?" He asked, knowing in his heart he wanted to comply with her request.

"I want to explain to you why I had to leave."

"You're just a few years too late, aren't you?"

"And I'm sorry for that. I am heading over to Bay Watch Resort. We have a four-bedroom suite there. It will give us privacy to talk.

It is located on 2701 South Ocean Boulevard, suite 1407. Please, just give me a chance to explain why I did what I did."

Chad wasn't sure about this. It sounded a tad too intimate for his liking. It wasn't that he didn't trust Vanessa. He didn't entirely trust himself. His pause prompted her to speak. "Chad, I owe this to you. Please don't deny me the opportunity to set the record straight, clean the slate so to speak. I probably need this more than you."

Against his better judgment he gave into her request. "Thank you, Chad."

Nervously, he shaved and showered, and then dressed in clean clothes thinking how he shouldn't be doing this. As hard as he tried, he couldn't win the argument. He had never been unfaithful in this marriage, but Liz had been right, she had not been his first true love. This had absolutely nothing to do with the Roth rivalry. He didn't give a damn about him. He needed closure and hoped to find it. He certainly didn't need a new beginning or an affair. Uncertainty held him in its grip.

28

The crowd gathered around the four pilot whales bobbing in the water on the stretch of secluded beach. None of them were alive. The overwhelming stench of decay had the onlookers covering their mouths and noses. Swarms of huge green blow flies occupied the airspace shared by feasting gulls, all laying claim to their share of the bloated bounty. One of the whales was missing a huge chunk of flesh from its midsection and a second had no tail, severed cleanly. No visible markings could be seen on the other two. Authorities had been called but had not arrived. While it was not uncommon for whales to beach themselves, these had done so obviously to escape some sort of attack. Unlike the dolphins that had been discovered days ago, these mammals had been viciously assaulted. Tourist posing for pictures uncovered their faces and held their breath until the shots were snapped, and then they scurried a safe distance away from the gut-wrenching smell.

Further down the beach a lone kayaker drifted just beyond the breaking waves. The bearded middle-aged man paddled only when repositioning himself for the next fishing cast. He had been trolling for better than an hour but had not received his first bite. He could see the commotion a half mile up the beach and decided to reel in his line and paddle in that direction. Curiosity had gotten the best of him. His strokes were smooth and hardly made a ripple. Something streaked by him just underneath the surface creating enough turbulence to cause his kayak to bobble like a cork. He stopped his paddling, peered over the side, and saw a second, a third then a fourth blur torpedoing just under the surface. The shapes as best he could tell were odd. They didn't resemble a dolphin or seal. They were brownish green in color and well over ten feet long. Astonished, he saw the trailing one better than the first three. It had a long slender neck and almost a bird like head. It possessed what looked like flippers and a short stubby tail. It almost reminded him of a sea turtle without a shell, but much larger and swifter. Blood streaked from an open wound on its side which explained why it was slower than the first three.

He placed the paddle across the bow of the kayak where his lap was positioned inside its hull. He scanned the waters ahead expecting the strange creatures to surface, but they didn't. He began slowly paddling again in the direction of the growing crowd on the beach, still scanning the horizon for any signs of what he had just witnessed. His buddies would never believe him not without proof. He knew what he had seen, and it wasn't anything he had ever seen before. He practically lived on the ocean and thought he had encountered most of the resident species. He removed a waterproof camera from his belt readying for another potential glimpse. Without warning something in the ocean opened like a vast hole and something snatched the kayak and pulled it beneath the surface. Other than a few trailing bubbles it was as if it had never been there. The fisherman did not even have an opportunity to scream. Seconds later, a large chunk of kayak bobbed to the surface followed by the other half. The occupant was gone, peeled from the tiny hull like a nut from its shell. The crowd gawking at the whale carcasses was too far away to have witnessed the kayaker's demise.

The wounded creature, unable to keep up with the others, now lulled about just below the surface, flapping its paddles like wings to hold its position. It watched frantically behind for any signs of the predator that had been pursing them. Even with its excellent underwater eyesight it could not detect the pursuer in the murky waters. After remaining as stationary as possible for a few more minutes, it slowly but deliberately paddled in the direction of the others of its kind. Blood still trailed from the open wound. With lightning speed, the predator scooped up the wounded Plesiosaurus in its jaws. The water bloodied only momentarily as it sped off with its prey. It was at the top of the ocean's food chain and feared nothing, not even man. Anything it could catch it would devour. Nothing in the oceans were safe or excluded from its voracious appetite.

29

Chad pulled into the hotel's underground parking area. After locating an open space, he turned off the engine and just sat there. His emotions ran the full gambit, excitement to apprehension. Vanessa stirred long lost feelings but visualizing her married to Roth quickly quenched the full effects of the fantasy. He still could not fathom why she had married the prick. A ride in an elevator is all that separated him from solving that mystery. He thought about just driving off, but he couldn't. He needed this meeting, if for no other reason than to heal old wounds. Why had she abruptly left college and why had she later married Roth Niederwerter? Why had she never tried to contact him instead? Exiting the car, he walked over to the elevator and pressed the 14th floor button. The elevator rumbled toward his parking level location and the door opened. He was thankful it was empty, and it zoomed to the 14th without stopping. He quickly located suite 1407 just a few doors away from the elevator.

He popped a mint into his mouth, crushing it immediately with his teeth. Taking a deep breath, he rapped on the door. He could hear her approaching, heels echoing off the tile floor. Suddenly remembering to breath, he exhaled. The door opened and there she stood, dressed in a low-cut tan blouse and olive cargo shorts, breathtaking as always.

"Glad you came," she said, stepping aside so he could enter. He brushed her as he passed by. He wasn't sure if that had been intentional on her part or his. She smelled wonderfully fresh.

"Can I fix you a drink?"

"I'll have whatever you're already having," replied Chad, observing the glass on the end table.

Vanessa made him a Rum and Ginger ale. "Have a seat," she told him. After he sat down on the couch, she sat on the opposite end.

Taking a swig of his drink, Chad wasted no time getting directly to the point. "Why did you really leave college? I don't buy that navy seal crap."

With not so much as a blink Vanessa responded, "I was pregnant."

Chad had not expected that response. He almost dropped his drink in his lap. He did manage to spill some directly on his crotch, creating an awkward strategically located stain. Wild eyed, he remained speechless.

"It wasn't yours if you're worried. We always used contraceptives and I was incredibly careful."

"So, when did you throw caution to the wind?"

"Remember that party at the lake, the one when we had that little disagreement."

"Yeah, I didn't realize asking you to get engaged would piss you off so, but I guess I loved you more than you loved me."

"Oh, I loved you and still do, but I wasn't ready for marriage, not with college to complete. We both were quite career minded."

"And so, when did that change? After you quit using contraceptives and got pregnant, and then decided to leave college, a career, and me?"

"It wasn't exactly like that."

"You laughed in my face when I pulled the ring from my pocket, if memory serves me."

"I wasn't laughing at you. The situation just blindsided me. I sometimes get hysterical in those situations."

"Those situations…how often have you been asked to become engaged?"

"I wasn't ready and that was the first."

"But you were ready for a pregnancy?"

"No, not hardly, but you left me at the party."

"That was after you laughed in my face, told me no way in hell were you going to marry me, or any other son of a bitch. You then topped that by saying we needed our space. Those were your exact words. I have them etched in my memory."

"I had too much to drink. I shouldn't have said it like that. I'm really sorry."

"You weren't drunk Vanessa and said exactly what you meant to say. I got it and Elvis exited the building. Is that when you spread your legs to reclaim your space?"

"Ouch, I deserved that one. Actually, I became extremely shit faced and was sorry I had said what I had said. Angered I had pushed away the most important person in my life."

"Touched, so who ended up being the lucky guy not wearing a condom?"

"Like I said, guilt ridden, I drank way too much that night. With you gone, I didn't have a ride."

"Oh, so you're going to make out this to be my fault??

"No. I take full responsibility for my actions that night."

"Except for the getting pregnant part…that would have required a willing body, unless you're into an occult specializing in artificial insemination."

"You're not going to make this easy, are you?"

"Been saving up for a long time I'm afraid, but please do continue."

"Someone did eventually take me home. The night was a complete blur. I woke up the next morning puking my guts out and with absolutely no memory of the particulars. I wasn't sure who had brought me home and really didn't care."

"Guess that's supposed to make me feel better."

"A couple of days later, the mystery was solved when I received a call from my designated driver saying what a wonderful time, he had with me, and he asked me for another date. We were still…"

"Having our space…" Chad finished.

"Yeah, so I agreed to go out with him again and didn't let on that I had not remembered a thing about our alleged first date. Early into the date and in the backseat of his car he tried to have his way with me. Only after I refused did I realize he had already had his way with me that other night. Still refusing to admit to him that I didn't remember, we eventually had sex back at his place. I made sure he used protection and I wanted to make sure I remembered it. He laughed, telling me he wished I would make up my mind. At the time I didn't get it."

"Telling me how many times you screwed your mystery man isn't really necessary."

"You've haven't asked me the identity? Aren't you the least bit curious?"

"You had your two night stand, so what. The thing that really got me was when you started dating Roth. You knew how he and I disliked each other. You could have picked anyone else but him, but then again, I figured that was your point."

"Roth treated me nice, special like you used to before I messed it up."

"Oh yeah, he's a real sweetheart."

"A little over a month later I found out I was pregnant. I was devastated and unsure what to do, so I confronted in the only possible father. He without hesitation asked me to get an abortion and said he would pay for it."

"What did gentleman Roth have to say about that, or did you tell him about your little indiscretion?"

"He's the one that asked me to have the abortion. He was the father. He was the one that had his way with me that night after the party. I still don't remember that night. I turned you away and then he did the same to me in my time of need. He said he loved me but wasn't ready for kids. It stung just like I'm sure it stung you when I said I didn't want to be engaged."

"This is insane, Vanessa."

She began to cry. Without thinking Chad slid to her side of the couch and held her in his arms. He kissed her on the cheek and tasted her salty tears. She tilted her head and pressed her lips against his. Caught up in the passion, Chad reciprocated and only released her as her sobbing subsided. "You allowed him to buy his way out of it."

She shook her head no. "I left college as you already know. I couldn't bring myself to have an abortion, but I wasn't ready to be a mother either. I decided to stay in hiding and have the baby, I placed my child up for adoption."

"So, you have a baby out there somewhere."

She shook her head no. "I had a miscarriage into my third month. I think all the stress killed my baby. College was out of the question. I could not return to you or Roth, not after all the bridges I had burned. I did eventually join the navy and did become a navy seal, a damn good one I must admit. I completed my education compliments of the United States government. Years later, Roth and I eventually found one another again. You were married. The rest is history."

"I hope this has cleansed your soul because it hasn't done a damn thing for mine. All the rhetoric about falling for Roth and getting pregnant happened after you broke it off with me, so what's the point?"

"The point is I still love you. I never stopped and regret everything from that very moment I turned down your engagement proposal. I'm sorry. I am so very sorry and hope you will find some way to forgive me. Excuse me. I need to go freshen up. Please make us another drink if you don't mind."

Chad reeling, couldn't believe what he had just heard. Roth had rubbed his nose in it when they had been in college. He had claimed to have plucked Vanessa from him and had often gloated about it. Then in her time of need, it had been all about what was best for Roth, his career, his reputation. Claiming the prize now and flaunting her in his face had been the icing on the cake for Roth. Vanessa returned a few minutes later wearing nothing but a bra and panties. She sat down beside Chad and began smothering him with kisses. She ran one hand underneath his shirt and hooked it under his arm and over his shoulder. She rolled backwards on the couch and pulled him on top of her.

"I love you Chad."

Chad pushed away and whispered, "And I love Liz."

She felt his arousal and whispered, "Maybe not as much as you think."

Chad sighed and then rolled off her and stood up. "I'm afraid I do. I am flattered. I'm sure a stroll down memory lane would be simply wonderful, but I'm not into one day stands. You are married to Roth and even if that means nothing to you, you made your choice. You best learn to live with it. Liz is my world now. She accepted my proposal and we are happily married. I can't return to the past and a life of what-ifs."

"You love me. I can tell. And you were just as excited as me."

"Don't confuse the two four lettered L words, love and lust. I have got to go now. "

"Chad, please come back!"

Chad ignored her. The ride down on the elevator took an eternity. Riders entered and exited at almost every floor. He thought about how easily he could have betrayed Liz. He thought too how easily he could have one upped Roth by screwing his wife and then flaunting it in his face. He was happy he had done neither. It had served as only a minor distraction for solving the mystery for what lurked off the Grand Strand. He still owed Roth for lying about the dolphin. That was next on his agenda, payback. First, he needed a shower to wash away Vanessa's scent, and then he needed Liz, to hold her and make love to her. Tonight, he would handle Roth. He wasn't sure how, but he would get even one way or the other.

30

"So, she actually met him at our suite," confirmed Roth, pacing as he talked on the phone "Where are they now? I see. She's still there and Chadwick has departed. No. There is no need to follow him. Thank you for your service. You shall be compensated for your discreet actions. I'll contact you if I require further assistance in the matter." That didn't take very long thought Roth. Lovers always find their way back into one another's arms. "I love it when a plan falls into place," he whispered.

The phone rang again. Roth listened patiently to the caller for almost a full minute before commenting. "Four of them you say and you're sure they have been attacked. The bite marks are that large. Possibly we do have our great white after all. Okay, I will send out a team to assist. Keep the area secure."

Interesting thought Roth, we do have a major predator in these waters. First the dolphins and now these Pigmy Sperm whales but are these linked to those attacks on the boats? Could this really be the work of one creature? This could be the chance of a lifetime if I can put such an animal on display at the aquarium. The investors would be most grateful and further my agenda along.

The phone rang again. "Yes Paige, she did indeed take the bait. Yes, if I know my dear Vanessa, she spilled her heart and guts. I am sure Chadwick now knows every little dirty detail of her illicit college affair with me. No dear, I have no regrets. I could care less if they screwed one another's brains out. A mere pawn in the battle. I grew tired of her long ago. Yes, we will move forward with that plan. You have done well, Paige. No, not tonight but we'll have time for that later."

The poor girl thought Roth, can not see the forest for the trees. I play with my toys until I tire of them. She has been a joyful experience but like all toys, we outgrow them, and then discard them. It is time to move on to the next best innovation. The new has worn off my dear Paige and she certainly has no place in my future; never actually did.

Roth made the next phone call. "Greetings Chadwick, I assume your vacation stay here on our beautiful Carolina Coast is going well for you and yours?"

"A beach is a beach. It's hard to beat the Keys."

"How does an esteemed oceanographer occupy his time? I don't take you for the lounge in the sun type sipping on fruity beverages."

"What can I do for you, Roth?"

"I was hoping you and your lovely wife Elizabeth could join Vanessa and me for dinner tonight."

"Sorry, we already have plans," answered Chad, painting a little white lie. "I'm sure even you can understand the importance of spending time with family."

"Family is indeed important. Their love and trust are the fiber of our being, isn't it? If not tonight, you choose a night that might best work into your schedule. I'm sure my Vanessa would be sadly disappointed if she didn't have the opportunity to spend time with you while you were here."

"I can't make you any promises. After all, this is supposed to be a family vacation and it would be quite rude if I bowed out of my obligations."

"Always putting others first. That is a commendable trait. I certainly would not wish to tarnish that image. But I am sure even family would excuse you and Elizabeth for a couple of hours. If dinner is out of the question, then possibly we could have drinks and discuss old times. I have a suite on the beach front with a fabulous view of the Strand."

"Roth, do we really have any old times worthy of discussing?"

"Don't sell yourself short my dear Chadwick, I'm sure we do. We share common interests after all...our love for the same lady...the ocean and what she has to offer us. Without her, we would surely live a most unsatisfied existence, don't you think?"

"What's really going on here? What do you really want? I sense you're fishing or at the least, playing another one of your demented games?"

"Why Chadwick, I thought we had discarded our college competitions and distain for one another. Surely you are still not holding me responsible for all your past failures, including Vanessa."

"I was wondering when you'd get around to that one, old chum."

"Quite touchy, aren't you? Bone excavation can often instill hostilities in those unable or unwilling to accept the circumstances. You have a wonderful wife. I would think that would be enough for you now."

"Look Roth, I really don't have time for this crap, so if you'll excuse me, I have to go."

"By the way, have you heard the news of the beached Pigmy Sperm Whales? Before you place that rescue ranger hat on your head, I must report that none of the mammals survived their beaching or a horrid attack. They will not have to undergo the prolonged agony of your persistent codling. Your bed side manner after all failed to save those poor dolphins."

Chad almost exploded but somehow contained his emotions. He wanted to call Roth out on the sole survivor but knew he would just deny the accusation. "Attacked, how so?"

"I have not seen the carcasses, but I did send a team to assist. Reports indicate exceptionally large wounds on several of the mammals, possibly those of a great white shark or another aggressive species; maybe an Orca."

"Where are the whales?"

"Now Chadwick, I will not contribute to your potential delinquency from family interaction. Please try to enjoy your vacation and leave these matters to the experts. Call me if you have time in your hectic family bonding schedule for drinks." Click, the line went dead.

"Bastard," whispered Chad.

"Not a pleasant phone conversation, my boy" commented Frederic, entering the den.

"It was Roth. He said there's been another beaching. This time a pod of Pigmy Sperm whales and evidence points they were attacked."

"Patterns point that a territorial predator is roaming these waters," stated Frederic.

"Did you make any headway with the autopsy research, sir?"

"As you have already confirmed through your preliminary examination, the bite mark from our severed torso wasn't that of a shark or any other known marine animal. We are contending with a new species of sea creatures. Your theory has been collaborated. Unfortunately, my contacts have not yet identified the perpetrator. They are broadening their research."

"How so, sir?"

"Any creature known to have roamed and dominated the ocean's depths," replied Frederic.

"Are you saying what I think you're saying, sir?"

"Possibly we have a species, for whatever reason, that isn't actually extinct."

"Care to elaborate. You are the expert."

"The sea once offered up many vicious creatures. My contacts are comparing those bite marks to all fossilized remains on record. Selfishly I hope for a match, but God help us all if we do."

"I think the death and destruction we've witnessed is self explanatory. We are already dealing with a creature man has never seen before and it is preying on new victims. Modern fishermen and Jurassic sea life have never crossed paths. It appears the oceanic team is winning thus far."

"If indeed we do confirm the existence of a once thought extinct monster of the seas, where has it been hiding all these millions of years?"

"We both know that so little of the ocean has ever been explored. They and other creatures could have possibly flourished in the depths. Who knows, maybe lack of food or some other natural phenomena has driven them from hiding."

"I don't think these creatures fear or hide from anything."

"What would be your guess, sir? What extinct creature could have caused the carnage we have witnessed and experienced?"

"Several come to mind," explained Frederic. "A Kronosaurus, possibly the Liopleurodon ferox, the Simolestes vorax, or any species of Pliosaurus. Any would have been formidable then and in today's oceans would portray the apex predator. They would only have to fear their own kind."

"I must admit. I certainly require a refresher course to visualize those you have named."

"They're quite similar actually, some larger than others based on fossil remains. Many arguments exist about size and their feeding habits but believe me son, there is nothing in the modern-day ocean that could hold a candle to any of them. Even the great white would be a quick meal."

"I guess we better hope that their continued extinction weighs in heavily then. What do we know or suspect of these creatures just in case your colleagues identify our culprit?"

"Plesiosaurs, the first of its species discovered, had already developed many of the characteristics of the marine predatory reptiles. That of a long neck, four flippers, wide jaws, and razor-sharp teeth. Picture a turtle with no protective shell and a much longer neck. Some suggest it probably even laid eggs on shore like the modern-day turtle. While proficient in capturing fish, it most likely became prey to the more vicious creatures of the sea. Many think the Loch Nest Monster is a Plesiosaurus."

"It doesn't sound like to me that this could be our predator."

"Just providing a little background and no, these were estimated to reach lengths of sixteen feet; however, the Superfamily, Plesiosauroidea, included the long neck version, the elasmosaurs and its cousin, the short necked polycotylid. This polycotylid gave way to a large headed and apex predator, the plesiosaurians. These creatures ruled during much of the Mesozoic."

"I'm thinking back to Captain Joe. They hooked something and his mate, Ken, shot it just before it broke free. His description matched what you have just described as a Plesiosaurus."

"Interesting, could it be that we have more than one species emerging along the coast? A Plesiosaurus could not have sunk our ship or could have been what attacked our cadaver, also resulting in that ship sinking. A Kronosaurus or Liopleurodon is our most likely candidate. That is if they are among the living."

"Just how large was the Kronosaurus?"

"Intriguing question, my boy," smiled Frederic. "This has led to much debate among my colleagues. First estimates placed them at over forty feet, but many argue that thirty feet is more accurate."

"And where do you land in this debate?"

"I believe they could have exceeded fifty feet, possibly even reaching sixty, but no fossils support my theory I'm afraid."

"But a living and breathing one would, now wouldn't it, sir?"

Frederic smiled. "That would be just a kick in the pants."

"Tell me more about the Kronosaurus."

"Picture an enormous lizard with four paddles, compact bulky torso, almost crocodile like in many ways, with huge teeth exceeding 7 cm. His bite would be easy enough to identify because his teeth were so large and conical. They did not have a sharp cutting edge. This would be a remarkable find if it is indeed our oceanic culprit."

"And what about the other one you mentioned, the Liopleurodon?"

"Now, my boy, we have the super predator of the Jurassic seas. Picture a cross between a shark and orca then increase a great white's three-ton girth tenfold. At thirty tons and fifty feet, you have the perfect predator."

"That would put it at about the size of an adult sperm whale."

"A sperm whale with an attitude and voracious appetite," added Frederic, "And again, arguments have put it at reaching lengths exceeding seventy feet. Actually, we can support this theory even if the scholars wish to quibble with fact."

"How so sir," asked Chad, intrigued by the possibilities.

"Liopleurodon ferox, a magnificent creature, even larger than the Tyrannosaurus Rex, its skeletal remains have been discovered in Mexico and has cast a shadow on those who argue against the creature's size. Dubbed the Monster of Aramberri, it is truly a magnificent discovery. Here, read this article that I printed out at the library."

Chad unfolded the paper and began reading…

Far larger than Tyrannosaurus Rex, the skeleton of this "Monster of Aramberri," nicknamed after the place in Mexico where it was located, is likely to throw light on the beast's last meal and the cause of its death. It used to hunt the ancestors of the modern shark and aquatic reptiles such as ichthyosaurs.

The skull, as large as a car, was found to have a huge hole in it, possibly made by a victim that fought back. The bones were discovered mingled with those of smaller ichthyosaurs, which the Liopleurodon had probably eaten, together with huge chunks of rock which it would have swallowed along with its prey as an aid to digestion or as ballast.

Leader of the research team Eberhard Frey, of the Natural History Museum in Karlsruhe, where the bones are to be shipped for reconstruction, said the specimen would help them to build the most accurate model yet of the creature. "A sensational find," says he, adding that "no other living creature in the sea could fight it successfully. They swallowed their prey whole."

Liopleurodon ferox, first identified by the French paleontologist H.E. Sauvage in 1873, belongs to an order of prehistoric marine reptiles known as the plesiosaurs, cousins of the dinosaurs that thrived in the Jurassic and Cretaceous periods, between 208 and 65 million years ago.

The creatures, whose collective name means "near lizards", were carnivores with four powerful flippers. Liopleurodon, which means "smooth-sided tooth", is one of a sub-group called the pliosauroids, which had large heads, strong jaws, short necks, and resembled whales.

Estimates prepared by the BBC series suggest that the largest of the creatures would have been even bigger than the 'Monster of Aramberri,' at up to 80 feet long and 150 tons, although most paleontologists are more conservative, particularly about its weight.

Liopleurodon's teeth measured up to 10in each and were so sharp that several members of Frey's team suffered cuts while it was painstakingly dug from the soil.

"Remarkable," commented Chad. "If we indeed have one of these fearsome creatures now sharing the oceans with us, how do we adjust? How does man live with something that views us as no more than a food source, mere morsels at that?"

"Very excellent question my boy and unless such a creature received immediate protection and became designated as an endangered species, it would surely be hunted and destroyed and face permanent extinction again. Humanity destroys what they fear and do not understand. This would certainly rate as the most fearsome man has ever encountered."

"I agree. If it posed a threat and we both know it already has, it would be hunted and killed."

"You should gain some pride from the possibility of such a creature still existing. It adds credence to your mother's work and her pursuit of the legendary woodland creature."

"Unfortunately, unlike your dinosaurs, no skeleton or fossil remains have ever been discovered of the elusive Sasquatch. That alone has caused my mother much grief and anguish in her pursuit and ability to substantiate its existence. She's actually off somewhere as we speak for the first time in a number of years, so one can never tell I suppose."

"Liz has shared with me your concern of the mystery surrounding your mother's disappearance in 1980 during the eruption of Mount Saint Helen. Does Mattie still refuse to discuss it with you?"

"Yes, mums the word. Whatever happened during that period when she had become lost in the wilderness forever altered her life. That's why I am surprised after all these years she had again has chosen to venture into the great northern woods. Allow me to sometimes share with you what I read in Matt McGregor's journal. She doesn't know I've I read it"

"Matt McGregor," questioned Frederic, "I'm not familiar with the name."

"My ancestor, a true mountain man from back in the 1800's and most likely the prime reason my mother has built a career around proving the existence of Bigfoot, but I'll save those tales for another time if you don't mind, sir?"

"I look forward to that discussion, my boy."

"I suppose we wait until another attack or incident or until your contacts identify our creature?"

"It seems it is our only course of action."

"Unless…we try to locate it first," smiled Chad.

"My boy, it appears you have a plan."

"Possibly, but I have a few other matters to tend to first if you'll excuse me."

"Certainly, my boy. I'll make a cameo appearance with Teal and the other ladies before they become too suspicious about our absence."

Chad nodded and then exited the condo, one thing in mind; confirming the condition of the dolphin and making Roth pay for his lies.

31

The captain beached the fifty-six-foot pontoon as was customary during the tour of Shell Island and informed 63 tourists they had an hour to tour the barrier island's beach area, collect shells, and take in the sights. He, however, warned them to stay along the beaches and not to venture inland and chance an encounter with the aggressive wild hogs, also native to the island. An abundance of shells, including conch, were always retrieved during the excursions. The captain, a native of the low country had navigated Georgetown's Winyah Bay, sharing tales and folklore of an area rich in history. The fifty-six-foot vessel offered unobstructed views of the scenery, with shaded deck seating and modern facilities, all handicap accessible. With open sides, one could take in the warm river breezes. The captain had pointed out numerous bald eagles flying or roosting high in the treetops along the banks. To his surprise they had not seen any dolphins and few times had that ever happened.

The folks filed out onto the beach. Most were a senior citizen church group. Less than twenty were made up of a hotchpotch of family, young kids ranging to middle age adults. The captain eased the pontoon back out into the bay once the last person had disembarked. He would remain just off the barrier island and return to retrieve his patrons after allowing them their hour to explore. Three elderly women decided to remain on the pontoon with him. They did not fancy exploring the beach.

"Ladies, might I offer you a soft drink or water," he asked, but all were content and had brought their own beverages.

"We'll be visiting the Winyah Bay Lighthouse on our return trip," he informed them, building the hype. "It is one of the oldest active lighthouses in the United States. We will also pass the Harvest Moon. You will be able to see its smokestack, the only portion of the vessel visible I'm afraid. It was sunk by a Union gunship during the Civil War. And because this is a two for one special, we will complete the second leg of our tour, the plantation and ghost tour. That will bring us back in about an hour after dusk."

On the island the tourist filed in one direction or the other, pausing to retrieve shells or wiggle their toes in the water, occasionally waving to those on the boat. The captain decided to venture just around the bend to give his three mates a view of the open ocean. Two small children scampered ahead of their parents, attempting to keep the pontoon in sight. The young parents walked leisurely along hand in hand enjoying the tranquility and each other's company. The captain paused just short of the breakers allowing the three women to take in the view. The children giggled, dodging the small waves lapping on shore while keeping the pontoon in view. Dad held mom in his arms oblivious to everything.

The pontoon tilted violently over on its seaward side, not normally an easy task, spilling the captain and the three elderly women head over heels into the river. Without life jackets the women were floundering for their lives. The captain regained his composure and swam frantically toward his pontoon. He paused only long enough to glance back and make sure the women were still afloat. He yelled out that he would retrieve them once he reclaimed his boat. Swimming crossways against the strong outgoing tide he found this more difficult than expected. He quickened his strokes attempting to regain lost ground. The deep dark cavity gapped open directly beneath him and as if being caught in a toilet flush he spun and disappeared into the waiting mouth, swallowed whole, no chance to fight the attacker. The women one by one, overcome by shock and the exertion required to remain afloat, none being extraordinarily strong swimmers, disappeared below the river's surface. The pontoon drifted seaward caught in the current of the outgoing tide.

The five-year-old girl and her three and half year old brother ran screaming to their parents, not sure what their young eyes had just witnessed. By the time their parents fully understood what they were trying to explain between sobs, the pontoon, a mere speck on the horizon, continued its trek into the awaiting ocean. The children had not witnessed the demise of the captain or the drowning of the three ladies, having fled back to their parents' arms after the boat breached on its side. The young father now aware of their situation felt helplessly abandoned on the island with the remaining 56 tourists. Without a radio and without cell phone reception, the situation appeared bleak at best. They were not even expected back for at least another three hours, having taken advantage of the great two for one tour deal. Furthermore, he still could not comprehend what sort of boating accident could have taken the lives of the captain and the three women who remained on board with him. He owned a pontoon back home and knew the difficultly in capsizing or sinking one. His children could offer no reasonable explanation. There was nothing left to do but inform the others. He was by far the youngest male and being a national guardsman would have to bear much of the responsibility for holding things together until rescued.

The captain did little to extinguish the creature's appetite, so it swam off in search of larger prey. Its senses were not homing in on anything of significance. This alone assured the next encounter would be more violent. Hunger instilled anger and lately the hunger pains persisted. Prey in these waters had become scarce, the aquatic wildlife wearier of the new hunter. Instinct drove it toward anything large enough to be registered by its sensory system. It feared no encounter. Nothing the sea had to offer had up until now posed a threat. It darted to its left and inhaled a seven-foot nurse shark just before returning to deeper water. This only served to fuel the hunger. The new apex predator of the ocean was on the hunt again.

32

Chad Reynolds purchased an aquarium ticket just like any would-be tourist. He diverted to a souvenir stand when he recognized one of Roth's men that would surely have been able to ID him. He meticulously toured all the viewing tanks not expecting to see his dolphin. He hadn't and surmised it must be in a holding tank somewhere not accessible to the general public. He surveyed the map on the aquarium brochure trying to pinpoint just where such a tank might be located, but it didn't offer enough detail to non-tourist areas. He noticed a commotion over near the shark exhibit and blended in with the onlookers to ease closer. A man with his back to him stood in front of the viewing window. A professional looking camera shouldered by another man faced him.

"Ryan, save that one for the edit floor. Now let's take it again from the top."

"Sure thing Lance, three, two one…we're rolling again."

"This is Lance Rocker reporting. We have taken the Rock Your World cameras inside this spectacular aquarium where we will be interviewing Roth Niederwerter, curator, and owner of the aquarium. Mister Niederwerter has confirmed that he is convinced that a rogue shark, possibly a rare great white is roaming the waters along the Grand Strand. It is his professional opinion that this shark has been responsible for numerous boat attacks and at least eight deaths, not to mention the beaching of dolphins and whales lately."

Chad recognized the man in front of the camera. He had a syndicated television show, somewhat of a weekly one-hour tabloid investigative circus. If memory served him, Rocker tended to offer credence to the bizarre. Chad remembered that Rocker's claim to fame had been his involvement in an incidence receiving national attention here in Myrtle Beach. He recalled it having to do with a serial killer. The details hadn't stuck in his mind though, not relevant for a Florida native. Rocker's persona and style had reminded him of a snake oil peddler or flim-flam man. The reporter's type of television theatrics had never held his interest.

Roth, as if almost on queue passed by Chad less than a foot away, but because he had been so focused on the interview, he had failed to recognize him. Chad backed a couple of steps until he blended in the second wave of people.

"Here's Mister Niederwerter now," said Lance, redirecting the camera. "Mister Niederwerter, please tell our viewing audience what evidence you have to support your theory of a man-eating shark terrorizing Myrtle Beach."

"Are we live, or can we pause for a second," asked Roth.

"Ryan, cut," ordered Lance. "We'll pick it back up when Mister Niederwerter responds to my first question."

"Mister Rocker, the coroner has failed to confirm the originator of the bite that took the life of that poor man from the Serendipity. I'm not sure why he has hesitated, and he did not enlist my assistance or any of my oceanic experts," explained Roth off camera. "He did bring in supportive testimony from a vacationer, a Mister Chadwick Reynolds, but I am uncertain if he is uniquely qualified to identify those creatures that habitat our waters. He is from Florida where the aquatic life is much different. After all, how much credence do we really want to place on a man whose mother believes Bigfoot exists. He probably thinks we have the Loch Ness Monster in our waters. I'm afraid delusional paranoia runs deeply in his immediate family roots."

"Great stuff Mister Niederwerter, I think we should include this dialogue in the opening interview."

Chad stepped forward. "Fact, I examined the body in the morgue at the request of Detective Stone. I confirmed the bites in no way resembled those of any known shark."

"Ah, we have Mister Reynolds in our presence, Mister Rocker."

"But the coroner stated the examination was inconclusive," stated Rocker, not missing a beat.

"He only stated it as such because I couldn't identify the bite marks," replied Chad.

"I suppose we don't have many dental records available for sea monsters, do we?"

Even Rocker tried to contain his smile after Roth's comment. "Allow me to recap for our audience. We have one victim, bitten in half but by what appears to be unknown currently. We have at least two sunken ships and the cause for these catastrophes remain unsolved. Five men vanished in the one or should I say four and a half. Three men disappeared from a shrimp trawler, it too unsolved. We have had beached dolphins, swirling accusations that one dolphin may have survived. I heard on my drive here that whales have been found beached and this too is under investigation. We either have a gigantic shark or a sea serpent responsible, dependent on whom you ask. Let's not forget our love triangle; more of which I will expose on my next segment. We do have plenty of finger pointing now, do we not? There is no love lost between Mister Niederwerter and Mister Reynolds. This is indeed the perfect storm and makes for a wonderful story line, doesn't it, folks?"

"Don't forget mother dearest, Professor Mattie Reynolds, the great Sasquatch seeker," laughed Roth. "And by the way, I have some of my associates investigating the whale incident. We'll get to the bottom of that beaching shortly."

"Okay, cut for now, Ryan," advised Rocker.

Chad was fuming and the smug look on Roth's face just made it ten times worse.

"You gentlemen take the prize," suggested Lance Rocker. "I didn't think anyone could top the Road Rage serial killings. It certainly makes for sensational television viewing and should skyrocket my ratings. We are going to wrap this segment up and edit for next week's show. You have my card. Please keep me posted Mister Reynolds if you identify Godzilla."

After Lance Rocker and his camera man departed, Roth continued his onslaught on Chad. "Just what the hell are you up to Chadwick?"

"What's that supposed to mean? I bought a ticket and decided to visit your little aquarium again. I am putting money in your pocket at the tourist rate. Do you have a problem in me supporting your local economy? You pulled me into this but this time you are dead wrong. I'll cherish bringing you down."

"I'm shaking in my boots, you pathetic loser. What are you and my wife doing behind my back?"

"Geez, you are one paranoid loser, aren't you? Now tell me, where's the damn dolphin?"

"And you're a psychotic idiot. What do I have to gain from hiding a dolphin? Then again, what do you have to hide concerning my wife?"

"I'm tired of playing your silly ass college games, Roth. People are dying in that ocean and we need to determine what's really responsible for all this death and destruction. Can't we put aside our petty differences for once?"

"I have no idea what you are insinuating, Chadwick?"

"Bull, cut the crap, Roth!"

"Might I remind you, you're on vacation. What happens here really isn't your concern."

"And it sure doesn't seem to concern you except for the sensationalism and publicity. Where is your compassion for the families of those already lost, and what about the safety for those who put money in your pocket by vacationing here?"

"Do you really think that this aquarium is my lifeline? It is a mere investment, part of my vast portfolio. You always did think small. That's why Vanessa left you."

"Vanessa left because of you. Roth. You couldn't man up and take responsibility. It's you first; always has been."

"What, you can't face the fact that you lost her to me?"

"Roth, you're pathetic and spineless. Revenge and spitefulness are going to take you to an early grave."

"Are you threatening me, Chadwick? I will call security and have you tossed out on your can."

"That wasn't a threat," replied Chad, as he round housed a right to Roth's chin, planting him square on his ass. "Now, that's how one completes a threat. Stay out of my business and out of my way or next time I won't be so nice."

"I'm calling security," whined Roth, attempting to upright himself.

"Call the Calvary for all I care," said Chad, using his foot to push Roth back on his back, "And better call an ambulance while you're at it because I'm not putting up with your crap anymore. Stand up and they'll be scraping you up off this tile."

Roth stayed put as Chad exited the area. He rubbed his chin, smiled, and then whispered, "Gotcha," as he glanced at the security camera in the corner.

33

Russell, along with his brother, had accessed the facility with Russell's keys and barcode badge. Russell sat down at the control panel and typed in his old pass code. It still worked. His fingers clacking the keyboard at lightening speed, he began reprogramming the filtration system for the main tanks.

"Are you sure you know what you're doing?"

Russell nodded to his biker bro. "I helped develop this system. I know it like the back of my hand. I have deactivated all alarm systems. I am recalibrating the standards which will alter the tanks' chemistry."

"What the hell does that mean?"

"I'm tricking the system to make false adjustments to throw the ecological balance out of kilter. Because I have recalculated the standard, the automated system is fooled now to continue making the wrong adds. The program will be attempting to reconcile the integrity of the self-contained ecosystem. With no alarms to alert otherwise, it will continue until we have a massive kill."

"Won't those monitoring the system be able to detect the changes?"

"It won't be visible until it's too late and the fish start bellying up. I have programmed the system to default to its original settings in 48 hours. By then, they will not be able to reverse the process in time to save the marine life. The program will be back to normal causing them to really scratch their heads. To throw them off the trail, we'll dump the contents of those jugs directly into the recycling unit."

"Just exactly what will this do to the little fishes?"

"It will totally screw up basic fish tank chemistry on a colossal scale. Ammonia levels will be off the chart as perceived by the computer monitoring system. It is the number one killer of fish in home aquariums. Without going into detail, the computer will overcompensate for all sorts of nonexistent imbalances, high levels of chloramines, nitrites, copper, ph, with all intended to over correct something that isn't real. By the time Roth's so-called experts realize what's happening the chaos will be in full gear."

"I know you want revenge, Russell, but I thought fish were your life."

"Lessons must be taught. There are plenty of fish in the oceans. A few sacrificed will go unnoticed, except by that bastard."

"Badasses we are then. Hope we don't get busted."

"Not to worry, I am covering our tracks, wiping clean the surveillance videos, working my magic in all the programming. I am good at this. That's one reason Roth hired me. He believes in surrounding himself with the best. Mistake though! Never cross the best. Dump the stuff and let's get out of here."

34

Chad walked into the condo and spotted Frederic hunkered over his laptop at the kitchen island. He could hear his father-in-law mumbling out loud and saw him shaking his head back and forth. Turning, he smiled to acknowledge Chad's arrival and then the frown lines materialized on his forehead.

"Are you okay, sir?"

"I've heard from my colleagues examining the bite marks on the torso of that poor gentleman."

"And," inquired Chad.

"They were unable to find a match when comparing it to documented fossil remains."

"So much for that theory then I suppose."

"Not necessarily. We may have a new sub species instead."

"You have my attention."

"Possibly a hybrid of the Liopleurodon, but the teeth are more developed and capable of massive flesh removal."

"I'm sure our man in the morgue could concur."

"They estimated the size to be that of a great white."

"Then it couldn't have possibly been responsible for sinking our boat or attacking the shrimp trawler."

"Unless it was a mere juvenile, my boy."

"Are you saying a pod of these things could be out there? You've got to be kidding."

"Possibly, something in the range of 40 to 60 feet seems likely to have sunk both charter boats and to have tilted the trawler.?"

"Okay, for the sake of argument I concede that we have a new species of mega creature patrolling the coastline. Why now and where did they originate?"

"Excellent questions, my boy, and just how large is this alleged pod? Even more troublesome, have they found an endless food source, tourist and locals alike?"

"Obviously, we either must capture one or at least photograph one to sell this to the media, so you're not incriminated as loony along with me. I'm already being pegged as a delusional freak because of the mere mention of my mother and her obsessive search for Sasquatch."

"Why has your mother's good name been dragged into this?"

"Roth planted the seed with that damn television celebrity, Lance Rocker. He's in town doing a segment about the attacks. Liz isn't going to like it at all."

"What does my daughter have to do with this?"

"Rocker is playing up this preposterous angle that Roth, Vanessa, and I am intertwined in a love triangle. Roth stirred the pot while on camera accusing me of it. If that footage hits his segment…"

"Is there any truth to these allegations?"

"Absolutely not," Chad defended his honor. "We dated in college. That's all. She invited me to their beach condo to explain a few things to me."

"Did you agree to this meeting?"

"Yes, and we've already met. Nothing happened, sir. She merely explained to me why she departed from college and joined the navy. She also justified her decision to marry Roth."

"And why did she feel compelled to confess these things to you, my boy? It appears you put yourself in a very compromising situation."

"I don't know. Women do screwy things sometimes."

"Do you love this Vanessa Niederwerter, Chadwick?"

Chad hesitated. "I did once but not now."

"Then why did she request this meeting and in such a remote and private environment? Does she still love you?"

"Not anymore," he lied. "And I assure you, I have been completely loyal to your daughter."

"I believe you, Chadwick and I am sure my daughter will feel the same way. I suggest you tell her before that segment airs."

"Thank you, sir. I intend to do just that. I'm sorry to have troubled you over such personal and private matters."

"Chadwick, you are my son-in-law. I appreciate your honesty and your love for my Elizabeth. I surmise we have just encountered one of those male bonding experiences I have read about. I must admit, it was quite refreshing and an escape from the ho-hum doldrums."

"I could use a drink. What about you, sir?"

"I do believe that would indeed complete the circle," chuckled Frederic, much out of character. "Then we must plot how we plan to thwart this Roth Niederwerter."

Chad laughed, "Sir, I didn't know you had such a devious side."

"My boy, it appears we both have a lot to learn about each other. See, vacations are wonderful tools after all. It brings a family closer."

"That will be our first toast," smiled Chad. "Then we must decide what to do about our possible new species. The women aren't going to appreciate us making this a working vacation."

"Once we explain the circumstances, I'm sure we'll have their full support."

"Sea monsters! Do you think they'll really believe us?"

"Sea monsters. How much have you two been drinking?" Robert Bornfreund was now standing in the condo's open doorway.

"Not nearly enough, Bobby boy," responded Chad.

"Care to enlighten me, Father?"

"This really doesn't concern you," spoke up Chad.

"If it has anything to do with us almost drowning then I beg to differ."

"Robert does have a compelling point, Chadwick."

Chad wanted to explicitly voice his disapproval of bringing Bobby on board but decided best to bite his tongue. He would find out sooner or later so he might as well hear it from them. "Okay, bring him up to speed then sir."

Frederic articulated the short version of what they had discovered and what they suspected. Bobby remained quiet and focused, something Chad found refreshing. Even afterwards, Bobby said nothing at first and poured another stiff drink. He topped off those of the others before finally responding.

"What do we do about it? A discovery like this could make us all wealthy and famous."

"Is that all you can take away from what your father just described? People are dead and missing. We are sitting on a potential powder keg if our suspicions are correct, and all you can think about is how you can make money from the carnage. You're no better than Roth Niederwerter."

"That's the aquarium guy, right? I knew I liked him."

"Peas in a pod," grumbled Chad.

"Bickering is not becoming of either of you," interrupted Frederic. "Robert, you must be discreet with this information and treat it with the utmost confidentiality."

"Fine, I'll leave the dragon slaying to the two of you,' said Bobby, exiting the condo.

Chad had a bad feeling about sharing too much information with Bobby Bornfreund. He despised his brother-in-law and didn't trust him as far as he could throw him. He had worried about becoming too bored on this little family outing, but he could dismiss that notion now. Just when he thought it could not get any worse in walked Liz, Teal, Corrine, Alex, and the kids. Each of the women gave them *THE LOOK* as only the female species has mastered, suspecting all was not well with their male counter parts.

35

Under the mask of darkness Marty Long maneuvered their eighteen-foot-long Jon boat through the murky black water while Wyatt Pope spotlighted the shore. The nearly flat V-hull aluminum boat cut through the water and was ideal for navigating the calm coastal streams and swamps. They used the quieter trolling motor as much as possible. Hunting alligator was not legal but good money could be made from the harvested meat and hides. Gator bites appeared on many of the restaurant and bar menus. Their clients never asked them where the gator came from, preferring to benefit from the discount prices cutting out the middleman. Tonight had been a queer one indeed noted Wyatt earlier. They had seen no gators, not even small ones. Using the spotlight, he scanned both sides of the narrow marsh waterway attempting to locate a gator's glowing eyes but had turned up no reptilian quarry. Stranger still, the two good old boys had not heard the typical night sounds of frogs bellowing and croaking. The silence had only been broken by the constant buzz of swarming mosquitoes.

"Marty this just ain't right," spoke up Wyatt as softly as his gravelly gruff voice would allow. "We always see gators by now. Hell, I haven't heard nothing even make a damn splash tonight."

"I been noticing the same thing, Wyatt. Gators don't spook easy, so maybe we're just not in the right spot tonight. We got time to head over and try that hole near the big water. We have plucked some big'uns outta there from time to time. One ole ten-footer would make it worth our while tonight."

"Maybe that splash of saltwater feeding inland gives them gators some sort of hormone boost," chuckled Marty, spitting tobacco juice in the water.

"Pass me a cold beer while you ain't got nothing better to do," said Wyatt pointing toward the Playmate cooler.

"I reckon you want me to pop the cap for you too," answered Marty.

"What's the matter, do you think I'm not going to tip you?"

"Screw you, Wyatt."

"You best throw that big motor in the water if we going to get to that last spot before daylight," barked Wyatt. "Don't make me come back there and bury my foot up your ass."

"And you better hold on to your sorry butt less I throw you in and give them gators something new on the menu," snapped Marty, dropping the 35 horse power into the water, firing it up, and heading toward their final destination.

Both sipped their beers quietly as Marty eased them from the neck back into the main river. It widened to about 40 yards. The channel up the middle was about 25 feet deep. Wyatt aimed the spotlight ahead watching for any debris but hadn't seen any, just like he hadn't seen any gators. Less than 20 minutes later they were within ten minutes from the spot where they had claimed their biggest gator, a thirteen-footer, nose to tip of its tail. That booger had put up a hell of a good fight until Marty had placed a 30-30 slug in its head. Hauling out a gator just a few feet shorter than their Jon boat had been a challenge, but they had cleared mighty good money for their efforts.

Wyatt held up his hand and motioned for Marty to kill the motor. He did and they slowly coasted to a stop in the middle of the channel. "Did you spot one?"

"I'm not sure. I did see a big ripple just ahead, but ain't seen no eyes surface," clarified Wyatt. He swung the light from one shore to the next then spotted something floating in the water just to their left.

"What do you see, Wyatt?"

"Must be two, no three gators over yonder, but something seems mighty peculiar."

"Good, we're finally getting lucky. Do they have any size to them?"

"Holy crap, they been all chewed up," answered Wyatt, as the boat coasted closer to the carnage in the water. "And it's a fresh kill. Damn, these were some big suckers too. Nothing does that to gators that big, Marty, except the mother of all gators maybe." Wyatt was now close enough to poke at them with a paddle. "This ain't right I'm telling you. This whole night is just too messed up to suit me."

"You got that right, Wyatt. I say let's call it a night. I sure don't want to tangle with what killed them gators. It wouldn't think a second about gnawing on us. What the hell is that," yelled Marty, pointing toward the bend.

"Ain't no such thing as a rogue wave on the river," commented Wyatt, now standing up to better spot the light on the ever-growing wave approaching them. "Whatever it is, it's coming at us like a bat out of hell."

"Sonofabitch, you better sit your sorry ass down, Wyatt. That there wave is gaining speed and about to slam straight into us."

"That ain't no wave, Marty! Get us out of here…pronto!"

Marty tried to engage the 35 horsepower to make an evasive maneuver, but time allowed no such move. The wave sporting an endless mouth full of teeth exploded, breaching the surface as it crested on top of them.

"Oh crap," shouted Wyatt, tumbling backwards, looking for an escape path.

"Holy mother," screamed Marty as the engine fired up, and then they were gone, hook, line, sinker, and boat, lost in the ripple of the splash.

Wyatt surfaced seconds later less than ten feet from the riverbank. Not much of a swimmer but he didn't have to because the spot where he ended up was barely five feet deep. Standing it came up to his chin. Wild eyed he scanned where the Jon boat had been. "Marty," he whimpered. "Marty…where are you, boy?"

He gulped loudly and began backing toward the shore, immersed in the darkness, only able to see a few feet in any direction. Chilled but aware of warmness on his right side, he attempted to lift his right arm from the water. No arm broke the water. He felt for it with his left hand fearing he had broken it, but shock set in when he realized his arm was missing from his shoulder socket. Blood gushed freely from where it had been attached. His scream broke the deathly silence and then the nightmare with teeth surfaced and reunited him with his missing arm. The twisted Jon boat bobbed to the surface, the only reminder that the two brave gator hunters ever existed. A ripple just below the surface indicated their adversary now returned to open water, its appetite yearning for more prey.

36

"Interesting Mister Bornfreund, so why are you telling me this?" asked Roth Niederwerter

"I don't really care for my brother-in-law and my father is a pompous ass. Neither are visionaries or profiteers. They are purely scientific buffoons. Somehow, I see you as an opportunist as I categorize myself. To coin Chad's analogy of us, we're two peas in a pod."

"And when did Chadwick make this assumption, we were the perfect alliance?"

"He did just after I tried to point out the monetary value of their alleged discovery."

"But all is circumstantial."

"My father's colleagues identified those bite marks. That should stand for something and what about the thing that sunk our fishing boat? This isn't a shark."

"Your father's colleagues didn't exactly identify anything. Theorizing that a new species roams the ocean is mere theory and that's all. Without tangible evidence to support it, we have nothing. There have been no sightings or substantiated encounters. Anything could have sunk your vessel," argued Roth, containing his actual intrigue in the revelation.

"Name one. Name something that could have sunk that charter boat."

"I still hold firm that a gigantic rogue great white is the greater possibility. I don't deal in myths."

"Did you examine the victim's bite marks?"

"The coroner did not request my professional opinion. That was a grave error on his part, giving credence to the likes of Chadwick Reynolds."

"Then you can't dispute what my father's colleagues concluded, can you?"

"Mister Bornfreund, I do appreciate your candidness and conviction, but what do you really wish to accomplish?"

"I pose that we go capture a sea monster and I want 50% of every penny earned when we put it on display in your aquarium. If we must kill it instead, I still want my share of anything we take in."

"Tell me Mister Bornfreund, are you an expert in these matters?"

"In what matters?"

"In capturing sea monsters. What do you bring to the table that warrants such a pricy compensation?"

"I thought you were the expert. You're the oceanographer, aren't you?"

"Seems I bring a lot to this table and you don't."

"That's where you're wrong. I have the inside track to Chad and my father's every move. That should account for something."

"How long do you think you will be their confidant once they discover you and I have talked?"

"And how will they discover our little secret? I surely don't intend to tell them, do you?"

Roth grinned. "Have you shared this with anyone else?"

Robert shook his head no. "Not even my wife, so do we have a deal?"

"It appears I will be financing this little venture, but I propose a 65-35 split on any revenue."

"And I share the billing, the discovery as a personal dig to Chad and my father."

"Peas in a pod indeed," grinned Roth, as he extended his hand.

"Shouldn't we document this, have a written agreement?"

"Does my handshake and word mean nothing to you my dear fellow?"

"To be blunt, I don't know you from jack. I have no idea how trustworthy you might be. I am not trying to be condescending, but I would feel much better if we had a written contract. I am not so sure we exactly have a blooming relationship and I'm not here to be your friend. I'm a businessman as I surmise so are you, Mister Niederwerter."

"Very well put Mister Bornfreund," Roth said, withdrawing his hand. "And I suppose being on a first name basis is out of the question?"

"Too chummy; let's just leave it as is for now. When can I expect to see this in writing?"

"Come back this afternoon Mister Bornfreund and we will formalize our merger. In the meantime, please gather any additional information that might promote our cause."

"You just have that contract ready this afternoon and then I'll be better prepared to divulge what I know."

"Very well, this afternoon. Shall we say three o'clock then, but not here. I have a beach condo. Here's the address and phone number."

"When do we go sea monster hunting?"

"In due time I assure you, but these things require proper planning."

"By the way, do you really have the dolphin that Chad has been bitching and moaning about?"

Roth just smiled.

"I thought so," added Robert. "Way to go. See you this afternoon."

Once Robert Bornfreund had departed the premises Roth beeped Paige. Seconds later she appeared in his office. She found her boss sitting at his desk scribbling on a notepad and knew better than to disturb him. She stood there patiently until he completed his task. "Here," he said, handing her the sheet of paper. "Acquire all items on that list immediately, no questions please."

Paige raised an eyebrow, rubbing her chin, and then gave her boss a quick. "Timeline?"

"No later than 6 AM tomorrow. I don't wish to hear any grief. Just make it happen, Paige."

"I'll take care of it. Here, I think you may find these most intriguing," she said, handing him a manila folder. "Photographs and details of the team's preliminary examination of the beached pod of whales. And there appears to be a missing kayaker in the general vicinity of the beached whales. Pieces of his kayak washed ashore with no signs of him. Tyson saw the debris and reported what appeared to be bite marks on the exterior of the hull; exceptionally large markings."

"Is Tyson here?"

"Yes sir."

"Summon him to join me. You are dismissed. Please make that happen," he said, motioning to the list in her hand.

"You'll have everything you require, Roth. This isn't a great white, is it?"

"No, it's not, Paige. This time ensure we have no publicity; at least not until I am ready to share my discovery with the world."

She nodded and exited his office. Roth examined the photos and the report, and then smiled, sea monster indeed.

37

"Permission to board, Captain Joe," requested Chad Reynolds, accompanied by his father-in-law Frederic Bornfreund.

"Granted, come on board. Join our merry crew," he nodded toward Captain Tommy and Ken.

"We have an idea of what may have attacked your vessel and sunk Tommy's Girl," stated Chad.

"You've got my attention," announced Captain Tommy, strolling over to where the two men stood. "My insurance company would be just tickled pink to have an explanation."

Frederic took a few minutes to bring them up to speed with his colleagues' analysis and a few sketches to give them an idea of what such a creature might resemble. His audience, while captivated by the revelations, remained speechless until he had completed his presentation.

"Fierce and formidable adversary," commented Captain Joe. "I assume that's why you're here. We're going after this creature, right?"

"Creatures and yes, with your cooperation and use of your trawler," answered Frederic.

"You really think there's more than one of those things out there," questioned a wild-eyed Ken.

"We think there's an entire family trolling these waters. How many could be anyone's guess," clarified Chad.

"And you guesstimate the big ones top out at over 60 feet."

"Sounds about right to me, Tommy," chimed in Captain Joe. "It would have taken something about that size to have tipped Salty Santa's trawler like I saw it up righted."

"A smaller version is responsible for the bite that took the life of that fellow that washed up on shore from the Serendipity, but I suspect one of its parents sunk the charter boat," added Chad.

"Where do you think they came from?"

Chad explained, "Ken, now this is just a guess mind you but possibly the Puerto Rico Trench. It is located between the Caribbean Sea and Atlantic Ocean, just north of Puerto Rico. That trench is associated with a subduction zone further south along the Lesser Antilles and the major transform plate extending west between Cuba, Hispaniola all the way through the Cayman Trench down to the coast of Central America. The coordinates are 19°50′9″N 66°45′16″W□ / □19.83583°N 66.75444°W□ / 19.83583; -66.75444"

"What the hell is all this subduction and transformer talk? Can you speak English my friend?".

"Sorry, Captain Tommy, geological terms," apologized Chad. "Basically, subduction refers to the process, that place as two boundaries converge. One tectonic plate moves underneath another tectonic plate," explained Chad, using his hands to illustrate one over the other. "Both sinking into the earth's crust as they converge. You can measure the subduction rate by how many centimeters of convergence you have a year, typically between two and eight annually. That's about how much your fingernail grows."

"Not so much, huh," commented Ken.

"To keep it simple, a transform fault is the boundary that runs along the tectonic plate. While some vertical movement may exist, horizontal movement is the primary vector."

"Whatever you say," shrugged Captain Tommy.

"This particular trench is about five hundred miles long and over twenty-eight thousand feet deep; a mere baby compared to some of the world's other trenches. It's still a vast and unexplored world and the deepest spot in the Atlantic."

Captain Joe fired off the logical question, "If this trench is located that far south from us, why wouldn't these creatures be wreaking havoc in the Caribbean Islands instead of populating our waters?"

"Could be that they prefer the cooler waters," suggested Frederic. "Or maybe this is some old and embedded spawning ground."

Captain Tommy asked, "Then what made them leave that trench?"

Chad attempted to explain. "An unprecedented Category 5 pre-season hurricane recently passed north of the Caribbean directly over the trench and then skirted the eastern Atlantic coast. It did not make landfall but possibly it churned up the sea and disoriented our species. It might have prompted them to relocate. Or maybe their prey had become scarce and they followed the sounds of migrating whales or were lured by other potential food sources of the course."

"In other words, you have no damn clue," quipped Ken.

"Let's be civil, Ken," warned Captain Joe.

"Well, he's right. Why have they stayed secluded and undetected is a mystery? These are just educated guesses at best. Until we have an actual visual sighting and can study them up close, we really don't know the reason," stated Chad.

"That brings us back to you gentleman," spoke up Frederic. "Can we rely on your services?"

"I had intended to hunt it anyway. We can always use a helping hand or two, and the money right now," admitted Captain Joe.

Ken then asked, "Is this a killing or catching mission?"

"Let's call it a locate and study mission for now," answered Chad, "Even with your trawler involved, I'm not so sure we're capable of capturing an adult version of this species."

Captain Joe tossed in his two cents, "What about a juvenile?"

"And piss off mommy and daddy," added Ken. "I don't like the sounds of that. Remember, I might have already seen one of these things' babies, but it didn't exactly resemble those drawings you have there. That creature we caught in our net had a much longer neck and didn't look much like something that would sink a ship even full grown. It was one ugly scary son of a gun let me tell you. I shot it but it broke free of our net."

Frederic penciled a quick sketch and asked, "Did it look more like this?"

"Almost the spitting image," nodded Ken.

"This species I am familiar with and it appears we have more than one species in these waters," confirmed Fredric. "Plesiosaurus, the estimated length of a mature creature is 16.5 feet. I agree. It would not have been capable of attacking and sinking a reasonably sized vessel. Small fish and other oceanic prey would be more to its liking, not humans."

Chad then added, "I wonder how many other species have awoken from extinction?"

"My boy, we are on the brink of a discovery that would compare to none. That is unless your dear mother uncovers undisputable evidence of the existence of Sasquatch."

"It would certainly make believing in Bigfoot more viable if we proved the existence of a Liopleurodon ferox cousin," added Chad.

"Bigfoot," repeated Captain Joe. "You folks must have quite the family circle."

"Fodder for further discussion once we reach the high seas," chuckled Chad.

Frederic interrupted, "Captain Joe, we have much preparation, but if we can acquire what we need, can we shove off at first light in the morning. And not to fear, I will finance our little expedition to compensate you for your troubles."

"We can leave as early as you gents see fit. I had planned to do this at my expense, but I will not turn away your offer. Speaking for the three of us, pickings have been thin of late."

"I promise, we'll earn our keep," added Captain Tommy.

"I have an uneasy feeling about this," said Ken. "The track record doesn't indicate that those that have encountered these sea serpents of yours have lived to tell about it. Money doesn't mean much to a dead man. How does it go; dead men tell no tales."

"We'll certainly respect your decision if you choose not to participate," replied Frederic.

"Live men do need money, so I'm in," smiled Ken sheepishly.

"Very well then, we have much preparation before daybreak tomorrow," stated Frederic.

"Indeed, we do," added Chad.

38

"What the hell are you talking about, Colby?" shouted Roth Niederwerter. "It is impossible that we have a major kill. Our systems are failsafe!"

"Tell that to those sharks gone belly up, along with too many other species to count," responded Colby over the intercom. "And it gets worse."

"Impossible, this can not be happening. I demand answers. Heads will roll."

"Dead fish, tons of them and it's not just localized to the main tank. We have confirmed failures throughout the facility. This is massive."

"There were no alarms, how can that be?"

"Not a single warning, Roth. We had no clue until we began noticing the dead."

"What does the analysis say? Damn it man, these samples are obtained automatically by the computer program and adjustments are made accordingly. It could not have shifted out of kilter. It's just not possible."

"We're still sorting through the data and we're troubleshooting the program, but so far everything looks normal," answered an extremely nervous Colby.

"Chadwick Reynolds, he was here. Could he be responsible? He might have contaminated our ecosystem."

"This goes beyond merely adding contaminants I'm afraid. Our systems should have detected any changes and prompted a reaction. We are talking total systemic failure. He doesn't have access to our systems and even if somehow he did, the programs would be impossible for him to hack unless he's some sort of hacking guru."

"Inside job then," fumed Roth.

"Could have been, but we need more time to confirm. Right now, we're focusing on reconciling the imbalance and saving as much of the remaining marine life that we can," replied Colby.

"Where do you estimate our losses?"

"Upwards of 40% and climbing. This is bad, real bad boss. Some of the exhibits are going to be irreplaceable and the costs will be astronomical. "

"Not to mention the negative publicity. Have you informed Paige?"

"Yes, Paige is aware of our situation."

"When you see her, send her my way."

"I'm right here," said Paige, standing in the doorway.

Roth depressed the intercom button and snapped, "What the hell is going on here, Paige? How could something like this have happened? I want answers and somebody's ass. You better already be working a media angle to ensure this does not escalate into a three-ring circus! My investors are going to be livid and the timing could not have been worse. This could cost me everything unless you do what I pay you to do. Do I make myself perfectly clear?"

"Perfectly," she acknowledged.

Pressing the button again he commanded, "Colby, you determine the damn root cause of this breach and correct it. Do what you can to contain and minimize casualties. Keep me posted on everything that transpires. Find whoever is responsible."

"Will do boss. I have called in all our resources. We're all over it."

"I want a name. I want the perpetrator's balls and you best deliver!"

"I assure you we're doing everything humanly possible."

"And in our world of computer technology that really isn't too adequate, is it?"

"I assure you we will get to the bottom of it…"

"Or I'll have your balls first on my platter," Roth finished he sentence.

39

"I can't believe how you're ruining our vacation," cried out Liz, fuming at Chad.

"Please do not blame your husband, Elizabeth, for circumstances beyond our control I assure you," replied Frederic, attempting to rationalize with his irate daughter.

"And you promised me, Chad," she continued. "How is any of this your problem?"

"Sea monsters," mocked Corinne Bornfreund. "What have you two been smoking and I hope you saved me some."

"Corrine, do not be condescending to your father," warned Teal.

"You sound like your mother, chasing mythical creatures, Chad. How can you possibly believe what you're saying?"

"Liz, my mother has nothing to do with this, so please stifle the cheap shots."

"You're not doing this without me," spoke up Alexis.

"What the hell are you talking about, Alex?" asked Corrine.

"I'm part of this. I was on that boat when this thing attacked. I'm going with them."

"Like hell you are," protested Corrine.

"Yeah, like hell you are," repeated Chad.

"Frederic, tell them please. You cannot deny me this. I am part of it. I was there with you and the others and for me it brings closure to the ordeal. I must face my demon...please."

"Indeed dear, you are part of this, but I warn you if I allow you to accompany us, I take no responsibility for your life. It is your decision and you bear the consequences."

Alex nodded she understood.

"Hold on a second," exclaimed Teal. "You're making this sound like some sort of death mission. I'm not so sure I'm going to allow you to go, Mister Bornfreund."

"Teal, I do appreciate your concern and your love means more than anything to me but I, like Alexis, will not be denied this opportunity. It might very well define my career. This is a discovery that could reshape paleontology. Do you not understand the significance of what we face here?"

"I understand that an extinct dinosaur could take your lives. If what you say is fact, this thing or things have sunk two boats and have eaten heaven knows how many people already. I'll not tolerate it having you, any of you for dessert!"

"Teal, there are dangers all around us. We have no control over fate," explained Frederic.

"Having control and tempting it is two different things. I know I'm wasting my breath, but I don't want your claim to fame to be the last meal of an extinct species."

Frederic embraced his wife and kissed her on the cheek.

"Father, you can't allow Alex to go with you. I forbid it," fumed Corrine.

"Why," chimed in Robert. "We're not stupid, sis. We all know why you brought her along, for just the shock factor. You will do anything to get under the old man's skin. She is just another one of your passing toys. You've certainly outdone yourself this time."

Chad thought, way to go there, Bobby, for once I agree with you, and I couldn't have said it any better; except I would not have said it in the presence of Alex. Nevertheless, the cat was out of the bag now. Let the fireworks begin.

"Bullshit, Bobby and you know it," yelled Corrine. "This is no dog and pony show. I'm not going to take that crap from the likes of you, Mister Underachiever."

"Calm down dear. I'm sure your brother didn't mean it," said Teal the peacemaker.

"Oh, I meant every word and she knows it," said Robert, as his wife Cody, mouth open in shock, eased into the background and sat on the sofa.

"Is it true? You were just using me to rile your father?"

Chad wanted to yell hell yes but decided to allow it to run its course. He could see the hurt wailing in Alex's face as she absorbed the shock.

"Alex...you can't possibly believe him. He'll do anything to take the pressure off himself."

"Lie to her if you think you can, sis," said Robert.

"I must admit I've suspected something ever since we've arrived, but I've been in denial I suppose. For the record, my love for you has been real," she said as she touched the back of her hand to Corrine's cheek and then she turned to Fredric. "When do we leave?"

"Alex, you can't," commanded Corrine, all falling on deaf ears.

"At first light, my dear. As for my daughter, I do apologize from the depths of my heart. I am not sure why she hates me so and why she would belittle you and embarrass herself. We certainly did not raise her to be disrespectful."

"Why do I act like this? Because you are not my father and mom is not the saint you make her out to be," spouted Corrine, determined to cast the final stone. "Yeah, you two are the perfect role models, aren't you? We should all bow in your presence and kiss your feet like we already kiss your asses. Dirty little secrets, Mother, it's time for you to confess your sins."

Chad watched as Teal dropped her head. He saw the tears rolling down her cheeks, obviously confirming the truth. Frederic stood there like a mighty oak, unaffected by the revelation. This had suddenly turned ugly and to make matters worse Robert said, "Hell I knew you couldn't be my full sister. You have got to be the product of a damn psychopath the way you've always acted. Who the hell's her daddy, Mother? I hope he was worth it to make you betray father."

Frederic did something completely out of character. He backhanded his son across the cheek. "You'll not speak to your mother in that tone!"

"I'm sorry," boohooed Teal. "It's my entire fault."

"Please my dear, don't fret yourself. I have known for some time about those skeletons. I just never understood why Corrine felt as she did toward me. I had no idea that she had uncovered the truth. In my heart she has always been my daughter and always will be."

"It's your fault that she turned to another man for comfort, father dearest. All you cared about was your work, your career. Family was well down the totem pole. Because she loved you, I was denied time with my real father. She kept her dirty little secret to protect you. Because of that I never had a chance to meet him or know him. It is entirely your fault. And guess what, he is dead. He has been dead for over twenty years now. I never had the opportunity to spend one second with him, all because of you. She would have told me about him if not for her fear of hurting the mighty professor and tarnishing his pristine reputation."

"I'm sorry you feel this way. Fact is I knew your father, Corrine. He was an exceptional man and a loyal friend and colleague. He admitted the affair to me when you were merely two years old. He asked for my forgiveness. It was not easy for me to swallow my pride, but I eventually granted his request after he shared with me his fate. He asked for me to be your father and raise you as my

222

own and I did. Corrine, your father was an extremely ill man and he realized his days were short. He could not give you the life you deserved as badly as he wanted to claim you for his own. I am sorry Teal. He did love you and confided in me to keep his admission a secret and not to hold you responsible for what had occurred between you and him. And Corrine, you are correct. I did put my work ahead of you, your siblings, and your mother for too many years. I have done my best to reconcile those errors in judgment. Apparently in your eyes I fell short and for that I am sorry, but you are my daughter just the same. I could not love you any less than I have loved Elizabeth and Robert. You came from your mother's womb. I held you in my arms in that delivery room. Nothing changes how I feel. I hold no resentment toward your mother or Mathew Mittelbronn for bringing you into my life."

"You've known all this time," said Teal. "And you never for once showed your disappointment in me for betraying you."

"I could never mistreat you Teal, but all wasn't easy at first. I am not without my dignity, but all I had to do is look at our Corrine and it helped me wash away my anger and hurt. For the first two years of her life I knew her as my flesh and blood. Finding out the truth did not make her any less my daughter or you any less my wife. Corrine is correct. I drove you into the arms of another by not being here for you, and much time transpired before I forgave myself. If anyone should apologize, it should be me."

Corrine now looked like the one that had been sucker punched. For the first time she had no smartass response. She took a deep breath and then exited the condo in tears.

"I'll go talk to her," said Liz.

"No, let me," spoke up Alex. "She needs a shoulder and just possibly mine might still fit."

"I'm so sorry, Frederic," sniffled Teal.

"For what. You gave me a wonderful daughter and for that I will always love you. These admissions and revelations change nothing

223

about the way I feel about my family. I'll not be excavating old bones this time," he said as he held Teal in his arms.

"Okay, if all the damn hugs and tears are behind us now, and my bastard sister has left the building, can we go catch this sea monster," asked an unaffected Robert.

Chad snatched Bobby up by his shirt collar with both hands and shoved him against the wall. "One more word from you and Corrine and Liz will be the only remaining Bornfreund children under this roof."

Robert eyed his father for assistance in putting an end to his brother-in-law's assault, but Frederic just shrugged. "Take your medicine like a man for once son. You do have a tendency of allowing your mouth to overstate your buttocks. I do believe we've heard enough of your insults."

"Listen to your father, Robert. He's a very wise man," added Teal, holding Frederic tightly.

Chad released him and said, "And another thing, you cause us any trouble on that trawler, and I'll be the first to convert you to chum, got it? You'll be overboard before you can blink an eye."

Robert pulled away and said nothing. He had more important things to tend to than this. He must phone Roth Niederwerter. He gave one parting glance as he too exited the condo.

"I think you two need a little breathing room," commented Chad, motioning to Cody and Liz.

He was thankful the kids had been in the bedroom and had not witnessed the circus. What a vacation he mumbled under his breath.

40

Robert Bornfreund wasted no time calling Roth Niederwerter. Within the hour he met face to face with him at the aquarium where total chaos still prevailed. Roth multitasked as he listened to the snitch's story. The revelation changed everything. Besides dealing with the aquarium catastrophic, he now had to expedite his plans for launching his own expedition to capture the creature responsible for wreaking havoc on the Strand.

"It will be difficult for you to update us from the trawler," commented Roth to Robert.

"I have no intention of being on that trawler with the likes of my brother-in-law. I'd prefer joining your crew, so I can witness the expression on their faces when we capture the sea monster."

"You sound as if you despise Chadwick as much as I do."

"He's just a suck-up intent on impressing the great Frederic Bornfreund. He relishes belittling me in my father's eyes. I have put up with his crap long enough. I plan to silence his thunder."

"Quite a family rift we have here," stated Roth.

"Fame and fortune heal all wounds as far as I'm concerned."

"Then welcome aboard mate but understand this is no luxury cruise. You will be required to pull your own weight. The price for fame and fortune doesn't come cheaply."

"Aye, aye, sir," Robert stood erect and saluted. "When do we shove off?"

"I plan to be on the water before Chadwick and his misfits leave the harbor. And you say they will be sailing on the Shrimp Cocktail."

"Yes, it's a shrimp trawler moored in Georgetown. Father and Chad are convinced they can save these creatures like it is their morale obligation. They're idiots with their modern day save the whales campaign."

"Chadwick has never been much of a visionary. He thinks too small. I'm surprised he has deceived your father."

"The old man sees this as a final feather in his career. He has studied old bones his entire life. Now he has the opportunity to go Jurassic Park and study a living and breathing dinosaur. Notoriety means everything to him. I intend to snatch that golden ring from underneath his nose. There's only room for one famous Bornfreund and it will not be him."

Roth smiled, thinking no Bornfreund will lay claim to this discovery. It would be his and his alone. He would not share the lime life with anyone else, especially this spineless leech. Accidents do happen at sea. Luck had placed the turncoat on his vessel. Things have a way of working out indeed.

"What will you tell your father about not joining them?"

"I have no intention of telling them anything. I will be gone before they rise and simply not show up. Trust me, neither my father nor Chad will care. Chad didn't want me to accompany them in the first place."

"Very well, be at the Murrells Inlet harbor by 3 AM. Until then, find out what you can about their plans. Do not raise any suspicions."

"I'll do what I can but I'm afraid I've already pissed them off."

"How pray tell did you accomplish this?"

"Family matter," responded Robert.

"Very well but I fear your family matters are just beginning," he smiled.

"You let me worry about that," stated Robert as he exited Roth's office.

Once he had cleared Robert Bornfreund's stench from his office Roth retrieved his cell phone and contacted Tyson. "I require you to call in that favor from your acquaintance. Yes, he is the one. Have him detain the departure of the Shrimp Cocktail from Georgetown Harbor in the morning. No, how he accomplishes this is of no concern. Just do not allow it to sail from that harbor. Do I make myself perfectly clear? The crew is of no significance to me. Merely lateral damages if they attempt to intervene. Just make this happen, Tyson. And Tyson, my name will not be associated with the incident, understood? Excellent, carry on please."

Roth accustomed to being in control had found himself in very unfamiliar territory in the past 24 hours and it brought out the worst in him. He blamed Chadwick Reynolds for his ill misfortunes, and it infuriated him to admit the bastard had shaken up his perfect world by meddling in affairs that did not concern him. This was no longer a game and he would pay dearly for interference.

Roth keyed in a number on his cell. "Kevin, assemble the crew. We make way by 4 AM. You heard me clearly. Kevin, have everything on board as I requested. Save your excuses. Just do it. We will have one extra passenger. No, extra provisions or accommodations will not be necessary. Our passenger will only be with us for a short stay. I am sure you do not understand, but I do not employ you to think or question my orders. Now do I? You just make sure we sail by 4. Do not disappoint me, Kevin. I am not in a very forgiving mood."

Fine thought Roth, dead or alive, one of these sea anomalies would most certainly thwart the negative vibes suffocating his world. He could right all wrongs in the eyes of the investors with such a discovery. Deflection. Divert their attention away from the aquarium and show case the next King Kong. He would not be denied. This would be his version of the Lost World. He would dispose of Chadwick Reynolds in the same breath…perfection is a gift indeed admitted.

41

It was late, almost 11 PM when Chad answered his cell phone. "Hello, Chad Reynolds."

"Chad, this is Detective Sly Stone. I hate to bother you at such a late hour, but I require your input on urgent matters."

"Not a problem. I'm on vacation and I am not one accustomed to seeing an early pillow. How can I assist you?"

"You heard about the beached whales I assume."

"Yes, I am aware of the incident."

"Your friend Roth Niederwerter and his team of marine experts became involved, unsolicited by my department of course, and he declared shark attack to the news media."

"But you don't agree, do you?"

"I'm not in a position to dispute the experts on such matters, but you still don't think we have a great white in our waters, do you?"

"Not a rogue one responsible for all these peculiar incidences, no."

"There's more," he continued. "We have a missing Kayaker. We found his kayak severed in half with what looked like bite marks to me."

"Without examining the marks, myself, I can't absolutely rule out a shark attack, but I don't believe a shark was responsible."

"You seem mighty sure about this."

"I have my suspicions. That's not the half of it. A touring pontoon boat in Winyah Bay down in Georgetown was…let's just say capsized or tipped over. The captain and three elderly women are missing, believed to have drowned."

"It's not easy to capsize a pontoon. You think there's something more to this incident, don't you?"

"Most of the sightseers had already been off loaded on shore to scavenge for shells as goes the tour agenda. The only witnesses to the accident were a couple of small children and this is where it gets weird. I suppose it's where a child's imagination can get the best of them. They say they saw a sea serpent tip over the boat. What do you make of that?"

Chad raised an eyebrow and just commented, "Interesting but given the circumstances, understandable."

"It gets a little freakier still. It seems we had this guy with military experience that recruited a couple of volunteers to try to go for help. They left in the direction of the bay following the shoreline and marsh. We haven't found them yet. We were able to follow their tracks until the three of them entered the water to cross one of the streams feeding the bay. We couldn't find any tracks on the other side."

"Drowned?"

"Tide was going out. No bodies have been recovered."

"What do you think happened to them?"

"I was hoping you could shed some light because my gut tells me all these incidences, including the two charters, the one you were on and the shrimp trawler, could be related. And there's more. "

"I'm listening."

"Georgetown game officials reported two men missing in a Jon Boat. A wife of one of them says they went out night fishing and never returned. They say these good old boys have been fined in the past for gator poaching. Possibly they met their match with a gator. But again, I'm not so sure given everything else that has happened. What's your take?"

"I don't think you're going to appreciate my take, detective."

"Yeah, I kind of thought there might be one of those Paul Harvey *and now for the rest of the story* moments. Lay it on me."

"Promise me you won't go public with what I'm about to tell you because we have no visual or convincing physical evidence to support our theory yet."

"Yet," added Sly.

42

The Ocean's Seven Odyssey and its team had already set sail 45 minutes ahead of schedule. The former research vessel of the German Navy had been restored and customized by Roth as the ultimate floating Mega Exploration Yacht, suiting his every need. At 80 meters long, its 262 plus feet were more than formidable for any challenge the ocean offered. Too large for any of the local harbors, it had arrived from Wilmington and they had taken a small skiff from Murrells Inlet out to join the captain and crew.

The vessel was powered by an extremely reliable diesel electric drive with four MWM main engines. It was equipped with an electric motor on the propeller shaft. Because the main engines were totally enclosed and especially mounted, the drives were almost noiseless and free from any vibration; a smooth ride indeed with a range of over 12,000 miles. The Odyssey was equipped with a landing platform. A helicopter hanger housed a vintage Sikorsky S-76 Spirit serving as the perfect multi-purpose commercial copter to meet Roth's needs. Two cranes on deck could lift over fifteen tons each. To add a splattering of luxury and comply with Roth's lifestyle, the vessel came equipped with a sky lounge, a mega sun deck, and running track. It had all the creature comforts of a cruise ship. An array of smaller vessels could be launched at a moment's notice. Roth had spared no expense thanks to his investors.

Captain Huey Horatio Long had been in Roth's service since the conception of the Ocean's Seven Odyssey. Long knew every inch of the vessel and its capabilities. He had personally handpicked the crew of fourteen men. There were no women on his ship as he believed it taboo to have female crew members. A throwback and seasoned sailor, he commanded respect and no one, including Roth, ever questioned his judgment in any matters of the sea. Roth had brought along seven, including Tyson, Colby, Kevin and the slug, Robert Bornfreund. He respected the captain's wishes and included no women. Paige would be running interference on shore and ensuring only the most positive publicity leaked to the media. He had no intent in disclosing the purpose of his mission until he had one of these creatures contained or killed, preferably captured alive.

"Is there any word on that trawler, the Shrimp Cocktail?" asked Roth, seated comfortably on his leather couch in his blush cabin.

"My man assured me he would have it disabled as you requested or at the least not seaworthy if it managed to set sail," replied Tyson.

"Excellent," smiled Roth. "I'll not tolerate any interference from Chadwick Reynolds or that ancient paleontologist father-in-law of his. The spotlight belongs to me. I'll not share this potential discovery with anyone, especially Chadwick."

A rap on his cabin door interrupted their conversation. Robert Bornfreund entered before being granted permission and that infuriated Roth. "Excuse me but we were having a private conversation in my quarters. Has your father taught you no manners, Bornfreund?"

"Just checking on our game plan, partner," said Robert, helping himself and pouring a cup of coffee.

Roth clinched his jaw. "You're excused Tyson but keep me posted on that matter we were discussing. Bornfreund, you're trying my patience with your abrupt behavior."

"Look. I have done everything you've asked of me, including betraying my family. Like it or not we are in this to the very end," he toasted and downed the coffee in one disgusting gulp.

The end cannot come soon enough for me thought Roth. "I do appreciate your interest in our expedition and in due time I shall disclose the plan. For now, please excuse me. I have more urgent matters to attend to, Bornfreund."

"Very well, partner. I'll be in that sky lounge of yours when you need me."

Not for long thought Roth. "I shall find you when the time is appropriate, I assure you." His thoughts returned quickly to the Shrimp Cocktail. This matter better be settled or else.

"Ahoy there, Captain Joe," greeted Frederic Bornfreund. "Did everything we ordered arrive?"

"I verified the manifest personally. All is accounted for."

"And good morning to you, Captain Tommy," said Frederic.

"Just Tommy, please, there's only room for one captain on a ship and this here one belongs to Captain Joe."

"As you wish," answered Frederic.

"Is this everyone?" asked Captain Joe, eying Frederic, Chad, and Alex.

"Yeah, looks like it," answered Chad. "It seems my brother-in-law has gone MIA. Most likely this mission isn't to his liking."

"I'm highly disappointed in Robert's behavior of late," said Frederic.

"And I'm sure you haven't been too pleased with mine lately, Father."

"Corrine, why are you here?" Frederic spotted his daughter standing dockside.

"I can't allow my father or my true companion to do this without me," she responded, nodding to Frederic and Alex.

"Come aboard daughter. That is if it is okay with our captain."

"Your charter, sir," replied Captain Joe.

"Too many broads on board" whispered Ken to Tommy. "This isn't right. It's supposed to be bad luck or something."

"Room for one more," called out a second figure emerging from the shadows.

"Detective Stone, isn't this a little out of your jurisdiction?"

"Chad, just taking a few days off to do a little fishing and learn the shrimping business. It can never hurt to have a back-up plan after retirement. I might just buy me one of these trawlers. Besides, I needed a break away from bike week. My superior was none too happy about it."

"Not to be rude," spoke up Tommy, "But this isn't exactly the Love Boat. It's going to be mighty close quarters for a crew of eight, don't you think Captain Joe?"

"I suppose it would be if we were shrimpin but we're not. We will make do. Come aboard, son," motioned Captain Joe. "You look fit enough to pull your own weight."

"By the way, I caught that guy snooping around here earlier," Sly pointed to a gentleman cuffed to a railing. "He had this bag of explosives and a timer. It seems someone does not want you to set sail this morning, but my friend over there hasn't felt so inclined to tell me who. I have a team on the way to pick him up for interrogation. I'll retain this as evidence for now," he said, holding up the disarmed bag of explosives.

"Roth," whispered Chad to Frederic. "He has become more ruthless than even I would have ever expected."

"Arson or even murder is rather a large leap from being a competitive college prankster, my boy."

"I have drastically underestimated him."

"Cast us off Ken," commanded Captain Joe.

"I don't have a good feeling about this," mumbled Ken, "Not a good feeling at all."

"Father, I'm sorry about everything."

"Corrine, there's been enough apologizing from everyone. We are family, always have been, and always will be. You're my daughter."

"Father, tell me about Mathew Mittelbronn. You said he was your friend."

"Indeed, he was, and you have your father's eyes and his smile."

"You're my father," she said giving him a hug. "I want to know about Mathew Mittelbronn, the man."

"Very well," he replied and so he began.

"Looks like things are working out," commented Chad to Alex.

"For her and her father, I hope so," answered Alex. "For us, we'll see. I still love her, but I am not so sure I'm still in love with her. I'm not one that fancies being used, so overcoming that might not come too easily."

"I'm sorry she hurt you. I should have told you I suspected she was using you, but it really wasn't any of my business."

"I probably wouldn't have believed you anyway. I was blinded by love of the first kind."

"Well, whatever happens, happens, I suppose," added Chad.

"Do you really think these creatures exist?"

"I suppose it sounds a little far fetched, but Frederic's colleague, the ones that examined the photos of the severed corpse and the coroner's report, seem to think so. I'll believe it when we have a confirmed sighting."

"And if we don't."

"Well, something is responsible for raising wholly hell on the Grand Strand. I'm convinced it is not a shark, even a Megalodon. While discovery of a new species would be a milestone, I am struggling with how mankind will embrace the existence of such a vicious beast. Driving it back into extinction might be the natural reaction."

"What happens if it turns out to be that species of super predator you've mentioned, and the species begins to flourish?"

"God help us because its introduction into our world would wreck the ocean's ecological system and jeopardize the fishing industry. It could even threaten man's coexistence on the open seas and immediate shorelines. We are not prepared for such a super predator. This could very well be the last stand on the Grand Strand."

"You're right. Humanity's way of dealing with things like this is always very inhumane. Kill first and deal with the consequences later. Last stand, I certainly hope not."

"While I would oppose such a reaction, there might be no alternative solution to this one. My mother has always faced this dilemma when researching the existence of Sasquatch. Would man destroy it if they ever found it? Funny thing is, in almost every documented case where an armed hunter encountered a Sasquatch, the hunter could not pull the trigger because they said the thing too resembled a human being. Such will not be the case if this new species of Liopleurodon does exist. No one will hesitate to pull the trigger on a sea monster, especially one that has already taken human lives."

"Sounds like we can count our blessing we didn't end up on the menu when it sunk our charter."

"I'm thankful but puzzled why it didn't. It surely took no mercy on that other charter or at least not that one particular guy. I suppose we have no proof that the others including the captain were actually taken as prey. They could have simply drowned. Possibly our cadaver flayed too much in the water and drew attention. A juvenile may have been drawn to the movement."

"Do you think we're safe on this shrimp boat?"

"Captain Joe says he witnessed the Holy Grail, another trawler tilt skyward and that crew vanished, but at least the boat did stay afloat. Detective Stone just last night told me about a sight seeing pontoon in Winyah Bay that was tilted in s similar fashion. The captain and three sightseers were lost from that one then later three more tourists disappeared from along the shore where they were shelling after being let off by the sightseeing boat."

"I see what you mean about your earlier comment."

"Combine that with a missing kayaker, two missing fishermen in a Jon Boat and a pod of beached whales and dolphins, we're painting a grim picture of our extinct animal's arrival along this coast."

"And you think they came from that trench you mentioned last night."

"Well, like I said, the **Puerto Rico trench is the deepest part of the** Atlantic Ocean and the closest to this coastline. I don't think they could have remained undetected otherwise. The question remains, what caused them to show up here now, and is there a possibility they will return of their own accord?"

"That would be the best outcome for all, wouldn't it?"

"For their good and ours," confirmed Chad.

"Hey brother-in-law, can I pry Alex away from you for a while?"

"Sure thing, Corrine, but play nice, or as nice as you're capable of playing." Chad then joined Captain Joe, Sly, and Frederic in the wheelhouse. "Where do we search first?"

"The captain and I were just discussing our best option. We have marked all the alleged attacks on this map with the assistance of the detective. The center of greater activity appears to be where the ocean and Winyah Bay converge. The whales and your dolphins were a little further north," pointed out Frederic.

"Simple, they stalked their prey in that direction. We don't seem to have any reports further southward. That tells me they remained well out to sea and for whatever reason were attracted to the body of fresh water. Spawning perhaps," inquired Chad.

Frederic nodded. "Possibly so…their much smaller cousin, Plesiosaurus were thought to have laid eggs like the sea turtle, but I'm not so sure about Liopleurodon. There's argument that they were completely ocean bound and were live bearers like a shark. Many believe they did have the ability to surge onto shore and take prey like the Orca from the beach or shallows."

"Could they have sought out streams for giving birth, possibly to ensure their young were protected from larger ocean prey until they were mature enough to return to the ocean?"

"Good assumption," replied Frederic. "They have the perfect access point through the bay. If they emerged from the Puerto Rico trench as you have suggested. This could have offered more protection than any of the Caribbean Islands. I suspect they prefer cooler waters, but still, why now."

"Could be that their reproductive cycle is much longer than other creatures or this isn't the first time they've been here. Maybe the area is more populated than in their previous visits or we paid no attention to similar incidences of beached sea creature. I will log into my laptop. I have wireless and can link into the internet via satellite. It might be time to conduct a little history lesson of the bay and surrounding area to see if we have signs of other visits or unusual activities."

Captain Joe interrupted, "Gentlemen, how do you propose we lure it out of hiding?"

"Who says we need to lure it at all? It seems to find us simply fine on its own; The Serendipity, the Holy Grail, and Tommy's Girl were easy enough targets. None were trying to lure it to them. It has a taste for sea captains."

"Point taken, Tommy," said Captain Joe.

"If an adult is as large as you suspect, what exactly will we do if we do encounter one? Aren't you afraid it might sink our boat?"

"Sly, given it didn't sink the Holy Grail or that sight seeing boat, and both are similar in length, I don't think we have that to worry about," answered Chad.

"But must I remind you, in both those incidences it plucked its prey from the boats. Seven people are still missing from on deck."

"I'm glad I'm captain then," chuckled Joe, "The wheelhouse seems to be the best chance for survival if attacked."

Sly then asked, "What if one of these things doesn't find us?"

"We have a plan B," smiled Chad. "Recordings of whales and dolphins, nature's very own dinner bell for an apex predator. Whales can communicate over large distances using extremely low frequencies. Dolphins usually use higher frequencies, which limits the distance, but between them we have the frequency covered and the perfect lure."

"Then what?"

"Captain, we have your nets and my tranquilizers," replied Chad.

"Didn't you say an adult could be upwards of 60 feet? How long is the trawler; 40, maybe 50 feet?" inquired Sly. "To quote Sheriff Brody in Jaws, *we're going to need a bigger boat*."

"Where are we going to haul one of these things if we do manage to coral one alive?"

"Now captain, I haven't exactly worked out that detail yet," answered Chad.

"But I do have my colleagues attempting to secure saltwater containment," spoke up Frederic. "There's a defunct ocean park facility located just above Saint Augustine that could be the perfect place to study the creature. It does have a tank large enough to support one if we're lucky enough to capture a youngster."

"And if we're not," asked Sly.

"Then we'll have to tag and release it," replied Chad. "With a tracking device of course."

"Mates, this vessel is not equipped to haul a monster the size you have described all the way to Saint Augustine," advised Captain Joe.

"My good man, we would make additional arrangements for transport, I assure you," replied Frederic.

"And I'm doing this on my days off, what the hell was I thinking," stated Detective Sylvester Stone.

43

"Good morning, Paige, rise and shine," spoke Roth, "Status report, aquarium?"

"Risen and I have been shining for several hours now," she responded. "The news isn't good. We're at 65% losses and Hendrik confirmed that programming had been hacked and modified so that changes would not have been detected. It had to be someone who knew our systems. The Dangerous Reef exhibit has taken the largest hit with losses at almost 80%. We should receive lab results on the contaminants later this morning. "

"And the news media?"

"I've leaked that the venue had been temporarily shut down for unexpected maintenance and so far, it has held. However, that Lance Rocker guy is very persistent. He worries me."

"From what I hear of his reputation with the female population you should be able to defuse our talk show host celebrity by using your astute powers of persuasion."

"Are you insinuating that I seduce him?"

"Don't act so naïve, Paige. Just do what is necessary, what I pay you to do, and if giving it up for Rocker keeps him at bay, then so be it."

Roth had personally had his way with her too many times to count, but he had never asked her to give herself up to anyone else. As much as she loved him, this was a little much. "I'm not a common whore, Roth."

"Paige, you're paid well for what you do and you will do what I ask," commanded Roth, not one to take lip from the hired help and that's all she was to him.

"But Roth," she pleaded. "You make me sound like a prostitute."

"Paige, a call girl doesn't pull down a six-figure income. Remember that. Wine and dine our Mister Rocker then cough up a little to reel him in. Keep him occupied until we have accomplished our mission and have our star exhibit in captivity. Do this for me Paige."

Absolutely not she thought. Her job description did not require her to do this. How had she been so wrong about him? Her hesitation did not go unnoticed.

"Paige, your silence frustrates me. Do I sense a bit of insubordination here? You of all people should know how that angers me."

"Roth, please don't ask me to do this. I…" She could not finish the sentence. She could not tell him how much she loved him. Right now, she wasn't even sure he understood the concept.

"You watch and choose your words wisely my dear."

"I'll meet with Lance Rocker and do what needs to be done."

"Excellent, I knew you would not disappointment me. Has there been any news concerning the Shrimp Cocktail?"

"Shrimp Cocktail," repeated Paige.

Roth realizing his mistake and having not brought Paige into the fold on this situation, clarified his question. "It's a shrimp trawler in Georgetown. Chadwick Reynolds chartered it. I am just curious. Please verify if it has left port."

"I will have someone check on its status immediately. Is there anything else?"

"Rocker, he's your top priority. Do what you have to do."

"I assure you. I intend to do just that."

Roth's temperature and blood pressure elevated, just at the mere thoughts of his nemesis, the forever thorn in his side. Ridding of him once and for all consumed Roth. That would come later. For now, he'd settle for delay tactics. He waited quite impatiently the news that the trawler had been disabled.

****

The reflection of the morning sun off the calm Atlantic prompted Chad to scramble for his shades. His sunglasses offered truly little relief from the glare though. They would be arriving shortly at their destination. Chad wondered if they would see one of these creatures or would he become trapped in his mother's personal nightmare, chasing an elusive creature that might not even exist. No, Frederic's cronies had examined the evidence as had he, and something different had taken that man's life. All evidence identified the likely culprit. Of course, Sasquatch footprints were a dime a dozen, yet no creature had ever been captured nor had any remains been found.

He had always vowed to never follow in Mattie Reynolds footsteps and be consumed by myth. Look at me now; he shook his head in disbelief. The difference, he was not in it alone as had been his mother after his father, Shawn, had died. He for the first time felt her pain and anguish and commitment, or was it mere obsession? Again, the trail was strewn with missing persons and actual attacks. He had personally experienced the power of the creature when it had sunk the charter. More than ever, he was convinced Mattie Reynolds had experienced something too. Maybe after this was over the two of them could have a sit down and cleanse their mortal souls.

"See anything out there," asked Sly, almost causing Chad to piss his pants.

"Nothing but another beautiful sunrise," he replied.

"I received a voice message from my squad leader, Detective Trudy Wagner. Game management officials have found the Jon Boat but not its occupants."

"Did it capsize?"

"Her message indicated that the aluminum boat was twisted and had strange punctures."

"Bite marks," said Chad.

"She didn't say, but she did say that this was no mere boating accident. Even stranger, numerous gator carcasses were found in the general area."

"Well, weren't these men supposed to be alleged poachers?"

"True but look at the photos she sent and you tell me," replied Sly, showing Chad the three photographs on his cell phone.

Chad examined the photos, but because of their size on the phone's display screen, it was tough to make out detail imagery. He could see well enough to get the point. The first, a photo of the badly mangled Jon Boat, and yes, he agreed this couldn't be the result of a boating accident. The second, a floating Playmate cooler and life jackets indicated that the men were not wearing preservers. The third, the most disturbing of the three was the carcasses of several alligators. The sheer savagery of the attack and shredded remains left no doubt that this was not the work of poachers.

"What do you think?"

"Your missing men most likely disturbed one or more of the creatures while they were feeding and became part of the main course."

"My thoughts exactly."

"Where exactly did they find the Jon boat?"

"A couple of miles up the Waccamaw River. So, what do you think?"

"I don't think prey would have prompted them to swim upriver. After all, they are oceanic creatures. My bet, they were there to have their young, start a new generation of apex predators."

"You think we have babies sprouting upriver. What happens when they become adults?"

"Hopefully, they return to the deep where I assume they came from in the first place."

"And if they don't?"

"We must learn to adapt, or more likely, mankind will proclaim open season until they are hunted back into extinction."

"What are you boys talking about?" Corrine was standing behind them, holding a mug of steaming coffee.

"Evolution," replied Chad.

Corrine just rolled her eyes and then asked, "Is it just me or is that Ken guy a little too creepy?"

"I think he's just a little too high strung. The anticipation of an encounter is getting the best of him. He wasn't too keen on coming out here," explained Chad.

"Why did he then?"

"Moral obligation to Captain Joe and most likely the money won out," chuckled Chad. "Have you mended your fences with Alex?"

"Let's just say I've strung up the first strand of wire."

"Hope it wasn't barbed."

"Time will tell. You boys want a refill?"

"Since when were you so accommodating?"

"Hey, I'm trapped on this boat. It's subbing for a confession chamber. I also have six extremely brave men or six sorry asses vowing for the Kevorkian achievement award. To top that, I am with a woman who thinks she loves me and we're hunting for extinct dinosaurs. I figured I might as well make the best of it."

"Allow me to go for coffee," said Sly.

"And where's Alex?"

"My nutty professor father has her full attention. She's really into to this reality show of yours; name that sea monster. Are you convinced there's something to this?"

"Afraid so. Something sunk our charter boat. It wasn't a fluke accident. It's no coincidence that too many peculiar things have been happening up and down the coast. We have something new feeding in these waters, the likes that mankind has ever known. Vegas odds, I'd bet the bank."

"Alex said you called this the last stand on the Grand Strand. That's a little scary. Why do you think it's yours and father's responsibility to capture or kill it?"

"I'm an oceanographer, and your father is a paleontologist. It seems like we are the right men for the job. Why are you here, Corrine?"

"I guess I might finally be acting my age and taking responsibility for my actions and my life. I have hated and blamed people long enough for my miserable existence. Maybe this is my way of exorcising my demons, a brand-new start. Father told me about my real dad. I believe I can bury him now and move on. I am undecided if Alex will be part of that journey. Whatever I decide, I will not string her along or hurt her. I don't think I'm cut out to be a full time lesbian. I still like men too much."

"Candid as always, Corrine," said Chad, rolling his eyes. He saw Tommy waving his arms and mouthing something on deck. He waved back and headed toward him. Corrine tagged along.

246

"Joe has something on the fish finder and it's pretty damned big. It is almost directly below us. I think it could be one or more of them."

44

The Ocean's Seven Odyssey had come to a full stop and had dropped anchor. A skiff had been launched to retrieve the floating debris. A crew member radioed back. "It's definitely remnants of some sort of boat. Francisco has recovered a larger section. Please stand by." After a pause, "We have confirmed the identity. It is the Serendipity or at least what remains of it, printed plain as day. Francisco says he thinks there is a tooth fragment buried in the wood. We're retuning to the ship with the tooth once he removes it from the wood."

Captain Huey Horatio Long asked, "Do you think this tooth belongs to your alleged sea serpent?"

"Hopefully," replied Roth. "Evidence would assist our cause."

"Captain, the skiff is gone, sir," came the scream on the radio from the observation deck's lookout.

"Gone, repeat, what do you mean gone?"

"Captain, it was there then it wasn't," repeated the lookout.

The inflatable sea craft had indeed vanished without a trace, the three men on board along with it. The observer continued to frantically search with his binoculars as Captain Huey and Roth arrived. He avoided direct eye contact with both men.

"Where did you last see them?" Captain Huey commandeered the binoculars.

"Position, 10 o'clock," he replied. "But they're not there now. They're not anywhere."

"Did they report any difficulties to the bridge?"

"No sir. You heard their last radio transmission as did I, that they were returning to the ship with the boat debris and a tooth."

"Excellent sailors, all three," commented the captain.

"And gone with them is my tooth fragment," fumed Roth.

The lookout eyed the captain for his reaction to that last comment, but Captain Huey held his tongue. His face expressed much anguish. Taking a deep breath, he gave the command, "Launch a second skiff, two men, search and rescue."

"Search and rescue for whom captain," asked Roth. "They're gone. We'll not waste more of my equipment or men on a futile recovery mission." Roth paused then said, "On second thought that might just be an excellent idea."

Captain Huey did not appreciate the tone in Roth's voice. This time he spoke what was on his mind. "You'll not use more of my men as bait, sir."

"You're absolutely right," apologized Roth. "Please hail our illustrious guest, Robert Bornfreund. Have him meet us at the second skiff."

"You can't be serious," Captain Huey boldly questioned his boss, wanting no part of his suicidal scheming.

"Deadly serious, I assure you. Ready the steel netting on the cranes. Be prepared to move them into position," commanded Roth. "Step to it man. I'll not request this a second time."

Captain Huey reluctantly gave the order to his lookout to do as Roth had asked. "Sir…" then the lookout thought better of it and excused himself from the bridge.

Roth picked up the ship's phone and hailed Tyson and Colby. "It's time, lock and load," he chuckled and then turned to the captain. "I've always wanted to say that. Lighten up captain. I will compensate you and your remaining crew handsomely once we successfully complete our mission. I'll even compensate those poor men's next of kin if it makes you happy."

"Sir, I'm placing you on notice. Once we have docked, I am prepared to resign from my post and report what has happened."

"You do disappoint me Captain Huey. I hadn't pegged you as a quitter or a snitch."

"Nor had I pegged you as such a murderous heartless sonofabitch."

"You've got balls after all," grinned Roth. "But you're one stupid bastard with absolutely no visionary skills."

Captain Huey leaned in close, nose to nose and said, "A promise Mister Niederwerter. I'll have you up on charges for the hierarchy you are about to pull if that man dies."

With not so much as a blink Roth replied, "You are screwing with the wrong individual, Captain Huey. When I finish with you and your precious reputation, you will not be able to operate one of those boat rides at a traveling carnival. Now let us prepare our guest for his little ocean excursion."

Roth and Captain Huey arrived at the disembark deck about the same time as did Robert, the bait of choice. Tyson and Colby were already standing by, near the skiff suspended by cables.

"Greetings partner," said Roth offering his hand to Robert Bornfreund.

Robert grasped his hand and asked, "Has one been spotted?"

"Not yet, we're going to search some wreckage we detected in the water earlier and thought you'd like to come along."

"Sure, anything I can do to help."

Roth extended his hand and said, "After you."

Captain Huey spoke up, "No Mister Niederwerter, you, first. After all this is your find."

What the hell was the captain trying to pull wondered Roth. He had no intention of clambering on board that death trap. "Please, partner, you, first. We shall share the spotlight."

"I insist Mister Niederwerter," stated Captain Huey, now waving an automatic pistol.

Robert looked at Roth and then the Captain. "What the hell's going on?'

"You stay put sir. Mister Niederwerter will be manning the skiff alone."

"Tyson, Colby, relieve the captain of his weapon," ordered Roth.

Captain Huey released the safety and pointed the pistol at them. "I think it's best you two join Mister Niederwerter in that skiff. He could really use your assistance. A man of his upbringing should not be required to physically exert himself."

"Fools! Don't let him bluff you. He has no intention of using that weapon."

With that Captain Huey fired the pistol and the bullet zinged just past the two cowering men. Both scrambled on board the skiff.

"You're making a huge mistake," threatened Roth. "You can't just desert us."

"I have no intention of deserting you. I'm merely assisting you in testing your theory. I will have the authorities waiting for you on shore."

"You can't be serious. This is murder, plain and simple."

"Take in what your partner just confessed young man," said Captain Huey to Robert. "He intended this to be your fate."

"I don't understand," replied Robert.

251

"I just lost three of my own men on the first skiff. It just vanished beneath the sea. Your partner is convinced that a sea monster took them down. He intended to use you as bait to draw it to the surface to capture it."

Robert took a deep breath and said, "Then I think it's time you lowered the skiff, captain. I'm done with this so-called partnership."

Colby and Tyson exchanged glances, wanting no part of this, but too late. Captain Huey had pressed the button engaging the winches. The skiff descended to whatever lurked beneath.

"Damn you worthless bastards, why the hell do you think I pay you? It's surely not to just stand there with your thumbs up your asses."

"He had a gun," spoke up Colby.

"And we didn't," added Tyson.

"Well guess what, none of us have a weapon on this little scuttle."

"We have this," said Tyson, holding the flare pistol.

"Wonderful," fumed Roth. "What the hell are you going to do, signal the captain to pick us back up? Once we hit the water, engage the motor and let us make haste toward shore."

"I hope we have enough fuel to make it," commented Colby.

"We have enough fuel. I just hope we have enough time," added Roth.

Once they touched the surface and the winch cables were released, they did just that, hauled ass toward the shoreline barely visible on the horizon.

45

Aboard the Shrimp Cocktail...

Chad asked, "Do you still have them in sight?"

"Look for yourself," said Captain Joe, pointing toward the large blobs on the screen.

Chad examined the objects diligently and then commented, "I think you're right. It looks like a pod; possibly two adults and a juvenile."

"Some junior," quipped Captain Joe. "It must be nearly 20 feet long. I place the other two at over 50, closer to 60. They're at a depth of about 150 feet and have been shadowing us for nearly 15 minutes now."

"I hope they're just curious and not hungry," said Chad as Frederic joined them.

"What do we have here, my boy?"

"We either have a pod of whales, which I doubt, or you're looking at a new species of Liopleurodon, the whole cotton-picking family."

Frederic smiled. "I ascertain this would be the appropriate time to launch our underwater robotic camera, don't you think?"

"Excellent idea. I'll prepare it while you keep an eye on our company."

Frederic asked, "You did say the other trawler had been attacked, didn't you captain?"

Joe replied, "I just saw it's under belly as it tilted backwards. If these things were responsible, they struck the Holy Grail from behind."

"Perhaps, they were attracted by what had been snared in the nets," added Frederic.

"Makes sense," replied Captain Joe, "The nets had been shredded from what I remember. You're saying that maybe we're not very appealing to them. They were just interested in the catch squirming in those trailing nets."

"Just a wild assumption on my part or they may have been confused by the girth of the vessel. It could have been a territorial reaction."

"Or they're just stalking and sizing us up," added Tommy. "Tommy's Girl surely prompted an attack but then again we were reeling in fish at the time. I'd still suggest we keep the nets out of the water."

"Your ship was much smaller, less intimidating," said Fredric.

"Same size as Captain Marvin's vessel," confirmed Tommy. "Why didn't they take us after she went down?"

"We remained calm and didn't splash about. Maybe after a taste of the hull it decided we were not prey," replied Frederic.

On deck, Sly assisted Chad with the robotic camera while Corrine and Alex kept watch for any breach on the ocean surface. All were quite antsy.

"Will this thing go as deep as they are right now?"

"Sly, she'll go three times that depth with the attached power cord and we control her from that computer and joystick," replied Chad. "It's almost ready to launch."

"Anything ladies," asked Sly.

"Not a ripple," answered Alex.

"And let's hope it stays that way," added Corrine.

"Okay, let's try to get a visual," said Chad using the mounted winch to lower the robotic camera.

Tommy yelled to them that the creatures were still holding their position portside. Once the robot cleared the surface bubbles and Chad had a perfect view on screen, he used the joystick to control the descent. Reaching depths of one hundred fifty feet were cumbersome. He called out the depth aloud every ten feet. Tommy confirmed the three creatures' location in the same intervals, watching the screen intently. The pod held their position and speed, mimicking the Shrimp Cocktail's movements. So far there were no signs of an imminent attack.

"We're at 80 feet," announced Chad. "Are they still holding their position?"

"Like ticks on a hound," yelled Tommy.

Frederic arrived on deck eager to witness the first confirmed sighting. "We could be about to set the scientific world on its pompous ass, my boy," he said, placing his hand square on Chad's shoulder.

"I must admit, it has me on an adrenalin high right now."

"It just plain scares the crap out of me," spoke up Corrine.

"Where's your sense of adventure, Corrine?"

"Somewhere between wishing I wasn't here and hoping we're not the dinner bell, Alex."

"Ninety feet," called out Chad.

"They're holding their position," yelled Tommy from the wheelhouse.

"Do you think this is all of them?"

"Sly, my gut tells me probably not. If I had to guess I would say we have a couple of females and a juvenile below us. I'd bet money there's at least one male if not more somewhere," replied Chad. "The male would not be sticking close to a female and her young, lack of interest and the female probably wouldn't allow him to approach. The second adult must not be in heat or we would see a male close by. Now I am basing my assumption on the behavioral habits of whales. One other possibility, the second adult could be an escort male. It isn't uncommon for a male whale to trail a female with calve, contemplating the next return to the spawning grounds, staking claim to the female a year in advance."

"Need I remind you, Chad, that these things aren't exactly whales. If they are what you and Father think they are, then they could act like nothing you have ever experienced," stated Corrine.

"Corrine, Chad is the expert on marine life, must I remind you," cautioned Frederic.

"Need I remind you father that these are extinct monsters of the deep. I don't think textbook assumptions really apply."

Frederic smiled. "But assumptions are all we have my dear."

"One hundred feet," announced Chad, "Visibility is less than ten feet."

"Still there," called out Tommy.

"You're gong to have to be up close and personal if you hope to make a visual, aren't you?"

"Alex, in these murky conditions it isn't going to be easy."

"I hope they aren't camera shy," she added.

"I hope they don't eat the damn camera," commented Corrine.

"Maybe we should have equipped that robot of yours with a hook and cork," said Ken, who had been watching in silence up until now.

"One hundred ten feet," called out Chad.

"They might have just spotted your robot," yelled Tommy. "They're at 140 and slowly ascending."

"Thirty feet separate us for something monumental, my boy," stated Frederic, his eyes glued to the computer screen.

"I just hope it's not menu-mental," quipped Ken.

The rest crowded around the laptop, all waiting to catch their first glimpse of an extinct aquatic dinosaur. "One hundred twenty feet," announced Chad.

"One hundred thirty-five feet," called out Tommy. "They should be just below and slightly behind your robot."

"Okay, I'm going to pull a 180 and drop another ten feet," stated Chad, working the joystick. "It's show time." Engaging the joystick, clicking the computer keys, he began the turn and continued to gradually lower the robot. "We should have visual contact any second now."

Frederic wet his lips with his tongue. Corrine and Alex almost huddled as one while Sly rubbed his chin, each mesmerized by the nothingness being displayed.

Ken broke the silence, "So, where are these mysterious sea monsters?"

"Right there," pointed Chad, as a fuzzy shape appeared on screen just on the outer boundaries of visibility.

A blur then a second shot past the camera. Chad yelled to the wheelhouse, "What's happening?"

"They're leaving like bats out of hell," yelled Tommy, "They're moving northwest. I can clearly make out the two large ones and the trailing smaller one now."

"Damn it," sighed Chad. "We were so close. Could you make out anything?"

"Not much, my boy. Certainly nothing to lay claim to our finding."

"Can we stick with them?"

"Joe says not a chance, Chad," yelled Tommy. "Best we can hope for is to stay on the course they were headed."

"Then do it," shouted Chad. "But not until I bring up the robot."

"My boy, that will take too long," replied Frederic.

"Sorry sir, but this equipment is too expensive for my budget."

"Very well," he answered. "How long?"

"Fifteen minutes, twenty tops," he replied.

Sly asked, "What do you suppose prompted that northwesterly exit?"

"Prey or some sort of creature distress call is my best guess," replied Chad. "Or maybe the dominant male is in the area."

"It could have been a blessing," commented Ken, wiping sweat from his face with a handkerchief.

"Amen, brother," chimed in Corrine.

"I can't believe you two," stated Alex. "The chance of a lifetime and you're acting like a couple of wussies."

"This isn't just fun and games, Alex" answered Corrine.

Ken just shrugged and made his way to the wheelhouse.

"We were so close," said Chad.

"We'll have another go at it," Frederic attempted to console him. "We're a step closer than we were before this morning. We should replay the encounter and advance it frame by frame. Maybe we will be lucky, my boy."

"I'll do that once I secure the robot."

"They're off the screen," shouted Tommy. "Captain Joe is locked onto their last position. Say when, and we'll set sail."

"Ten more minutes," confirmed Chad, ten exceptionally long agonizing minutes he imagined.

46

Three men in the inflatable motorized skiff had taken aim on the shore.

"Is this the most you can get out of this piece of crap?" Roth was furious and taking it out on Tyson.

"Don't blame us, Roth. We had nothing to do with the purchase of your exploration vessel and all its toys. Russell oversaw equipping it, remember. He selected these, not us."

"Russell, I bet he's our damned aquarium saboteur," barked Roth.

"Could have been," answered Colby. "He knew the aquarium systems better than anyone."

"And he was not a happy camper when you canned him," added Tyson.

"Remind me to have Paige play up that angle when we return. I'll crush that weasel."

"Speaking of Paige," said Colby. "We heard a radio broadcast, a promo for that Lance Rocker's show just before you hailed us to the skiff. It said something about not missing the next telecast; breaking story about local aquarium catastrophe."

"And you're just telling me this," yelled Roth.

"We had a gun pointed at us and it didn't seem very important at the time."

"Damn Paige, she dropped the ball."

"There's more," spoke up Tyson. "The promo mentioned you and your pursuit of the Grand Strand's very own Loch Ness Monster."

"Get me to shore, now! Paige has screwed up everything!"

Something struck a glancing blow from underneath the speeding water craft, launching it several feet into the air and wildly sideways. It landed, almost flipping over, but Tyson's quick maneuvering set it back on course. Problem, they were minus one occupant. Colby now treaded water 45 yards behind them, waving and yelling for them to return.

"Leave him," ordered Roth.

"You're crazy. I'm not leaving him," answered Tyson, banking a turn to rescue Colby.

"Leave him," shouted Roth, now resting the flare gun against Tyson's forehead.

Colby eyeing the skiff as it veered back in his direction began to swim toward it. Tyson had brought it to a stop no more than 25 yards away. Colby could see Roth with the flare gun aimed at Tyson. He swam more frantically trying to close the distance.

"Look," pointed Tyson. "He's right there. We can have him back in the skiff in less than a minute. Come on sir. You're not so cold bloodied that you'd allow a man to drown like this. Please."

Roth sighed and removed the flare gun from Tyson's head. "Fine, get him but quickly."

Tyson hailed Colby, "Hang on. We're coming."

Roth and Tyson stared helplessly as the ocean exploded underneath Colby and massive jaws took him in one quick snap. Liopleurodon or some derivative of the mega ocean beast was no longer extinct. Although the two men had only caught a glimpse of its head and vicious jaws, they both knew they were in an extremely vulnerable and perilous predicament.

"He's dead. It got Colby. What do we do now? Your aquarium is not equipped to house something that large," shouted Tyson.

"Stifle your whiny comments and get us the hell out of here. Tyson just stood motionless; mouth gapped wide open. "Tyson, I said go."

Tyson snapped to and completed the 180 and gave the skiff full throttle. Roth scanned the waters behind for any signs of the creature. He clutched the flare gun so hard his knuckles were aching. He ignored the pain and maintained his vigil watch. A flash just beneath the water less than 20 yards behind the skiff told him what he didn't want to know. The creature streaked effortlessly just below the surface and it was gaining ground. Roth guessed it must be at least 70 feet in length.

"Tyson, we need more speed."

"She's maxed. Toss out everything that isn't nailed down."

Roth began jettisoning everything that he could, but the craft held truly little equipment, no significant weight to gain them any advantage. The sleek reptilian torpedo would have them any second. Roth got rid of the only thing remaining. He grabbed Tyson by the arm, spun him, and shoved him overboard. He then took command of the skiff. Glancing back in the wake, he no longer saw his adversary. He hoped that didn't mean it was now underneath him. He got his answer. Those same horrific jaws plucked Tyson from the surface.

Roth hoped that the momentary pause bought him the precious time he needed to make his escape. He glanced at the fuel gauge and realized that he would probably run out before he could reach the safety of the coast. He had no more sacrificial offerings for the hungry beast that pursued him. Captain Huey had indeed deserted him. He could see his ship heading northward on the horizon toward Wilmington. Survival was in his hands and his hands alone. The odds were terribly skewed not in his favor. Looking behind he didn't see the thing, but he knew it had to be there, somewhere close.

47

Back on the Shrimp Cocktail...

"Okay, robot has been secured," shouted Chad to Tommy, standing in the wheelhouse entrance way.

"We're good to go, captain," Tommy relayed the message to Joe.

Captain Joe eased the throttle, but the shrimp trawler was not built for hot pursuit. He held the course where the creatures had last been spotted. "I regret I got you into this, Tommy. Hell, I'm regretting getting myself in this mess as well," spoke Captain Joe.

"Adventures on the sea have reached a new level my friend and not to worry, I have no regrets. One of those things took down Tommy's Girl. I had my obligation to her to take vengeance."

"I'm not sure we're equipped to take vengeance," chuckled Captain Joe. "Some things might just be well enough left alone. Our sea monster hasn't survived for millions of years to be taken by the likes of two old salty dogs I fear."

"The way I see it, it's never had to tangle with salty dogs before, so it might have met its match," laughed Tommy, patting Joe on the back.

"Best open us a can of spinach, mate. I think we're going to need it, "grinned Captain Joe.

On the deck, the remainder of the crew huddled around the laptop screen as Chad forwarded the video frame by frame, hoping to catch a first look at the once thought extinct behemoth. So far, only the depth's murkiness filled the view.

"Some technology," quipped Ken.

"Give it a rest," snapped Corrine. "You've been bitching and moaning ever since we left the dock."

"There," pointed Frederic. "Stop."

"What is it?"

"Alex, you're looking at the dental work of the most fearsome predator of the Jurassic seas," stated Frederic. "Liopleurodon, which means smooth-sided tooth, and it does not apply here. Look at the serrated edges. This is definitely an uncategorized species of Plesiosaurus."

"Amazing," commented Chad. "Let's move it forward." He advanced the frame and eventually an enormous eye came into focus. The skin surrounding the pitch-black eye appeared almost greenish grey. Advancing the next frames, the creature's body blocked out the screen and it seemed to pass forever, and then the ocean's murkiness reappeared.

"That's it," proclaimed Chad.

"That footage doesn't prove squat," commented Ken. "I don't see you convincing the world they are real just from that. It's no better than those fuzzy pictures you always see of Bigfoot."

"He does have a point," said Sly. "I wasn't even sure what we were looking at until you pointed it out."

"Father, I don't think you have enough there to convince the skeptics."

"I'm not convinced identifying them with indisputable evidence would be in these creatures' best interest," said Frederic.

"I agree. I'm not so sure anyone will want to place them on an endangered list if they're munching on the activists," added Chad.

"I don't envision cries of save the Liopleurodon," said Corrine.

Captain Tommy called out from the wheelhouse, "We're receiving a mayday."

Chad joined the two seamen to listen in.

"Is there anyone out there? I need assistance, low on fuel, and in a perilous situation, two men already dead," screamed a distraught man.

"I recognize that voice," said Chad. "It's none other than Roth Niederwerter. Do you have his location?"

"The dumbass hasn't depressed the button so we can ask him. He's been in a panicky hailing mode," confirmed Captain Joe. "Tommy, take a gander through those binoculars and see if you can spot anything."

Tommy began his 360 sweep and halted suddenly and then said, "We have some sort of craft, small one at that, directly ahead, less than a mile. I can't make out much though."

"That puts it directly in the path of those things if they stay true to the course. The fellow needs to take his finger off that microphone button so we can warn him what might be heading his way," said Captain Joe.

"Too late! I think they've already arrived," said Chad, listening to Roth's screams.

"Oh, my holly mother," he kept repeating. "Please no…please no…."

Standing in the entry way Frederic commented, "Possibly the creatures were drawn to that other vessel sensing easy prey."

"Two men dead, sounds to me that they've already punched their meal ticket," said Tommy.

"Good, he finally released the button," said Captain Joe. "Ahoy there. We have you in our sight at 3 o'clock. Stand by, and after you speak, take your finger off the button so we can communicate."

Chad instructed Captain Joe to tell him to cut the engines and remain perfectly still. He did but Roth spouted back. "Cut the engines, are you insane?"

"You know him. Maybe he'll listen to you," said Captain Joe, passing Chad the microphone.

"I doubt it, but I'll give it a try. Roth, this is Chad Reynolds. We know what we're talking about. These creatures are attracted to the movement and sounds of your vessel. Cut the engine and try not to move until we arrive."

"Chadwick, impossible, you can't be out here."

"Why, because your goon was supposed to blow us up? Don't worry. He's in custody and I suspect he's already incriminated your sorry ass by now. Right now, you need to listen to me. Contrary to you, I am actually trying to save your worthless soul. Cut the engine, Roth."

"You don't understand, there's one chasing me right now. It's killed five of my men and has already sunk one skiff."

"What you don't seem to get Roth is there are probably three more on a collision course with you this very moment."

"Here already," yelled Roth. "They took a bite at me when I just zoomed past them. Stopping is not a viable option."

"Can you see us?"

"Bee-lining your way as we speak, but are you sure that trawler is going to offer any better protection?"

"It's better that what you have. I'm all ears, Roth, if you have another idea."

"My skiff is deflating. One of them must have punctured the craft."

"Hold your course, Roth, we're coming as fast as we can."

"I'm…" then the speaker blared with Roth's screams.

"Can you see anything?" Captain Joe asked Tommy, binoculars glued to his eyes.

"Too much," replied Tommy. "Two of them have surfaced and are shaking that skiff like a ragged doll, scary looking mothers at that. Their heads like some sort of gigantic gator. I think your friend is probably dead and the Shrimp Cocktail might just earn its name as an appetizer."

"You don't see him," shouted Chad.

Tommy shook his head no. "I don't think there's anything we can do for him."

Captain Joe asked, "What about those whale and dolphin recordings of yours? Could we lure them away?"

"I wouldn't waste my time with that either. That boat is history and they are already gone," said Tommy, lowering the binoculars.

"We'll make a pass by just to make sure," said Captain Joe.

"What for? The man's dead. Why would we want to enter the jaws of hell if we don't have to?"

"Ken, we have a moral obligation as men of the sea responding to a mayday," stated Captain Joe.

"They're not paying us enough for this gig," fussed Ken.

"They're paying us what we agreed to," replied Captain Joe. "Go back on deck and stand by."

"They should be paying us a hell of lot more," mumbled Ken, heading back on deck.

Chad should have held no remorse for the demise of Roth. After all he had attempted to have them blown to smithereens only a few hours ago, but he was saddened by his untimely death. "Anything on the screen?"

"I don't see them," answered Captain Joe.

"Hopefully, they're long gone," said Tommy. "I'm not so sure tangling with the likes of these things is justified revenge for the sinking of Tommy's Girl. I might just be willing to call it all square if we can reach shore in one piece. We are heading back, aren't we?"

"That's left up to our paying customers," replied Captain Joe.

"I'm with your mate, captain. Money doesn't seem that important right now," stated Tommy.

"I agree but I do have an agreement to oblige."

"You're too honorable for your own good, but I'll stick by you whatever you decide. You were good enough to let me earn my keep, so I do owe you. Plus, you rescued us. Hope they're still not hankering to catch one though."

"That little one is all my nets could possibly manage and then I think we would have a fight on our hands from those big'ons."

"Maybe they'll be content with some picture taking," commented Tommy.

"I hope so."

"Look, there's something in the water," hailed Tommy.

"Where?"

"Six o'clock, starboard. Not moving though, but it looks like it could be a person in a life vest."

"It could be what's left of that Roth feller. I'll pull along side and you see if you can latch on to him."

"What's going on?"

"Detective, we got a bead on something in the water ahead and it might just be that feller that yelled for help or a chunk of him maybe. You might want to keep the gals to the stern until we know for sure. This could be messy.

"What's up?"

"Chad, they think they've spotted something in the water where the skiff went down. It could be Niederwerter," explained Sly. "Captain said to keep the women back just in case we have a bloody mess on our hands."

"Pulling along side," announced Captain Joe.

Tommy extended the boat hook to snag the life jacket with what appeared to be the corpse of a man bobbing on the surface. He snagged it on the second try and began pulling it toward him. The body remained motionless. "Help me pull him on board," said Tommy, signaling to Ken.

The two men grunted as they towed the lifeless body up and over the railing, smacking the wood noisily. He appeared in tack, no missing limbs or torso. Like a springboard Roth scrambled to his feet, wild eyed and breathing frantically.

"Son of a sailor, you're alive," exclaimed Tommy.

"Damn right I'm alive. I have been doing just what Chadwick proposed that I do. I played dead, remained perfectly still and miraculously I did not receive so much as bump or sniff. I owe Chadwick my life."

"Don't blame me for you being here," spoke up Chad. "They would have probably regurgitated you if they had woofed you down. Crap leaves a bad taste in your mouth."

"You're the expert, Chadwick. You've been eating mine for years, but my gratitude just the same."

"Tell us, Roth, how did you end up out here in nothing but a skiff?"

"That bastard Captain Huey deserted us in my exploration ship after that creature attacked and sank the first skiff. Three men died on board. That spineless captain, good as murdered my other two men when he sailed off leaving us to fend for ourselves."

Frederic poses the obvious question, "Why did the dear captain desert you?"

"Spineless, like I said. He wished no part of tangling with the creature. I'll have his balls when we arrive."

Chad wasn't buying it, but he played along. "What about those other two men? What happened to them?"

"It attacked, rammed us from below, and tossed both overboard. It took them time they hit the water."

"So, you've seen it," asked an excited Frederic.

"Just a glimpse," replied Roth. "That was enough."

"Liopleurodon ferox," asked Frederic.

"Possibly, but something about it didn't resemble the depicted drawings or skeletal remains," replied Roth.

"And just when did you decide you weren't hunting down your great white?"

"Come now, Chadwick, we can certainly put our petty differences aside for once, can't we?"

Chad retrieved the satchel full of explosives and dangled it in Roth's face. "Petty indeed. Premeditated murder is not so petty."

"What are you insinuating? Get that out of my face."

"Explosives intended to take us out of the water. I should toss you back overboard and allow nature to take its course."

"I assure you I know nothing about any explosives. I'd never do anything so repulsive, not even to you."

"Play it close to the vest Mister Niederwerter if you wish, but we have your man in custody and we most likely already have a confession," spoke up Sly.

"And who the hell are you?"

"Detective Stone, Horry County police and I apprehended your demolition's expert red handed, attempting to set the explosives on this trawler."

"Detective, I assure you I had nothing to do with this preposterous accusation of yours."

"I have the Coast Guard online," announced Captain Joe. "They heard the mayday and our response. What should I tell them?"

Frederic eyed his companions before posing his scenario. "Bringing in the Coast Guard now serves no purpose. We have retrieved the sole survivor. We certainly do not need them to go off have cocked and muddle up this astounding scientific discovery. Please, I employ each of you to stand firm and allow us to study these magnificent creatures before mankind attempts to destroy them."

"I'm not sure I can stand by and do that," spoke up Sly. "I'm sworn to justice and protecting the people."

"Please, what harm can a few precious hours cause? Allow us enough time to at least film them."

"Frederic, no one wants to protect them any more than me, but let's face facts, these creatures are probably responsible for a dozen deaths and who knows how many more they may claim if we allow them to escape," said Chad.

"But we have them in view and if they remain here with us then they cannot be feeding elsewhere," continued Frederic.

"Would you rather them feed on us, Father?"

"I don't think your father is saying that Corrine," spoke up Alex.

"Please…decide something…the guard is not going to wait forever," interrupted Captain Joe.

"Allow us time, please. I beg you. If they depart then we contact the authorities immediately and warn them."

"Only if everyone is on board with this," said Chad. "We watch and we wait, but the first signs of them disappearing off screen and we call the Calvary…understood?"

"You can't be serious," commented Corrine. "You saw what it did to Roth's skiff and heard what happened to his men. How can you even consider staying out here?"

"Corrine, this is the chance of a lifetime while the world doesn't know they exist. Once they do, these creatures will be hunted back into extinction."

"It doesn't sound like such a bad idea to me, Father. These things eat people. I have no desire to be part of the so-called last stand on the Grand Strand."

"He's right Corrine," added Chad. "Once the cat is out of the bag, these creatures will be killed."

"It saddens me to admit it, but I agree with Chadwick," spoke up Roth. "I've taken on more loses than any of you, losing five men, but this is undeniably a remarkable opportunity. We can all be part of it."

"First signs of them vanishing and we make that call…agreed? But we must find them first and I set that time limit as one hour. We don't find them by then, we make the call," said Sly.

"I'm in," said Alex.

"I don't know," whined Corrine.

"Do it for me," said Alex.

Corrine rolled her eyes and reluctantly nodded okay.

"Captain," said Frederic.

"This is Captain Joe of the Shrimp Cocktail. We have rescued the survivor of the mayday. His skiff has sunk. This person has been identified as Roth Niederwerter. He is unharmed. There is no need to send out a cutter. I repeat; all is under control."

"Very well captain. Sounds as if we should recruit you for service in the guard. This is your second rescue this week."

"Don't be giving no metals just yet but thank you just the same," said Captain Joe.

"Thank you, captain," whispered Frederic.

"I hate to break up this little love fest, but we just met your first stipulation, detective. We have company," shouted Captain Joe. "We have two…no three…make that four visitors just off our port side. Depth, 50 feet. They are holding their position. What would you like me to do?"

Ken leaned over the port side straining to see them. "I can't make a visual. It's too murky."

Without warning and with such effortless lightening speed, one of the creatures launched itself like a cruise missile to the surface and snatched Ken cleanly from the trawler. Corrine fell backwards into Alex's arms, both women landing on their butts.

Captain Joe, pale faced and mouth hanging open, eventually managed to mumble, "It happened so fast. I have never witnessed anything move like that. One minute just hovering there then…"

"It's not your fault, Joe," said Tommy. "We're dealing with science fiction here."

"Now I know how it got Ken's nephew from the Holy Grail. It just plucked him from the deck."

While everyone was preoccupied with the circus, Roth eased back inside the wheelhouse and disabled the radio by shorting it out with a bottle of water. The crackling and popping let him know he had succeeded. But for good measure, he severed the microphone cord near the bass and then tied it back together stuffing it back underneath. Reluctantly he decided he would be willing to share the spotlight with this assortment of misfits, if any of them were fortunate enough to survive the venture. Falsely making nice with his nemesis had its perks.

"All bets are off now," said Sly. "I can't stand by and bear witness to more deaths and carnage. Captain, contact the Coast Guard, please."

Captain Joe gave the hail but noticed no signal. He began turning the knob, changing frequencies, but still no signal. He noticed condensation, no, a puddle of water underneath the base. It didn't make sense.

"What's wrong Captain?"

"Detective, the radio is dead. Very queer. It is wet. Impossible."

Roth dissolved into the crowd of perplexed onlookers. Tommy ran his fingers along the radio and confirmed what Joe had said. He spotted the open bottle of water Roth had staged and picked it up. "Here you go, here's your culprit. No cap."

"Impossible," denied Captain Joe. "I always keep my water nearby and the cap secured tightly until I need to quench my thirst."

"There was a lot going on," said Chad. "Accidents do happen."

"No. I don't have accidents. Not at sea. I assure you. I replaced that cap, snug as a bug."

Chad looked around until he spotted Roth. He couldn't prove it, but suspected Roth had been responsible, but why? What could be gained from severing radio contact? What did Roth have up his sleeve? He couldn't risk taking his eyes off him now and decided to recruit a little help. He knew just the person to ask. Alex. Roth would never suspect her as a watchdog. He had to first pry her away from Corrine.

"Cell phones," shouted Corrine. "We can use our cell phone to call for help."

"Good luck," said Tommy. "Typically, we have no signals this far out."

"Nothing," sighed Corrine.

"Mine either," added Alex.

"Ditto," said Sly.

"Half a bar on mine," said Chad. "Never mind, it's gone."

"No reception," confirmed Frederic, checking his.

"I suggest we cancel this little expedition and head back to port," suggested Tommy.

"It's not our call," stated Captain Joe. "But I lean heavily in that direction too gentlemen," eyeing Frederic and Chad. "Obviously, these things are too large to capture with my vessel. Might I add, they are too many of them as well."

"We can't go back without even trying," blurted out Roth.

"Is that why you were here?"

"The Odyssey has everything we require."

"But they deserted you, remember," said Chad.

"Let's not be too hasty here. Surely, we can develop a new plan," advised Roth.

"I tend to agree to some extent," stated Frederic. "We should at least attempt to obtain photographic evidence of their existence."

"I don't exactly think these things are ready to smile for your camera," commented Sly.

"We still have the whale and dolphin distress recordings," Frederic reminded them.

"That's like ringing the dinner bell, isn't it," said Tommy. "Do we really want to do that given what we know now?"

"Excellent idea, possibly we can snare the smaller one with the nets," said Roth.

"Then what? Do you think these others are going to let us haul it back in just like that?"

"Corrine, capturing one is out of the question now," stated Chad. "Are they still there?"

"The three original ones are still huddled just off our stern at a depth of 120 feet. The new one, the largest is on the move, sort of encircling us at a depth of 60 feet," replied Captain Joe.

"Something's not right," said Chad to Frederic. "Do you think this is the male? I would have thought the female to be the larger of the species."

"I've been dwelling on that very same point, my boy," said Frederic. "Possibly this is the alpha female and those other three are just smaller females, one with an offspring. I don't envision both genders traveling as one unless breeding is involved."

"It certainly seems to be the aggressive one of the group."

"It was the big one that took Ken," confirmed Captain Joe. "And hold onto your horses it's surfacing again, this time abaft."

"Abaft, where the hell is abaft?"

"The rear of the boa, Corrine," yelled Chad.

"Everyone amidships," shouted Tommy.

"Middle, even I get that one," yelled Corrine.

The behemoth exploded to the surface landing its massive head on the stern, tilting the ship backwards at almost 45 degrees. Chad viewed the creature closer than desired, its ominous jaws as he skidded toward it, only managing to stop his plunge into those snapping jaws when he snagged a cleat. It shook its head back and forth until finally sliding back into the sea.

"New species for sure, more evolved than Liopleurodon or Kronosaurus," commented Frederic. "Serrated teeth, no doubt about it now and its neck, although thick and bulky, is much longer than either of them. Kronosaurus had more of a gator snout while Liopleurodon was like a cross between a shark and the Orca. Did you note that spiked collar at the base of its cranium? That has never been found in any of the fossils. The pigmentation, not as I suspected either."

"Black as pitch, almost seal like," stated Chad.

"A marvel," said Roth. "The world has never seen anything like this wondrous creature. Those eyes were the eyes of Satan, reddish, flaming, seductive, almost mesmerizing."

"The perfect killing machine is now in our ocean," added Chad.

"Gentlemen, we can not allow such a unique and magnificent species to be destroyed," advised Frederic. "And surely those who do not understand would do just that because it has taken the lives of men. Humanity reacts by killing what they do not understand. Man is not their main prey. We did not exist when they ruled the world."

"But what about now, Father? We are here and so are they. Our paths will continue to cross if they remain in our waters."

"Indeed, they will and have," agreed Frederic. "There only chance of survival is to return to where they lived and thrived, or they will face inhalation."

"I don't think you can force them to go back where they came from, Father."

"The best way to protect them is place them in protective custody," spoke up Roth.

"You still want to catch one, don't you?"

"I want to capture all of them," answered Roth. "How better can we protect and study them? Chadwick, what were you planning to do?"

"I admit. I became caught up in this but not anymore. Roth, even you can't be serious, now that you have seen them. Your aquarium couldn't support the smallest of the brood."

"We could construct one that could. Investors would leap at the opportunity."

"And where would you keep them until, even if we were fortunate to capture them?"

"You're consumed by details Chadwick, thinking too small as always."

"Brace yourselves mates, she's coming back. This time starboard," warned Captain Joe.

"I know, just move to the center and hold on," yelled Corrine.

"Oh crap," yelled Captain Joe. "The other two large ones are surfacing and splitting up, one at our stern and the other abreast, left side."

"Interesting behavior," whispered Chad to Frederic. "They're reacting almost pack like."

"What we're learning speaks volumes," replied Frederic. "We'll be rewriting what we once knew."

"If we survive," added Chad. "I think we may have jumped the gun on this one. What the hell were we thinking?"

"Opportunities my boy, phenomenal opportunities," answered Frederic.

"Ladies, inside the wheelhouse, pronto," yelled Chad.

Sly stood in the middle of the open deck with his revolver in hand. Roth clung to netting and waited patiently for the creatures to appear.

"All right sir. I have the handheld and will attempt to video this attack, God be willing" stated Chad.

"Our detective is not planning to use his weapon, is he?"

"Self defense, professor. This is the only gun we have on board. I don't condone shooting them but I'm more opposed to dying. We are outnumbered and outsized. We're as good as sunk if they choose to sink us."

"I believe for now that the trawler's size intimidates them," commented Frederic.

"But once they determine we are vulnerable; all bets are probably off. I think that's exactly what we're witnessing. They are feeling us out. Worse, with the taking of poor Ken, they now identify us as a food source."

Batten down and secure yourselves mates," yelled Captain Joe.

Bracing for the worse, the band of shrimp boat misfits held their breaths watching anxiously for the pending onslaught. What happened next shocked everyone. A thud, then a second, a third, none of them was hard enough to move the vessel. A fourth then a fifth ensued.

Corine whispered, "What the hell are they doing?"

"They're circling us like Indians around a wagon train and bumping the hull," whispered Captain Joe.

"Determining if the trawler is eatable," stated Chad. "They're sampling, tasting the vessel."

Alex asked, "And if it isn't, will they go away?"

A harder bump, this one moved the vessel. A second one rocked it even more.

"They're working through the equation," remarked Roth. "These creatures are more intelligent than any of us ever gave them credit. We must preserve them. It is our duty."

Chad shook his head. "You mean capture them and cash in, don't you?"

"I agree with Roth, son. This is the opportunity of a lifetime," spoke up Fredric. "It would be an injustice to allow their destruction."

"What about our destruction?" Corrine now clung to Alex.

"They're submerging, all three adults," announced Captain Joe.

"Maybe we're not so tasty after all," chuckled Tommy.

Everyone breathed a sigh of relief and began ambling about the deck. They had dodged a profoundly serious bullet. The creatures had apparently satisfied their curiosity and had gone according to the fish finder.

"What you say we head toward shore, mates?"

"Sir, is that okay with you?" asked Chad.

Frederic nodded reluctantly. Chad signaled to Captain Joe to head in.

"I can't believe you," snapped Roth. "We can't just sail away and leave them behind."

"You still think we can capture one, you damn fool. Captain, please take us to port as safely and quickly as you can."

"Best news I've heard all morning," said Sly. "I'll think long and hard about my next days off."

"What tales we'll have to share," cackled Tommy, slapping Joe on the back. "This should be worth our weight in rum." Tommy expected a quick quip from his sea mate but instead the lines on Joe's face illustrated anything but harmony and glee.

Captain Joe yelled, "They're back and they're surfacing again, all of them, brace your...."

48

Chad lay flat on his back counting the stars encircling his point of vision. Cautiously sitting up and shaking the cobwebs, he thankfully realized he remained dry and the trawler was still underneath him. He remembered little else about the past few minutes if indeed only a few minutes had expired. The back of his head ached terribly. Rubbing his hand through his hair he felt a sticky wetness, blood but not enough to appear life threatening. He took a deep breath and attempted to focus on his surroundings. His father-in-law lay motionless on his stomach just a few feet away. A puddle of blood formed beneath his upper torso.

Chad eased over on his hands and knees, crawled, and closed the distance to Frederic. He nudged him but he didn't move. "Sir, can you hear me?" No response, so he felt for a pulse. Weak but he located one. He spotted the source of the bleeding. Frederic lay on the wooden shaft of a boat hook and the hook had punctured the frontal portion of his right shoulder. He had lost considerable blood. He flipped him over and the hook dislodged itself increasing the blood flow. Chad removed his shirt and attempted to plug the hole, applying pressure to restrict the bleeding.

Glancing around Chad saw Roth entangled in the shrimp netting hanging there like a marionette's puppet. He appeared to be breathing and coming around, blinking his eyes, and turning his head. "Are you hurt?"

Focusing on his voice, Roth blinked a few more times and wiggled his fingers of both hands. "I don't think anything is broken. Do you recall what happened?"

"Obviously, we were attacked but things are a little fuzzy to me too right now."

"I know what happened. I was inquiring if you remembered."

"Not after the first few jolts from their ramming. Can you get free?"

"Don't you think I'd already be if I could? How's the old man?"

"Unconscious, trying to stop the bleeding to a wound in his shoulder," confirmed Chad.

"Let me give you a hand," said Captain Joe, emerging from the wheelhouse, shaken but apparently uninjured.

"Get Roth down first. What about the others?"

"I'm not sure. We took one hell of a pounding and rocked and rolled with vengeance. It only lasted a couple of minutes then they dove again. They are at about 20 fathoms and holding right now. That would be about 120 feet."

"Enough of the chatting, free me damn it." Within less than a minute Joe had freed him and moved on to Corrine huddled near the portside.

"Are you okay, lassie?"

"She's gone," mumbled Corrine. "She's gone. She's gone."
Sly stood a few feet away aiming his pistol toward the ocean surface. "The second jolt tossed her in the air and overboard. One snatched her up in midair like tossing a treat to a begging dog's mouth. The poor girl never had a chance. It smacked its mouth shut and disappeared, gone in one single bite. I never got off a single shot."

"Put that weapon away you stupid prick," yelled Roth. "We don't wish to kill them."

"Speak for yourself," yelled Tommy, near the stern, sporting the Shrimp Cocktail's flare gun in one hand and a boat hook in the other.

Chad sighed at the loss of Alex. It could have been a lot worse he suspected. As it stood, Frederic had been severely injured, but he had managed to stop the bleeding. Corrine appeared deeply in shock but unscathed otherwise. Everyone else just had scratches and bruises.

"Keep an eye on them captain and yell if they mount another attack," shouted Chad. "How's the trawler?"

"I haven't checked below to make sure we're not taking on water, but the engine is idling fine."

"I'll give her a look," said Tommy, making his way below.

"Soon as we have an all's clear, we'll make haste for land," stated Captain Joe. "That is if they're willing to let us."

"We absolutely can not pass on a chance to capture at least one of these magnificent creatures," fumed Roth.

"We have a man down in case you haven't noticed and two people dead on this vessel alone. Staying out here is insane and suicidal and it's not an option," yelled Sly. "I'm not really interested in your opinion or wishes, Niederwerter."

"You work for me less you forget, to serve and protect."

"And that's exactly what I'm trying to do; protect you and get you to safety before you're served up on a silver platter to our hungry guests."

"I personally know the mayor and I'll have your damn badge for this."

"Would you like to hold it right now," said Sly, retrieving it from his pocket. "It's worth nothing to me dead."

In the meantime, Chad tried to get through to Corrine. "Corrine, I'm sorry for your loss. Alexis was a wonderful person, but your father needs you now. He is injured. Please, Corrine, come with me."

Corrine stared blankly at Chad as he led her by the arm. She had only one minor cut above her left eyebrow and couple of bumps and bruises on her left thigh and forearm; nothing serious. Her worse injuries were emotional. She turned and glanced back at the ocean where Alex had disappeared and mumbled, "I used her and for that I'm so sorry."

"It's okay," responded Chad.

"It's not okay," she replied, twirling to face him. "I use everybody. I always have. I'm a selfish, self serving, self centered bitch!"

"Everyone has to be good at something," said Chad, attempting to break the mood.

"You think so too," replied Corrine, taking him seriously instead.

"Come Corrine, let's check on your father."

Frederic still lay almost motionless with only the slightest signs of his chest moving as he breathed. The blood flow had stopped but his complexion was extremely pale. Chad wasn't encouraged by his condition. Corrine squatted by his side and grasped his right hand. He felt cool to her touch. That snapped her back to life.

"Is he going to be okay?"

"He needs a doctor. We're heading to shore. Stay with him and make him comfortable."

Sly had joined Captain Joe inside the wheelhouse. Both stared intently at the screen tracking the creatures' position. Their expressions told the story.

"All right give me an update on their position," said Chad.

"The three tend to huddle just below at 80 feet and the big one continues to circle maybe 20 feet deeper, wide circles, almost like it is contemplating the next move."

"These things are much smarter than I would have ever given them credit," commented Chad. "Are we in any condition to be on our way?"

285

"I can answer that," said Tommy, poking his head from the floor hatch. "We're not presently taking on any water but we're just a couple of hits away from it. We can't take much more of this battering. The engine is fine, so I suggest you make haste, Captain Joe."

With that Captain Joe fired up the engine and set course for Georgetown harbor. As he completed his turn and headed more in a northwest direction so did the blips on the screen; the larger one racing ahead. "They're not going to make this easy on us. The big fellow is cutting us off."

Roth couldn't believe they were actually giving up, abandoning this goldmine, and leaving it potentially to someone else to reap the benefits. He had to do something to ensure these creatures stayed put and he had the perfect plan in mind, the distress call tape. He had to activate the whale and dolphin calls he had heard Chadwick and the old man mention. This would guarantee that the creatures followed them. Discreetly he began searching for the apparatus, the vessel for activating and delivering the signal. It didn't take him long to find what he was looking for, but he had to access it without anyone noticing if he expected to be successful. This required a diversion. Before he could devise one, the perfect diversion fell in his lap. The old man began wheezing and spitting up blood. That drew the attention of his fellow shipmates.

With little effort he scooped up the transmitter and underwater speaker system and eased to the rear of the trawler. He fed the line attached to the compact underwater speaker off the stern and then switched on the playback. He gathered up some loose netting and concealed the recorder-player. Roth then nonchalantly strolled back to the bridge where the others frantically worked to assist the old man.

"Something's happening," yelled Captain Joe. "Better come take a look."

Chad reluctantly left Frederic's side to the care of Sly and Corrine. There really wasn't much he could do anyway that they couldn't. Captain Joe pointed to the screen. "What do you make of that?"

The creatures had broken pattern and had fanned out. The larger one stayed just ahead of the others and now at depths varying from 20 to 30 feet. Each of the remaining two smaller ones flanked them, the smallest one trailing just behind the assumed mother. Chad swallowed. "They're hunting."

"I thought that's what they've been doing," stated Captain Joe.

"No, before they were testing us to decide if we were normal prey, edible. Even after taking Ken and Alex, they were still leery because of the trawler's size and texture. For whatever reason, they are no longer confused. This attack won't be like the others. They intend to mortally wound their prey."

"We better batten down the hatches best we can then," replied Captain Joe. "Never mind, they're bearing down on us. Brace yourselves. God be with us." Everyone but Roth heard the warning as they huddled near the wheelhouse.

Each weighing greater than 30 tons and matching the size of an adult sperm whale charged the trawler of similar length but not girth. Fortunately, they did not ram the hull from beneath, instead they broke surface and crashed starboard, stern, and port. The trawler still took a beating. The larger female's width matched the vessel's beam and she struck first at the stern, almost causing the trawler to plane. The other two females stuck starboard and aft, bobbing the vessel like a buoy. It ebbed underneath the tide manufactured by these behemoths. The old boat creaked under the pressure created by the beasts slamming it relentlessly.

Roth had been knocked to the deck on his belly and slid this way and that from each thunderous blow. He scrambled to gain a foothold but came up short. Corrine lay across her father trying to hold him in place but all for naught. The two were launched airborne, Corrine ending up underneath her father, his wound reopening and bleeding freely. The trawler held together but could not withstand a steady dose. Sly grabbing for hand holds tried to make his way to Corrine and free her from her entrapment under her father, He found himself reeling backward instead of forward and making truly little headway in her direction.

"What's got them so riled? It's like they're pissed at us," shouted Tommy.

"Hungry, they appear to be in feeding frenzy, not unlike sharks when blood is detected in the water" yelled Chad.

Captain Joe gave her full throttle attempting to bulldoze through the onslaught, but there was no bulling his way through these sea monsters. Three to one they were overpowered and outmatched. The pounding was sure to take its toll if it continued. The trawler would be torn to pieces at this rate.

"Got an idea," yelled Joe to Tommy. "Drop the nets, maybe we can confuse them."

"What if you entangle them instead," questioned Chad, hanging on for dear life.

"Then we go down sooner than latter," barked Captain Joe. "But we at least put up the good fight."

Sly had managed to reach Corrine. He flipped over Frederic, freeing her from his dead weight and dead he was, observed Sly. He had simply lost too much blood. Roth had made his way to their location, crawling like a reptile glued to the deck boards. Once Sly had dragged her back inside the wheelhouse, Roth acted evasively and dragged the old man's body to starboard. They were still under assault. Roth then hoisted him up and over the side. The creature dropped back to claim its prize, attracted by the smell of fresh blood. The other two ceased their assault hopeful of laying claim to some of the prize, a mere morsel for them at best.

Chad had witnessed the disgusting act and as soon as the boat leveled, he charged Roth, tackling him at the waist, knocking the wind from his sails. "You, worthless piece of crap," yelled Chad as he pinned Roth on his back.

"The old man bought us some time," he wheezed, just before Chad slugged him and continued to slug him until Sly pulled him off the now unconscious Roth.

"I should toss his ass overboard now," shouted Chad, still held firm by Sly.

Tommy yelled from the stern, "Mates, you better take a look at this."

"Make it fast boys, they're bearing down on us again at eleven o'clock," shouted Captain Joe. "We can't outrun or outmaneuver them I'm afraid."

"I found our problem." Chad switched off the player-recorder emitting the distress calls and retrieved the speaker from the water. "Now I know I'm going use that bastard for chum."

Sly grabbed him by the arm. "Hold on. Does this thing operate on battery?"

Chad jerked his arm free, took a deep breath and said, "It has a battery back up for short time use. What do you have in mind?"

"We toss it overboard instead of Niederwerter. It might buy us some time while they follow it instead of us."

"How about we strap it to Roth and toss both overboard."

"Is it waterproof?"

"Limited, it wouldn't survive long being submerged," he replied, taking a deep breath, while eyeing Roth still out cold.

"Got it," chimed in Tommy. "We seal her in a Ziploc, weigh her down and then toss her over."

"If we're going to do it, we better do it quick before they arrive for seconds," said Captain Joe. "They're going to be all over us in less than two minutes."

Corrine sat on the floor motionless by the captain's side, having drifted back into shock. Luckily, she had not witnessed her father being tossed overboard or it would have sent her further over the edge. Captain Joe had no time for her now though. The creatures were closing ground. He wasn't sure if the Shrimp Cocktail would survive another assault. He tried the radio again, but it was dead as a doornail. He let the microphone drop by his side and it fell to the floor. The cord had been severed. He for an instant agreed that tossing this Roth guy overboard wasn't such a bad idea.

Tommy scrambled down the galley steps, and then frantically began opening drawers and cabinets in search of a plastic bag large enough to contain the transmitter. Luck was not shinning on him as he came up empty. "There's got to be something," he mumbled.

He spotted a Tupperware cake holder turned upside down next to the refrigerator. Popping the top, he smiled when he realized Captain Joe had been using it to stash his stockpile of Nutty Buddy bars. The old sailor had a sweet tooth. Dumping the contents, he hurried back to the stern, passing a puzzled looking Captain Joe seeing him carrying the cake holder.

"We need weight," shouted Sly.

"I still say we use Roth," fumed Chad.

"Got it covered," shouted Tommy, pointing to a bin loaded with heavy lead sinkers.

"Take hold," yelled Captain Joe. "They're back."

The first ramming creature struck from the starboard side, causing both Sly and Chad to drop to their knees. "The signal is off so why are they attacking us so aggressively now?"

"Afraid not, I had to switch it back on before placing it the plastic container."

"But the speaker's not in the water," commented Sly.

"I'm sure they can still sense the calls just the same," replied Chad, as a second creature crashed into the port side.

Tommy steadily prepared the huge sinkers for anchoring the transmitter while Chad placed the transmitter inside the Tupperware enclosure and securing it with duct tape. The creatures continued the plummeting of the trawler hampering their progress.

"I've got another idea," said Sly. "Why not attach that satchel of explosives, set the timer and launch it with the transmitter."

Chad took a deep breath. "I really don't want to harm them."

"Let's face it Chad. It's either them or us and I'm really pulling for us," replied the detective.

"He's right," chimed in Tommy. "Once they devour this transmitter, they're back at us for sure. The explosion might just be a game changer. It could take one or more of them out and provide plenty of chum in the water. If they've been fed, they might cut us a break."

Chad deplored taking this course of action and if Frederic were alive, he would protest killing them too. Their survival hung by a thread and he knew it. The third creature surfaced; its head landed over the back railing. Its long gator like snout struck Tommy, sending him sprawling face first onto the deck. It moved its snapping jaws from side to side, hoping the scoop one of them up. Both Tommy and Sly managed to dive away from the three and half foot-long mouth full of razor-sharp serrated teeth. This attacker was one of the two smaller ones. Tommy righted himself and swatted it across the nose with the wood end of a boat hook. It immediately slid back into the sea, none to happy about the lick it had received.

"Stop farting around mates, lock and load this bomb, and launch it before we're all treading water in the open ocean," yelled Captain Joe.

Roth opened his eyes and propped up on his elbows. He spotted what the men were doing and grabbed the starboard side railing to right himself. In Tommy's haste, he had laid the flare gun on a crate just a few feet away from where Roth now stood. He snatched it up and aimed then yelled, "We'll not be exploding any of my sea beasts."

"I told you we should have used him for a boat anchor. I don't want to do this anymore than you do, but because of you we're as good as sunk. Where would you rather be, here or out there with them?"

"We're not killing them," shouted Roth, waving the flare gun in their direction.

The creature's appeared to Roth's right, extending its head sideways to claim its prey. In just that instance Roth was pushed to the deck by Corrine having failed to have seen the sea monster lurching over the side. Her focus had been on stopping Roth from firing the gun at the others, but Roth trigger happy finger fired the flare. The massive jaws snapped shut snagging Corrine's blouse on the serrated edges of four-inch-long teeth. Jerked backwards she pulled off a Houdini escape evasive maneuver to cast off her blouse before being yanked overboard. Luckily, her blouse had not been buttoned in the front and she had worn it over the top of her sleeveless tee shirt.

Captain Joe had not been so lucky, the flare exploded in the doorway where he stood, consuming him in a firestorm. Screaming and flailing about he did the only thing he could and flung himself overboard to save his boat from going up in a blaze. The others could only watch in dismay. Chad rushed to the edge of the railing, but the sea captain was gone just like that.

49

Sly restored order, binding Roth and then quickly returning to the task at hand, preparing the lure and explosives. Captain Tommy had taken the helm, cursing the likes of Niederwerter. For once he agreed with Chad, they should toss the bastard to the hungry sea creatures. The stench of charred flesh burned his nostrils. He would sorely miss Joe.

"Timer set," said Sly.

"Okay, let's do it," said Chad. "And hope the distress signal sounds the dinner bell."

"They're on us again. You better do it now," yelled Captain Tommy, viewing them on the finder.

Chad fed the device over the rail, allowing the line to slip through his fingers. Tommy announced it had caught their attention. They were converging, four distinctive silhouettes. The fake whales were soon 40 yards behind the boat. Sly held his watch up and began counting down from 30 seconds. Chad took a deep breath, having reached the end of the cable. Sly counted down from ten with his fingers. The ocean exploded behind them. Tommy let out a whoop from the wheelhouse, hopeful it had hit its mark.

Chad and Sly ran to view the screen. Three creatures remained in view below them. Their plan had apparently worked but had only taken out one of the smaller females. The other three were now dropping back, either dazed or confused by the explosion, figured Chad. What he didn't know was that they were feeding on chunks of their kind. Blood in the water had only put them in a frenzy state. The trawler was not out of danger yet.

"I demand you untie me," shouted Roth.

"Not a chance," yelled Detective Sylvester Stone.

"For all I care, untie him and toss him overboard. Let him tread water and pose as a distraction. It would serve him right."

"Give me a break, Chadwick. The old man was deceased. Certainly, you can't fault me for buying us some valuable time as you've so eloquently suggested."

Corrine turned to Chad. "What is he talking about? Captain Joe was not dead." In her frazzled state, she had not witnessed the event or at least had not remembered seeing her father being tossed like garbage over the side by Roth.

"Not now Corrine. We have enough on our plate. In due time I'll fill in the gaps for you."

"He was talking about my father, not the captain, wasn't he? Where is his body? I haven't seen his body. I can't remember what happened. Why can't I remember, Chad? Where is his damn body?"

"Corrine…please…trust me…this is not the right time for total recall. Please do something for us. Check the galley for anything we can use for bait."

"Bait, are you still going to try to catch one of these things?"

"Not hardly but I have a new plan."

Almost robotic like, she did as asked, still stressed that her father was gone. Where had he gone, though? Alex, sweet Alex was gone too. Find bait. Yes, that's what she must do.

"Let's hear this new plan," inquired Sly.

"It's a long shot but we're running out of options." He then explained what he had in mind.

Corrine returned as the two men huddled near amidships. She retrieved a wadded up piece of paper stuffed in her bottoms and read, "A pork roast, maybe four or five pounds of burger, a whole chicken and a couple of packs of boneless pork chops; oh yeah, and three cans of Spam and five cans of Vienna sausage, and plenty of potted meat, whatever the hell that's supposed to be. Now, tell me about my father. Where's the body?"

"They're on the move again and trailing us, closing ground," yelled Captain Tommy.

"Are we wide open?"

"Joe might have been able to squeeze another knot or two out of her, but I got her doing all she'll do. This baby was not built for speed. She's a workhorse. Now Tommy's Girl, she could motor along."

"What's happening? You cannot just bind me like this. It's inhumane."

"Can it," snapped Sly.

"Sly, please assist Corrine and gather the provisions from the galley. We may need that other diversion very shortly."

"Why do they keep chasing us and just where the hell did these nightmares come from?"

"Sly, unfortunately, Frederic was the expert on these matters. "I'm a marine biologist. I deal with known living and breathing oceanic creatures. I'm familiar with endangered species but not extinct ones."

"If you ask me, we're tops on that endangered list right now," sounded off Sly.

Chad bit his lip and nodded.

"Me and my stupid intuitions," sighed Sly, heading towards the galley. "Take a day off and go to the dock and snoop around, great idea detective. I don't even like fishing or seafood."

"I for one am glad you are following your gut," said Chad. "You stopped that guy from blowing us up."

"That's it," said CaptainTommy. "I don't think we can hold this speed for very long without her protesting. Make the best of it, men. Looks like they are just off starboard, 135 feet deep but definitely trailing us now. The big one is leading the way."

"I don't suppose we have any arsenic or some sort of tranquilizers on board, do we?"

"Well, she's not my vessel but I wouldn't count on it, lad. We could sure use a good harpoon."

Corrine and Sly arrived from the galley carrying a gunny sack. "All right, everything we could find is in here," stated Sly.

"Even that mushy potted meat," added Corrine. "Who in their right mind would eat this crap?"

"Southern cuisine my dear sister-in-law," answered Chad.

"Hey, don't put that off on me," protested Sly. "I'm a southerner and I don't even eat Spam or Treat or mountain oysters or chicken feet. I'm sure I could name a lot more. I'm steak, well done with baked potatoes, loaded."

"What do you have in mind with all this stuff? Given the size of those things I don't think this would qualify as an appetizer."

"Corrine, do me one more favor," said Chad. "Check the first aide or any cabinets that may contain medicine. Bring me anything you can find."

Sly asked, "What now, you want to drug them?"

"Be honest with you, I'm flying by the seat of my pants and grabbing at any straws. I'm open for ideas if you have any. Remember what Captain Joe said, rest his soul, this ship can't take another beating."

"Well look on the bright side, they're only three of them now," pointed out Sly.

"But the biggest bad ass on the block is still out there," said Chad. "Frederic said Liopleurodon was the most fearsome predator to terrorize the Jurassic seas 150 million years ago. I remember him saying that if this pack leader was upwards of 60 feet then it could possess a ten-foot-long jaw and enough bite to crush a granite slab. You have seen what I've seen. These things are definitely a relative or revolutionized version of that creature and now they're alive and hungry in our ocean."

"Sounds to me this is no longer a save the whale speech," remarked Sly.

"Sadly, it quit being that once it plucked poor Ken from among us," confirmed Chad.

"And Niederwerter still has the notion we can capture and transport one to a destination to be determined."

"And that's why his ass is still tied up where he can't act on those idiotic assumptions," smiled Chad.

"The worse case scenario we go down with the sinking ship. Do you want me to untie him?"

"If that happens, I don't think it much matters. It might be more humane not to untie the bastard, but let's not cross that bridge just yet and jeopardize jinxing our pathetic situation."

Corrine returned. "I found these," she said, dumping the contents.

Chad read aloud the bottle labels "Tylenol, Ambient, Darvocet, Valium, Sominnex, Caritin, BC Powders and Viagra; quite an assortment Captain Joe kept on board. I don't think even if we mixed them all together, we could come up with a concoction that would do us much good."

"Sorry, that's all I could dig up," said Corrine. "The Valium is mine."

Captain Tommy announced, "Gargantuan is directly below us now no deeper than 10 fathoms."

"Fathoms?" squinted Corrine. "Please cut the sailor boy lingo. Speak English."

"Sixty feet, one fathom equals six feet."

"Aye, aye, sir," she saluted. "Just say 60 feet next time, how about it? You guys still haven't told me about my father's body."

"It's overboard," Chad finally gave up and admitted.

"Burial at sea?"

"Damn it, Corrine. I wish you'd stop pressing this," snapped Chad.

"Fifty feet," yelled Captain Tommy.

"Why don't you go ask Niederwerter," blurted out Sly, Chad giving him the evil eye for doing so.

Corrine looked over at Roth. "What does he have to do with it?"

"Less than 30 feet. Everyone better brace themselves," warned Captain Tommy.

"Tommy, can these nets be set free manually?"

"I'm not a shrimper, so I'm not exactly sure, but I bet we can cut them free if need be. What do you have in mind?"

"Can you leave your post for a few minutes?"

"I'd feel better if we idol her down a bit before I do."

"Then do it and come on out. Make it pronto please. Our visitors are definitely back."

Chad gathered the troops, minus Roth and spelled it out. "Here's my plan. We bait the nets with the assortment of meats, launch them, and then just before the creatures take the bait, cut them loose and pray for a miracle that they become hopelessly entangled."

"And if it works, it buys us the time to get the hell out of here," added Sly.

"Not perfect but it's the best I can come up with," stated Chad.

"What about the drugs," asked Corrine.

"Hell, toss them in for all I care," replied Chad.

"Best act now," said Captain Tommy, pointing to the blips on the screen.

"Corrine, you man the wheel. Tommy we'll need your help."

"You really want a female at the wheel," she grinned.

"Just hold it steady and straight, gal. You'll do just fine as a first mate."

"Like this," she illustrated, grabbing the wheel.

"Perfect," he replied.

Chad interrupted, "Gents snap too. Let's get this party started. They are bearing down on us. One has already surfaced behind us."

"Set me free. I can assist," pleaded Roth, as they passed him on deck.

"You can assist by climbing inside one of these damn nets," blasted Chad. "Save it for someone who gives a rat's ass."

"Don't insult the potted meat by allowing him to share their net," exclaimed Sly.

"One more thing," mentioned Chad. "I want to mount the underwater camera on the cable just before the netting. I may never get another opportunity to film one of these things."

"I certainly hope that will be as up close and personal as it gets for your Kodak moment," replied Sly.

Before they could complete their tasks, they were slammed from beneath, the creature crashing into the hull, the jolt knocking them off their feet. Scrambling back up, they began planting the meaty morsels inside the netting and securing the camera. Seconds later Chad gave the okay for Captain Tommy to launch the trawl nets.

Chad had not paid much attention to the net's configuration until now but remembered the nickel tour offered by Captain Joe just before they departed the port. The conical bag-like trawl net was connected by lines to what he remembered Captain Joe calling doors. The doors were connected by lines to the mouth of the net. Bridles controlled the angle of the doors and regulated the spread of the net's mouth and these kept the trawl on the ocean bottom. He examined the trawl bridles and how they independently operated the towlines that connected the net to the vessel. Other lines at the mouth served as weights to keep the net on the bottom. Floats added buoyancy. Joe had said the floats tickled the little shrimp from the ocean floor and into the awaiting net. That was shrimpin-101 as he recalled it.

"Earth to Chad, come in," said Sly, noticing that his sea mate had drifted off into la-la land.

He snapped out of it to the whining sounds of the winch lowering the net. The irritated sea monster rocked the vessel again. They clung to whatever they could to remain upright on the deck, all but Roth and he sat, still bound, and cursing them for all his worth.

Chad rushed to the wheelhouse where Corrine held the wheel on course and steady. He eyed the blobs on the fish finder's screen. They had not yet taken the bait. The behemoth was still directly below and the other two were trailing just a few yards behind it. The footprint on the screen indicated the apex predator did indeed appear to exceed 60 feet, possibly if 70 feet. The other might reach 30 or less, and then the small one had to be a youngster. Chad held firm to his belief that neither of the larger ones were males, just gut instinct. The camera recorded only bubbles and net.

"The net is out 40 feet and holding," yelled Captain Tommy.

"Still no nibbles," Chad returned the shout. "They're shadowing us."

"They must not be fond of potted meat either," shouted Sly.

"Hold it. Looks like the smaller one is dropping back," announced Chad, looking like a spectator at a tennis match, attempting to view the fish finder and laptop's screen.

Suddenly the winch began screaming from the additional weight and the trawler was jerked from one side to the other, the engines laboring against the monster's force. "Appears that Nessie number two is entangled in the net," yelled Captain Tommy.

Chad stared in amazement as he did indeed get his first look at the entire mass of the evolved Liopleurodon. The sleek black body was almost camouflaged with a broken pattern of lighter gray. The long thick teeth studded jaws were those of a supreme hunter. Massive flippers were perfect for propelling the beast effortlessly. It resembled some sort of freak mutation, a cross between a shark and orca with a splattering of crocodile thrown in for good measure. At better than 25 feet in length, it made a great white appear no more intimidating than a bottlenose dolphin. It must have weighed better than 15 tons and this was the smaller of the adults.

Chad continued to stare at the computer, oblivious to the escalating events. The more the creature struggled, the more it became hopelessly entangled. The larger one had dropped back sensing the smaller version in distress. The calve trailed the net. Suddenly it came into view on camera. Chad dropped his jaw at the shear size when compared to the one in the net. The camera didn't do it justice. It began snapping at the net attempting to free the smaller version of itself, a most intriguing and stunning reaction for reptilian type creatures.

Captain Tommy broke the silence. "The net, we've got to set it free, lads, or we're going to be towed under!"

"Screw those nets," yelled Roth. "Set me free, I beg of you."

Chad sighed, not wanting to end the scene playing out before him. He finally took a deep breath and yelled, "Do it."

Sly reached for the ax, but the much larger Nessie had changed strategy and now charged the trawler. The impact on the vessel's stern threw him sideways and onto the deck. The snared creature wreaked havoc on the net and the trawler. The engine began smoking and grinding but no one was below to witness the carnage taking place. They had their hands full battling the two sea serpents, one caught in the net and the other serving as a battering ram. Sly made a second attempt to grab the ax but instead was almost catapulted overboard. Chad seeing the dilemma unfold deserted his post to intervene. He hustled for hand and foot holds as the monster relentlessly attacked from just below the stern.

Captain Joe had been dead on; the old trawler could not withstand repeated punishment. The weakening steel hull gave way to tiny breaches spurting water. The engines continued to labor against the tugging Liopleurodon hybrid entangled in the net and its behemoth counterpart's ferocious bombardments. Chad scooped up the ax, but before he could take his first swing, the gigantic Liopleurodon's head slammed down over the railing on the port side, jaws snapping for any human morsel in its reach. Chad missed his opportunity to land on the menu by mere inches, tucking and rolling like an acrobat, dropping the ax out of his reach. He needed no photographs to remember these images.

Corrine screamed but no one heard her except Roth. "What the hell are you boys doing back there? I can't hold on to this damn wheel. This heap is freewheeling so much that it's about to break both my arms. Do something please or come in here and take over. There's smoke coming from below. We're screwed. I just know it!"

"Free me. I can help her," shouted Roth, his pleas falling on deaf ears.

Captain Tommy wrestled with the winch, losing the tug of war battle. Both Chad and Sly had regained their sea legs and simultaneously reached for the ax. Chad gave way to Sly still trying to avoid the mammoth head and jaws seeking retribution for imprisoning the other creature in the net. Sly held the ax over his head aiming carefully while he still could. His attempt missed the mark, grazing the cable and succeeded in only frazzling some of the twisted cable strands.

Corrine losing the battle at the helm fought off fatigue, exhaustion, and injury opportunities. She became more frantic by the minute, viewing the monster in the net blotting out the laptop screen and the continued smoke spiraling from somewhere below. To compound matters, the engines began to sputter. She screamed again for help but as before none arrived. Roth was still furious about his captivity. He sat helplessly mesmerized by the scene unfolding before his eyes. Selfishly he pulled for the magnificent creature to pluck Chadwick from the deck. He watched as his nemesis narrowly escaped the sharply serrated chomping teeth snapping to claim its prey. Another of the Liopleurodon had been netted and if he had overseen this cluster, he would have secured it and towed it in. He wasn't sure what these dumb asses had in mind for the trapped creature. All he could do for non was sit here and take it all in and wait for an opportunity to change the game. A second then a third chop with the ax had been delivered by Sly, but he had not succeeded in severing the winch cable. He had landed on his butt between tries. "Let me give it a try," shouted Chad, pulling the ax from his grip.

Two swats split more twisted strands. The third, the charm, the cable snapped and twanged overboard. No longer needed at the winch, Captain Tommy rushed to the wheelhouse to relieve Corrine. He smelled the engine smoke before he saw it and recognized the source immediately.

"You got her girl," he said, nodding to the wheel.

"I have now," she responded, no longer fighting control for the wheel with the netted creature now released.

Captain Tommy plunged below and was greeted with ankle deep water. He throttled down the smoldering engines before searching for the source of the invading water. Four tiny leaks pissed streams of sea water into the innards of the trawler. He had expected much worse. He could deal with these tiny punctures. He engaged the bilge pump. It should easily stay ahead of the incoming ocean. Captain Tommy returned to the engines to inspect for damage. Not an expert on the trawler's mechanism, he still felt rather good that they should power them home safely, providing the serpents from hell let them be here on out. He climbed topside and spotted Chad at the helm, having relieved an exhausted Corrine. He gave him the short version of the damages.

"The large Liopleurodon has disappeared off the screen, probably trailing the netted one. Hopefully, this has bought us our time. Give me what you can and let's get the hell out of here," Chad informed the new captain and heir to the Shrimp Cocktail.

50

It had been an hour since they had successfully netted the smaller Liopleurodon hybrid and so far, there had been no signs of the giant version. That had been wonderful news for the worn-out remaining crew of the Shrimp Cocktail. However, the bad news, they had been idle in the water for the better part of that hour. Previously undetected hull punctures had seeped more water into the lower compartments. Captain Tommy had shut off the engines temporarily to avoid water damage as he attempted to stay ahead of the rising water. It was now almost knee deep near the stern.

Corrine monitored the fish finder and kept a weary eye on Roth who had been set free. Chad figured without the nets; Roth could no longer wreak havoc insisting they must capture one of the creatures. Common sense said this was an impossibility given their shear size. So far Roth had played it low key and had offered no resistance, but on the other hand, he had contributed very little either. He sort of stood watch, a self-imposed duty, scanning the ocean for any signs of his beloved creatures.

Chad and Sly worked feverously to develop a plan B just in case the Liopleurodon returned. So far this consisted of fabricating harpoons from the boat hooks; neither overly confident that they would work affectedly. Chad had too much time to think about the losses of his father-in-law, the renowned Frederic Bornfreund, and former British Playboy model Alexis Clarke. She had been so smitten by his sister-in-law Corrine. It appeared they had mended their fences just before she had been taken by one of the resurrected extinct sea serpents. He struggled through the thoughts of breaking this news to Teal and his wife Liz. Then there was Captain Joe and Ken. Both would most likely still be alive if not for he and Frederic charting the old shrimp trawler for this ill-equipped suicide mission. Why hadn't he left well enough alone? He was on vacation and this was none of his business. Too much like his mother, he could not turn his back on the discovery of a lifetime and for what…four people dead and they were certainly not out of the woods yet.

The cell phones still had no signals meaning their survival rested on their shoulders. Chad's shoulders were feeling the strain, not convinced that the Liopleurodon had abandoned their wounded prey. If they remained floating aimlessly, they would be sitting ducks on the pond.

Sly broke the silence. "And you still have no clue where these things have been hiding?"

"Big ocean but my bet is still on the Puerto Rico Trench. It's deep enough for their species to survive undetected, but it still doesn't explain why they've remained there until now. What drew them to the Carolina Coast instead of the Caribbean Islands? I still think that early season Cat 5 Hurricane Hilda that careened through the Caribbean's open waters had something to do with their appearance."

"It might have been the key to opening the deep's Pandora's Box," spoke up Roth. "But I think our coast is an ancient spawning ground. Fossil evidence points to the Megalodon preferring nursery sites in coastal waters. That's why so many tooth fossils have been discovered in the Intracoastal Waterway, specifically in South Carolina and Georgia. As you are certainly aware Chadwick, many of these teeth belonged to juveniles."

"Explain, Roth, if that's the case, wouldn't Liopleurodon have been making frequent visits here before now? Encounters with man would have been prevalent."

"Your hurricane theory holds some merit. Let's purpose our creatures have survived and thrived in the Puerto Rico Trench, secluded in some unknown and confined abyss and dear Hilda somehow disturbed their little haven, possibly disrupting their food chain or opening the door to Pandora's Box literally. Possibly once they surfaced primal urges imbedded in their genes drove them to the coast."

"We're grabbing at straws. Without extensive studies we can be certain of nothing."

"We can be certain they are here, alive and well, unless you're driven to destroy them."

"Roth, I had no intent in harming them. Frederic and I wished to study them, possibly capture one for scientific purposes. Unlike you, we had no interest in profiting from their captivity. We sadly underestimated their size, numbers, and furiousness of their primal instincts. Our survival hinged on us fighting back. Destroy them or perish, pretty damn simple math."

"Possibly we can still accomplish this, Chadwick."

"Sly, gag and tie him back up before he has a chance to spew senseless garbage from that pie hole of his."

"Please hear me out. We can lure them into the coastal waterway using whale recordings. I shall have my men there with tranquilizers. Once subdued and contained, I offer use of my aquarium where we can indeed study them. We'll share the discovery."

"You're one delusional bastard, aren't you? You've seen how large these creatures are and what they're capable of and you still think you can corral one. You tried using the recordings and almost got us killed in the process."

"Look around you," added Sly. "This boat couldn't outrun them on its best day. And right now, we're taking on water and barely keeping the engines from being flooded. You switch on that whale dinner bell and we are as good as dead. How about this. We give you a life ring, toss you overboard and tow you behind as bait."

"That was my original suggestion hours ago. I just wasn't planning on wasting a life ring."

"This is an opportunity of a lifetime, gentlemen," stated Roth, as he fell to his knees.

Corrine stood behind him waving a boat paddle. "You worthless piece of crap. I remembered. That's right. I remembered how you threw my father's body overboard. I'm all for letting you tread water, or stay on board and I'll bash you brains in." She lifted the paddle for a second swat, but Chad stepped over Roth and grabbed it.

"He's not worth a murder rap, Corrine."

"Who'll know? He'll just be one more casualty of those freaking monsters out there."

"I'll know and off duty or not, I'm still a police officer; not that he's really worth saving."

"Give me the oar," pleaded Chad.

She reluctantly handed it over to him, but not before she kicked Roth in the rib cage for good measure.

"Watch your back, asshole."

"Keep your crazy sister-in-law away from me Chadwick."

"Or what?" Corrine stood defiant.

"Or you'll be joining your father," replied Roth, grabbing her by her ankle and flipping her on her backside.

With that, Chad jerked him up by his shirt collar and to his feet. He then tossed him toward the railing. He held him firmly two thirds hanging over the side. Sly didn't try to intervene. "You pull crap like that again and I'll be the one to toss you overboard. I'll make sure our fine detective doesn't witness you slipping and losing your footing."

"I certainly can't be held accountable for accidents. Those sort of things happen and aren't a criminal offense," added Sly, pretending to look the other way.

Chad jerked him back and then slugged him with a left hook, sending him sprawling on deck, nose, and mouth bleeding. "I should have never untied you. You mess with us again and I will personally tie you up and tow you behind us in a life raft. What happens then will just be left up to chance."

Roth, fuming, wiped the blood from his face with his shirt tail but remained quiet this time realizing the numbers were not in his favor. Chadwick and this woman would pay. He would make good on that promise. He eyed the detective's pistol. Once he had it, the odds would shift his way. The bitch would be the first to tread water.

51

The huge female circled her entangled counterpart, the smaller female resting on the ocean bottom, unable to free herself from the shrimp boat's nets. The circling Liopleurodon hybrid's senses were being stimulated by the younger female's stressful situation and the luring scent of bait contained inside the netting. Cannibalism among their kind not uncommon, the weaker often supplemented the nourishment to ensure the survival of their species.

The calf hung close to the net, helpless with its mother's confinement. Without warning the oceans gargantuan struck, snagging the youngster in its jaws, devouring it in large chunks. The entrapped female recognized the huge one's aggressive behavior and struggled to get free, but the net only tightened its grip. Her sibling and offspring had already perished. She had shared earlier in her sister's shredded remains. Unless she somehow freed herself, she would meet the same fate. Seventy feet long, three times her length, the giant swam above her, gliding like a seal as she darted near the netting and then away, becoming more stimulated by the situation.

The younger female, in early stages of her pregnancy, would not conceive this litter as had her sister. The Liopleurodon hybrids sexually matured within their first three years, evolution paving the way, postponing their extinction. If given the opportunity she would have tripled her size over the next five years and most certainly have birthed a litter of pups every other year. Unfortunately, she would never see her first offspring fighting for their place in the ranks. Swiftly, the seventy-foot behemoth delivered the deadly bite, diving from above, engulfing the head of the trapped female, the only portion of her torso protruding from the netting. Blood gushing into her mouth and down her throat sent the behemoth into a feeding frenzy, much like those displayed by sharks. She ripped and tore at the lifeless body through the netting snagging large portions of flesh until the creature no longer resembled their kind. Momentarily getting her fill, she remained close by, protecting her prize. No challengers appeared. This new ocean belonged to her.

52

Chad had gotten an update from Captain Tommy. The news had not been good. More leaks had sprung in the hull. While none of them were exceptionally large, combined they were overwhelming the bilge pump. It was losing the battle to contain the encroaching sea. While he had slowed down its march toward the engines, thus far Tommy had not been able to successfully contain or corral the rising water. Corrine and Sly had joined the battle, utilizing anything at their disposal to mount a blockade, garments, life jackets, rags, and assortment of sundries from the galley. The sea refused to be denied its prize.

Chad gave the command. "Fire up the engines and let's get as far as we can. How long before they're flooded?"

"At this rate, less than 30 minutes of running time before we're kaput; if we're lucky," replied Captain Tommy. "Give me a few minutes and I'll shout when all is ready."

Chad dreaded the next question even more. "How long before we…"

"From skillet into the fire," stated Roth, "Chadwick, what's your ingenious plan for saving us now? Being a leader tests one's fortitude, doesn't it?? But then again, leader isn't on your resume, is it?"

"Okay, so we don't like one another, Roth, I get it. Another time how about it? Right now, we best collectively do what we can to prevent the inevitable."

"Poor Chadwick, spouting the inevitable validates your admission of defeat," smiled Roth. "I'd suggest you not show your fear to the others if you value their continued support and wish to dispel outcries of a mutiny."

"Until you're ready to contribute something constructive, you can stick a sock in it, Roth."

"Profound statement your lordship," mocked Roth.

"One question if you are capable of responding honestly; what did you do with that dolphin? The one that survived the beaching?"

Roth smiled, reminiscent of the Cheshire Cat toying with Alice. "You so caringly nurtured the poor mammal, didn't you? You held it to your bosom as your very own, while the others died around you. Did you think yourself God like, choosing the single dolphin that should live another day over those less fortunate? Saving it changes what? The dolphin made a conscious suicidal decision rather than face death delivered by the jaws of the Liopleurodon. The creature possessed logic, reasoning out the lesser of the two evils and you interfered. You always interfere, Chadwick. Why is that? Your dolphin is dead. It died only moments later. You have no special gift, no divine powers for resurrecting the dead or saving souls. You are less than mortal and have always been a mere pimple on my ass; no more. This is just another example of your pathetic behavior. Your friends face certain death and you fret over a dolphin." Roth embraced the lie, making Chadwick think that the dolphin had died, knowing it had even survived the saboteur's attempt to contaminate the aquarium. Chadwick would never be privy to that information.

Chad sighed, unsure why the dolphin's survival held so much importance, except for the game. Roth had won again. Evil over good had prevailed. Why worry about a dead dolphin now? He had to focus on the lives of those on board the floundering trawler. Like the trickling of sand in an hourglass, time did not weigh in their favor. Whether the Liopleurodon returned or not it didn't really alter their situation. It just added another twist to their fate. Making it to shore safely in the inflatable raft with a small horse powered motor did pose a challenge, but it offered a better option than merely floating on the open sea in life vests.

"Roth, you and I will prepare the raft if you have no objections."

"And if I do," responded Roth.

"Feel free to stay on the trawler and fulfill your fantasies. Catch one of these magnificent creatures with your bare hands."

"Testy, aren't we?"

"Look Roth, we keep beating this same dead horse. You don't like me. I don't like you, but circumstances have placed us both in a very vulnerable spot with potentially deadly consequences. Frankly, I'm tiring of your bullshit. We can have a knock down drag out if you want, but let's continue this after we've reached the safety of land. How about it…truce?"

"Sleeping with the enemy for the greater good, you're so predictable, Chadwick. Have it your way. We will tolerate one another until we set foot on shore, but I have but one request before I agree."

"And that would be…"

"We wipe the slate clean this very moment. Anything that has occurred up until now on this vessel remains between us, no lawsuits, no criminal accusations, no retribution for any acts. Do I make myself clear?"

"So, I'm expected to forget how you almost got us all killed, summoning the creatures to attack us without our acknowledgment or permission? I'm supposed to wipe the slate clean, free you from incarceration and the conviction for Captain Joe's death? I'm supposed to just erase the fact that you tossed Frederic Bornfreund's body overboard, treating him like common chum to keep your monsters interested in us as quarry? I'm supposed to forget how you've single handily put us in jeopardy for the sake of the 'all mighty' dollar and chance at fame and fortune? Oh yeah, and you hired someone to blow us out of the water. Not to mention that you are obsessed with ruining my life at any price. Your deal is too pricey I'm afraid. Here's plan B. Stay the hell out of my way, or I will toss you overboard without a preserver. That's no threat. It's a promise. You will rot in jail for the grief you have inflicted on my family and this community."

"Sounds all too personal to me," smiled Roth, never flinching. "Then best we prepare the escape pod and duel this to the bitter end later as you have requested, Chadwick."

"Corrine, I need you to man the wheel please. Are you ready yet, Tommy?"

"We have a bit of a problem. The water is rising faster than expected. This vessel continues to spring leaks and interesting enough it's forming a bite pattern, a very large bite mark. What do these things have, titanium teeth?"

"Can you not stop any of them, plug them with something?"

"Detective Stone has found a caulking gun and is attempting that task as we speak."

"And…" inquired Chad.

"Give us a few minutes and I'll let you know."

"What about the engines?"

"We'll know that in a few minutes too because if our detective can't cork these tooth holes, we're done for, engine will be flooded."

"We're readying the raft. Do what you can."

"We're doing just that."

"We're pretty much screwed, aren't we?"

"Corrine, don't put us down for the count so soon. We're not that many miles offshore and we do have the raft. Once we maneuver closer to shore and have phone signals, we can call the Coast Guard."

"And what if those things come back, then what?"

"Let's tackle one catastrophe at a time," smiled Chad.

"Where's that bastard Roth?"

"He's preparing the raft as a contingency plan."

"I can now understand why you dislike him so. That sonofabitch is going to pay for what he's done."

"I agree whole heartily. I've told him as much."

"I'm worried about Mother. This is going to devastate her. She's been so dependent on him."

"Your father was a great man. Teal is stronger than any of you give her credit."

"And sis," she said, trying to fight back the tears.

"Liz will step it up for your mother as will I."

"Why do you suppose Robert chickened out?"

"I hate to give him credit, but your brother came out of this like a bandit by not joining in on the fun."

"I wouldn't be so quick to underestimate Robert Bornfreund," interrupted Roth. "Your brother is quite ambitious and self serving."

"What's that supposed to mean?"

"Young Daniel Webster had his price, bartered his soul with the devil so to speak," chuckled Roth.

"If you have something to say, cough it up," demanded Corrine.

"Chadwick critiqued me for my lustful tendencies for fame and fortune. It seems those roots grow deeply amongst your flesh and blood, dear."

"What are you implying?"

"Your brother is a turncoat, willing to cannibalize his own for the sake of the mighty dollar and celebrity stature. He posed as my insider."

"What the hell are you saying?"

"Paid informant," smiled Roth. "He was a mole, my dear. How does that quaint expression go; he tossed you under the wheels of the bus."

Corrine took a swing at Roth, but he blocked it with a forearm. "Please, refrain from assaulting the messenger, my dear. Save your energy and frustration for brother dearest. He sold you out. Blood is not thicker than water it appears."

"Where's Bobby now?"

"The spineless bastard is on the Odyssey, my exploration vessel, with my captain and his mutinous crew."

"The mighty Roth Niederwerter lost command of his vessel," laughed Chad. "Now that's just priceless. What prompted that?"

"It doesn't concern you. My lawyers shall reconcile the matter."

"Could it be that they had no taste for your ruthless ways, and they decided to cut their loses. Priceless, they deserted you, didn't they?"

"Chad, we may have a temporary reprieve," hailed Captain Tommy.

"Talk to me, Tommy."

"We had enough caulking material for the detective to plug about half the holes. It's given the bilge pump a fighting chance. We're gaining some ground over the incoming sea."

"Wonderful news, how soon can we be on our way?"

"Ready when you are," he replied.

"Chad," screamed Corrine.

Chad's heart dropped at the sight of Roth now in the water with the raft, the rat deserting the sinking ship. He smiled and waved.

"Captain, fire them up," commanded Chad.

"Are you going after that asshole?"

"Sort of, we're heading the same direction; toward shore, but I doubt if he has enough fuel to make it. We do if we keep the engines afloat."

"I say we run him over then," demanded Corrine.

"Let's not stoop to his level just yet," replied Chad.

Sly had joined them on deck, pistol drawn. "Just say the word and I can probably put a couple of holes in that escape craft."

"Tempting but save your ammunition for something more worth while."

Sly holstered his weapon. "Bringing him up on charges might even be better."

"Houston, we have a problem," butted in Corrine.

53

The Liopleurodon ceased her feeding. Its alerted senses detected the vibrations emitted by the trawler's engines. Territorial instincts now engaged. An intruder threatened her kill and she must fend it off. She and the pod had previously encountered the adversary with the tough hide. It had been a worthy opponent. She had ripped morsels of flesh from it and would do so again to protect what belonged to her. She would not share her kill. Homing in on the odd but exhilarating sounds she plotted her return course.

She closed the gap quickly. It had hardly moved from where she had last launched her attack. It moved slowly but loudly now treading much water in its wake. Swimming 100 feet below she circled, measuring the odd creature's underbelly, remembering how tough it had been to grab its slippery hide. Her most successful attacks had occurred from the surface. There she had plucked fleshy chunks from the wounded creature. Oddly, she sensed no blood from the wounds. This did not deter her from her primal urges to attack.

Another odd sound distracted her, smaller and moving ahead of the larger prey. She continued to shadow the larger one while utilizing her senses to examine the tinier creature splashing in the ocean. She decided the larger one posed more of a challenge and ignored the whining sounds, focusing on the creature laboring above her instead. She had only a brief history with this odd creature, so she cautiously observed it, searching for any signs of weakness. No fins or flippers or legs extended from its bulky torso making it a formidable foe to grasp. She sped along waiting for just the right moment to attack.

"They're back," announced Corrine, pointing to the screen.

Chad sighed, "It's the mother lode, the seventy-footer. I'd recognize that blip anywhere. She's alone this time."

"Is there no end to this? I feel as if we're the doomed cast of Jaws 5 in 3D." Corrine watched the screen fearing the inevitable.

"Captain Tommy, we have company. Big and bad is back and directly underneath us. She is mirroring our speed. Is this all the vessel will do?"

"I can squeeze a little more out of her but matters little. We can't outrun your sea serpent."

Corrine posed the question, fearing the response, "Do you think it will attack us again?"

"I'm certain it's not sightseeing down there," replied a watchful Chad.

"Why doesn't it go after the raft?"

"Sly, it might be that we intimidate it more or possibly it views us as a larger meal ticket. Everyone stay in the wheelhouse. No one on deck where it can pluck us off like ripe grapes on the vine."

Sly asked, "Shouldn't we warn Niederwerter?"

"Hell no," spoke up Corrine. "Let him try to round up his prize with that motorized raft."

"Unless Captain Joe has a megaphone stashed around here, we have no method of hailing him anyway. Besides, we're not gaining on him. He made his bed. We have our own issues to deal with and it is 70 feet long, packing plenty of tonnage and a mouthful of razor-sharp teeth."

"Niederwerter foiled plan B by stealing the raft. I don't suppose you have a plan C up your sleeve, do you, Chad?"

"I'm fresh out of ideas. What about you, Sly?"

"I'd just like to live to tell my grandkids about this."

"You have grandchildren."

"Not yet. I hope to live long enough to have a bushel of them though," he smiled.

"Funny, I never thought much about Liz and I having kids until now. I might just have to work on that when we get back."

"Welcome to Romper Room," chuckled Corrine. "Me, I have no desire to squeeze out any bratty little rug rats and ruin this perfect body. I may just stick with women from here on out though. Less wear and tear."

Sly and Chad both burst into laughter. They needed any form of stress relief right now. Short lived unfortunately. The blip on the screen had risen to within 60 feet of them.

"What about some sort of oil or fuel slick," suggested Sly. "Could that possibly discourage our friend from paying us another visit?"

"Not a bad idea," said Chad, patting him on the back. "It might leave a bad taste in that crocodilian mouth."

"Okay then I'll…."

"Crap! Hold on! She's surfacing and coming up on the port side," yelled Captain Tommy. "It's better portside than from below. The hull's not going to survive another pounding. You mates stay low and away from the rails."

Sly propped in the doorway, holding his pistol in a two-handed grip. "Just maybe I can nail it a few times and make it think twice about attacking us."

"Aim for its eyes. Maybe you can blind it," encouraged Chad.

"Good thinking, the eyes it is," replied Sly, as the creature's enormous head appeared at port, just ahead of the wheelhouse doorway.

Resting its head over the rail, its sheer weight caused the trawler to list heavily portside. Corrine unprepared for the maneuver found herself airborne and crashing into the portside wheelhouse window. Glass shattered around her as she covered her face with her forearms. Chards of glass now embedded in her arms bled profusely. Luckily, none severed a major artery, but her wounds were serious. The bone in her left wrist had shattered, forearm broken. Two fingers on her right hand were bent in the wrong direction. She lay on the floor unable to right herself. Just as well, the creature continued to rock the boat with vengeance, head crashing down repetitively. Down below several chunks of the caulking had given way. Water spurted from the reopened wounds. Captain Tommy suddenly had his hands full monitoring the water, maintaining the engine, and bouncing off the walls from the thumping being inflicted by the attacking Liopleurodon.

Top side, Sly tried to steady his aim but firing at those demon eyes proved to be a challenge on unsteady legs. As previously advised by Chad, he tried to use his ammo wisely. Restlessly the creature bumped the side of the trawler and leaned its head over the side snapping at anything within its grasp. Chad manning the wheel held on for dear life, finding it extremely difficult to maintain a true course. Corrine still lay in a heap at his feet. He was in no position to offer her help, caught in mortal combat with the deep sea monster.

Sly timed his shot between the creatures jerking head movements. He squeezed the trigger and his bullet harmlessly ricocheted off the creature's long snout. He had missed just an inch in front of the eye he had targeted before being tossed off balance again. The second shot hit its brow, another glancing blow. The Liopleurodon appeared undisturbed by both, which highly perturbed the detective. Taking a much wider than normal stance and leaning his back against the doorway, Sly fired a third time. This time hitting pay dirt. The orb exploded and the enraged creature disappeared. The attack had ended abruptly. Sly yelled triumphantly while Chad let out a sigh of relief. All returned to normal or as normal as it had been in the past few moments.

"Please see to Corrine," motioned Chad to Sly.

Crouching over her, Sly asked, "Are you okay?"

"Do I look like I'm okay?" Corrine held up her deformed fingers while her other arm lay limp by her side.

"I nailed it. It's not so evincible after all," bragged Sly.

"Don't celebrate too much quite yet. It's sticking with us just off the starboard side, depth at seventy. I hope we didn't merely piss it off."

"Maybe it's bleeding to death down there, sort of like what I'm doing right now," commented Corrine. "Assistance please if you don't mind."

"I tell you. I hit my target, bull's eye," said Sly, while looking around for a first aid kit.

Captain had returned below to check the damages during the assault. "Chad," he shouted from below. "Is it gone?"

"Not exactly, but Sly did land a shot. How does it look down there?"

"Barely holding our line in the sand I'm afraid to report. We have more leaks than plugs. How are the damages up there?"

"Superficial, busted railing, and missing cleats on portside is all that I can see. Keep those engines running and give it all you can."

A pause then Tommy answered, "How far to land?"

"Under 20 miles best I can guess."

"You better hope we have phone service real soon then."

Chad decided he did not wish to know the rest of the story, so he didn't ask. "Do the best you can, Captain Tommy."

"You mates, watch your back up there."

"Okay, I finally found the first aid kit, but I'm not sure it's going to help a whole lot," stated Sly, examining Corrine's injuries.

"Work on the bleeding and then splint me or something," demanded Corrine. "I don't suppose we have anything for pain, do we?"

"Afraid not. We loaded the net bait with any narcotics we had at the time."

"Here, try this," said Chad, handing them Captain Joe's bottle of Brandy. "Best we have for now."

"With her mangled fingers and broken wrist and arm, Corrine could not hold the bottle. "Looks like I need a sippy-cup," she managed a little forceful smile.

Sly held the bottle up to her lips. "Say when."

"When it bottoms out," she replied, commencing to gulp loudly and un-lady like.

"Our friend is still holding its position, below us and now to our aft," announced Chad. "Has anyone tried a phone lately?"

Corrine pushed the bottle away and said, "Get real."

Sly retrieved his cell phone. No bars appeared on the screen. Corinne motioned to her purse. Sly retrieved hers, no bars either.

"Mine's the same," confirmed Chad. "And my battery is about gone."

"Corrine's is low too," verified Sly. "Mine has half a charge. I think being out here with no signal strains our batteries."

Chad scanned the horizon but saw no craft of any kind. Worse still, it appeared a weather front might be heading their way. Storm clouds were brewing to the west. He could make out flashes of lightning. Vacation, who needs them he thought.

54

Roth had lost sight of the trawler but sadly hadn't spotted land either. He utilized the compass he had found on board the rubberized raft to plot his course toward the shore. Any chunk of land would serve his purpose. He checked the fuel tank. The gauge indicated less than a quarter of a gallon remained. He had the engine on full throttle which consumed fuel at a dangerous rate. He didn't care. He just intended to put as much distance between him and the others as quickly as possible. The reserve tank held another gallon. If luck be on his side, maybe it would be enough. Thankfully, he had not encountered a Liopleurodon. Once he reached land and again took command of his exploration ship from his soon to be unemployed captain, he would return and claim his prize. That is if Chadwick and his hoard didn't do something stupid to harm or chase them away.

Roth mentally compiled his to-do list. Fire and sue the mutineer. Pay off all witnesses to the sinking of the skiffs. Fire Paige. Destroy Chadwick and the others if they managed to survive. His main priority capture a Liopleurodon. Why hadn't he noticed it before now. The skiff had a short-range radio. He switched it on. It appeared to work fine. Now was not the time to use it, but in due time it would come in handy. And better still, he had a flare pistol with three rounds. Glancing back, he spotted storm clouds building up. He couldn't tell if the weather pattern was headed his way. Having efficient time to ponder, he played through his head, what if Chadwick and the others survived? They would surely concoct the tale making him out to be the villain. Normally that would not bother him, but this time indictment of criminal activities could result. Accidentally setting that captain to flames was still a far cry from cold bloodied murder, and there had been no surviving witnesses on the second skiff.

Hopefully the Liopleurodon would make quick work of the trawler and its passengers, and he could strike that one off his list. Let them fatten up his next exhibit. The reef aquarium would be a tight squeeze for the larger of them. Possibly his team could capture one of the 25 or 30 footers. Having an extinct creature of any size would be a guaranteed draw. Something splashed the water alongside. Roth nearly jumped from the raft. Wide eyed and hardly breathing he scanned the surface for the source. Thirty seconds later and 15 yards ahead, porpoises broke the surface. He exhaled loudly, grabbing his chest, and letting out a little chuckle.

55

Sly had patched up Corrine the best he could. He had placed splints on her warped fingers and had secured her wrist, putting her arm in a sling. He had cleaned and bandaged her superficial wounds from the glass, removing the larger chards. "I'm no doctor but I think you'll be okay until we get to a medical facility."

She held up the empty pint of Brandy and with a slight slur said, "I don't suppose we have more of this, do we?"

"I don't think so, but I'll take another look. You just stay put."

"What else would I do? I can't even drive this boat now."

"Steer," Chad corrected her.

"Heifer," she giggled.

"No, I mean you steer a boat, not drive one."

"Look at me. I can't do either. I look like *Evil Knievel* after a missed jump."

"I can't argue with that."

"But I'm a hell of lot better off than Father or Alex," she began to tear up.

"It's on the move again and closing. Tommy, hold on, it's back."

Chad watched as the creature closed ranks…50…45…40…35 feet, eventually holding at 25 feet directly below them. "Tommy, I don't like the looks of this. Prepare for another attack on the hull."

"I don't know if the hull will take any more strikes."

"I'm not sure we can either."

"This thing appears way too smart to me," commented Sly.

326

"I'm not following you," said Chad.

"We successfully wounded it topside. Now it remains below and strikes us from the bottom. It learns quickly. Are reptiles supposed to act like that?"

"Hard to say. We have no experience with this species, and I wouldn't actually categorize it as reptilian."

"If it stays submerged, we're screwed, aren't we," spoke up Corrine.

"Only if its reason for doing so involves it mimicking a battering ram," answered Chad.

"We're not going to get out of this, are we?"

Chad did not answer. He focused his attention on the blob on the screen, on the move again. He yelled to keep Tommy in the loop. "It's directly underneath you Tommy."

The blob on the screen remained glued to the trawler's underbelly, but still nothing happened. It maintained their speed shadowing the vessel.

"What's happening?"

"Still there, directly under you, but it's doing nothing."

Sly chimed in, "What does this mean?"

"I'm not sure. This is very peculiar behavior," answered Chad, rubbing his free hand though his hair.

Almost two minutes expired, and the creature still held its position.

"Have you felt any bumps at all down there?"

"I wouldn't even know it was there except for you telling me," replied Captain Tommy. "Does this seem natural to you?"

"Not in the least, but then again wounded animals often act oddly. Possibly that shot hurt it worse than we anticipated."

"We can only hope I suppose," replied Sly.

"Hold on, it's dropping back and submerging deeper." He counted off the distance as before until it disappeared off the screen. "I think we just dodged the bullet."

"Maybe Sly's shot did the trick," added Corrine.

"I doubt it but maybe it's searching for easier prey," answered Chad.

"If I had a drink, I'd drink to that," slurred Corrine.

"Tommy, we're in the clear. How does it look down there?"

"Holding our own. I think we are going to be fine if she leaves us alone. At least she should hold together until we dock her."

"All right then, Georgetown here we come," smiled Chad.

"And facing Mother," added Corrine. "All she's going to remember is how crappy I acted yesterday. She doesn't know we patched things up before…"

"I'll tell her you were both square. Not to worry. Then next on my agenda is Roth."

"Save some for me," said Corrine.

"Putting him in cuffs will make my day," added Sly.

"Holy Mother," yelled Chad, his eyes fixed on the fish finder's screen and the locomotive steaming toward them from directly bellow and almost on them already.

The impact lifted the trawler out of the water catapulting the unprepared crew. Just as quickly it was over and the charging Liopleurodon had vanished again. Chad had managed to keep one hand locked on the wheel but had still been whipped sideways slamming his hip against the control panel. Corrine now lay on the opposite side of the wheelhouse face down and not moving. Sly was not in the wheelhouse at all. Chad heard him groaning from the deck. He first checked Corrine for a pulse. Relieved that she was not dead, he then called to Captain Tommy but received no answer. He tried a second then a third time, but the man was not answering. Suddenly it dawned on him, the engine was not running. They were dead in the water.

56

Roth Niederwerter kept a weary eye on the surrounding sea as he changed out the fuel tanks. His raft had sputtered to a stop, now bobbing up and over the waves like a fisherman's cork. He frantically rushed to switch over the other one-gallon tank, having run the first one empty. Finished, he attempted to start the tiny outboard engine pulling the cord. Having run the fuel lines dry, it refused to fire. A splash startled him. He completed a 180, flare gun in hand, finger on the trigger, almost losing his balance and stumbling overboard. He identified the source, merely water lapping against the raft causing a slapping sound. He retuned his attention to the outboard motor. The smell of gasoline flooded his nostrils, burning his eyes. He had apparently flooded the choke.

He cursed loudly and repeatedly kicked the sides of the raft. The thumping sounds did not go unnoticed. Senses heightened, the predator paused to take in the odd sounds, some oceanic creature obviously in distress. A couple of more thuds and it had homed in on the source of the sound and effortlessly torpedoed toward it. Roth attempted again to start the motor, pulling the cord time after time, but to no avail. It simply refused to fire. His impatience worsened his situation and he banged the motor with a boat oar. He eyed the radio thinking now might be the time to hail a mayday. If he did and the Shrimp Cocktail was still afloat, then he would be guaranteeing their rescue too

Alerting the Coast Guard would surely expose the existence of the beasts. The general public would scream bloody murder and most surely launch an all-out assault on his creatures. This was something he absolutely would not tolerate. This situation required sufficient time to nurture. He must first convince the governing authority to side with him. Play the endangered, previously thought extinct card to protect the Liopleurodon's most certain slaughter. Man, always destroyed what he could not understand. The creature's ravenous appetite and fondness for human flesh would not paint a flattering picture that humans and these creatures could live in harmony. Rogue creatures were always put down. Animals could not attack man and live. No, it was not time to radio for help. He was not prepared to plead his case just yet. There were too many loose ends to tidy up.

The raft wobbled and this time it had not been the result of his overactive imagination. Something had passed underneath the raft; something large enough to displace the water. A swirling wake appeared on the opposite side of his rubberized island, but as hard as he strained his eyes, he could not identify the source. Obviously, he was no longer alone. He began yanking the cord on the outboard, but it refused to cooperate. Whatever it was, it passed underneath again, rippling the water, almost taking the raft with it.

Taking a deep breath, Roth grasped the mic from the radio and fondled it, contemplating making a distress call. The sudden bump landed Roth on his ass and dislodged the mic from his hand. He sprang back up and instinct prompted him to reach for the flare gun instead of the radio's mic. Rescue would take a while, and this called for more evasive maneuvers. While he cringed at the thought of having to fire a flare at one of his sea creatures, dying was not an option. He would only shoot if life and limb were in jeopardy. He desperately hoped he had sufficient time to make the appropriate decision.

It bumped again from below, harder than the last time. It was curious, attempting to evaluate if the raft was really a viable food source. Roth suddenly realized his bladder felt as if it was about ready to burst. His nerves were getting the best of him. He despised playing cat and mouse, especially when he had been designated the role of the rodent. "What are you waiting for? Roth slapped the boat oar on the ocean surface before really thinking the ramifications. He jerked it back to his bosom almost as quickly.

Standing in the raft was ill advised. The craft rolling with the waves tested one's acrobatic skills. Roth compounded the adventure by constantly shifting his position, searching for any signs of his uninvited guest. After a full minute with no visual or physical contact, he resumed his attempts to start the motor, ignoring the radio. It attacked from below launching the raft airborne. Roth careened off the rubberized side, resembling a kid bouncing off a trampoline. He landed in the water almost ten feet away, completing an excellent belly flop. Surfacing and paddling, spinning like a top, he frantically searched for his attacker. It did not take him long to spot the caudal fin encircling him. The twelve-foot tiger shark sized him up as well. Unbelievable thought Roth. How could it possibly end like this, with him being taken by a common variety shark and not by a Liopleurodon. He had falsely warned of an invasive killer shark along the Grand Strand. Now he had one. A tiger, not a great white.

The tiger shark passed within three feet and darted off. Now or never, surmised Roth. He swam fast and furiously toward the raft that had drifted some 20 feet away. The splashing sounds alerted the shark and it immediately veered back toward its prey. It closed in for the kill. Roth knew it pointless to look and stroked like a mad man, closing the distance to the raft. He only chanced a quick peek once his hand had touched the raft. The fin rising above his head closed less than six feet away. Roth held out his hands hoping to deter the attack. He could see the tiger shark tilting sideways, mouth open, eyes rolled back and realized he would not be victorious. The ocean exploded in a fury, the turbulence almost washing him underneath the raft. White foam quickly transformed to blood red as the shark head decapitated from its body landing inches from a floundering Roth. The Liopleurodon made quick work of its prey. It was there, then it was gone.

Roth spewed the ocean from his mouth and nostrils. He had been prepared for the shark's arrival but had been totally taken off guard by the sudden attack of the grim reaper. One hand still clinging to the raft he searched frantically for any signs of the much larger beast. He only spotted the bloody morsels of tiger shark. He sighed, realizing he had once again been spared from certain death. Assured now that a greater plan awaited him, he scampered back into the raft, feeling more invincible than ever, but admitting that a cat only has so many lives.

Roth sat back for a few seconds catching his breath and gathering his wits. He decided now would be an excellent time to mayday the Coast Guard. Why push his luck. He reached over and grabbed the microphone and calmly pressed the button. "Mayday, mayday, this is Roth …." The raft disappeared below the surface, plucked from beneath like a ripe piece of fruit. Bubbles erupted on the surface, air hissing from the deflating vessel. Seconds later Roth broke free coughing out the sea once again, but still very much alive. With no life preserver he treaded water frantically to stay afloat. He turned a complete 360 scanning for anything he could cling to, but he remained the only spec in the sea. Smiling he thanked his lucky stars, having dodged fate one more time, but faced an even larger challenge. Swim or drown and no land in sight.

Roth wondered how many more times he would cheat the grim reaper. He received his answer swiftly. The Liopleurodon delivered the message, devouring him in one single bite. Roth Niederwerter was not a cat after all, and no grand plan awaited him. He would simply go down as lost at sea without a trace, a fitting destiny for one ruthless and heartless bastard.

57

Seeing to Corrine first, Chad flipped her over on her back after again verifying a pulse and checking for any obvious additional life-threatening injuries. She did have a knot appearing on her temple and remained unconscious, possibly from a concussion. Sly staggered into the wheelhouse, blood dripping from a cut on his chin and his left eye almost swollen shut. He waved off Chad, saying he would see to Corrine, freeing Chad to go below and verify Captain Tommy's condition.

When he arrived in the little engine room area, he spotted Tommy already rising to his feet, rubbing the back of his head. "Kamikazed us, didn't she."

"Anything broken," asked Chad.

"Just my pride," smiled the crusty old sea captain. "Spirit still barely in tack, how are the others?"

"Corrine is out like a light and I'm not certain to the degree of her injuries. The detective is seeing to her. He appears to have just a few more bumps and bruises. What's the status on the engine and the boat?"

"Let's just take a look see," he replied, suddenly realizing the water flow had greatly increased.

Chad stood patiently, peering over his shoulder, not liking what he could see. Tommy scratched his head and then rubbed his chin before replying loudly, "This baby is kaput. Too much sea water is unhealthy for the best of engines. Bilge can't possibly stay ahead of these new leaks."

"How long do we have?"

"I would say less than two hours unless the bilge pump stops working all together. Our hull has more holes in it than a colander. This would be a good time to pull a miracle out of your ass, mate."

"Roth departed with my plan B. I don't suppose we have another floatation device squirreled away somewhere, do we?"

"Not much I can do here, so what you say I work on us a life raft of some sort."

"Just let me know how I can help.'

"I might just take you up on that offer once I figure that out," smiled Captain Tommy. "I'm sure not much of a captain; fixing to have a second ship go down in less than a week. My reputation is going to be shot. I'll be colored as a jinx."

"You get us out of here, save us from drowning, and I'll hire you to sail anything I own."

"Mighty nice of you, lad, but let's not forget that drowning might be the least of our problems. We still got ourselves a mighty fierce sea monster out there. Once we're in the open sea we'll be easy pickings. Maybe if that Roth fellow somehow makes it to shore, he'll send help our way?"

"I wouldn't hold your breath on that. He could care less about us, especially me. He wants the Liopleurodon. He wouldn't hesitate to use us for bait."

"We should have allowed you to toss him overboard just like you first suggested. Best we stop all this jabbering and work on something that floats."

"I'll go check on the others. Utilize anything you can find that might serve as a raft."

"One thing's for sure, this ain't my ship, so I don't plan to go down with her. What's going to happen is going to happen to me out yonder in that ocean."

Chad winked and patted Tommy on the shoulder and then headed top side. Greeted by a pleasant sight, Corrine sat upright but woozy. Sly was nursing the bump on her head with a cold compress.

"How's Captain Tommy?"

"No worse than the rest of us, and are you two okay?"

"Cross shrimping off my bucket list," spoke up Sly.

"Mine too," added Corrine.

"Makes three of us. The engine is shot. We're taking on too much water."

Corine asked the obvious, "Does this mean we'll have to abandon ship?"

"I'm afraid the Shrimp Cocktail is going to abandon us."

"What do we do now?"

"Sly, we need to build something that will float until we can be rescued. Tommy is working on that hopefully."

"So, we're boat builders now," replied Corrine.

"We better learn to be improvised fabricators unless you'd prefer bobbing around out there in a life vest."

Corrine stood shakily to her feet and said, "Where are our emergency boat building tools?"

"Better still my dear sister-in-law, scrounge around for water and food. We could be out here for awhile. Sly, please search for ropes, nets, wiring, cable, anything that we can use for binding our flotation contraption. I'll grab life preservers, anything that will float."

"How long do we have?"

"Not nearly enough, Sly, couple of hours at best says Captain Tommy."

"That is if that thing leaves us alone," said Corrine.

"Nothing we can do about that, so let's focus on what we can control."

"Now that you mention it, what about weapons? I'm out of ammo."

"I think we've already thrown everything at it but the kitchen sink. Let's focus on an escape pod first, and if we have anytime left, we'll worry about our weaponry," said Chad, glancing out at the sea, realizing they would soon be sitting ducks if they were lucky enough to construct a seaworthy craft.

Not a time to reflect, but one tends to do just that when one's life seems to be slipping away or at best hanging on by a thread. Chad thought about Elizabeth and the fact they had not started a family. Their careers had gotten in the way. How stupid they had been. Even Bobby and Cody had made time to produce kids. His brother-in-law, Bobby **Bornfreund**, the turn coat, had been good as responsible for the death of all on the Shrimp Cocktail, including his own father. He owed him big time, but now was not the time to plot revenge. Revenge and Roth, one in the same. He wasn't sure who he wanted worse, Bobby or Roth. Maybe he should promise to forget and forgive if the Lord would grant him and the others a safe return. Making deals with the Lord was not his style though. A man promises too much when faced with death. Most men don't follow up on the bargain. Chad did not want to be one of those men.

Captain Tommy jolted him back into the now. "Found this, might just come in handy," said Tommy, dragging a section of shrimp netting from the hatch. "Can you give an old sailor a hand?"

Chad scrambled to help him pull the heavy netting on deck. "Are we in the shrimping business again?"

"Not in my lifetime, but I got myself a brain fart," smiled Tommy. "Round up everything we got that floats."

"I was working on just that," answered Chad, holding up a couple of life vests.

"That will do for starters but we're going to need a lot more. Water's up almost three feet deep below now. Not sure if we have those two hours before we go under. Pump is losing the battle."

"Let's hear this plan of yours."

"Time for that in a few, but right now we need to be scrambling," he said, pointing to a large cooler. "Dump that. We can use it."

Chad nodded and followed the captain's orders. Any plan was better than no plan at all. Not a quitter by any stretch but he was a whipped puppy for the moment. He tried to maintain his poker face for the others, especially Corrine.

"Gentleman, we have company again," yelled Sly from the wheelhouse.

The familiar signal on the fish finder left no doubt that their worse nightmare had returned and now hovered less 100 feet directly below them. Chad sounded like a deflating balloon and looked to the heavens for some sign of redemption. The heavens did not respond and in a fleeting moment he thought, we are the ones facing extinction now.

"Enjoy the view;" spoke up Captain Tommy. "Battery won't be with us much longer."

Corrine stared blankly at the idle object. "It's not going to let us escape, is it? You damn ocean demon! How much does it take to fill your belly?"

"Switch off the finder, conserve the battery," commanded Chad.

"What for? The engine won't be firing back up and we have no radio. What difference does it make unless you don't want to see it coming?"

"Just do it, please. Shut down anything that relies on the battery."

"That sparkle in your eye tells me you're onto something, mate."

"Butt flapping in the breeze is about all I've got but like yours, better than nothing," answered Chad.
"Corrine, Sly, assist the captain while I work on our diversion. Captain Joe's Shrimp Cocktail is not going down without a fight, that I promise."

"That's the spirit, lad. We'll fight this booger with our last dying breath."

"I was with you until you started spewing this death talk," said Corrine. "I'm not buying this Custer's last stand crap,"

"Come on Corrine, let's put that rage to good use," encouraged Sly. "I plan to live long enough to draw my pension."

"Let's do it for those who went before us," boasted Captain Tommy. "Let not their deaths be in vane."

"This is for my father, Frederic J. Bornfreund and Alexis Clarke."

"For Captain Joe Wilson and his first mate, Ken Simpson," added Captain Tommy.

"And Roth Niederwerter, your ass belongs to me and don't you forget it," said Chad, as they each placed their hands-on top of one another's, pep rally style. "And I'm going to kick your brother's butt for good measure too."

"Stand in line. I get first dibs on brother dearest, the worthless money hungry turncoat."

A few minutes later Captain Tommy announced, "Okay, everything that was pulling any juice is now off. Cross your fingers we don't receive a surprise from below."

"I do believe we have searched every nook and cranny and have found anything that has a prayer of floating," stated Sly.

"And what you see is all the water and perishables we have other than a few items that require refrigeration," added Corrine. "No potted meat or Spam remains in the cupboards it saddens me to report."

"How are you holding up?"

"Better than being dead I suppose. Arm hurts like hell but no need to whine about it. We don't have the time or accessories for a pity party. When are you two gentlemen going to share your grand plan with us peasants?"

"Mine is simple," spoke up Captain Tommy. "We're about to construct our raft, a down and dirty no frills get her done floating bam-a-jama. The netting will be our floor and everything that floats will be attached to form our sides. I don't expect it to win first place for show but hopefully it will prevent us from bobbing out there like a buoy marker."

"With that mesh bottom we'll make one hell of a smorgasbord for that thing circling below," commented Corrine.

"That's where my plan comes in to play," Chad began explaining.

His three shipmates remained silent until they heard his scheme. Corrine, the skeptic commented first. "That's it. Whether it is hungry or not, you're just going to ring the dinner bell."

"It's all in the timing my dear skeptic."

"Its or ours," she replied.

"Yep," Chad smiled.

"Looks to me this will be a one-shot deal, lad."

"What have we got to lose," spoke up Sly. "The boat is going to sink anyway and once we're in that net, we will be easy pickings."

"We may as well lure the fly into our web," said Chad.

"This is the mother of all flies and I don't think the spider had this in mind," added Corrine.

"Step to mates. We have a raft to build first, before we invite our extinct friend to dinner."

58

The Liopleurodon continued a short circular pattern below, maintaining her watchful vigilance on the strange prey above, still searching for any signs of weakness. The tough hide had proven to be formidable thus far, frustrating the apex predator. Any other adversary would have already been an afterthought and a certain meal by now. This surface-dwelling anomaly, 25 feet shorter and many tons lighter than the prehistoric behemoth, both intrigued and infuriated the gigantic female. Its prey emits no distress signals and the salt water being cycled through the sea monster's nostrils detect no presence of blood or other animal fluids typically associated with aquatic inhabitance. While the female harbors no fear, she remains cautious. Attacks on the top dweller's under belly have opened no bloody wounds. Attacks from the surface have been more effective, plucking morsels of nourishment from the floundering invader of her domain.

Her hunting pack consisting of two female offspring and a juvenile have been eradicated, so she understands the dangers of taking this creature too lightly. After consuming one of her own, she is not driven by hunger. Instead, instinct has taken over and her need to protect her territory has all but consumed her. She will not give way to any beast in her waters and she claims the entire ocean as her territory.

The peculiar weather patterns of many days ago had disrupted her world in the deep fathoms of the trench. Her pack disoriented, had surfaced for the first time into unknown waters, temperatures much warmer than what she and her kind had been accustomed. Long forgotten primal urges had emerged driving her to lead the pack northward to a spawning ground once inhabited by her ancestors. The Atlantic coastal waters of South Carolina had pulled at them like an invisible magnet. An endless supply of aquatic life had quenched their hunger pains making it easy to pick and pluck their quarry.

Primal urges satisfied; the pack had begun a return trip to the trench when this odd creature had perked their interest. Assessing it to be a slow-moving lumbering meal, the apex predator had underestimated its foe. She possessed no concept of revenge. Only driven by rage and territorial urges the female had lingered in the area, determined to mortally wound, and take this creature. She watched and waited, searching for the surface dweller's weakness, still puzzled by its dormant state. If not for the occasional sounds from within its bowels, she would have thought the creature lay dead. Purging more sea through her nostrils she searched for any signs of a fatal wound but still detected nothing.

She feared nothing, but this creature was not like anything she had ever encountered before. It fought back and refused to be taken by her massive jaws and razor-sharp serrated teeth. More sounds emitted, odd, and almost guttural. The creature remained motionless, not splashing about, and much too peculiar for a sea animal that should have sustained horrific life-threatening wounds by now. Her sensory system registered another presence, but it moved rapidly away from her and her prey, heading in a northerly direction. She dismissed it as a threat and returned her focus to the floating invader directly above her. The strange internal sounds continued. She dove then swam upward within 30 yards before slowly drifting away. The creature if it had sensed her approach had not flinched. She wondered if it could already be dead, but the odd sounds convinced her otherwise. She remained cautious, not something she was accustomed to being.

59

Captain Tommy stepped back to admire his creation. "Well," he said rubbing his chin. "She's far from a work of art unless you look at her through squinted eyes, but she should be seaworthy."

"We're supposed to plop down on that netted bottom," questioned Corrine   .

Tommy nodded.

"We'll be advertising to come and get it, won't we?"

"Not if the lad's plan works."

"Chad's plan and your raft compliment one another pretty damn well. I don't think either have a chance in hell in working."

"Oh, ye of little faith, sister-in-law," spoke up Chad.

"Just stating the obvious," she replied.

"Captain, I think she's a fine vessel," smiled Sly.

"A keen eye, detective. She'll fair better than the sinking one we are standing on."

"Load the provisions and let's prepare to put our plan in motion," said Chad.

"What about some sort of weapons," asked Corrine.

"I still have my revolver and I did locate one extra cartridge," said Sly. "Thought I was out of ammo but guess I lost it on deck during some of the excitement."

"And the flare gun, two cartridges, but we'll need one of them," added Chad.

"I took the time to straighten these boat hooks best I could in a pinch. Close range they'll serve as crude harpoons," said Captain Tommy.

"If we're close enough to use those, we're probably on our way down that things gullet," said a pessimistic Corrine.

"I regretfully have to agree," said Chad. "If plan A isn't successful then plan B, doing hand to flipper and teeth combat certainly spells our doom."

"For once I wish you wouldn't have agreed with me, Chad," said Corrine, punching him in the shoulder with her good hand.

"We're one pathetic bunch of misfits, aren't we, my dear sister-in-law?"

"But we're alive and kicking," said Sly.

"For the moment," added Corrine.

"How much longer before this tub goes bottom feeder?"

"She is already heavily favoring the portside," answered Captain Tommy. "I'd give her another 20, maybe 30 minutes tops."

"Timing is everything," advised Chad. "If we launch this so-called raft too soon, I'm sure we'll draw its undivided attention. Too late and we might go down with the Shrimp Cocktail or worse."

"A waiting game it is," nodded Captain Tommy.

"Vegas odds must really blow," stated Corrine.

"Shouldn't we fire up the finder to verify if our sea monster is still around? If she's gone, your plan might not be necessary, lad."

"I suppose it wouldn't hurt to take a peek, but let's not waste too much of the battery, we'll need it to power my system."

"Here goes," he said, all huddled around him, eyes glued to the monitor.

The huge green blob, a dead give away hovered less than 80 feet below, dead astern, an ominous sight indeed. She looked even larger than they had remembered.

"What's it waiting for, an invitation?"

"Corrine, I certainly hope so. I have one engraved in gold for her. Switch it off, Tommy. Save the battery. We have our answer. We are not alone."

"I need a drink," spouted Corrine.

"Let's hope it will be one we can all share later in celebration ashore," replied Chad.

"I don't relish entering the water in the captain's homemade raft," said Sly. "Nothing against your workmanship captain, I'm just not looking forward to being in the open sea with that thing and one chomp away from filling its belly."

"Son, you don't have to explain or apologize. This is a sticky-wicky for us for sure. I have seen firsthand what it can do to a sturdy vessel. My ship is already resting on the bottom as a result."

"Same here," added Chad. "If my plan fails…"

"Perfect time to say if, don't you think," interrupted Corrine. "And while we are playing the *what if game*, what if there are more of these things out there? Let's face it. We started with four, who's to say there aren't a herd of these things just out of range of that finder."

"Guess we'll have our answer in a few more minutes, won't we."

"I really do hate surprises, brother-in-law."

"Best make way with your plans, lad, she's about to go under."

"Prepare the raft. I'll set the bait."

"You're really going through with it, aren't you?"

"The ship is going under regardless," confirmed Chad. "May as well use it to our advantage."

"By calling that thing to come and get it sounds pretty idiotic to me," she sighed.

"Getting it here and getting rid of it is a dice roll I do agree, but if we don't try something, we're just going to be sitting ducks," Chad defended his plan.

"I sure hope this is just a bad nightmare and I'm about to wake up," replied Corrine.

"Me too," winked Chad. "Head over to the raft."

"What about you?"

"Save me a spot. I've got to toss out the welcome mat first."

"Don't you make a widow out of my sister, Chad Reynolds?"

"Just be ready to abandon the Shrimp Cocktail," he replied.

60

Chad's plan was quite simple. Lower the extra speaker into the water, engage the whale distress call recordings and summon the creature to the dinner table, that table being the Shrimp Cocktail. Hopefully the Liopleurodon would take the bait and assault the boat. The second part of his plan had not been flawlessly perfected. He intended to blow up the boat while under attack and with it, terminate the sea beast. While confident about luring the creature, he wasn't so sure his visions for destroying the boat would work, and as he had explained to the others, timing was critical. The boat must explode while the creature mounted the attack and while the tanks held sufficient fuel to do the job. Igniting it in a timely manner did carry its share of risks and uncertainty. It would have to be done manually by him and still allow him time to distance himself from the potential explosion. Too many variables overwhelmed his thoughts.

Another problem reared its ugly head, the makeshift raft. If they launched it too soon would it prompt the creature to attack it instead of the boat. If they did not launch it soon enough could they distance themselves from the explosion. If all came off without a hitch, the boat destroys the creature, the raft and he survived. Still, they would be marooned in the makeshift raft with no mechanical means to reach shore or hail a mayday. With the Shrimp Cocktail's sinking inevitable, what other options did they really have? Damned if you do and doomed if you don't.

Chad had taken time to handwrite a couple of last farewells to his wife and mother just in case he didn't escape the explosion. He had discretely passed the notes along to Detective Stone not wishing to fret Corrine. To his mother he had shared the discovery of the extinct species, realizing she would appreciate and relate to this, being that she had spent much of her life seeking evidence of the existence of Sasquatch. Matt McGregor's chronicles had convinced him the creatures, if not now, had once existed back in the 1800's. He shared his regrets for having been forced to destroy the sea creatures, but explained that if he hadn't, they would have most certainly devoured he and his party. A mother would understand his dilemma.

To his wife, Elizabeth, he expressed his failure to have put off starting a family, placing career ahead for far too long. He expressed his sorrow for the loss of her father, Frederic J. Bornfreund and that he had died doing what he enjoyed best. He explained how he had seen the sparks ignited in the infamous professor's eyes, discovering a species long thought extinct. He asked her to convey this to Teal. Foremost, he pledged his love to her and encouraged her to seek happiness with another, not to morn her loss, to move on as quickly as possible.

Chad glanced to the heavens seeking God's hand to guide him and reassure him that this would work. He felt a calm come over him, his prayers obviously answered by the divine power above. He snuck a peek at Captain Tommy and the others standing patiently awaiting the signal to abandon ship. He then ventured below, pail in hand, to open the fuel valve to set the table for the pending fireworks. Sea water almost waist deep greeted him, instilling a panic attack because he could not see the valve submerged somewhere beneath. The rising water now prevented him from filling his pail, his primary instrument in preparing the ignition fuse. Why hadn't he done this sooner?

He removed the flare pistol from his waist band and placed it on a shelf as he began to fumble blindly for the fuel valve in the murkiness. Slightly disorientated at the shock of the water's depth he became his own worse enemy, now breathing hard and struggling to maintain his composure. God's reassuring hand had apparently abandoned him, or Satan had intervened when he ventured below just to rattle his cage and announce he still had some say in the outcome.

Chad took a deep breath and mumbled to himself, "You can do this. Just calm down and do it. The others are depending on you Chad Reynolds."

Just like that, his hand struck gold, the valve touched his fingertips. He put the death grip on it, turned it, and immediately felt the pressure from the released fuel. He then smelled the overpowering fumes of petroleum. Reality reared its ugly head when he realized the escaping fuel now engulfed him, making him a potential human torch. This was bad on so many levels and the clock did not tick in his favor. His original plan of pouring a fuel fuse along the deck from the engine's fuel tank and then igniting it with the flare gun just before making a dive for the raft, had been foiled. He presently had no second option and the boat would not stay under his feet forever. Firing the flare into the opening at this close range would almost certainly spell doom for him. He would never be able to escape the potential explosion. He had understood the risk involved in his original plan, but he at least had a glimmer of hope, He wasn't sure he was prepared to become a suicide bomber for the greater good.

Standing on the deck it did not take Captain Tommy long to determine the lad had that whipped puppy expression on his face. He hurried over and asked, "Did something go wrong, mate?"

"It's flooded down below."

"Happens all the time when a boat is sinking," answered Tommy.

"I opened the valve but…" Chad held up the empty bucket.

Tommy frowned. "So, we blow up the Shrimp Cocktail some other way then."

"Any suggestions? I'm drawing blanks."

"That fuel laced sea will come bubbling on deck soon enough, and then you'll have your target, but hauling ass will reach a new level if you catch my drift."

"Ready the raft and leave the ass hauling to me."

"Aye, aye," saluted Captain Tommy. "My fat ass is best suited for raft sitting anyway."

Chad switched on the fish finder to sneak one more peak at the creature before implementing his scheme. "Oh no," he exclaimed, not seeing the familiar huge green blob.

Had it gone? And if so, why risk calling it back? How could he be certain it was not lurking out there somewhere just out of range? He didn't know and that scared him more than knowing its whereabouts. He stared to the heavens questioning why things had become so complicated. Water lapped at his feet and the smell of fuel permeated his nostrils. What to do, what to do? He really had no choice but to ring the dinner bell, because if he didn't, and it was still out there, a lost opportunity surely spelled their demise. He took a deep breath and mumbled, "It's show time."

61

She had finally lost interest in the creature floating on the ocean's surface, instinct convincing her it posed no threat to her territory. Not driven by hunger, she decided to trek her way back toward her former habitat, the Puerto Rico Trench. Almost a half mile now separated her and the Shrimp Cocktail. She cruised at 160 feet below the surface, the perfect swimming machine. She glided through the ocean depths effortlessly but with senses always on alert. A school of dolphin broke the surface directly above, but the tiny creatures posed neither a threat nor a flicker of interest. They had sensed her presence and fled in the opposite direction. She swam with her mouth open, amplifying her sensory system. Nothing ominous lay ahead. She should have been extinct 150 million years ago but yet she lived in an era far removed from her Jurassic seas. A magnificent specimen, her serrated teeth, evolution at its best, had replaced those smoother ones of her ancestral cousins. No fossils had ever been found to identify her as the new and improved ultimate predator of the seas. Suddenly she veered off course and completed a one eighty, her attention drawn to the whale song that jolted her senses. The creature sounded again loudly, and she sensed it rivaled her own size. That jeopardized her territory. Instinctively she homed in on the creature's location and soared toward the source, intent on destroying the interloper. The sea belonged to her.

****

Chad had powered up the second smaller player-recorder and dropped the back-up underwater speaker off the portside at two fathoms deep (twelve feet). He had cranked up the volume for full affect. Now he waited on deck in nearly knee-deep water. The Shrimp Cocktail was leaning heavily to starboard where Captain Tommy, Corrine, and Sly held their ground for easy access into the ocean. Chad focused on the fish finder screen for any signs of the Liopleurodon. The screen remained blank as precious time expired. He could see the mixture of fuel and sea splashing about on deck and wondered if the smell might deter the creature if it did make an appearance. Chad registered disappointment at the prospect that it just might not return, when he should have been cutting cartwheels, thanking his lucky stars it had vanished back into obscurity. He looked over at his three shipmates and shrugged.

"Thank goodness," yelled Corrine. "This nightmare is over."

The screen began to flicker. Either the battery was growing weak or the water was taking its toll. Suddenly it went blank all together. Chad checked the player-recorder, but it remained playing. It dawned on him it had kicked into battery back-up.

"Son, face it, she's gone, and we are truly blessed," yelled Captain Tommy. "May as well join us and let's launch this fine craft of mine before the shrimper takes us all under."

She crashed to the surface and landed a third of her body over the railing of the portside catapulting Chad toward her snapping jaws. His right hand caught a cleat, his legs flailed just inches away from a most certain and horrific death. The raft and three startled crew took an unpredicted tumble: Corrine receiving the worst of it with her one arm in a sling. Captain Tommy first up, grabbed her by her good arm, yanking her to her feet. Sly mesmerized by the thing clambering on board still sat flat on his ass, oblivious to the actions being taken by Tommy.

Tommy managed to land a glancing kick off the side of his shoulder, jolting him back to the task at hand, launching the life raft. With the starboard side now clearly tilted away from the ocean, this became much more difficult to pull off. Just maintaining a good foothold posed a challenge to the would be raft launchers. Chad still clung to the cleat and had problems of his own. Luckily, the flare gun remained secure inside his waistband, but it hurt like hell in his somewhat dangling precarious position.

The creature inched further on board and that prompted Chad to attempt a most dangerous maneuver. He released his hold on the cleat and at the same time kicked off the side of the railing like an Olympic swimmer pushing off the wall of the pool. Spinning and sliding across the deck he barely avoided the creature's humongous serrated teeth. He crashed into the stern half knocking

353

him self coo-coo. The flare gun dislodged from the sudden jolt. Sucking in fresh air Chad tried to regain his composure. Somewhere beneath the incoming wash rested the gun. He fumbled and felt everywhere as the boat succumbed to the weight of the behemoth hastening its rendezvous with Davey Jones. Chad struck pay dirt and held the flare gun by its barrel. He righted it, finger now firmly on the trigger. "Now," he yelled to Captain Tommy.

Adrenalin at maximum overdrive the three managed to shove the raft over the side and plummeted inside. Chad balanced on the stern railing and fired the flare gun toward the wheelhouse as he back flipped off the floundering Shrimp Cocktail. The backlash from the flames sucked the oxygen from the surrounding air just before the explosion rocked their world. Debris rained from the sky for what seemed like forever, inflicting more cuts and bruises on the three raft survivors. Once the hailstorm ceased, Corrine began frantically searching for any sign of her heroic brother-in-law. She screamed his name, but no one answered. Sly clutching his revolver propped up on his knees scanning the sea for their nemesis, its nightmarish image still vivid in his mind. Captain Tommy said nothing, only shook his head in disbelief, refusing to believe Chad Reynolds had not survived the carnage.

The creature's bloody head surfaced less than five feet behind the raft. Sly opened up, blasting holes in the lifeless eye sockets, causing the bodiless head to spin on its side. He sat back in the raft gasping for air and then laughing out loud, realizing Chad's plan had worked almost flawlessly. He wished his newfound friend could have witnessed the outcome, but it was not to be.

"Shouldn't we search for him," begged Corrine.

"Look around you," replied Captain Tommy. "Do you see anything worth searching through?"

Sly asked, "What now?"

"Shore is that way," pointed Captain Tommy. "Will your hands fit this paddle?"

"If his won't, mine will," stated a familiar voice, clinging to the decapitated Liopleurodon head.

"Holding onto your trophy, mate," smiled Captain Tommy.

"And a perfect specimen it was until Sly shot out its eyes," replied Chad.

"I didn't like the way it was looking at me," grinned Sly, reaching over to lend him a hand up.

Once on-board Tommy asked, "Do you want us to haul in your find?"

"Nah, I think what's extinct should remain extinct unless Corrine would like us to dedicate the discovery to her father."

"I think father would feel the same as you. He was a bone man after all, and this might put his fellow paleontologist out of business."

"Too big for my apartment wall," added Sly.

"Chum it is then. Let's get the hell out of here," replied Chad.

"Row, row, row your boat," sang Captain Tommy.

"I like five hundred bottles of beer on the wall better," said Corrine.

"I think we have plenty of time to do both," laughed Chad.

Epilogue

Chad slipped out of bed, but not before kissing his pregnant wife on the cheek. Liz sucked in air and snorted before letting out a sequence of sputtering snores. He smiled and slipped on his shorts, retrieved a cup of coffee and the morning paper before stepping out onto the deck overlooking the everglades. It had been almost five months since their ordeal, but in ways it seemed like only yesterday.

Corrine had moved in with her mother. Teal had been an emotional wreck after losing Frederic. The family had all but banished Robert after discovering his alliance with Roth Niederwerter and blaming him for the professor's death. Cody had found the courage to take the kids and leave Robert. The divorce settlement and child support would certainly put the final nail in Robert's coffin. He had tried to capitalize on the sea monster story but was discredited as conniving gold digger.

Roth had disappeared without a trace on the second inflatable so had explained Captain Huey, saying the man was obsessed with capturing a great white. Vanessa would eventually take control of his business and liquidate it once he could be legally declared deceased. The Aquarium never reopened. Paige had a brief affair with Lance Rocker and while neither could prove the existence of the sea monsters, the unexplained disappearances, and alleged attacks, it made for good television and substantial revenue. Paige began pinning a fictional book utilizing the likes of Roth Niederwerter as the antagonist in her sorted tale of crime, corruption, and illicit passion. Lance moved on to rock someone else's world.

Captain Tommy had moved to Montana and opened 'Tommy's Got It All' hunting and fishing shop, having gotten his fill of the sea. Detective Sylvester Stone returned to a life as part of Horry County's finest. He remained in touch with his fellow survivors. None ever confirmed the existence of sea monsters along the Grand Strand. The mob believed a competing family had been responsible for the sinking of the first charter boat. Sly and the police department left it at that, unsolved.

The attacks and sinking of the other boats had been explained as the result of a rogue whale, a modern-day Moby Dick. The alleged whale had drowned during the encounter with the Shrimp Cocktail, entangled in the trawler's nets. Only the survivors on the Shrimp Cocktail had seen the perpetrators and they stuck to their fabricated story. Neither Bobby or Captain Huey Horatio Long or his crew had witnessed what had taken the first inflatable vessel. A rogue whale could have been the culprit. After all, there was no such thing as sea monsters or prehistoric extinct ocean serpents roaming the seas. The beaching of the dolphins and whales were not uncommon and were chalked up as unrelated to the other incidences. Chad with the cooperation of Vanessa, had seen to the release of the only surviving dolphin.

A casino boat out of Little River, South Carolina mysteriously and without any warning disappeared off the coast during a nighttime cruise three months after their ordeal. No survivors were found, and extraordinarily little debris was recovered. There had been no mayday. The search lasted nearly a month and remains a maritime unsolved mystery. News of the missing casino boat had not received national attention. It had been overshadowed by another despicable crime story along the Grand Strand, the second in recent years. Detective Stone had been distracted as well during this high-profile case. Detective Trudy Wagner was again in the limelight for all the wrong reasons, as was Lance Rocker.

Hatchlings began migrating from Bull Island for a trip that would take them back to their origin. Children from a local school found fragments of the eggshells there, the teacher pointing out that they probably belonged to loggerhead sea turtles. The teacher instructed them to not touch the shells. Phil did not heed her warning and had discovered one egg in tack. He slipped it inside his backpack and would later toss it into the trash after his parents instructed him that having turtle eggs was illegal.

Chad's mother, Mattie Reynolds, against her better judgment, had followed a lead that would take her to Willow Creek, California in search of evidence that her ancestor's Bigfoot still existed. A woman in the area alleged she had been feeding a family of the illusive creatures blueberry muffins. Chad had yet to tell his mother about the sea monsters he had encountered. Maybe some day both would confess their encounters. Chad hoped the Liopleurodon would never return.

Last stand on the Grand Strand, maybe…maybe not…only time will tell if other supposedly extinct sea creatures lurk in the ocean depths.

About the Author

T. Allen Winn was born in Abbeville, South Carolina. He began publishing his books in 2011 through Prose Press Publishing. His first seven books were published under this brand. He now publishes his books via his publishing brand, Buttermilk Books. T. Allen and his wife have called the Myrtle Beach area their home since 2005. Follow him on Facebook at T. Allen Winn. His books are sold on Amazon or where books are sold online, at Southern Succotash in Abbeville, S.C. and at Grapefull Sisters Vineyard in Tabor City, N.C.

Two Old 'Ts'

Fiction from T. Allen Winn
The Detective Trudy Wagner series

Road Rage
North of the Border
Tithes and Offerings

Bigfoot Series

Foot, Tree Knockers and Rock Throwers
Another Foot, What Really Happened to D.B. Cooper

More Fiction from T. Allen Winn

The Perfect Spook House
Dark Thirty
Lou Who
Raw Ride, a Wild West Zombie Apocalyptic Shoot'um Up
The Man Who Met the Mouse
Mister Twix Mystery, a Cat Scene Investigation
The Lord's Last Acres, Birth of the Bugsters
The Tenth Elemental
Come Here Getouttahere, Tyler's Tail Wagging Tale

Non-Fiction from T. Allen Winn

Being Bentley, A Dog Like No Other
It's All About the 'A', Faith, Family, Football and Forever
to Thee
with coauthor, Benji Greeson
It's All About the Angels in the Backfield, Dawn of a
Dynasty
with coauthor, Benji Greeson
December's Darkest Day, While I Breathe, I Hope
The Hardwood Walker of Port Harrelson Road
(based on true events in Bucksport, S.C.)
Cuz, My Brother, Life is Good, God is Good
The Endless Mulligan, Short Shots from the Golf Whomper
Clay Page, Somewhere In Between

Memoirs

The Caregiver's Son, Outside the Window Looking In
Cornbread and Buttermilk, Good Ole Fashion Home Cooked
Nostalgic Nonsense
Don't Sit Naked in A Grits Tree, More Nostalgic Nonsense

Short Stories

For Your Amusement featured in Beach Author Network's
book titled 'Shorts'

Ciled Me a Bar featured in friend and author, Danny Kuhn's
Headline Book's *Mountain Mysts*, Honorable Mention in Fiction
at the 2015 London Book Festival and the book
is endorsed by *Joyce Dewitt* of the sitcom *Three's Company*

Short story about his Granny Bowie in friend and author
Robert Sharpe's book,
The Heart and Soul of Caring, about caregivers
and their challenges